Praise for the Philip K. Dick award nominated
Compas Reach,
the first volume of
The Secantis Sequence.

"Compass Reach is space opera for those who've outgrown starship battles and phoney heroics. Complex, mysterious and engaging, it's reminiscent of the early work of Samuel R. Delany. Mark Tiedemann is a fine writer, and this novel proves that he's of the best new SF authors on the scene today."—Allan Steele

"Compass Reach is a rousing, inventive, far-future adventure by one of the most distinctive new voices in the field."— Jack McDevitt

"A vivid and unexpected view of the underbelly of interstellar society.Mark Tiedemann writes with an engaging energy, gritty realism, and a genuine concern for his characters. Here's a new writer worth watching!"—Jeffrey Carver

METAL OF NIGHT

BY

MARK W. TIEDEMANN

VOLUME TWO
OF THE SECANTIS SEQUENCE

Meisha Merlin Publishing, Inc
Atlanta, GA

Metal of Night Copyright © 2002 by Mark W. Tiedeman

METAL OF NIGHT

Published by Meisha Merlin Publishing, Inc.
PO Box 7
Decatur, GA   30031

Editing & interior layout by Stephen Pagel
Copyediting & proofreading by Teddi Stransky
Cover art by Ed Cox
Cover design by Kevin Murphy

ISBN: 1-892065-65-7

http//www.MeishaMerlin.com

First MM Publishing edition: June 2002

Printed in the United States of America
0 9 8 7 6 5 4 3 2 1

Table of Contents

Introduction to Mark W. Tiedemann's
Metal of Night
by
Jack McDevitt

I'm not a military SF fan. In fact, with a few exceptions, I don't care much for military novels at all, of whatever breed. Too much blood. Too many characters who literally seem to enjoy combat. Too much celebration of destruction.

What usually happens in military novels, whether mainstream, historical, fantasy, or science fiction, is that the characters get lost in the carnage. Banners wave, squadrons of cavalry (or starships) charge the enemy flank, and the protagonist executes all sorts of incredible heroics. And almost always without a scratch, and without a thought for his (or her) own safety.

The war is inevitably waged against the most vicious sort of antagonist. One usually has no difficulty from page one determining who is on the side of the angels. Even among the great novels, there is rarely an effort to put a human face on the enemy. Tolstoy gives us a cold emperor who places medals on the tunics of his soldiers but leaves inferior officers to affix them. Norman Mailer and Herman Wouk are stuck with World War II, which really was a collision between good and evil, so there wasn't much to be done. Mailer's Japanese are visible only behind their machine guns. Wouk allows one of Hitler's generals to discuss the strategy and tactics of the war from the German point of view.

It might be that the World War II experience and the shadow of the Cold War influenced the entire family of late twentieth-century military novelists to create scenarios that divided quite cleanly between darkness and light. That have made it difficult to recall that war has more often been complicated and messy and morally ambiguous. Or it might be that it's simply easier to arrange everyone as agents of darkness or light.

Mark Teidemann, in *Metal of Night*, gets past this obstacle and shows us both sides of a conflict. The action is set in the world of his superb Freerider novel, *Compass Reach*. We are caught up in a revolution on a world out on the perimeter of an interstellar federation, whose base is Earth. The political system is anchored by the Armada, a terrestrial fleet of over-whelming power. Various shadowy alien civilizations are out there, wielding influence for good or ill. (It's hard to know, not because the reader can't see what they're doing, but because he may still be making up his mind where his sympathies lie. The uncertainty seems to stem from which viewpoint charac-ter is on stage. And that is a striking accomplishment.)

The book's heroine, Cira Kalinge, is a pilot with the Ar-mada. Which tells any experienced reader that the Armada is ranged with civilization and decency. But Tiedemann has dem-onstrated in earlier work that he has a gift for playing with the reader's assumptions.

Who are we rooting for? It's usually easy to know. Good guys here, evildoers over there. The world, Tiedemann seems to be telling us, is a messy place, and just not all that easy to sort out. Especially when the shooting starts.

It's not always clear how a given war starts. And it's not always obvious what forces keeps it running once it does start. We used to think the munitions makers planned World War I. And I once heard a rumor that the architects and the con-struction industry planned Hitler's war.

We also make the uncomfortable discovery that there are good people on both sides, just as there are barbarians on both sides. And people caught in the middle, where often the real drama in armed conflict can be found.

While reading *Metal of Night,* I found myself thinking of people in the border states during the Civil War, where fami-lies divided North and South. Or in the colonies during the American Revolution, when the population split more or less evenly into thirds, loyalist, rebel, and neutral. It must have been a tough time to be neutral.

So Tiedemann gives us a martial epic that plays out the way real wars do: a thoroughgoing catastrophe for all who touch it. No banners fly, nobody organizes parades, the heroics are never exhilarating, and sometimes, when the act of derring-do has been committed and a character is grateful simply to walk away alive, the reader is left to wonder whether the price has not been too high.

Military science fiction has a habit of giving us two-dimen-sional heroes. They take out an enemy battle cruiser with a particle cannon and move on to the next challenge with a glib comment and a wry smile. Tiedemann's characters change as they engage in or are affected by combat. They erect a wall around themselves. They become more skeptical. More frightened. More desperate. They feel a sense of loss without knowing precisely what has been lost. And throughout the action, they and we are left to wonder precisely who is directing the fighting, and for what purpose.

But none of this touches on what, from my perspective, is the most unusual aspect of *Metal of Night*. Some years ago I was sitting on a panel during which we were discussing how to make villains believable.

I've never liked villains. Not because they twirl mustaches and serve to keep the action rolling when the author can't think of a better way to throw obstacles into the path of his hero. The problem with villains is that, with rare exceptions, they are boring. They're hard to make believable because once you do, they become human and the reader discovers affinities for them, and then they're not villains anymore. There's nobody duller than a homicidal maniac. And if it's true I wouldn't think so if he were after me (as a member of the audience pointed out), it's also true that I wouldn't have him over for dinner. Even if he were disarmed. Can one really spend an entertaining evening with Ming the Merciless?

Every standard military SF novel has a homicidal maniac stashed somewhere. Usually at the top of the enemy force. He glories in conquest, in torture, in pure malice. He is the focus for the hero's efforts, and we know that, in the final pages, the climactic confrontation will surely come. And we know also who will win.

There's no such character to be found in *Metal of Night*. There's one hopeless looney running around, but Tiedemann shows us how he got to be the way he is. And because we understand the motivation, and the context, we tend almost to sympathize.

I'm not suggesting these are noble people. What they are is *ordinary,* which makes them compelling. They've been hardened and damaged by ongoing conflict. People they love have died, sometimes in exceptionally brutal ways. But they hang on, most of them. They do what people have always done, stay out of harm's way while forces no one understands roll over them. They react as one would expect, sometimes out of fear, sometimes out of desperation, but always we recognize why they behave as they do.

This is all by way of saying that both the conflict and the characters are fully realized. They are true. The reasons behind the war are clear enough, and yet there's a murkiness to it all, a sense of invisible machinery somewhere taking the decisions out of human hands. A kind of inevitability that suggests the conflict is really a kind of gigantic bus accident.

But the illusion of a rationale is always present. The Armada, if nothing else, is making a statement. And what precisely is the statement? Here things get nebulous again. The reader will be recalling one or more of a half-dozen recent American interventions.

I have never been in combat. But it doesn't take much imagination to grasp the central fact that war is a horrific experience. A novel that is true to the reality necessarily makes for painful reading. Not only in the body count, or the injuries, but in the damage to the human spirit. People never come whole out of a war. One grows up quickly when the shells start landing and body parts begin to rain down. It's a maturing process with permanent scars.

There's a trap here somewhere for both the reader and writer of science fiction. The probability is that there will never be interstellar warfare. It would be nice to think it won't happen because at some stage we'll grow up. That's a happy possibility. But it's not the point. Interstellar war will never occur for the same reason interstellar commerce won't. The stars are too far apart, and the chance of finding short cuts across space is remote. No conqueror will be so crazed as to be willing to sit inside a tin can for 50,000 years simply for the opportunity to raise hell with the Vegans.

Consequently, those of us who think we might be getting a portrait of what future warfare will be like are deluded. But that's not where Tiedemann is headed. Aside from wanting to create an emotional ride for the reader, he has a few points to make. Good novelists, when they write about combat, are not writing about Spartans and Persians, or about the Armada and the rebel fleets on Finders. They are writing about *us* and the nature of war. And how we behave under stress.

Metal of Night doesn't waste our time with a detailed account of the politics behind this conflict. The politics are imaginary and irrelevant; the conflict is *real*. It is the animosity between individual characters in the contending forces that interests us, and, conversely, the impersonality of the forces that drive the war. Tiedemann has given us a compelling novel that is true to itself. For that reason, it won't be to everyone's taste. Readers who prefer mindless heroics, or who like their warfare without brutality, will want to look elsewhere. For the rest of us, who are willing to take our chance with an experience that, for all its unworldliness, is quite realistic, and might even leave a bruise or two, this one's a good bet.

Jack McDevitt
March 2002

What is a "Sequence"?

Labels are two-edged instruments—useful and deceptive simultaneously. We live by categories but reject their implied limitations, and rightly so. Labels might provide a useful starting point in understanding something—or someone—but it's all to easy to forget (or never know) that a label doesn't come close to exhausting the content of what it describes, nor does it set any kind of natural limit on where something—or someone—can go.

As long as labels are descriptive rather than proscriptive, they're useful. But they tend to become a shortcut in aid of taste, a cheat, a passive—but powerful—arbiter of aesthetic choice. They begin doing what titles ought rightly to do—suggest actual content.

Content itself is a tricky concept. What does the work contain? Will one reader actually recognize the same contents as another? The title is there to give entry to the aesthetic potential of the story, maybe suggest something about the concerns of the story, but it's not possible for the words on the cover to tell us what is actually in the story. What does *Gone With the Wind* actually say about what is in the book? Or *Wuthering Heights*? Or *The Stars My Destination*? At best, a title becomes, after reading the work, a handy mnemonic by which memories of the reading experience trigger.

But a category label?

Science Fiction Contained Here.

And what does that actually mean? That any ten, five, or even two SF novels are the so much the same that you know by virtue of the label that the reading experience will be the same (and therefore don't waste you time...)?

Does *The Left Hand of Darkness* actually share anything remotely in common with *Ringworld*? Or *The Demolished Man* with *Triplanetary*? Would you expect an identical experience with *The Female Man* after having read *The Space Merchants*? Are the Galaxies of Asimov's *Foundation* stories and Banks' *Culture* stories the same place?

Likewise the more general labels you run into with large works. Trilogies, Dekologies, Series, Sequels, Prequels, Spin-offs, and the like. Some, when precisely used, do describe something distinct. "Trilogy" goes back to the ancient Greek and describes three tragedies on a connect subject. It has come down to us fairly intact—any group of three works about more or less than same subject. Of course, very often now we have trilogies about the same people but dealing with distinct themes in each book, so the drama is not so much connected as the *dramatis personae*. A series is a group of works featuring the same characters or set in the same locations. Trilogies and quartets are specific kinds of series. (A series can also be a publishing format—books on mathematics, say, by different authors, but done in uniform volumes.)

What about a Sequence?

Well, generally the term is used to describe poetry united by a single theme, containing similar or related elements.

I've chosen to call these stories, beginning with *Compass Reach* and now continuing with *Metal of Night*, a sequence. The background is similar, the politics connected, but I intend each work to be readable in isolation from the rest. Nevertheless, they are related by a set of common themes, questions, interests. So far only one character appears twice, the settings of the stories are different, and the point of departure in each is unique. Over time, they will construct a common tapestry.

But I most specifically wanted to write them in such a way that no one will be forced to buy and read the rest in order to understand any given volume. Or short story. (Yes, there are a number of short stories in the Sequence; eventually they will be collected.) But I also wanted to be able to present a richer examination of this universe with each additional volume.

I didn't want anyone trapped—or locked out—by a label that obligated them to do more than what they wanted or kept them from reading any of it at all for fear of being required to commit to other books. It is not a trilogy—you don't have to read three books. There are no direct sequels or prequels— you don't have to hunt the previous volume down or wait impatiently for the next in order to get the entire story.

Unless the entire story you become interested in is the overall universe in which these tales take place.

The Secantis Sequence is a history. It has a shape and a backstory and a direction—several, in fact. But like real history, the stories about the people—or the aliens—do not require that you know all of history to understand.

So it is both a title and a label, but only in the most limited sense—a name to remember, a point on a map, a destination. It doesn't describe what is within the story, only a placemarker where you can find a story, in this case a particular kind.

But what kind? I leave that for the reader to decide.

Mark W. Tiedemann
March 2002

METAL
OF
NIGHT

Prologue

Cira Kalinge drummed her fingertips against her thigh and read the letter over again.

"My Family—I regret that I did not see you at my graduation. It would have made the achievement worth so much more."

She took a drink, let the whiskey burn her mouth, her tongue, her throat. No. This will not do, she thought, and deleted the two sentences.

"Don't apologize," she said aloud as her fingers rattled against the keypad. She leaned back and scanned the new text.

"My Family—it is regrettable that you chose not to attend my graduation. You would have benefited from the experience; perhaps you might have come to understand what it is I want to do."

"A little harsh?" she wondered and swallowed more whiskey.

She looked to the left, at the broad transparency that, combined with the dim glow from the terminal screen, provided the only light in the room. Beyond, a big megacorps liner floated, snug against the Armada segment, a long boom that extended nearly two kilometers from the main body of the station. The liner was half-again the size of an Armada cruiser, two of which drifted close to the larger ship. Special convoy, a secure shipment. Not her transport.

"I will be boarding a ship tomorrow <affix adjusted date and time for Homestead local> for my first assignment as an officer of the Armada. Any communications you send—"

If you send any, she thought sourly, if you don't stand by what you've already said about never seeing me again.

"—will go through Armada secure channels, following me from posting to posting. I ought to get it quickly, but it will be viewed by strangers. This is the last time we may communicate privately."

This is the last time we may communicate.

She wiped at her eyes impatiently and drew a deep breath. More whiskey. She emptied the glass and poured two fingers from the decanter. She did not like being drunk, but this time she found the sting of the liquor oddly helpful. It distracted her from the past, centered her on the now.

"I want you to know that I do not consider anything finished. I am not leaving forever."

She closed her eyes and remembered her father, thunderously quiet, pronouncing her prodigal. She had applied to the Armada against his wishes, left the family stead after he had forbidden it, and seen the course all the way through even with at first daily then weekly admonitions against pursuing what he called her defiant madness. She had paid for a special courier to hand deliver the announcement of her graduation and her commission to the stead, but there had been no reply.

At least, she thought, the damn card didn't come back unaccepted.

"I want you to be proud of me. I want you to understand. Perhaps you cannot understand *what* I am doing, but I do not believe it is too much to ask that you understand that I *want* to do it. If you love me, that ought to be sufficient."

If you love me...yes, she mused, that is the question, isn't it?

She deleted the line and tapped the pad.

"That alone ought to be sufficient reason."

Yes, it ought to, but it never was. Cira drank and remembered all the times that it had not been. "Want doesn't mean ought," her father had said, and she had come to accept that, even understand it. She understood him, or at least understood that he was who he was because he could not be otherwise. She wanted the same in return.

But that's who he is, isn't he?

She read the letter once more and wondered if it would do as a final missive. The last words of a prodigal daughter to her family.

But I'm coming back...

"*You've cut the bonds, you'll go and go and go and never come back. If that's what you want, then be prepared to pay the cost. The cost is that we don't know you. This isn't home, you've rejected that.*"

"*Why can't you see what I see? Why does it have to be your way or nothing?*"

"*Some things are just impossible. You can't be a wanderer with a permanent home.*"

"*But—*"

"Enough. It's done. You've made your choice."

Cira laughed sharply. Remembering it now it seemed so comic, so melodramatic. But that was her father. He never conversed, he made pronouncements. He never talked, he declaimed. He never let things be, he either embraced them or rejected them.

That's not me, she thought, and added a last line.

"You say I'm never coming back. Maybe. But that's your choice. I, at least, keep the possibility open. I still consider you family."

Her eyes burned. She squeezed them shut, rubbed them, then swallowed a mouthful of whiskey. As it seared a path down her throat, she signed the letter and stabbed SEND before she could change her mind.

"It's up to you now," she croaked, and stood.

What really hurt was the way everyone else had simply stood by and let him speak for the family. She could see that they disagreed, most of them, but no one else said a word.

When Maitha was alive, she thought, it would've been different. Or would it?

She gazed out at space, the ships, the parts of the station she could see, and let herself be lost to it. She loved this. Since she was small she had wanted to go to space. But she was a farmer, farmers do not go to the stars. So, she decided one day, I will not be a farmer.

Now I've got it...

I shouldn't have to feel shitty about it.

The polycom chimed and she jerked. She stared at the terminal. Incoming message?

She rushed up to the machine and fell into the seat and pressed ACCEPT.

"Goodbye."

Hours later she woke up. The word still glowed on the terminal screen.

Cira's head throbbed dully. She reached out and cleared the board, then went to the hygiene cubicle. She showered, took a couple of antox pills, and pulled on a new uniform.

The polycom chimed again. When she touched ACCEPT the official seal of the Armada, the stylized sword across the sphere of a blazing star, flashed on the screen. She watched her orders scroll up. When it finished, she downloaded it into a disk, slipped it into her jacket pocket, and shouldered her duffel.

She gave the room a last look from the doorway. Everywhere else in this section the graduates of her class had partied, talked to friends and family, spent a last night indulging childish excess in celebration.

"Goodbye," she said, and walked away.

Chapter One

Alexan Cambion stepped between the technicians jostling for room as they worked on the pilot suits. The prep room stank of oil and ozone and sweat, the insufficient ventilators unable to keep the air properly scrubbed. The faces he saw were rigid. The carrier had not been called to out-system duty in so long that minor break-downs proliferated, becoming major problems. Worse still, the techs had to overhaul the *Castille* while en route to a combat zone. Alexan believed they were doing the best they could, but the stress showed. Probably none of them had pulled shifts this hard since their training.

His pager sounded. He unclipped the disk from his belt and thumbed ACCEPT. The message scrolled over its small pearl surface. "Please report to Task Commander Palada, sub-bridge."

Alexan made his way to the exit. Across from the hatch, he boarded a shunt and directed it to the sub-bridge. A deep groan coursed through the ship, as if it were protesting—protesting the speed, the destination, the purpose. He sympathized. Everything on board the *Castille* was old, much too old and undermaintained for battle.

The shunt let him out on the carpeted expanse of the sub-bridge, one deck below the main bridge. The wide chamber was a maze of couches, roving trolls, and small clusters of neatly-uniformed officers. Alexan self-consciously zipped his tunic and tugged its hem. He had been working the last six hours in the armory section and he was sweaty.

He made his way through the loose collection—a troll stopped suddenly at his approach, an unsecured keypad sliding loudly over its flat metal tray, waited for him to pass, then rolled on—to the wide fuzzy blue privacy shield that hulked near the lift to the bridge. He pressed his comm disk into the air-soft surface.

"Come."

He stepped through the field.

Task Commander Palada lounged in a high-backed chair. Sitting on a nearby couch, Security Chief Tovak, distinct in his dark grey uniform, intently studied a portable ops board. Standing against the wall between them, thumbs hooked in the pockets of a dark green civilian jacket, was a man Alexan did not recognize. Cira Kalinge looked up from where she sat on the deck on the opposite side of Palada with a quiet smile and a nod. Alexan smiled in return.

"Lieutenant," Palada said. He spoke with the drawn-out vowels of Nine Rivers, a drawl that irritated Alexan. He wondered how a person could stay away from a place for three decades and fail to lose an accent. Alexan suspected Palada affected it because he knew it gave a false impression, which Palada used skillfully. "I asked you both here," he nodded at Cira, "both my wing leaders, for two reasons. We'll be arriving at Finders in, uh…" He looked at Tovak.

"Seventy-six hours," Tovak supplied without looking up.

"Seventy-six hours. Our orders are for full assault deployment, then wait for Micheson's task force to arrive with the ground forces. She's due in…"

"Twenty hours after we arrive," Tovak said.

"Twenty hours later."

Alexan glanced at the civilian, who raised an eyebrow, mouth puckered to suppress a smile.

"Will your wings be prepared to deploy?" Palada asked.

Cira nodded. "My people are running final checks now," she said. "I see no problems."

"I've been overseeing all checks personally," Alexan said. "We'll be ready."

"Very good. Well, the second thing." He waved a hand at the civilian. "This is Co Tory Shirabe. Co Shirabe is a journalist with the Ares-Epsilon NewsNet. Co Shirabe, you've already met Lieutenant Kalinge; this is my other wing leader, Lieutenant Alexan Cambion."

"Cambion?" Shirabe stepped forward, smiling politely, hand extended. His face was slightly rounded and his short-cropped hair was ivory-colored. He had dark brown eyes. He gripped Alexan's hand firmly, briefly.

"Who knows how," Palada continued, "but Forum Oversight has given Co Shirabe a clearance for the Front. He's going in with us."

"Sir," Tovak said, "I still recommend we check that out. This is hardly the appropriate time or place for public coverage."

"Your opinion is noted," Palada said. "I personally don't think it's such a bad idea. Forum Oversight's not out here, they don't have any notion what they're sending us into, and likely as not wouldn't give a damn if they did know. Now, Lieutenants, what I want you to do is give a little time to helping Co Shirabe do his job. See if you can get him a live feed for the operation."

"Sir—" Tovak began.

"Noted, Chief, noted and noted again. Credit me with a little awareness please."

Tovak glared at Shirabe, then nodded curtly.

"Less than seventy-six hours and we enter a combat situation," Palada continued. "I don't know what we're going to find. I expect not much. I understand you're from Finders, Lieutenant Cambion."

"Yes, sir."

"Anything there of any strategic value?"

"None that I can think of, sir. There's a Vohec shrine on the planet, which was the subject of part of the settlement treaties. Several mines, a dense mineral-rich asteroid field, one transit station that still hadn't been completed when I left."

"Hm. Not much. The only thing I can think we're doing is making a show of force out among the Distals. Finders has declared itself in secession. We have to start bringing them back into the fold and I guess Finders is where the Forum has decided to start."

"You don't sound much in sympathy with the policy," Shirabe said.

"Frankly, I've never been much in sympathy with any policy, Co Shirabe. I'm Armada. I do what I'm told, leave the rationalizations to the politicians. Take you, for instance. Tovak's right, it is irregular and possibly unadvisable to have a civilian—a journalist besides—in on this operation. My opinion aside, you've got the authorization from the Forum, that's fine. Not my butt on the line if anything goes wrong."

"You're not concerned that I may discover some irregularities on your side of the relationship?"

"Can't do anything but make the Armada better. Anyway, I have other things to discuss with my officers. If you'll excuse us, Co

Shirabe, Lieutenants Kalinge and Cambion will get in touch with you later and see to your needs."

Shirabe nodded politely. "Pleased to have met you," he said to Cira and Alexan. He stepped through the blue field and evaporated from sight and sound.

"May I speak freely, commander?" Alexan asked.

"Of course."

"I don't really have the time to shepherd a journalist through this operation. I don't think Cira—Lt. Kalinge—does either."

Palada nodded, folding his hands in his lap. "All I want you to do is make good p.r. for the Armada, stick him in a surveillance node, and leave him alone. An hour at most, Lieutenant. You can certainly spare that for a little good will gesture."

"Now," Palada continued, "to the other matter. We left Valico in rather a hurry. Consequently we didn't do as thorough a job with crew profiles as we should have. We may have some…associational difficulties with some crew. Chief Tovak has been catching up on evaluations. Chief?"

Tovak stood sharply and faced Alexan and Cira. "Overall, we have excellent profiles. Armada isn't usually very lax in culling counterproductives from the ranks. But this situation is unique. Factors that weren't important before the Riot have now become important."

The Riot. Alexan had not heard anyone refer to it so directly since the orders for deployment. He still found it difficult to imagine Earth as a battlefield, torn apart by factions no one could have guessed existed. At least none he had guessed. Then the secessions began and so they were going to war.

"Give them an example, Chief," Palada said. He reclined in his chair, gazing ceiling-ward.

"An example would be the Morgan-Kols Mega. Old, well-established Vested family, with holdings throughout the Pan Humana. In the last fifty years Morgan-Kols began making heavy investments in the Distals. A franchise was established at Skat, well outside the Secant. A family segment was allocated and the standard lines were established within the Pan Proper. With the death of Chairman Tai Chin and the subsequent Riot, there has erupted a schism within Morgan-Kols between the mega proper and the segment. The ties are complex, the associations difficult to trace. Members of the mega are under suspicion as Distal sympathizers. Family associations were not a problem prior to the Riot, now they can prove untenable."

"A lot of Vested send their young through the Armada," Cira said.

Alexan glanced at her, but she was paying attention to Tovak. He clasped his hands behind his back and kept his expression carefully neutral.

"And security," Tovak continued, "now has to decide which are uncompromised. It's difficult. We're not used to thinking in these terms. Vested are vested, we shouldn't have to question their loyalties."

"Their loyalties are where their capital is," Alexan said.

"Yes, but where exactly *is* that?" Palada said. "Morgan-Kols is all over the Pan, even the segment established on Skat. Their capital is spread everywhere, interconnected, entwined. How do you decide where that is when it's in fifty systems?" He shook his head. "I'm grateful that I'm a career officer and my family is just *in*-vested. Politics!"

Alexan was startled. He was unused to seeing Palada riled, less comfortable with seeing him express it. Perhaps he was groaning with his ship, complaining about the use and abuse.

Tovak cleared his throat. "We've run profiles on the crews of every ship in the task force. We've found forty-one members of vested families, fifteen with segment ties to the Distals. There are three of those on *Castille*." He pulled three datachits from his pocket, handed two to Cira and one to Alexan. "We need to get some sense of their loyalties."

Alexan accepted the chit uneasily. "Why not just order them to stand down for the duration?"

"I'd love to," Palada said. "Unfortunately, there would be repercussions. If I have the word of my subordinate officers that there could be a problem, I won't hesitate to pull them off duty. But I can't be arbitrary. Not yet. This isn't exactly a war at the moment. It's an 'action'—nice ambiguous term that means I can't exercise full wartime prerogatives. If it turns into a war, then I can put them in detention without any explanation to anybody."

Alexan nodded. Appearances. He looked at the chit. Mila
Salasin. He swallowed hard. Mila Salasin was one of his better
pilots. He pocketed the chit.

"I want to know," Palada said, "who will fight and who will
not."

Tory Shirabe took a corner booth in the omnirec and ordered a
glass of Valico mosel. He took out his notebook and scanned the
meeting with Task Commander Palada, his chief of security, and the
two wing leaders of his fighter squadrons. Tory shook his head,
dismayed at the fact that this carrier still deployed *in situ* piloted fighters. No VR, no telelinks, no station-to-station teleoperation, but real
live pilots. He glanced around the omnirec at the crew gathered—
mostly, he noted, pilots from Cambion's beta wing—and wondered
at the bravery or lunacy of these people.

The meeting was all in temp memory. He looked it over and
decided that there were interesting questions scattered throughout
the conversation. Unfortunate that he had not been permitted to
stay for the rest. He transferred the text to permanent storage. His
wine arrived and he settled back to watch the warriors and think
about his options.

He still did not know how his company had managed Forum
approval for his assignment and that bothered him. Tory liked to
know for whom he was working and under what conditions, always, but he had had no time to investigate, nor did he want to lose
the opportunity by asking inappropriate questions. Word came a
day before the task force was scheduled to depart Valico and he had
managed to get on board the *Castille* a scant two hours prior.

Later he would ask how. For now, one-hundred-thirty hours
out from Valico, he had more immediate concerns. He had managed to compile a healthy selection of research material and until
Palada had called him in he had been covering background.

As yet he had not found any but the most cynical reasons for an
operation against Finders. Skat would have been a better target, or
Etacti or, best of them all, Mirak itself, which seemed the likeliest
system from which to direct the secession. Mirak was the most
industrialized, the crossroads of trade between the Pan and the Seti
Reaches. It was the oldest of the Distal colonies, and as such the

headquarters for the majority of the corporations operating throughout the Distals and into the nonhuman regions. Why not Mirak?
Why not strike immediately at the core?

The Valico Task Force left dock very publicly, in a wash of
media coverage. Tory's guess was that Finders was a feint, nothing
but distraction. The important assaults no doubt had left their ports
shrouded in security and secrecy, targets unknown but, he imagined,
undoubtedly more important.

Tory watched the warriors in their fine pale blue uniforms toast
each other and strike unconscious poses of heroic grace for each
other and laugh with each other. He pitied them. They appeared to
have no idea that they were merely decoys or, at worst, sacrifices.

But, as Palada had noted, there was little worth the trouble at
Finders. It was doubtful Finders could field much of a defense.

Cambion and Kalinge entered. Glasses were raised, nods made
in deference, more laughter. For a few moments they talked with
the pilots, grinning confidently. Tory watched their performances
and, still riding his cynicism, judged their quality.

Of the pair, Kalinge seemed the most at ease, with herself and
the pilots. She was tall, slender, dark skin like polished wood. Her
confidence showed in the way she stood, moved, the way she occupied space with an unaffected surety. Cambion, by comparison,
was stiff, formal. He was powerful, capable, aware of his abilities,
but without the confidence of those abilities. He held it all in his
hands, shared none of it, and those around him knew it. He was
with them but not of them.

Cambion saw him. He leaned toward Kalinge and spoke and
Kalinge looked over, too. After talking a while longer, they ex-
cused themselves and came to Tory's booth. Tory switched on his
notebook.

"Co Shirabe," Kalinge said. "May we sit?"

"Of course. Call me Tor, though, please."

"Tor," Cambion repeated, sliding in on one side while Kalinge
took the other. "Isn't that an old word for a mountain?"

"That's me. A mountain of useless information. Tory is my full
given name, but sometimes I feel like a twelve-year-old using it."

"Well," Kalinge said, "Tor, you can call me Cira. No cer-
emony here."

"All right. And you?"

"Alex. And why would a journalist carry around a mountain of useless information?"

"Because you never know when any of it will link up with another piece of information that will make it useful."

"So what kind of useless information do you have that might become important to this operation?" Kalinge asked.

"We-ll...I know that the *Castille* is sixty-four years old and has been the in-system Armada base for Valico for the past twenty years. In that time it's been out-system once, on an official diplomatic mission to Mirak, and that was eleven years ago. For all practical purposes, the *Castille* has been serving as a transit station. I know that Palada was assigned command eight years ago because he irritated the wrong people. He has a talent for that. I also know both of you were assigned here exactly one month after the Riot and that you both saw action in Sol system during the Riot." He raised his eyebrows, soliciting a response. "Not enough? Okay, how about I know you both went through OTS together and that you, Cira, are from Homestead and you, Alex, are from Finders."

"None of this sounds particularly useless," Cambion said.

"It is until I have something to make it all connect. What difference does it make to anyone where anyone's from?"

Cambion and Kalinge looked at each other. Perhaps his cynicism acted as interpreter, but that look seemed meaningful. Did it now matter where someone was from? Tory was from Earth and that impressed many people, but Tory had never felt particularly unique on that account.

"So," Tory said, "are we ready?"

Cira raised her eyebrows. "You said yourself the *Castille* is sixty-four years old. That should tell you something."

A vibration rattled the glass on the table, setting Tory's teeth on edge.

"What *is* that anyway? I lost count how often that happens."

"The envelope generators are slightly out-of-phase," Cambion said. "They resonate against each other periodically. Nothing too serious, nothing that won't get us to Finders. But it needs to be realigned."

"Poor maintenance."

Cambion shrugged. "This is the first time *Castille* has been out-system in eleven years, like you said. What do we need properly-aligned envelope generators for if we 'll never go anywhere at translight?"

"Will this ship be able to fight an engagement if it comes to that?"

"Of course," Kalinge said quickly. "The fighters are old, but they, at least, are in excellent condition. We 've got plenty of fire-power. And we have four assault cruisers, plus two smaller carriers. Valico Task Force will be able to deploy four hundred fighters and cordon off the system with the cruisers. Any secessionist forces...well, I doubt there *are* any. It 's an old task force, sure, but it still over-matches anything in the Distals."

"What if the seti deploy ships?"

"They already said they wouldn 't get involved in our civil war," Kalinge said.

"You believe them?"

"Sure. It makes perfect sense for them to just sit back and wait for the shooting to stop. Why get bloodied in something that doesn 't concern you?"

"It 's been suggested that this does concern them. After all, the Riot occurred during treaty negotiations that were supposed to ei-ther shut them out of the Pan or open the borders further."

"You believe that?" Cambion asked.

"You don 't?"

"It 's been less than a year. We were there, we were involved. It was all action against Distal ships and very human insurgents. The conference was going on, but that was just coincidence. The reason for the Riot was simply a power struggle." He tapped a forefinger on the table, hard. "This is an internal issue. It doesn 't concern nonhumans."

"If this task force and, I presume, others are successful, the seti will be closed off from us. Don 't you think that might concern them?"

"I think they 're eager to stay out of it. They closed down all their embassies in the Pan. The Rahalen, Coro, Menkan, Ranonan, Cursian, Distanti, Vohec—all gone. They didn 't even protest."

"They might have withdrawn in accordance with military intentions."

Cambion shrugged again.

"The seti are too smart to get involved in this, Co Shirabe," Kalinge said. "I repeat: if any secessionist elements meet us at Finders, it will be a slaughter."

Cira studied the schematic, then moved two elements from one feed trunk to another. She typed in a requisition and waited for the system to respond. She rubbed her polyceramo-capped fingertips together impatiently; the *Castille* did not possess any direct-link systems. The journalist had guessed it, though he had not said anything blatantly. The whole ship should have been retired decades ago. This was not the task force for such a mission, even if no serious resistance was expected.

Her comm sounded. She looked up at the monitor and saw Alexan waiting outside the privacy shield. She touched the release and he stepped through the pale yellow mist.

He came up behind her and hesitantly touched her hair.

"What are you doing?" he asked.

"The live feed for Co Shirabe. I'm tying our oversight systems into one relay and splitting off a signal for him. He can get gross movements, some telemetry, and a lot of confusing detail he'll never sort out. That should satisfy him and Tovak."

His hand had slipped to her neck and kneaded her muscles. She closed her eyes for a moment and concentrated on her breathing. A pressure began to build in her chest and between her legs. She reached up and pulled his hand from her neck, forward, and kissed his knuckles.

"This is not a good time," she said. "Sixty hours left. You need to be drilling your pilots, I need to finish this and do the same with mine, we both need to coordinate with the *Poitiers* and the *Minsk*."

"Details," he said grumpily. "I hate details."

"Is that why you insist on going over every single one of them with your wing?"

Alexan sat down. "If I don't, one of them might bite me." He reached over and stroked her wrist.

"If you don't stop distracting me, *I* might bite you. Ah." Her requisition approval appeared on-screen. She tapped in more data. "Just about finished…"

"You are so beautiful."

Cira entered the last sequence and smiled at him. "I'm pleased you think so. Did you go over the datachit Palada gave you?"

Alexan scowled. "Why are you evading me?"

"Because we agreed to wait till after Finders. There's too much to do and I don't want to be distracted by an aching crotch."

"We've got sixty hours."

"No, we don't. We agreed. And I think it's a good idea. I promise, afterward I'll sweat you half to death. Right now we have jobs to pay attention to."

Cira leaned back and watched Alexan work through his disappointment. He was not the best at it that she had seen, but not the worst by far. He pouted a few seconds, then seemed to brood for almost a minute. Suddenly he shrugged and straightened in the chair. Done. Cira admired him for that. Some lovers stoically buried their feelings; intentionally, she believed, to make her feel bad. All it accomplished, though, was to undermine her trust in them: if they hid that kind of disappointment and hurt that well, what else did they hide from her? Alexan showed his feelings. Briefly, though, just long enough to relay them, and then he moved on.

"No, I didn't go through it, but I know Mila," he said. "I doubt we have a security problem with her. What about yours?"

"I'm recommending both of them be suspended for the term of the operation."

Alexan started. "Both of them? What did you find out?"

"Nothing Palada didn't hand me. I won't have a liability like that on my record. If Tovak suspects them of questionable loyalty, I'm recommending suspension."

"But—we're supposed to make a determination—"

"I have. I don't trust them, therefore I won't have them. I suggest you make the same decision regarding Mila."

"You haven't thought this through."

"Of course I have. Look: if we leave them behind and nothing goes wrong, we gain by appearing cautious and prudent. If we risk taking them and nothing goes wrong, we gain, but not as much. We failed to defer to the judgement of our superiors. Makes us popular with the crew, but looks bad on a transcript. If we leave them behind and something goes wrong, we can't be held responsible for risking the mission by trusting a potential traitor. If we take them along and it goes bad, we get full blame. The only option that looks good to me is to leave them behind."

"That's hardly fair to them."

"Fair left when Tovak handed us those chits. The little we could do would be token fair. Worthless."

Cira looked at her screen. The link was set up. All she needed to do now was let Co Shirabe know how to operate it. That would take about an hour. Too little time, too much to do.

"I'll think about it," Alexan said. He stood. "I better go down to the bays and see how prep on the fighters is going."

He slid a finger under her chin, across her cheek. The contact was warm, energizing. She looked up at him and wished he would leave or that someone would call this whole operation off.

"Go take care of your people," she said.

He smiled. "Sweat me half to death, huh?"

She grinned and swatted his thigh. He laughed and left.

"Lieutenant."

Alexan looked over his shoulder. Tory Shirabe came up behind him. Alexan wished he had activated his privacy shield, but he rarely used it anyway. He did not slow down; the journalist matched his stride with apparent ease, though he was a full head shorter.

"I'm on my way to the fighter bays, Co Shirabe."

"Tor, please. May I walk with you?"

"And ask questions?"

"It's what I do."

Alexan shook his head. "Odd profession."

Shirabe did not respond. They walked down the corridor for a time in silence. Crew passed them in both directions, a few nodding in salute to Alexan, many too busy, some hidden within cloudy privacy shields. Since the order to deploy, Palada had kept everyone busy. It seemed possible *Castille* would be nearly up to its best by the time they arrived.

Alexan entered a shunt. Shirabe squeezed in with him. Alexan felt uncomfortable. He thought about Mila Salasin and glanced at the journalist.

"This is the first time I've ever been through one of these ships," Shirabe said suddenly. "How do you remember where everything is?"

"It *is* big, isn't it? After a while you just learn. How do you remember where everything is in a city?"

"Point taken. Do you like this duty?"

"What? Carrier duty?"

"Well, that, sure. More specifically line officer duty."

"I like it quite well. Why?"

"Curiosity. You were slotted for a staff position, weren't you?"

"No."

"Really? But you took classes in Fleet Master Bonnel's track and your first position after graduation was on Commander Lariton's staff. That's diplomatic corps—"

"And I transferred to a perimeter unit to get field duty, which is how I happened to be involved in the Riot. Is this more useless information?"

The shunt opened and Alexan stepped out into a narrower corridor.

"I'm just curious," Shirabe said, "why someone with apparently an inside line to a lifetime position in main staff would volunteer for hazardous duty."

"You could be a staff writer for your company, nice office somewhere and access to a huge library, and write editorials or features that would never require you to leave that nice office. Why choose to be a field journalist?"

"Point taken again."

Alexan palmed the door and stepped through. Behind him he heard a sharp intake of breath. The hexagonal chamber stretched before them. Nestled within skeletal frameworks on all six sides the fighters looked like massive sleeping insects, gleaming chitin shells of black and sapphire. Their cradles trapped them within an embrace of cables and struts. Six strips of light ran the length of the bay, throwing harsh shadows around the diminutive humans that tended the somnolent giants.

"At deployment," Alexan said, pointing, "the outer doors louver away. All the ships are facing outward. The wing peels away from the carrier from aft forward, forming a six-armed star."

"There are two hundred fighters? That's thirty-three per row, two left over..."

"Command ships are on opposite sides," Alexan indicated his own, near the middle. "Those two rows contain thirty-four." He grinned at the journalist. "It's an incredible sight."

"I imagine."

Alexan shook his head. No, he did not think Shirabe *could* imagine, nor could the journalist imagine what it was like to be in the link with a fully-telelinked wing—which these were not.

"Are all these tied into a sensory trunk?" Shirabe asked.

Alexan was surprised again. "In a way...these are older ships, the new type links aren't part of them. Instead we have a constant-feed data net tied into the VPAC—"

"Velocity Position Attitude Coordinator?"

"Right...so we get continual, on-command updates on the situation of each ship in the deployment."

"How come no full-sensory links?"

"Like I said, these are old ships."

Shirabe nodded slowly. Alexan watched him study the bay, eyes flicking from place to place. The journalist's evident knowledge annoyed him. Perhaps it was part of Shirabe's job to understand such things, but...

"Lieutenant," Shirabe said suddenly, "this entire task force is old. The *Minsk* is older yet, about eighty years old, the *Poitiers* is fifty-six, the cruisers are all over fifty. The last systems upgrade any of these vessels received was eighteen years ago and then it was a new sanitation system."

"Not true. The cruisers are all armed with fairly new deflectors."

"Sure, but Palada didn't acquire those through channels. He impounded them off some Distal independents caught smuggling. For all intents and purposes, the Valico squadron has been ignored by the Armada and treated like an embarrassment. It's not the only instance of that kind of neglect, but it's a fact that most procurements and budget allotments go first to the Primary systems, the old worlds where most of the Vested live."

"Do you have a question?"

"Yes, lieutenant, I do. Is this task force up to the mission?"

Alexan laughed sharply. "You seem stuck on that question. Just what is it you expect us to encounter, Co Shirabe?"

"The settlement treaty Finders has is with the Vohec. They represent the military aspect of the Rahalen Coingulate. They may consider Finders theirs. You tell me."

Alexan looked down the row of fighters. A few techs nearby were giving them sidelong glances. Shirabe was keeping him from his work. It would be simple, he knew, to end the conversation with that excuse.

"Come with me, Co Shirabe."

He nodded to the techs as he walked. His tech chief, Sibbs, stood with two others near the far end.

"Any problems?" Alexan asked.

Sibbs looked up. Her wide face briefly registered surprise. "Uh, no. We're just doing a final alignment on the secondary data trunk. Just about finished."

"Fine. I'll be in my office if you need me."

"Yes, sir."

Alexan stepped through the hatch and ducked left, into a cubby barely bigger than a storage closet. A flatscreen monitor flashed continual datafeed from the bay. The small fold-down desk was uncluttered and a single lamp glowed coldly from the center of the ceiling. Alexan sat in his chair and indicated a fold-down seat for Shirabe.

"All right, Co Shirabe, what is it you really want to ask me? Do you want to know how it happens that the Valico System squadron gets called up to deploy in a Distal system when it is clearly an obsolete squadron? Or do you want to know how it is that the son of the man who almost owns that particular system is part of that deployment?"

Shirabe's eyebrows rose. "Could it be you missed your calling, lieutenant? Those are both good questions. And I'd like answers to both of them. But to start, sure. What would Maxwell Cambion think of his son barging in with an Armada task force to prevent his move for secession from the Pan Humana? And why is his son so willing to do it?"

"I'm disappointed."

"Oh?"

"There's one more question that precedes both of those."

Shirabe regarded him narrowly, then nodded. "Of course there is. Why would Maxwell Cambion send that son to serve in the very organization that would one day come and make him mind."

Alexan burst out laughing. "'Make him mind? I *like* that!" He rubbed his eyes. Despite himself he warmed toward Shirabe. "Oh, yes. That's the question. And to tell you the truth, Co Shirabe, I'd like the answer to that one myself. But think about it for a moment: does it seem reasonable that, given the fact that he *did* arrange my commission, my father is a secessionist?"

"It is odd. But how do you account for the fact that Finders proclaimed itself in secession?"

"I don't know yet. I'm on my way home to find out."

The image on the screen overlapped the impression through the interface. Cira smiled.

"Good," she said, "it's something. An edge, maybe." She took her fingertips from the panel and looked over at the thin tech at the next simulator. "I'm impressed, Reeg. Any possibility you could install these before deployment?"

He shook his head. "No way. What I was thinking, though, was maybe tying the command fighters into the sensor net through this."

Cira pursed her lips. The link was makeshift, nowhere near as rich as a fully functional sensory interface, but it was something extra.

"Do it. I'll talk to Lt. Cambion. Can you do two?"

Reeg nodded absently, tapping data into his clipboard.

"What about general readiness?" she asked.

"Everything works. Since DuChamp and Ben-Verion are standing down, I've even got back-ups."

Reeg's tone was neutral, matter-of-fact; Cira heard no intended criticism. Still, it nettled. For a moment she considered asking Reeg what he thought, if in his opinion she had done the right thing. The moment passed. Wing leaders commanded, they did not canvass for consensus.

"Good," she said. "Let me know when you have it installed. I want to run a simulation before deployment."

Reeg nodded again, still intent on his notes.

As Cira left the lab, she thought about the wasted talent at Palada's disposal. Reeg was a first-rate tech. He had cobbled together a functional interface in the time since the task force had been ordered to stand ready. There were others. Many of the pilots in her wing were superb. If they had the equipment, modern tools, she would have no qualms leading them into combat. The tools, though—that part gave her doubt.

The next posting, she thought, *I* choose. Alexan had talked her into this one. After the Riot they had had several options. Alexan's logic had been sound: the Riot was a consequence of the policies regarding the Distals and open communications and trade with the nonhuman Reaches, therefore the action would be along the Secant. Of the three postings open, Valico and Palada's outfit were closest to Finders, and that had been the part Cira should have questioned. Alexan was persuasive, though.

And after all he had been right. They had taken their new posts a short forty-four days before being ordered out. Palada's task force would be involved in some action, even if it was only a demonstration of Armada presence in an inconsequential system. Another step on the path, she thought. Front line duty, if she was lucky some combat engagement. Do the job, make no big mistakes, it all looked good in the transcripts.

And I'll be a goddamn flag officer by the time I go home again…

Alexan's office door was closed. She entered her own office, opposite his, and closed her door. She accessed the data on Finders and sat down to study it once more.

Finders' orbited a red giant, Deneb Kaitos, a big bloated ball fifty-nine light years from Sol. As a fairly young system, the star had once been Main Sequence, very hot, blue-white, and quick-burning. Now it was entering its late middle age; only fifty or sixty million years left to it before going supernova, plenty of time to strip the system bare and move the population elsewhere.

Stripping it seemed the only reason to be there. Nature had conspired to create a perfectly exploitable environment. Everything in the system was rich in heavy metals, exotic minerals, and isotopes. Ore was the major export. Even the surface of Finders was mined, the expense of shipping out of the gravity well made acceptable by the superabundance of the ores and the fact that the highest indigenous life form was a kind of quick-spreading bacteria that covered a good deal of the land area.

Cira keyed images of the planet. Mountainous, the lowlands nearly black under the orange-ish light, the sky yellow to green-blue, streaked with ashen clouds from numerous smoking calderas. Bleak, she thought, remembering Homestead's lush green and azure skies. She tried for a moment to imagine growing up on such a world, how it might shape a person, and how that person might become Alexan Cambion.

Since Officer Training School, she had puzzled over Alexan. In many ways he seemed so simple, so uncomplicated. It was not innocence, Cira did not believe in innocence, but as if whole parts of him needed completion. He did not seem to possess many of the basic components of human personality and, she believed, he knew it. He was driven, that had been the attraction for her. She understood driven, knew its appetites, its consequences. But the causes were different for everyone—except the primary cause, the first principle of the driven soul, to be *something else*. Cira understood her own impetus, knew the something else she wanted to be. But she did not think Alexan knew what he wanted to be, only what he did not want. Consequently, he had made a number of erratic, senseless choices. He had been handed a position on Lariton's staff, an opportunity for advancement through diplomatic corps into a high echelon job, and he had transferred away from it into field duty, which was the only door that had been open to Cira.

She glanced at the chronometer above the flatscreen. Fifty-six hours. She drew a lungful of air and thought about Alexan. The pressure in her torso traced a slow, aimless path. When she had an opportunity, she decided, she should transfer away from him. She hoped it could be soon. The longer it took, the worse it would hurt.

Tory listened intently to Lt. Kalinge as she explained how the direct-feed link worked. Tory was not fitted with the polyceramo contacts she owned that allowed mind-to-medium interface with polycom data systems—systems the *Castille* and, indeed, this entire task force, lacked—but she had cobbled together a mechanism that gave him a considerable degree of access through an optical link. In fact, he noticed wryly, too much. She had overloaded him. If he relied exclusively on the sensory feed he would end up with a general impression of the operation with little specific detail. He smiled appreciatively.

Twenty-one hours to go. Palada had refused to see him again. He had been dumped on Cambion and Kalinge and they had largely ignored him unless he insisted—typical Armada attitude.

"I can't think of anything else," Lt. Kalinge said. "If you come up with questions, I suggest you ask them in the next five hours. After that, I doubt I'll have time, me or Tech Reeg."

Tory ran through the briefing in his mind again. "This is all standard gear? I'm amazed."

"I wish we could do better. Actually, some of it's obsolete, but that's the best we could do on short notice. It works."

"Yes, I can see that." He turned in his couch toward her. "I asked Lt. Cambion, let me ask you. Is this task force ready for this?"

She folded her arms, leaned back against the railing that surrounded the small work station. "You keep asking that. Ready for what? What do you expect us to encounter, Co Shirabe?"

"Tor, please." He shrugged. "This close to the Seven Reaches, who knows what kind of deal was made between secessionist and seti?"

"I doubt we'd have been sent if anybody expected us to encounter a seti force. Finders is pretty much a nothing world in a nothing system. Besides, we were closest. I can't speak for why *Castille* hasn't been decommissioned, but the fact is it hasn't. And as an active duty vessel, this is part of the job."

Tory looked at her narrowly. "You're not that convinced."

"What difference? We're twenty hours out and no turning back." She shrugged.

"You know Lt. Cambion's father is there? He practically owns the planet, controls the largest mining operation, the shipping company—"

"I'm aware of Alex's lineage."

"How do you feel about that?"

"Did you ask Alex how he felt?"

"Yes."

"Then whatever he said will have to be enough. I don't particularly care. This is a deploy-and-secure mission. No more, no less, nothing complicated."

"I'm surprised Armada is letting him remain in command of his wing, though. That kind of relationship could be a problem."

"I don't see why."

"You've ordered two pilots to stand down based on consanguinity. Lt. Cambion's ordered one. You don't see how family relations pose a problem?"

"He wasn't on the recommended list. If the Armada feels he's fine, I have no problem with their judgement."

"You're from Homestead, aren't you?"

She nodded.

"How did you get into the Armada?"

"I joined."

Tory smiled politely, waiting.

Lt. Kalinge lowered her arms and sighed. "I got in through scholarships," she said. "I earned my way in. No special affiliations, no political favors to anyone, just a lot of hard work. My family is in agriculture, small shareholding."

"Did they approve?"

"That's hard to say. They're proud of me, certainly, but my leaving was a hardship for them. It's a family 'stead, four generations, and no one had left before." She shrugged. "I don't know if they approve. It doesn't matter."

"No?"

"I'm here, not there."

Tory nodded. He looked over the array of equipment. "This took a lot of time. Thanks."

"Commander Palada said to do what we could for you."

"This is a little more than he expected, I'm sure."

"If you're going to do something…"

A sharp tone sounded from her belt. She pulled a small disk from her right side and studied it for a moment.

"I have to go," she said, returning it to her belt. "Any questions? Make it quick."

Tory raised his hands. "No, I think you've done well for me. Thanks again."

She nodded once more and hurried off. Tory pushed back from the console and watched her stride down the narrow corridor toward the shunt. She moved smoothly, but every gesture was under control, and not the self-conscious exhibitionist sort of control Tory expected in people of Kalinge's background: people who had mined their own path up out of family-made crypts of expectation through the indifferent bureaucratic strata to the light of their goals, people who wanted something badly; wanted it from the soul, but could never believe they were good enough and that the work and effort qualified them; people who needed to impress everyone around them with a competence and confidence that they did not really possess. Kalinge did not move that way at all. Instead, she exuded genuine confidence, a match to her evident competence, and very little self-doubt. He watched her till she was gone, admiring her, enjoying for the moment the luxury of respect.

"I really hope you live through this, Lieutenant," he whispered.

Tory pulled himself back into the small alcove of equipment. He slipped his notebook from its pouch within his jacket and opened the back. Selecting a pair of wire thin cables and a set of jacks, he started looking for a way to connect to the array. If combat occurred, the speed and density of incoming data would quickly overwhelm his abilities to comprehend events. Tory made a series of requests until he found a diagnostics routine. The program proved to be very helpful. Connecting his notebook was a simple matter.

Then he started searching for a way into the command trunks. Tory tried whenever possible to get the entire story.

Alexan stepped through Palada's privacy shield and stood there for several seconds before he recognized all the people present. Mila's bitterness worked on him like adrenaline, leaving him furious and depressed in waves. He had listened wordlessly while she catalogued all the reasons she did not deserve being pulled from duty, and he thought many of them were excellent reasons. It was not, he believed, appropriate to debate with subordinates and so he expected her to run down and give up without requiring a response. However, she cited regulations that set aside Alexan's notions of Armada decorum. He was obligated to give a reason and she had the right to challenge that reason.

Cira stood near Palada, hands clasped behind her back, watching him. Alexan tried to trace the decision-making path back and found, as he had when Mila stood before him in an identical stance, that he could not explain that he had done it because Cira had told him to. He could not accept that explanation himself, even less offer it to the person suffering for it. The answer he had given—that his confidence in her was impaired due to her familial status—seemed shallow, certainly inadequate. Alexan did not know if his own family connection was common knowledge, but he had sensed that Mila knew and that knowledge was in the forefront of her thoughts as he finished his explanation. If so, she had said nothing, held back by discipline or decency.

"Lieutenant, are you with us?"

Palada gazed at him blandly. Alexan nodded, glanced around at the gathered officers. Besides Cira, Tovak was there, with his portable keypad, Harolston, the engineer, McShiros, the carrier defense coordinator, and Palada's exec, Stroikos.

"Very good," Palada drawled. He stretched for a moment and looked at each officer in turn. "We're less than twenty hours out now—"

"Eighteen thirty," Tovak supplied.

"Eighteen thirty," Palada continued. "I want to know and I want you all to know that each of you is prepared."

Everyone indicated readiness. Alexan pronounced his "Yes, sir" firmly, with none of the quaver he felt in his arms or lightness in his legs.

"All right, then," Palada said. "Stroikos?"

Stroikos stepped forward. "Final instructions, details will be relayed once you take your stations for deployment. No action is to be taken against the planet itself. We're to secure the immediate space around the transit station. Search and locate any and all merchanter class vessels or larger in the system and render them immobile, search for any multigigawatt power sources scattered throughout the system and take them out, then wait for Micheson's task force. Upon arrival, we're to provide them with protection while they first secure the transit station itself, then stand by to give cover for grounding on Finders. Any questions?"

"Do we have any intelligence on what we're likely to encounter?" McShiros asked.

"We have no intelligence, major," Palada said. "Somehow that wasn't part of the package. For all we know they've got a seti fleet sitting there. Be prepared for any contingency."

Stroikos waited a few seconds, then asked, "Any other questions? Fine, then get to your stations and stand ready. Anything not duty-related you haven't done waits till it's all over."

Alexan stood still for a moment, then turned.

"Lt. Cambion."

He looked at Palada, who crooked a finger for him to stay.

Cira brushed by and squeezed his hand. The pressure was warm, welcome. Then he was alone with Palada and Tovak.

Palada sighed. "Major Tovak, you can leave us alone."

Tovak started, then frowned at Alexan. Reluctantly he tucked his keypad under his left arm and strode out of the circle of privacy.

"Sit down, Lieutenant. This is off the record and I hate formality anyway."

Alexan sat on the sofa, opposite where Tovak had been. He felt suddenly self-conscious and young.

"You recommended Mila Salasin be taken out of the wing," Palada said, "and I approved the recommendation. You ought to know that she's filing a grievance, challenging the recommendation. Won't do any good since it won't get her back into the action here. Unless you withdraw your recommendation."

"Are you asking me to do that, sir?"

"Your decision, Lieutenant, your prerogative. But I do wonder why you made the decision in the first place. If I were to give advice, I'd suggest a rethink, maybe weigh the consequences of a challenge. Under normal circumstances a court that found unwarranted prejudice might transfer the demerits to the superior officer."

"These aren't normal circumstances, though," Alexan said. Besides, he thought, she was on Palada's list. Or was this an issue between Palada and Tovak?

Palada shrugged. "Depends on how this action is later defined. It might be within normal law enforcement parameters, in which case they are normal. I really doubt that, though. But if I were you I would reassess. Personally, I think you made a good call, but it can't hurt to know all your reasons."

"Yes, sir."

"Now, the reason I wanted to speak to you, off the record. We're going into action in your home system."

"Yes..."

"Your father's still there. A lot of people evacuated just after the Riot, came in away from the Distals. A lot of Finders citizens, but not Cambion."

"My father is...obstinate. He's put a lot of his life into Finders."

Palada nodded slowly. "I can understand that. My family is from Aqual originally. Freelance agrotechs, good at rehabilitating unworkable soil, making it pay. My grandfather moved to Tabit and bought a stead, tried to remake the Paladas into landed invested. Didn't work real well, we didn't have it in us to stay put. But he stayed with the property, died on it, even when he couldn't tug a subsistence living out of it. Stubborn. But investments are hard to surrender. Takes a certain kind of honesty to know when it really is time to leave." He leaned forward. "But I have to know if that's really what Maxwell Cambion is like or if I have something else to worry about. You mentioned there's a Vohec shrine on Finders. How did that come about?"

"I'm not really sure about the history, sir. Diphda borders their sphere. When the settlement was first established there were negotiations with the Vohec."

"Where is that shrine?"

"Southern hemisphere, in the mountains—"

"On whose land?"

Alexan frowned. "Ours, technically, the Cambions. But the Vohec have an indefinite lease."

"Mm. And what kind of a relationship does your father have with the Vohec?"

Alexan wanted to leave then. He suppressed an impulse to shift in his seat, scratch his nose, his ear, look away from Palada, to squirm.

"You want to know about my father, Commander, and I honestly can't tell you."

"Oh?"

"I don't know him very well. I saw him once, maybe twice every fifteen days. I was raised in the city, by caretakers and tutors."

"What was the reason for that? If you don't mind my asking, Lieutenant."

"Maxwell Cambion is a builder, sir. His life is his work and he spends most of his time on that. He owns the largest mining concern in the system. It takes all his attention. I think he intended me to one day assume control of the shipping business. That was the thinking behind my commission."

Palada nodded slowly, eyes fixed on Alexan. Palada covered his thoughts and feelings very well from what Alexan had seen, but now there was no hiding the extent of doubt in Palada's eyes. Alexan swallowed hard and hoped for the end to the interview.

"Very well, Lieutenant," Palada said casually. "You may go. And remember, make sure of your reasons for Salasin's stand-down."

"Yes, sir. Thank you."

The task force dropped out of translight at the rim of the system. Tory felt it in his bowels, squinted into the chaotic spectacle the direct feed provided. For an instant he was nauseated, then the adrenaline rush overrode every other sensation. The dazzle of light, streaking, multi-hued, disordered, was impossible to comprehend, but he tried. His notebook recorded what it could and maybe, later, he might match up what he saw and felt now with what the data told him. Maybe. It was like diving into a pool of light that shattered into crystals on impact, then reformed into a solid. Not exactly an image numbers rendered any clearer.

There were only three planets orbiting Diphda. The bloated orange sac spun a charred rock, a medium-sized gas giant, and Finders round itself, plus two large asteroid fields, one between the rock and Finders, the other just inside the orbit of the gas giant. The cometary cloud was not dense—too much had been boiled away when Diphda was younger and hotter. The data system provided Tory with a general reference indicating the current positions of the planets. The same schematic showed him the entry point of the task force; Finders was just ahead of the gas giant in its long orbit and the task force was coming in at an angle to intercept.

Tory touched a contact on his notebook. A moment later the chatter of the command trunk whispered in his ears.

The task force was splitting up. The *Castille* continued on a straight line for Finders, velocity at about seventy percent *C* but slowing fast, while the *Minsk* and the *Poitiers* peeled away in opposite directions to take up wide flanking positions. Two of the cruisers filled the gaps between the three carriers while the other two took positions "above" and "below" the *Castille*. Deep scans searched the asteroid field. Tory winced at the quantity of information—sizes and shapes, relative velocities, composition, densities, and spikes of exotic readings indicating alloys and artificial structures—and pulled back his attention. Let the notebook record all that, sort through it later.

Crisp, efficient command signals raced through the task force, blood in circulation bringing life to the machine. Velocity fell away. As they passed the orbit of the gas giant they traveled at barely thirty-five percent *C*. The scans probed deeper, started searching Finders itself, and the lump of the transit station in wide orbit, just now coming out of Finders' shadow. Caution, now, the tone of the commands urged, the asteroid field was still unscanned, the greatest potential danger.

The carriers deployed their fighter wings. The bay doors opened and the ships unfurled gracefully, extending the defensive arms of the carriers. To Tory, they seemed such fragile, insufficient guardians. But as they sped forward, accelerating ahead of the largest ships, he sensed the power each contained. The cruisers had already slowed and moved even farther away, taking positions for widest possible surveillance and covering fire. The task force, old as it was, suddenly seemed a model of efficient might. Tory felt foolish questioning its ability to meet the challenge. What difference did age matter when dealing with raw power and control on this level?

The fighters had almost reached optimum deployment, hundreds of ships, distributed for maximum effect. Despite himself, Tory was impressed.

The asteroid field shifted. Tory stared, awed, as thousands of asteroids ceased to exist. The information flow multiplied, scans shifted abruptly, retasked automatically by this sudden change. No error, there *had* been something there, reassessment clearly showed hard sensor data, varied configurations, complex arrays of compositional description—the system told itself that it had made no mistake, there was too much real information stating that there should be asteroids where now there was nothing.

No, that was an error. Something remained, many somethings, much smaller, and moving. Tory followed helplessly while the entire sensor analysis system tried doggedly to match what remained behind with what it believed should be there. It only took a part of a second for the massive and overwhelmed system to discard expectations and reassess. It only took another part of a second for the reassessment to absorb the new scanner data and derive a new conclusion. Before a full second went by, the task force data systems recognized the somethings as ships moving to intercept.

But at thirty-five percent C the entire task force had moved one hundred five thousand kilometers closer. The attacking ships were accelerating, the command to compensate ate up another fifty thousand kilometers, and by the time the fighter array began to break up to meet specific targets another quarter million kilometers was left behind.

For a few seconds the ships danced complex reels, finding position. Tory understood little, but the Armada fighters moved so fast, with clear confidence, that it seemed in control.

The pinpoints mingled then. Tory watched, dismayed, while nothing happened.

Then space filled with light.

Tory pushed himself back from the console, squinting, afterimages pulsing behind closed eyelids. He shook his head and rubbed his eyes. Around him the ship was quiet. He frowned at the silence, then pulled himself back against the board and pressed his face against the feed.

The novae were gone for the most part. A few here and there, sizeable, but hardly blinding. As he watched, hundreds of pinpoints converged on the task force. It was over, the fighters were returning to their bays. The enemy was beaten…

The points were arrayed in groups of six, and they flew erratically. Tory did not understand for a moment. Then he saw the lancing fire from the cruisers, then from the carriers' own weapons, picking at the pinpoints, and he knew then that there were no more Armada fighters. The battle of Finders was already lost.

Chapter Two

Cira felt the bite of air. Damaged, the fighter did poorly in atmosphere, but she only required it to get her down onto the surface.

The fire control system knew how many enemy ships she had killed but Cira had stopped counting at six. Her hands shook from adrenaline exhaustion. The biomonitor screamed warnings at her—the ship was crippled, impaired systems borrowed time and space on other systems, and the deficit was beginning to accumulate toward complete breakdown—but she needed alertness and overrode the failsafes to get more stimulant pumped through the skin patches in her suit.

She thought about the Riot in Sol system and the Shiva dance she had done linked to that fighter, one with its systems, its sensors her eyes, its weapons her own taloned hands and arms, its engines her muscles. The only thing Reeg's makeshift link had given her was an immediate sense of the death of her wing. Ninety-seven pilots.

Finders came up at her, thick clouds over dark lands, green seas, orange-peaked mountains. The ship bucked. Her ears burned and a distant whining began. She dropped through the stratosphere, into an ocean of cloud.

She was alone. The battle once joined had lasted less than five minutes. Cira wanted to believe her abilities had saved her, but she remembered little. There had been so many of them. No one had told her, no one had mentioned the possibility that they would meet such a force. After the false image asteroids had disappeared, thousands of signals came toward them. When they engaged, many of those targets disappeared, also false images, but to her overloaded systems so real! It became a guessing game which to fire on, which to chase, which to run from. Too little time. Cira had stopped trying to think it through. She let go, fell into a fugue state, a shell that fought. She did not recall the moment her personal Shiva took over, only that she danced through the fight, striking blows like delicate touch-points, spinning from one target to the next, untouchable.

Almost. The fighter was failing, she was lucky to be this close to grounding. Fugue had dissipated. A simple request from the fire control system and she would know the tally, but she refrained.

The passive-scan envelope signaled a breach. Cira requested identification. Another ship was dropping from above, quickly, the hull very hot from the sharp angle of descent. The polycom computed trajectory and displayed the projected line on a screen. It would miss her, fall on, and, unless it changed delta vee, would end up at the foot of the Hobic Mountains.

Cira hesitated to signal it. She could surrender to an enemy or link up with a friendly. Which was it?

She dropped below the cloud deck and transpared the canopy so she could see. Spread below her was the continent of Whale. To her left rose the Hobics, far to the right the Throne Mountains. Between lay the wide plain where most of the settlements were, a dark land streaked by lighter patches. Smoke covered vast stretches of the Throne Mountains from the numerous calderas, and the bone-jagged back of the Hobic glistened yellow and orange with ice and snow.

The other ship dropped from the cloud a thousand meters to her left and plunged toward the land like a rock. It was a black point lost quickly in the dark landscape before Cira identified it. She checked the recorders and found the image, backed it up, and froze it. She requested an ID match—WAIT flashed on the screen—and several seconds later the system identified it as a friendly.

Maybe not alone, she thought. Unless, she added wryly, it lands like a rock. She locked onto it and initiated autotrack, then followed it down.

Nothing worked. Alexan tried each system, one after another, hoping one of them functioned. Everything was dead, except the biosystems and part of the weapons module. He suspected, but could not discover since the diagnostics routines did not work either, that even his life support was about to give out. It kept warning him that his heart rate and blood pressure were too high, but Alexan felt calm, relaxed.

He could not opaque the canopy, so he drifted, slowly turning, within a vast field of debris. He imagined his own ship looked like the bits and pieces around him, twisted and burnt chunks of once sleek machines, streams of cable and wire, little collections of nodules and chips, cracked and scored sections of hull. An arm spun by, pink ice rimming the socket where it had been attached to a body.

The field looked like a shattered mirror in a black-walled furnace. Dante could not have imagined a bleaker place. Or perhaps he had; this was Acheron, and the armies had broken each other in their senseless charge.

He checked the weapons systems again and was startled to find that he had a fully charged particle beam at his disposal. But he had no way to target it. If something drifted into his line of fire…he laughed and looked out at the desolation. There was nothing left to defend against, nothing to attack.

Far to starboard he saw a black oval against the stars. He asked the fire control system if it could identify anything. The screen cleared then said YES: he could tap into the sensor array through the tracking system. Alexan grunted, surprised, and requested a scan of the black oval. After a few minutes he realized that he had been lied to; the system only thought it could work.

The black patch grew larger. It seemed to possess a definite shape and appeared to be moving in his direction through the field of debris.

Alexan felt a faint shock and the ship began to roll. He glimpsed half of a fighter moving away as he came around a hundred and eighty degrees—it had been sheered almost exactly in two, down its axis, and the tightly packed guts glinted dully, giving it all a viscous appearance, like organs—and beyond the gas giant was a clear blue disk. For an instant he imagined himself back in Sol system, above Earth…

The roll brought him full circle and now the black patch covered several degrees of space. His heart rate stepped up a little and he patiently tried to coax his sensors to tell him what it was. The fire control system told him to wait again and again failed to follow up. Alexan became convinced that the system had told itself what was out there and that was enough to satisfy Alexan's request. He slapped the console half-heartedly as he rolled away.

By the fourth roll the oval filled a quarter of space and Alexan could see its shape clearly. It was easily three times the size of a carrier, with a gaping maw that scooped up debris.

By the eighth roll, the biomonitor prescribed sedatives, but that part of the system no longer functioned. Alexan pushed against the console and stared disbelieving at the impossible cave that was sucking in space. He entered near the rim. The edge was pocked and eroded like rock. Just within, at the border of complete darkness, he made out huge rounded clusters of machinery. Then he was inside. He impacted several times, changed pitch and roll with each collision, and spun lazily into the abyss. Once he came around to see back out of the mouth, a giant fishy orifice framing stars and junk. Then he rolled away into total darkness.

The dim lights on his console seemed to sit far off. He could not see his gloved hands unless he held them right over the board. Collisions multiplied, became constant, and then ended. He began to relax, exhausted. He tried to activate his external lights.

Suddenly the canopy flared into light and he gaped up. Pressed against the transparency was a bas-relief mountain range, deep gorges and valleys, wrinkly and twisted, blue, red, violet, green, silver, and gold, smears of black and white. His metabolism shot up again and he tried to hunch down in his couch. He threw his arms up to fend it off, certain that he was plunging down a gravity well.

He swallowed hard and opened his eyes. Perspective shifted and he recognized metal and plastic, wreckage, surrounding him. Alexan switched off the external lights. Easier to sit alone in darkness than see clearly that there was nowhere to go.

The biomonitor finally stopped warning him constantly and prescribing things it no longer provided. He slept fitfully. When he opened his eyes, four hours and twenty minutes had passed.

The ship vibrated, then shuddered heavily. He turned on the lights. Nothing had changed, but he felt a steady rumble. The mass shifted. One section dropped out to reveal a pale orange light. Diphda gave light like that. For a few seconds Alexan thought—hoped—he was back out in space.

Another section vanished directly in front of him, leaving a gap about two meters wide. He blinked. Through the hole poked a mass like an oversized bunch of black grapes. The individual nodules shifted, some submerging within while others surfaced, and the entire assemblage turned. As abruptly as it had appeared, it withdrew. The orange light remained, but Alexan could see no details.

All at once, the rest of the wreckage fell away. Alexan gasped. The light seemed to have no source. Without a point of reference he could not tell the size of the chamber. Irregularly shaped black objects herded collections of debris into large floating clusters. It seemed the universe had been turned inside out and Alexan was staring at the lining.

The movers had sorted the wreckage according to size and material and the clusters hung suspended in a loose grid against the orange background. One of the machines raced toward him and stopped short. It extended another mass of nodules. The mover floated slowly around the canopy, holding the array about half a meter from the surface, then dropped beneath the ship.

Torn parts of the task force streamed into the chamber from somewhere above and to his right. More movers gathered around and began cutting out individual pieces and sending them in the direction of the growing clusters.

The black machine reappeared above him. The nodules retracted and the mover seemed to draw back and shift into a stand-by mode.

Soon three other movers came toward him. The first took position directly above the canopy and the newcomers flanked him at forty-five degree intervals. He was moved forward.

After nearly two minutes they turned left and angled between a large cluster of nearly-intact fighters and an equally large cluster of bodies. Alexan made out severed limbs, twisted torsos, shredded shipsuits, helmets. They had been removed from their ships and stacked here, like another type of debris. Alexan realized then that this was a seti ship and that the task force had not been defeated by humans.

He pressed the fire stud for the particle beam. No beam shot out but the screen cleared, turned green, then sought out and locked onto another target. Alexan fired again. The system selected still another target without discharging the beam.

In the seamless orange, a point of white appeared, then dilated. The movers shoved him into the bright chute. The ship was sucked down a spiral. Alexan tried again to opaque the canopy. He no longer wanted to see where he was going, wanted no clue what was about to happen. He was exhausted. He noticed then that his biomonitor no longer functioned. The canopy remained transparent.

The chute flared and he slid onto a cradle. Arms raised from the smooth bed and gently gripped the fighter. Above stretched a walkway beneath a cream colored ceiling. Alexan counted eight people standing there, leaning on the railing, staring down at him.

They looked human. He punched at the dead contacts on his console, trying to bring up a scanner so he could get a closer look, but the ship was now completely powerless. He panicked, believing that they would leave him inside till his life support gave up and he suffocated in his own CO_2.

One of the arms attached to the canopy while another cut around the base. Alexan stared, amazed and frightened, at the apparent ease with which it sliced through the polycor.

Air hissed into the cockpit.

He groped for the pistol in the field pack stored under the couch.

The canopy came away.

"Excuse me, co."

Alexan turned sharply. A pair of men—human men—stood alongside the fighter. They wore soft blue shirts and darker pants. Alexan's heart slammed in his chest and his fingers continued to feel for the pistol.

"You're all right, co," the righthand man said. "No one's going to hurt you. Please come with us."

Alexan breathed deep, heavy. The helmet plate began to fog. Black pinpoints danced at the edges of his vision. He abandoned the search for the pistol and frantically worked the seals of his helmet.

The air was cool, oxygen-rich. The two men reached in to help him out of the cockpit. For a moment Alexan felt profoundly sad to be stepping out of the dead ship, as if he were betraying a lover, turning his back on a promise or a friend.

Then his boots touched the cradle and he slumped in their arms. They held him easily and walked him away from his fighter. Alexan's vision tilted, seemed to slip loose for an instant. He closed his eyes and worked his legs until he got his feet solidly under him. He looked back over his shoulder, at his ship. The shiny carapace was dulled and scarred; several holes went all the way through and a section just behind the canopy looked molten.

They turned right, down a narrow passageway, and came onto
a broad walkway. Alexan craned his neck to see out over the railing.
His escorts veered closer; he almost thanked them.

Below stretched another huge chamber. Machinery covered
the deck in neat grids. Bright sparks danced, a river of molten
metal or plastic or composite flowed down the center, smaller
channels split off at regular intervals. Through smoke and harsh
blue-white lights he made out people, tiny and indistinct beside the
big equipment.

He stepped through a tall doorway that cut off the scene. He
looked down a long row of roofless cubicles. His escorts brought
him into one.

"Strip off, co," one of them said.

The cubicle contained a diagnostic bed, a biomonitor, a fold
down desk and three chairs. It smelled, as all such places did, of
alcohol and cotton and antiseptic fluid.

"Come on, co, we have to make sure you're all right."

Slowly, woodenly, Alexan undressed. Naked, he shivered. One
of them handed him a soft robe. He sat on a chair and stared at the
biomonitor. It appeared to be a common model, standard throughout the Pan Humana and the Distals. His two escorts, who stood
just outside the doorway, seemed perfectly human.

So did the two meds who came in. One went directly to the
biomonitor and began making adjustments, the other sat on the
edge of the bed and took out a notepad.

She looked up. "Hello, co. Welcome to Finders. I'm Shela, this
is Mari. What's your name?"

"Alexan Cambion."

Shela hesitated a moment, then entered the name. "Rank?"

"Lieutenant."

"Place of birth?"

"Finders. Specifically Downers Cove."

Mari glanced at him, frowning.

"Okay, co," Shela said, jumping to her feet. She patted the bed.
"Up here, please."

Alexan stood and let the robe fall, then stretched out on the bed.
A few seconds later he heard the hum of the biomonitor. Mari
leaned over him with a hand scanner.

"Nothing broken, nothing irradiated, no brain damage," she announced.

"Blood pressure's up, heart rate up, presence of endorphins but no stims," Shela added. "Good. You're very lucky. I think you're the only survivor."

Alexan sat up and glared at them. "For how long?"

Shela laughed sharply. "That's up to you and Commander Shinnick. But you're not slated to die, if that's what you mean."

"Is there any way I can see my father?"

They busied themselves with their equipment and did not answer. Alexan watched them, weighing the chances of escape, the efficacy of protest, the benefit of silence. Before he decided, one of them opened a drawer beneath the bed and pulled out a disposable set of utilities for him to wear. He shook the flimsy yellow thing out and frowned. The shoulder bore the stylized mountain and drill-bit logo of Thayer-Cambion Industries.

"You've got a clean chart," Shela said. "I'll see somebody talks to you soon about disposition."

"What about seeing my father?" He stepped into the legs, pulled on the top, and pressed the seal closed.

Mari leaned out the door. "Take him to detention."

His escorts walked him back the way he had come. They crossed the bridge over the factory section and through the opposite doorway.

Here the cubicles were fewer and roofed and not so fragile-looking. Most were open and unoccupied. They took him to one and waved him inside.

Somewhere behind him, a hatch slid open; the sound of voices—human voices—echoed through the corridor. Alexan hesitated, then looked around.

A small group headed down the corridor, away from Alexan. The man at the center of the group talked animatedly, his hands chest high and formed in a gesture that suggested he held something small and precious at his fingertips. He walked with long strides, a slight swagger.

"All right, co," one of his guards said, "in you go."

Alexan nodded, his eyes still following the talking man. He could not hear the words, only their tone, and in that brief exposure Alexan recognized a confidence he ached to possess.

Then the man turned to speak to someone on his left and Alexan stared at his profile.

"Hope you like the accommodations," the other guard said. "You probably won't be here long, co."

It was only a glimpse, but enough. The man was—could have been—Alexan's twin.

Hands gently took his arms and guided him into his confinement. A moment later the door closed and the locks hissed as they sealed.

The fighter had gouged a half-kilometer long wound in the ground, near the foothills of the Hobic Mountains. A convoy of some kind was heading south a few kilometers to the east of the wreck. Cira climbed high and waited till there was at least ten kilometers between them and the crash site. Cira circled twice before setting down near the wreckage.

She initiated the security net, took the pistol from below the couch, and opened the canopy. The cool air smelled faintly pungent. She jumped to the ground and activated her bodysheath and sensor perimeter. The mountains rose to her right, a great presence that pulled at her attention. Homestead had few mountains and those she had never seen except as images.

The foothills resembled giant slabs pushed up from below by roots. The amber, maroon, and oddly flesh-colored earth and stone was smeared by huge carpets of black spongy matter that squished under her step and released a sickly-sweet fragrance. Cira played with the filter control on her helmet until the odor was gone.

The crashed ship rested in a bed of piled up dirt. Behind it, in the distance, she saw where it had skipped once over the hump of a low spur. All around it to a circumference of about fifteen meters the black sponge smoldered, the sulphurous smoke bathing the site in foggy tendrils. The bodysheath diverted most of the heat around her. She rested her left hand on the butt of the pistol and mounted the swell around the crater.

It was buried a good six or seven meters and only the aft section still resembled something that once flew. The nose accordioned back against the cockpit. The canopy was missing; the console was cracked in two and both halves shoved against the couch. Shards of hull mingled with the remains of the machinery it once protected and the amalgam jutted up and out at tortured angles.

Cira swallowed dryly and activated her scanner. The entire area was still hot. She did a search for traces of organic matter. In the false colors of the scan she picked out a streak of blood on the right side of the couch, but nothing else. She climbed down onto the broken hull and rummaged along the sides of the couch, working her hands in where she could. The pistol was missing and so was the portable medunit. Looking up, she switched the imaging to radar and pattern recognition. It was a loose match, but she saw, in the wall of torn-up dirt, regular impressions that looked like toe marks. These same depressions were marginally cooler than the surrounding earth.

She rifled the rest of the ship, the parts she could reach, and pulled out another medunit, a pack of batteries, and the stash of emergency rations. She could not get to the weapons locker on the port side, nor could she pull the bivouac out through the partially crushed access hatch. Some power still traced its way through the equipment. It operated nothing, too much was damaged, but Cira drained it all, by the book. When she climbed back out of the crater with her salvage, the ship was an inert mass of metal and polymers.

Cira stood at the edge and tried to imagine how far an injured pilot might get. She looked up at the Hobics that dominated this part of Finders. The sky, where not streaked with yellow and orange clouds, was more green than blue. The mountains were pewter grey tinged sepia and streaked with black tears. They were young mountains, recently thrown up, the scars unfaded. Finders was young. Why people wished to come here was not a mystery—the system was mineral-rich, exotic ores almost on the surface waiting to be exploited, and no indigenous sentient life to worry over—but why people would then want to settle here and live out their lives baffled her. Why they would want to fight a war for the privilege was incomprehensible.

There were faint tracks leading away from the crater. From the spacing of the imprints, the pilot had run, in the direction of the Hobics. The convoy could have picked the pilot up.

Cira hoisted the salvage on her shoulders and headed back to her ship. Gravity was higher than Earth-normal, higher still than

Homestead; her legs burned and her shoulders ached by the time she had everything loaded.

She settled in her couch and pulled up the data on Finders. She located her position and studied the map.

Thirty kilometers east was the Tameurla Road, which ran north and south, loosely following the contours of the Hobics. The closest township was Orchard Crest, north, then further east on a spur road, perhaps two hundred kilometers. Tameurla ended six hundred kilometers north at the port city Emorick. Two main roads ran east and west out of Emorick—the High Eastering headed east, the Aquating ran west, cutting through a pass in the Hobics to the coast and a township called Terralaq. A coast road was under construction, but incomplete.

South was Crag Nook, about four hundred kilometers, nestled between two great legs of the Hobics, and two hundred kilometers south of Crag Nook was the Cambion Corporation enclave. The Hobics widened there, spreading east, and an old road, the Champ Du Terre, ran southeast from the enclave. The Eastering Road headed straight east from the enclave toward the Orca Mountains, then veered north to cut through the narrow valley between the Orcas and the Gallics.

Cira scratched her cheek. No one seemed to like to live close together here. On Homestead there would be a town every twenty kilometers.

The southern half of the continent seemed nothing but mountains with small valleys scattered about. Surveys had been made, but no settlements were listed.

Give them time, she thought, somebody will try to live there.

She did not have access to the survey satellites in orbit—she could easily be traced, even if she managed to access them past any security codes—so her ability to search was limited to fly-overs or guessing, which gave little chance of success.

She activated the agravs and the ship lifted. Two hundred meters up, she paused. She looked down at the crater and the scar it trailed; east at the thick smoky clouds hugging the horizon; south at wide black and amber plains; west at the wall of the Hobic Mountains. North was Emorick. It seemed reasonable that any kind of coordination centered there, at the spaceport. When the

Armada returned—she had no doubt it would—Emorick was high on the priority list to be taken and secured. On the other hand, they might just bomb it flat.

Cira sighed and headed south, hugging the contours of the mountains.

Nicolan Cambion stared at the monitor. The man displayed sat placidly in the small detention cell in a set of drab yellow utilities.

"Who is he?" Nicolan asked.

"He claims," Shela said, folding her arms and raising her eyebrows skeptically, "that he's Alexan Cambion, born on Finders, son of Maxwell."

Nicolan grunted, a sound that was half laugh, half disgust. "Well," he said after a pause, "he's got the face for it."

"I was struck by a certain likeness."

"Did you do his DNA?"

"Not yet, Mari's running the work-up."

"I'd like to see that when she's done."

"A brother you never knew?"

Nicolan shook his head thoughtfully. "It wouldn't be like Maxwell."

"To keep it a secret?"

"No, to make a mistake like this. He hates loose ends." He gazed at the monitor silently for a time, then shrugged. "How many other survivors did we pick up?"

"Fifteen so far. Four died before we could get them into a medunit. The remaining eleven are recovering." She frowned. "I didn't expect it to be so easy."

Nicolan glanced at her uneasily, then tapped the monitor. "Let me know about this one, Shela. Thanks."

"No problem."

He hurried down the long line of roofless cubicles that comprised the med center. Cross corridors intersected the main aisle and gave access to the eight hundred small rooms. Nicolan had expected at least half of them to be filled now with injured secessionists. No one, he reflected, thought it would be easy.

Nor had it been, he reminded himself, troubled by his own willingness to accept good fortune as no less than their due. The

planning alone had consumed months and the negotiations with the
Vohec almost as long. Contingencies were worked over repeatedly,
variations on contingencies, and variations on the variations. The
outcome had been a consequence of taking pains, but even so it had
been an unexpectedly quick victory. The danger now was in com-
placence. Secessionist casualties totaled less than a hundred; Nicolan
found himself wishing more of their own had been killed and injured. They had hardly received a bruise compared to the slaughter
of the Armada task force.

How did one stop overconfidence? And did he really want to
blunt it? Equal to planning and equipment and training was audacity,
and that came either from desperation or confidence.

At the perimeter of the hospital section, footbridges spanned a
gap up or down or straight across to other sections. The layered array
seemed to hang suspended in the midst of a huge cavern. Through
the gaps, mazes of apparatus were visible, lining the walls of the cavern like lichen. Small black nodules flitted among the contours, sometimes leaping to a floating section—messengers, like trolls, but faster,
more sophisticated. The sections—islands really—were held stable by
some kind of stasis field that buffered the interior from any action or
impact on the outside. The hull would have to be torn open for any
harm to fall on those within. Nicolan's awe of the vessel was slowly
diminishing, but it was a long process. He had been intimidated few
times in his life, and then rarely by an object. This ship, though, and
what it implied about its builders, disturbed him.

He took an ascending bridge and stepped onto a broad platform, workstations strewn across it like chess pieces.

"Co Cambion!"

Several faces looked at him, suddenly anxious. Reports waiting
to be heard, requests, clarifications, orders to be given. Nicolan
gave a brief salute and strolled from station to station, talking briefly
with the crews. At the opposite side, he crossed another bridge to a
small platform from which several walkways rayed.

From there he took a descending bridge to a section covered
with opaque bubbles. Narrow passages snaked among them; the
light here was somehow simpler, dimmer but cleaner, less complicated. Soft. He found his way to a large bubble near the center of
the array.

Within, tables occupied small circles at various levels, connected by a twisted spiraling sculpture that at the same time isolated them from each other.

"Nic."

Nicolan looked up and spotted the speaker about ten meters above. He waved and sprinted up to join him. The man wore a pearl-grey shipsuit and a light brown jacket. A glass nestled in his left hand, near a bottle of pale blue liqueur. At a distance his age was indeterminable—somewhere between thirty and ninety, two deep lines connecting cheekbones to chin, wide-set dark eyes beneath sharp black eyebrows, a nose that had been broken more than once and never properly repaired, a vague smile that signified nothing—but as Nicolan reached the table, the lines filigreed around those eyes stood out sharply, grey streaked his dark brown hair, and his hands, thick-veined and heavy-knuckled, showed long, hard use.

"Sean," he said, straddling an empty chair.

The man pressed a spot on the table and a moment later a clean glass floated down from above and came to rest beside the bottle. Sean poured and nudged the glass toward Nicolan.

"You look tired, Nic."

"No." He sipped the liqueur—aqual, semi-sweet and thick—and wondered how it came to be on board a seti ship. "Not tired. Troubled."

Sean nodded. "This came off too easy. Everybody's going to relax, open themselves up for a shitkicking later."

"How soon?"

"Well, some of the Valico squadron got away, which is good. Let them spread the word that an Armada unit got beat, but not totally. It'll irritate a lot of them, but then the fact that there were survivors, more than a few, will work on them and they'll realize that the fight hadn't been carried off as completely as Armada tradition dictates. Believe the mythology, the Armada never quits a battle, fights to the last co. Shit."

Nicolan smiled.

"So," Sean said expansively, "the back-up that was heading this way will stop. Assessment and all. Maybe get a new task force to come up, replace Valico. You might have ten days."

"Where will you be when that happens?"

"My orders say I'm supposed to be all the way the hell over by Skat in four days. Armada wants a report from someone on-site about activities there. After that, I don't know. Probably back to the Inner Pan." He shrugged. "I won't be here, that's a guarantee." He raised his glass in mock salute. "Find adventure and career opportunity, be a double agent. Hah! I can't wait for retirement."

"It would be a big help if we knew exactly which task force would be here next."

"It would, wouldn't it? But I don't know right now. If I figure a way to find out and let you know in time for it to do any good I'll see to it. But..." Sean took a drink. "So what else is bothering you?"

Nicolan shifted uncomfortably. "Nothing I want to talk about right now. When are you leaving?"

"Soon as the clean-up is done. Maybe tomorrow. Anything you want me to bring back from the Pan? This succeeds, now, there won't be an open trade route anymore." Sean grinned. "Very lucrative for the less ethical among us. I imagine smuggling will be the first major industry of the new empire."

Nicolan looked at the man intently, turning the glass of aqual between his fingers. "It doesn't bother you, does it?"

"What?"

"Betraying the government, the Pan."

For a few moments Sean's face lost any trace of humor. His eyes narrowed and his mouth compressed to a thin line. "As a matter of fact, it does. In my opinion this is lunacy. People will die because of a policy that's nothing but fear dressed up like politics. But nobody asked my opinion, so all I'm left with is somebody else's situation. I had to choose a side." He took a drink and his features began to relax. "I just haven't told everybody whose side I've chosen."

"How did you choose?"

"I have more friends on this side."

"Like my father?"

"Like your father." He reached across the table and patted Nicolan's arm. "And his son."

"Son. One son." Nicolan watched Sean's face, waiting for a reaction.

"A good one, you ask me." Sean shot him a look. "You're not moping over being the only one, are you?"

Nicolan shook his head. "No. In fact, that's one of the best parts of being Maxwell Cambion's son."

Sean laughed.

Nicolan finished his aqual and stood. "Let me know when you get ready to leave. I'll let you know if I need anything."

Sean nodded and raised his glass.

Nicolan felt relieved. If anyone would know about another son, Sean would, and Nicolan sensed nothing from the man to indicate that he had been lying. That was a problem dealing with Sean—he had been an agent for Armada security for nearly forty years; he was very good at his craft—but Nicolan felt confident that he could tell.

Which left only the question of who that pilot really was. And why "Alexan" and not "Nicolan"? Why change the name?

He shook his head. Other matters needed his attention. He made his way back to the bustle he had just fled, his mind a little clearer.

Alexan rolled over on the narrow cot and opened his eyes. The wall was dim greenish-grey. For a few seconds he could not tell how far away it was. He yawned, stretched, rolled again.

The doorway of the cubicle was solid black. In the low light he made out the shapes of the sink and toilet. Alexan blinked, trying to remember why he was in the brig. Then he remembered and closed his eyes.

A faint hum came from across the cubicle. Alexan started to sit up as the door faded from black to grey.

Black forms rushed in, hands grabbed his arms and legs. Alexan reflexively pulled himself into a ball, prepared to kick. A fist slammed into his stomach, then into his kidneys. His breath exploded and they jerked him straight out, turned him. He opened his mouth to cry out, then felt the cool patch against the skin of his neck. The numbness spread like water over his whole body. He felt himself relax completely just before he lost all feeling.

They laid him back on the cot, face up, and stripped off his clothes. Alexan was aware of everything they did, even though he did not feel it. In a way he seemed to be watching it from elsewhere. His limbs were pliant. They replaced his yellow utilities with heavy black ones, then pulled a hood over his head. They picked him up and carried him from the room.

When the hood was pulled off he was in another small room. Above him arched the ribs of a bare storeroom, the kind common in the shuttles that trafficked everywhere in the Diphda System. He heard the constant chatter of a commline, occasionally the shift of a body, footsteps. Once someone laughed.

Feeling returned like a million cold needles all over his body, but he could not move to rub or scratch. He groaned. The needles became spikes, became cramps. His legs drew up sharply beneath him, the pain quick, deep. He tried to reach down to massage away the agony and found his hands cuffed behind him. He clamped down against the scream at the back of his throat; sweat cooled on his face, pooled at the small of his back. The pain reached a limit, the muscles unable to squeeze harder, and gradually subsided. He unfolded his legs carefully—there was nowhere for his arms to go—and let out his breath, loudly.

"He's awake."

Alexan jerked his head up in time to see a man move away from the narrow hatch. A few seconds later a woman peered in at him.

"Good," she said and left.

Alexan closed his eyes and writhed until he found a more comfortable position. Then the chills began, waves of them. He rode them out silently, or at least he hoped so. When they passed he was exhausted.

"Come on, co."

Someone was shaking him. Alexan blinked. His head pounded and he squinted. He was pulled up to sit on the edge of the cot.

"Drink." A woman's voice, sharp and nasal.

A straw poked his lips. Automatically he drew on it and cold water filled his mouth.

"How much did you give him?" An older male voice, deep and gravelly. Familiar.

"Full patch. Didn't have time to be precise."

"Lucky he didn't go comatose on you."

Alexan opened his eyes. The woman who had looked in on him before stood next to a shorter man with thick black-grey hair and wide, staring eyes.

"Michen," Alexan breathed. Water trickled down his chin.

"Hm," the old man grunted. "Bring him along."

The woman gestured behind her and two men appeared. One on each side, they pulled Alexan to his feet. He felt shaky, but his legs—thankfully—supported him. Each step seemed difficult, though, as if he weighed more.

The old man—Michen—led the way out through the hatch and down a short, narrow corridor that opened into a large cargo bay. Alexan was pleased to see that he had been right—one of the in-system shuttles. A couple of coes in dirty brown worktogs directed four robots unloading cargo nacelles.

The woman fell into step alongside Michen and they spoke quietly. They descended the wide ramp to the mottled blue-grey floor of—

Alexan started. One of his escorts tightened his grip.

The bay had been cut into the rock, the floor leveled, tracks for the cradles running out to the switching platforms. Robots and people hurried in and out of a dozen shuttles squatting with their tails toward the loading zone, disgorging cargoes, taking on new. Under a shelf of jagged stone overhead, holding pens had been built for livestock, elevators for grains, freezers for perishables. Beyond, the cavern opened out into a vast inside-out world. Bright starpoints of floodlights shined high against the black roof.

"Home..." Alexan said. "Michen!"

The old man looked back, but his expression was a mix of disinterest and disappointment.

"Michen, it's Alexan! What the hell's going on?"

He was hustled into a tramcar, the middle seat between his two escorts. Michen and the woman took the one ahead. Alexan tried to turn to see if anyone sat behind them, but he could not. The car started with a lurch and picked up speed quickly.

It was all underground, more than he remembered. The mines had always been extensive, much of it cut by the initial colony groups for habitats, but he got the impression they had expanded tremendously since he had left seven years before. They rolled past new tunnels, widened chambers, storage areas with tons of new equipment, braceworks and gantries supporting the fresh wounds of newly-begun tunnels. Alexan shivered briefly.

The tramcar turned down an older tunnel and soon pulled up against a platform. Michen and his companion climbed out. She gestured and four men, all armed, came forward. They helped Alexan out of the car, then fell in around him and walked him down a short passage. At the end was a single door.

The room was twice the size of the last two he had occupied. Next to the bed stood a hygienic cubicle. Against one wall was a large medunit and biomonitor. The floor was carpeted.

Two escorts remained with Michen and the woman. Alexan was growing annoyed that he did not know her, though she looked familiar. He was still more annoyed that Michen gave no sign of recognition.

The cuffs were removed. He let his arms hang at his sides, twisted them slightly. His elbows ached and the tendons in his wrists felt bruised. His shoulders began to tingle.

"Take off your clothes," the woman said, stepping toward the medunit. She touched a few controls, then glanced back at him. "We can always relax you again and do it for you."

"Come on, Alex," Michen said tiredly. "Do as she says. It won't hurt a bit."

Alexan flexed his arms and began undressing. He smiled at Michen, who only stared at him.

"I've already been fully immunized," he said.

The woman came toward him, a small porcelain-white object in her left hand. She gently pushed him back to the bed. When the backs of his knees touched it, he sat down.

"Like the doctor said, this won't hurt a bit." She pressed the object against his right arm. It snapped delicately and she removed it. "Now relax. I have some tests to run."

He frowned at her as she went back to the medunit. "Michen..."

"I never thought this would happen," the old man said. He shrugged. "Hm. Well, can't manage everything."

"Michen—"

"Shut up, Alex. I'm not going to explain anything."

Alexan straightened, angry. "Where's Max?"

"He'll be along. Now, please."

Alexan looked at the pair of guards at the door, at the woman's back, the medunit, then again at Michen, who sat slumped against the wall looking weary and bored. He felt like a child, under suspicion of violating the rules, not sure which rules were in question, isolated and chastised without a hearing. He glanced down at himself, saw a man's body, well-muscled, hairless in the fashion of the inner Pan, but unfashionably tatooless. A contradiction to his feelings: he was home and it was as if he had never grown up.

The woman concentrated on her work for what seemed like hours. Michen snored once, startling Alexan out of his own light sleep.

The door opened. Alexan's pulse sped up. Maxwell Cambion stepped in.

Alexan felt: joy, relief, resentment, a combination of envy and pride, a twinge of hatred, a sudden eagerness to please, embarrassment first at his nakedness then at the fact that he had been captured then over his incarceration, shame at whatever violation of whatever rules he had inadvertently committed, gratitude, validation, a small desire for revenge, anticipation, fear. He felt all this in a rush that welled up inside his chest and skull and left him with too many choices for first words. He knew he was grinning, wide-eyed, and perhaps even flushed.

Maxwell looked at him for a few seconds, then went directly to the medunit.

"Well?"

The woman nodded. "Confirmed. Alexan."

Michen sighed, infinitely tired, and pushed himself to his feet.

Maxwell stood before Alexan, hands clasped behind his back, and Alexan looked up at his father. Maxwell's expression, as always, was unreadable. A virus early in his life had cut the path between his brain and the muscles in his face. He could talk—those were different muscles—and his eyes moved normally, but he could give only this blank mask to the world. Alexan remembered all the times when he was young that he aspired to someday make Maxwell smile. He had planned things, worked out details, imagined possibilities that might come with adulthood. He remembered what that journalist had said on board the *Castille*, that Alexan was returning home to make his father mind. No, Shirabe, he thought, I've come home to make my father smile. Once, out of pride for what I've accomplished.

Alexan sat straighter, smiled up at Maxwell.

Maxwell shook his head slowly. "Can't you do anything right? What in the name of perdition are you doing here?"

Twenty kilometers north of Crag Nook Cira ditched her ship. She set down in a defile high in the foothills and unloaded everything she thought she might need and buried it, keeping aside a field pack with the portable medunit, food concentrates, power packs, a beacon, her sidearm, an extra bodysheath and another change of clothes. She buried the balance—more batteries, more food, the spare beacon, a field com, the recorder from the ship, the salvaged bivouac, various other items—higher up still, with a low yield radioactive marker. She climbed to the crest of the wall around the pocket in the mountain. The fighter gleamed darkly, eerily incongruous against the rock. Cira sighed sadly and touched the contact on her belt.

A few minutes went by before the first wash of heat reached her. She stepped up the power on her bodysheath and flipped her visor down. The fighter suddenly glowed dimly and began to sag in on itself. Smoke rose from the rocks beneath it. The bodysheath deflected most of the energy, but she still began to sweat. After fifteen minutes the entire ship was an ugly slag of smoking black goo.

Cira turned her back on it and hurried away from the site.

The cloud cover had dissipated, leaving a metallic turquoise sky. Diphda was high over the eastern horizon and fiercely bright. Cira mounted an outcrop that gave her a view of the plains. It all looked burnt, black scarred by amber. The Tameurla Road was a streak of yellowish white. Cira adjusted the filters on her visor, correcting for Diphda's red giant spectrum. The black became lush green, the amber turned chalky brown, the road was pale blue-grey. Now it appeared as it would under a more hospitable sun and it looked rich and fertile.

Cira flipped up the visor. It was too distracting, too reassuring to see Finders in familiar light. Better to see it for its bleak self.

She picked a path carefully down the rocks. As she came onto a long low slope of earth she was sweat-soaked; her legs burned and her shoulders ached. She checked her handscan. Background radiation was a bit higher than normal, oxygen content a bit lower, but the ambient temperature was a cool eleven degrees centigrade.

Cira slipped the handscan back into its pouch and started down the slope. She walked south, about one hundred meters off the road. She quickly fell into a rhythm, and, though they continued to burn from the effort, her legs grew no worse. A few weeks of this, she thought wryly, and I can take up mountain climbing.

Just inside her helmet, on the right, a small green light winked on. She pulled out her handscan and turned toward the mountains. She picked up two signals coming from the northwest. Vehicles from their speed. Cira loped to an outcrop of reddish rock, glancing over her shoulder. As she reached the rock she could see thin wisps of dust in the distance.

Within a minute the sporadic puffs resolved into a large, blocky ground effect vehicle. Cira flipped down her visor, canceled the filtration, and increased magnification.

The machine was a standard surface transport modified with three large guns, projectile weapons of some sort. A cab had been added to the rear. Cira enhanced the image and counted six people huddled under the canopy, two at the console, and one each on the three guns, and another with a rifle.

Beyond, following at about fifty meters, was a second GEV, much like the first. They were dark, nearly black, with smears of amber and ocher dust, moving at a swift hundred and fifty kph. The lead vehicle veered onto the road and picked up speed south. The second almost overshot the road, corrected, and accelerated to match velocity.

They disappeared with distance, and Cira emerged. As she started south again, the heavy crump of an explosion came, then another. The handscan estimated it at five kilometers distant. A third concussion followed.

The walk took an hour and a half. Cira saw the smoke from two kilometers, inky black and drifting east. At half a kilometer away she flipped down her visor and climbed back into the broken terrain. Cautiously, she crawled to a point just above the scene and scanned. She picked up a signal heading southeast quickly, but no one seemed nearby. She pulled herself up onto a spine of sharp stone and looked down on the site.

The two vehicles were overturned, the lead one burning, belching out a thick funnel of smoke. She squatted motionless and carefully surveyed the entire area until she was satisfied no one was waiting in the jumbled outcrops. She moved down slowly, continuing the survey, weapon drawn. Until she smelled burnt flesh she did not think about her actions. There was no need for her to inspect the wreckage, she was sure everyone was dead. The odds of capture were high, but…she paused and looked back at the mountains. She needed to see that they were human. Even dead ones would be more reassuring than if she found setis.

The burning GEV had been hit twice, once directly in the prow, a second strike in the belly, which had started the fire. The other one had been hit in the side, near the front. The cabs were peeled away and as she came around them she saw the bodies.

They lay scattered, as if, already lifeless, they had been spilled from the overturned transports. Most were face down, several were stripped of overgarments. Two women had been dragged further away and left face up and gutted. Cira walked slowly among the corpses, looking for any sign of life—breathing, a moving limb, anything—unable to look away. Where a body had fallen on bare ground, the earth was moist and black. She stared at the women's bodies and her left hand moved to her own pelvis. Anger and nausea mingled at the back of her throat. She jerked her head around and staggered toward one of the male bodies. She flipped it over with a kick. It, too, had been gutted, the genitals split in half and the intestines dragged out across them.

She squeezed her eyes closed and waited while the shakes passed. She turned the body at her feet back over and walked away. Pressure built behind her eyes, in her chest. The sensations were not new, she recognized them, but they had never been so intense. She remembered ruining an entire batch of vesaleaf milk and the reaction of her parents. Lost income, lost profit, a major part of the season wasted because Cira had not checked the temperature of the distillator. Hopeless, helpless, wishing to make it right, to go back and do it over, but that was not possible. It was like that, but worse, far worse. More like when she had found Sheppie, their dog, gored to death by a wild pig, and all she could do was stare at the drying wound and the insects claiming it for their own and the weird gaze Sheppie gave the copse of ferns right in front of her. Like that, but worse still.

Mistakes, disasters, missed chances, wrong turnings, choices made in haste and ill-considered, and wanting to go back and undo all the heartache and embarrassment and expense, but knowing it was impossible, that time had locked it in and left it to be discovered by strangers. Like that...worse. Though she had killed people in the Riot, shot up their ships, holed the hulls of enemy vessels, they were machines she had destroyed. She had never seen the bodies. And now the pride she had felt at doing her duty as well as she had soured on her, turned to one of those embarrassments she wanted desperately to go back and undo.

But they *were* humans.

Cira swallowed, breathed deeply, and pulled out her handscan. At the outer limit of the scan, the signal she suspected was that of the ambushers who had done this moved swiftly away. A moment more and it was out of range. She picked up no other tracks.

She sniffed, put away the scan, and turned back to the transports.

It was sunset before she finished gathering the corpses into a pile and setting them afire. The eastern sky was a wondrous wash of reds and golds, shifting layers of cloud and sky alternately struck by the long-setting sun. Diphda was easier to look at now, but bloated and gluttonous.

She sat on the upturned side of the unburnt transport watching the funeral pyre she had built, cradling a salvaged rifle across her lap. That and the long overcoat and the heavy vest and a wide-brimmed hat she now wore were the only things worth recovering. The transports had been thoroughly scavenged. The rifle's breach was partly melted and a crack ran lengthwise through the stock, separating two halves of an ornate carving. The intricate weave of symbols meant something, she was certain, but it looked like nothing with which she was familiar. It was a small calibre, high velocity s.p., solid projectile, chemical slugthrower. Useless with the slagged breech, but it was the only one she had found. She cradled it, occasionally studied it, wondering about the people who had made it.

She needed to decide what to do. She watched the fire and the smoke and felt drawn to it, all thought distracted by the bright release of flesh to carbon. It was easy to embrace the flames and delay the next choice.

In the morning, she told herself. The morning would be soon enough to decide and even as she dropped to the ground and found a place within the wreck to sleep she knew the basic shape of her decision. Crag Nook was nearby. There was nowhere else so close. The decision was uncomplicated, but it seemed better to actually make it in the morning.

Cira huddled in the overturned transport, far back against the rear seats, and watched the cremation. She did not know if it guttered first or she simply fell asleep.

She came awake with a start. Orange slivers glowed in the remnants of the blaze. Above, the sky was awash with stars. Cira drew a lungful of Finders air and let it out slowly. For the first time she noticed the slightly acrid tang, the sulfur taste of a foundry. Her uncle had operated the smithy on the stead, back home. She had always enjoyed sneaking in when she had other chores to do and watching him, sweat smearing soot over his arms, his broad face lit like Vulcan, his large, powerful hands often taking over when the robots failed to achieve the precision or "rightness" he sought in the pour. It was strange to be reminded of home so far away, under such bizarre circumstances.

She stretched and climbed out from under the broken vehicle. She turned up her suit heat against the morning chill and looked up at the mountains. A pale, pale salmon glow traced out the ragged peaks, first hint of dawn.

Cira fished out a ration bar and pulled the long straw from the recess in her pack. She drew a mouthful of cold water and ate. Halfway through, she hoisted the pack onto her shoulders, picked up the broken rifle, and started south along the road. She hung her helmet from the pack and adjusted the hat, which was slightly too large for her head.

Morning was as long in coming as night had been. There was a leisurely quality to sunrise, minute gradations in brightness and color impossible to recognize until long after they appeared.

By the time the sky had acquired its turquoise hue, three transports had passed her, two heading north. She paid little attention and kept walking. Somewhere in the night she had abandoned her trained caution. She intended to enter Crag Nook in full light, instead of stealing in under cover. The overcoat hid most of her flight suit, she carried a native rifle, let the rest take care of itself.

The fourth transport—heading south—stopped.

Cira draped the useless rifle over her left arm and slid her right hand inside the coat to grasp the butt of her pistol. The vehicle was half the size of the others, a little sleeker, but just as grungy. Corrosion had etched mandelbrots over its panels. It had come to a halt less than twenty meters away but no one climbed out. Cira could hear its low hum, generators on standby, a slight ticking from cooling metal and plastic.

The pack was heavy and her feet hurt. She tightened her grip on the pistol and circled wide, well off the road, coming up on the transport's right.

"I don't bite," a smooth tenor voice said.

"I do," Cira said. She came even with the passenger door and peered into the transport.

A man sat at the controls, aiming a pistol out the window and smiling slightly. "I assumed so," he said. "Take your hand out of your coat, please, so I can see that it's empty."

Cira complied, slowly. The man's smile widened.

"They introduced a worm," he said, conversationally, "oh, about forty years ago, a special adaptation to chew up the uncharitably thick topsoil here and turn it into loam. Damn things have jaws like emergency leak seals, just large enough and powerful enough to take a body's foot right off. A lot of them went wild, no real way to prevent it, and for the most part they stay well below the surface, but it's not a bad idea to keep a weapon handy."

"Just in case?"

"Exactly. Would you like a ride?"

"Where are you going?"

"Crag Nook. You don't look like the type to go further." He seemed to examine her coat and rifle. "I passed an ambush ten K back. Survivor?"

"Bystander."

"Mm. Unusual, we don't have many of those anymore." He set down the pistol and touched the console. A panel in the side of the vehicle popped open. "Stow your possels, get in."

Cira hesitated, then shrugged. She unslung her pack and shoved it into the compartment, then added the rifle. When she slammed the lid, the passenger door had opened. She climbed in.

"I'd get the designs changed on the stock as soon as possible,"
he said as he pulled back onto the road. "Family markings like that
in the wrong hands, especially after an ambush, could get you quickly
killed." He glanced at her. "My name's Venner."

"Cira."

"Pleased."

The transport rattled noisily just before it reached cruising speed,
then settled into a loud buzz, making it necessary to shout for conversation.

"You're not a Founder," Venner said.

"What?"

"Thought not, you don't know what that means." He gave her
a quick look, head to lap and back. "Got to be Armada. So you *are*
a survivor."

Cira looked out at the swiftly passing terrain. "I get the feeling
no one does anything here anymore just out of friendliness."

Venner laughed. "Sure, they do, if they think they know who
you are, which side you are."

His weapon rested in a dash-mounted holster, in easy reach. Cira
slipped her hand back beneath the coat, touched her own pistol.

"I expected more traffic," she said. "Finders is supposed to
have a population of two million."

"About half a million left with the evacuations, six months ago.
The rest are at war."

"War?"

"The civil kind, where they fight over who gets to name the
place. Panners and partisans." He made a spitting noise. "Can't wait
personally to get off this rock."

"Is that what the ambush was about?"

Venner scowled. "No, that was pure opportunism. Any civil
disruption lets loose the parasites, out here is no different."

"You're not Finders either?"

His eyebrows went up. "No."

"You have a way off?"

He nodded slowly.

"Do you have room for a passenger?"

His eyes narrowed. "Maybe."

"How far is it to Crag Nook?"

"Another six K."

Cira nodded, tightened her grip on the pistol. "Wake me when we get there."

"Ten minutes."

"Wake me."

She slid sideways against the door, drew the hat down over her eyes, and eased the pistol from its holster.

Nicolan glared at the vacant cell. The techs had finished minutes before, but he did not expect to learn anything from their sweep.

"Middle of the third watch, prisoner removed, no one sees or hears anything," he muttered. "Sounds too trite to be real, but..."

"Actually, we do have a record of the abduction," Shela said. She held a notepad up for him to see. "Three hundred shiptime, five coes in full camo, took him with minimum struggle and left on an uncoded shuttle for Finders. We even have images. They sedated him. The only thing that didn't work was the alarm."

Nicolan took the notepad and ran the transcript. The enhanced, bas-relief figures moved in jerky real-time reconstruction on the small screen. The abductors appeared as empty shapes, parodies of people, all outline and no detail.

"Co Cambion?"

Nicolan looked around. A tall spindle waited just outside the cell door, a blue light shining softly at its peak.

"Yes?"

"Lovander Casm wishes congress," the Vohec device said.

"I'll join him when I'm finished here."

The spindle drifted back a few paces, then shot off down the corridor.

"Casm," Shela said. "Must be important."

"He'll wait." He handed the notepad back and gave the cell another quick survey. "Maxwell..." He shook his head and stepped out into the corridor. "What about the DNA scan?"

"Well...he appears to be related to you. Brother, I couldn't say. But close. Still, there are things that don't add up."

"Like what?"

"I can't say exactly yet, but there are a lot of coding anomalies. Like sequences that do the same thing they do in your code, but inserted differently and buffers in place to compensate for the displacement."

"I don't quite follow."

"DNA gives a pattern for proteins to follow. It's largely sequential, but the importance of placement isn't as great as, say, the placement of a code sequence in a machine algorithm. Segments control outcome, not linear commands. Still, placement isn't *un*important and where a particular segment is in the string can make a difference in the expression of that code command. A lot of problems used to arise when sequencing was shuffled. Birth defects, developmental disorders later in life, things like that. We learned to add buffers that rerouted some of the sequencing or rendered placement less important. Well, this Alexan Cambion has a lot of your code—enough to legitimately claim consanguinity—but a lot of those buffers seem to be in place and I'm not altogether sure they weren't additions. I'd need to do more tests, take a few samples from his hormone factories—"

"None of which you can now do because he's gone."

Shela shrugged and nodded.

"So he's probably related to me, possibly my brother."

"I can't say he's not."

Nicolan gave the cell one final annoyed glance. "I have to see Casm. See what you can do on what samples you've got."

He spun sharply and strode down the corridor in the wake of the seti troll. By the time he reached the Vohec section he had decided that a long conversation with his father would be a good idea.

He walked up the ramp to the island. A privacy shield encircled it, a dull grey absence of anything reflective, no detail, no shadow, no light, nothing, a wall of nether. A troll hovered at the top of the ramp.

"Nicolan Cambion to see Lovander Casm."

"Proceed."

Nicolan walked through the veil.

Each time he entered the Vohec segment, Nicolan had the indistinct impression that everything he saw had been—and was being—created just as he entered. Objects seemed to solidify as he looked at them, objects which a moment before he turned his full attention on them had been insubstantial forms, approximations of what he subsequently saw. Even what he did see he felt unsure about—the towers in the distance, what *seemed* like distance, *seemed* like either a city kilometers off or columns of some apparatus not many meters away—but the detail was just sufficient to make him doubt his interpretation rather than the substantiality of what he saw.

Lovander Casm stood waiting before a long bench. As always, he wore a midnight blue bodysuit with a short lighter blue jacket. His eyes, set wide in a squarish, hairless head, were solid green from corner to corner. He was taller than Nicolan, and thin without seeming gaunt.

"Co Cambion," he said, bowing his head slightly.

"Lovander," Nicolan returned the bow.

Casm invited Nicolan to sit on his right and sat down himself.

"Food, drink," Casm said.

A tray appeared near Nicolan with an assortment of foods and several carafes of liquids.

"Your generosity is recognized," Nicolan said. He selected a bottle and poured a goblet of dark red liquid. He offered it to Casm, who held his hand up, declining.

Casm waited till Nicolan had tasted the wine. "Within three hours," he said, "we will complete collection of the debris. Sorting, decomposition, remolding are proceeding. What do you want us to do with the organic salvage?"

"Can you store it for us and transfer it to the surface?"

Casm nodded. "You anticipate casualties."

"There were casualties this time."

"The Coingulate is making inquiries into the action here. Our motives are in question."

"We very much appreciate your help. Have you explained that no Vohec were directly involved in the action?"

"Of course, but action is a variable term. Supplying you may have violated our agreements with the Coingulate."

"Without those supplies the Armada would now be in control of this system. Finders would belong to the Pan Humana."

"Which is not a tolerable situation for us. This was understood in the first place. Our problems with the Coingulate will not involve you, but they may affect you. We can promise the presence of this ship until the battle debris has been reformed into usable materiél. After that, we may be required to withdraw our support. We hope this will not be the case."

"What if you do have to withdraw? What happens then?"

Casm was silent for a long time, his head cocked as though listening to something in the distance.

"If you lose Finders, the Vohec may be at war with the Pan Humana. If we are at war with the Pan, the Coingulate will repudiate us and we will likely be at war with the *Sev N'Raicha*. In that event, we will all lose."

Chapter Three

Alexan curled up on the cot and stared at the mottled wall, contemplating his sins. According to Maxwell they were legion.

His father's anger struck him as so many fragments of a broken whole, incomplete, but dizzying in its multitude. Details again. Alexan felt ashamed that his words could not transcend the details that comprised Maxwell's disillusionment and disappointment. He had done what he thought was right and it was all wrong. Alexan felt like a child again, because that was how he felt as a child. His own decisions, his own choices—inadequate at best, dead wrong usually, and he never deciphered the code that would tell him what to do. Simpler to ask, easier to seek direction, abandon responsibility to obedience.

He gnawed his lip, tasted blood, and blinked at the tears. Patterns shifted on the wall as light refracted through the sheen of salty liquid. Details obscured.

The door opened. Alexan listened to the quiet, shuffling gait cross the floor and stop.

"Michen?" he asked.

"Yes."

"Tell him I need to talk to him."

Long, papery sigh. "He's not interested, Alex."

"But—" He swallowed, throat dry, and choked. He rolled over and coughed, hard. When he looked up, Michen stood before him with a water bottle. Alexan took it and sucked on the straw. Michen shuffled back to the workstation, a faint scintilla of violet light dancing around him as he passed through the shield.

Alexan leaned back against the wall and watched Michen move slowly from place to place, his ancient face intent.

"I'm not carrying any diseases, Michen, you don't have to keep me quarantined."

Michen glanced up. "I'm not concerned about diseases."

"So why—"

Michen raised his hand, fending off Alexan's words. "Enough. I don't want to listen to you anymore. I have things to do. Now be quiet or I'll have you sedated."

Alexan threw the water bottle. It slapped sharply against the shield and bounced back, bursting open on the floor. The emptying container rolled against Alexan's foot, leaving a trail of spreading water.

Michen sighed again and leaned heavily on the console. "You're twenty-eight years old. Tantrums aren't endearing from you anymore."

"Then let me out of here!"

"Or what? You'll throw the bottle again?"

"I want to speak to Maxwell."

"Maxwell doesn't want to speak to you. He already did."

"No, he didn't! He spoke *at* me! He ridiculed me, shouted at me, humiliated me, but he did *not* speak *to* me!"

"Conversations must by definition be mutual. Your being here now shows that you and Maxwell have never had a conversation."

"That may well be true. Maxwell prefers giving orders. Is that why you like working for him, Michen?"

"Oh ho! Not bad. Pity all you learned during you sojourn among the defenders of the realm was adolescent banter."

"It was Maxwell's idea for me to join the Armada. What did he expect me to learn?"

"He didn't. He expected you to already have learned. The Armada wasn't suppose to be a school."

"What was it then?"

"An opportunity. Obviously you missed it."

Alexan crossed the room and stopped close to the shield. "I'm a very good pilot. I was in line for promotion after this campaign. In ten years I could have command of my own ship."

"Wonderful. Just what we needed, another ship captain."

"Then what was the goddamned *point?*"

"The 'goddamned point'," Michen shouted, his face darkening, "was that by now, had you *listened* to your father, you'd already *be* a goddamned *captain* and on your way up the tower of command! You were sent there to be important! Combat personnel are *not* important, contrary to their own opinions!"

Alexan scowled, frustrated. "You mean that job in public liaison? That was a nothing position, no chance for distinction, no possibility for decoration, for action—"

Michen raised his fists. He held them over his head, shaking slightly as if locked in a struggle for control. Finally he lowered them and glared at Alexan, his eyes bright with moisture.

"The Riot brought the entire Pan Humana to the brink of revolution. It won't take much to topple the government and when that happens the only organization with sufficient cohesion and authority to step in is the Armada. It will be those closest to the capital, to the center of power, who will have their hands on it, and that will not be combat elements. It will be the political arm. If you had taken that 'nothing position' you would have found yourself in due course among those taking control."

Suddenly Michen reached through the shield and grabbed Alexan's shirt. With surprising strength, he dragged Alexan against the shield. Alexan closed his eyes, but still saw brilliant sparks. Where he pressed against the shield he felt an intense raw vibration, a million studs in a wide, fast-spinning track rolling across him. Michen held him in place.

"You would have been *useful!* You could have done us all some *good!* Instead you volunteered for a combat unit and wound up shot down in your own home system, completely *useless!* And *that* is why Maxwell doesn't want to speak to you! You didn't listen to anything he or I tried to teach you all this time! You wasted yourself! Useless! Useless! *Useless!*"

Michen released him and he shot backward from the shield. He tried to catch his balance, but slipped on the wet floor and crashed onto the cot.

Michen's hands shook slightly as he wiped a thin trace of spittle from his mouth, glaring at Alexan. Alexan could not recall ever seeing him so angry. It seemed that Michen had been with him more than Maxwell, had taken the more detailed part in Alexan's upbringing. Odd, Alexan thought, that he had never recognized that before. But it was Maxwell Alexan had always feared disappointing, not Michen.

"I'm sorry," Alexan said softly.

Michen turned away. "I know you are. It's…all right. We'll soon forget about it. All of it. Now leave me alone. I have things to do."

Alexan watched the old man give himself over completely to his instruments with familiar concentration. After a while, Alexan stretched out on the cot. He stared at the ceiling and tried to reconstruct his childhood and adolescence, searching for the point at which Maxwell became the center, even while Michen had supplied the ground. Perhaps it was the moment his mother had died. He closed his eyes and tried to picture his mother, but the image remained elusive. Details drifted.

Cira's face coalesced in his imagination and with it all the sense impressions she had left on him. He caught his breath, startled at the cloying twist—almost-pain, almost-pleasure. He drew his lip in, tasted the blood, and rolled away from Michen to face the wall.

"Nicolan is on nine."

Maxwell glanced up from the flatscreen in his lap. Sunset washed his office in reddish light. He rubbed his eyes—they burned insistently; he had been reading reports for too long—and nodded.

"Let it through," he said.

He set the flatscreen on the table that was covered with cups, papers, other flatscreens, and datachits. Maxwell searched for a few seconds and located the most recent cup of coffee, plucked it from the chaos, and crossed to his desk. He hesitated over the window control and looked out at the view. The Eastering Road ran straight to the horizon. The Orca Mountains were a thin violet line. A thick plume of smoke sliced across the lower edge of Diphda and dissipated over the distant peaks. Maxwell touched the control. The windows polarized quickly to dense smokiness, till only the oblate sphere of Diphda was visible as a coppery disk.

He set down his cup and touched another button. Nicolan appeared on the small raised dais to the left of the desk.

"Nic."

A second and a half pause. "Maxwell."

"You're still way out."

Pause. "Yes, but we're on our way back in. I wanted to tell you myself that we've finished collecting the debris. By the time we get there, the material will be half-way through reprocessing and ready for manufacture. Six days and we'll have our ship strength back to norm and then some."

"Good, good."

"We have a problem. A couple problems."

"Just a couple? We're fortunate."

Nicolan grinned. "I think I'd trade these for a few tens of small problems. Lovander Casm informs me that the Vohec may be required to withdraw their support. It's possible they're in violation of the Coingulate Accords."

"All they've done is provide us materiél, advanced against future payments."

"Still, the nature of the materiél and their presence here put the legality of their actions in question."

"Will Casm complete the remanufacture?"

"Yes, that's no question. But resupply during an extended engagement is doubtful. If—when—the Armada returns, if we don't have an open supply line there's no way to sustain a defense."

Maxwell nodded. "Not unexpected. Frankly, I've had the feeling all along that the Vohec *Qonoth* is aiding us for reasons that have nothing to do with anything concerning the Pan and the frontier."

"As if our needs just happen to coincide. Political serendipity. Yes, I've gotten that feeling from Casm."

"When you make orbit, I want you down here. We'll talk this over in person. What's the other problem?"

"I think we may have Pan loyalists on board."

"Infiltration is always a possibility. Does this have to do with anything specific?"

"I've lost a couple of prisoners. Kidnapped. Very efficient abductions, too, right in front of the monitors and under staff noses. As far as we've been able to determine, they are no longer on board, which means they've been taken down to Finders."

"A couple?"

"Three, to be exact."

"Why would they kidnap captured Armada?"

"Symbols. Rallying points. Maybe just to show us they can. I don't know, but I'm not pleased."

"No, you shouldn't be. Have you tightened security?"

"I've asked Casm to supply us with security trolls."

"Vohec trolls? I'm not sure I approve."

"I haven't got the people to go around. Besides, we'll be at transit station in a couple days. I wanted to tell you this so you could check *your* security."

"Mine is—thanks, yes. I'll look into it. Any updates that I haven't gotten yet?"

"I doubt it. Nothing that can't wait till I'm there." Nicolan frowned. "Maxwell, we might have to evacuate."

"I've made allowances for that."

Nicolan started, then laughed. "Of course. I'll see you in a couple days."

"A couple days. Doesn't that thing move any faster?"

"When it has to."

"All right. A couple days, then. Take care."

Nicolan's image winked out. Maxwell stared at the empty dais, thinking the conversation through, taking parts of it and matching it to other parts. Finally, he looked up at the window. The copper disk was lower now, its bottom just beginning to touch the horizon.

"Station One," he said.

"Yes?"

"Where's Venner?"

"Co Venner left Emorick yesterday. He should now be in Crag Nook."

"Contact him, tell him to comm me at his earliest convenience. And find Co Rike, put him through soonest."

Maxwell depolarized the window several degrees. The land was matte black now, Diphda dipping into the mountains, coloring the sky blood red.

"Co Rike on six."

"Put him through."

Another man appeared on the dais. He stood easily, his body wide and powerful, a native-born Founder. "Yes, Co Cambion?"

"You only took the one prisoner from the command ship? No one else?"

Rike's face compressed slightly, as if he felt insulted. "Just the one, Co Cambion. We didn't have time for more."

"Do you know if any other abductions were authorized, by other teams?"

"I don't believe so. But Co Venner keeps things close, you realize. He might have ordered another team up, we'd never know."

"Very good, Co Rike. Thank you." Rike winked out. "Station One, find Co Harias, put her through."

"Co Harias on five."

A tall, gaunt woman with severe grey hair appeared. "Yes, Co Cambion?"

"Did any other shuttles leave the command ship in the last eighty-one hours besides the one with my imprimatur?"

"No."

"Your reports indicate only one passenger with the team on that shuttle. Is this confirmed?"

"Yes."

"Thank you, Co Harias."

She vanished. Maxwell turned toward the window to watch the sunset. He mulled over the possibilities. If Nicolan was lying, what was the motive? Nicolan had never lied to him before, not about anything important, so why would he start now? None of the answers felt satisfying. One, that Nicolan had somehow come in contact with Alexan, was the most troubling, but the odds seemed too great, even though Nicolan might legitimately wish to inspect the prisoners; Venner's people should have effectively screened out that possibility, and if they did not then it was Venner's mistake. Of course, no one had expected to find Alexan in the first place. Damn bad luck. Of all the dead, Alexan had to be one of the few survivors.

He had to wait to hear from Venner. In the meantime, there was the evacuation to think about. As he watched Diphda sink out of sight—a long, long process, infinitely soothing to him—he thought how much he would miss this place if he had to leave it.

Night came finally and Maxwell turned to his desk. If he had to leave it, the absence would be short. At worst a year and he might have to rebuild this office, atop the main tower of the Cambion mining complex. A year…

He sighed. "Station One, where is that comm from Venner?"

"Co Venner has not yet been located."

"Hm. Probably in some omnirec or nightclutch. Continue search, I still want to talk to him."

Maxwell picked up his coffee and returned to the couch. He scanned the disarray on the table, chose a flatscreen, and settled back to read.

Since Venner had turned onto the spur off the Tameurla Road, Cira had kept her eyes slitted. The road widened as it sloped upward.

She saw the city first, then the gate, which was nothing more than a pair of tall weather-blued metal pylons.

Crag Nook looked as if a vast hollow had been scooped out of the side of the mountain and a jumbled assortment of prefabs had been spilled in to fill it up. The components had then been simply pushed aside to make narrow streets, the walls and floors straightened. New windows and doors had been cut, ramps laid, bridges thrown, and new structures built around clusters of prefabs. Long streaming banners slapped colorfully from below the bridges, hung from windows, decorated rooftops. Around the rim at the top of the hollow windmills spun.

"A bit different than home, isn't it?" Venner said.

"A bit...a lot..."

Venner chuckled and Cira gave him a quick look. He drew his chin down against his chest when he laughed and caught his lower lip beneath large teeth. Cira felt anger rise, tainted by impatience. She drew slow breaths and looked forward.

A pair of broad red tents flanked the road just outside the gate, clusters of people sheltered within. As Venner pulled up and slowed, several figures stepped into the road. All of them carried rifles, most wore long overcoats like Cira's. She saw metallic glints on their shoulders and around their sleeves.

Venner stopped, lowered his window, and extended a small chit to one of the guards. She crouched down and peered at Cira.

"Yours?" she said. Her face was still, eyes young but brittle.

Venner glanced at Cira, then said: "Refugee."

The girl stared at Cira. Finally, she pulled a handscanner from beneath her coat, straightened, and inserted the chit. A moment later she tossed it back into Venner's lap.

"Take her to the Hall, reprocessing."

She stepped away and waved and the line of people moved back. Venner gunned the transport and lurched forward.

"Welcome to Crag Nook," he said as they passed between the pylons. "Population—variable. Major export—partisans." He glanced at her. "They love refugees. Gives them moral validation for sending out 'recovery missions' to scavenge the countryside. You might find work in that line."

"Why would you think that?"

"You might be good at it. I can put you together with the right people."

"People at the Hall?"

He laughed again. "I'm not taking you there. Not unless you want me to. The Hall—that's the Council Hall, or used to be—has been converted to a sorting pen where they separate loyal Panners from partisans. Try to, anyway; they make a lot of mistakes. 'Reprocessing' amounts to either being fed and armed and put to work or being interred and disposed of."

"Won't somebody check?"

"Does this look that efficient?"

People huddled at the edges of the streets or moved sluggishly close to the walls, most of them carrying backpacks or hastily-assembled bundles slung off a shoulder. Often the bundles included a child or two, their small faces struck ogling and immobile by the disarray, peering out from tightly-closed hoods. The adults looked only slightly less stunned. All the clothes were fading inexorably toward that non-color clothes become when worn too long at a stretch through too much, sort of brownish-black or cinder-grey. Here and there Cira spotted a bright splash of fresher, cleaner color, a red or gold or teal or even white.

As they moved deeper in, Cira began to smell something faintly familiar. For a while she could not place it, then she remembered: her one day of duty on the ground, on Earth, at a refugee camp outside the ancient city of Prague, thousands of displaced people crowded together for days without services, and the odor of long-unwashed bodies and raw sewage treated with wide-spectrum disinfectants where it lay...

The street turned and widened into a small plaza. Suddenly the first scent was completely covered in the mixed aromas of cooking food and antiseptic. Stalls rimmed the plaza, smoke rising from beneath the multi-hued awnings. People milled about a

central fountain—dry, the smooth carved lines smeared with grime—
protecting bowls and eating quickly. Several clusters of two, three,
and four adults ringed in groups of children who ate more slowly,
less frantically. Lines formed at all the stalls. Cira licked her lips, the
mix of odors teasing her hunger. She held back from digging out a
bar and eating here, where some of these people might see her. She
felt mildly embarrassed that she had her own food. The thinness she
saw, the drawn, post-desperate look of so many among them disturbed her more than the corpses at the ambush site. She had never
seen anything like this; at least at the camp near Prague there had
been ample food. Hunger was indulged in the Pan—a fad or a
discipline, a chosen condition. She had never seen a skinny person
who was unhappy to be skinny.

"Most of them," Venner explained, "are from Emorick. There's
been fighting there for almost twenty-five days, maybe more, mainly
around the port. Factions. Makes for a disorganized mess."

Venner pulled around the fountain, picked out a street, and angled
away from the plaza. The cooking scent diminished and Cira sniffed
for that other smell, but could not find it.

Venner ascended the sloping avenue till he took a left turn onto
a narrower street, empty of people. Cira craned her neck to look
up at the passing windows. She glimpsed faces smeared in shadow,
some quickly withdrawn, others, young, transfixed, watching. The
street curved into a lazy upward spiral. They came around the turn
and Cira saw squeezed between heaps of modified prefabs a structure like a domed spire that had been cut in half, open to the street,
facing a break in the line of buildings on the opposite side. Benches
filled the dome. People huddled far to one side. A few hurried
away at the approach of Venner's transport, but most remained. As
they rolled past the gap, Cira looked out over the center of town.

Venner turned left again, into another cramped lane. Here, along
this empty stretch, the street-level openings in the buildings had been
foamed shut—hastily, too, by the way the foam ran and pooled.

"This used to be a loyalist section," Venner said. "Most of these
people left right around the time of the Riot."

"They all lived in the same section?"

"No, not all. Most."

"Where are we going?"

"Not far now. Nice thing about this situation, a co has the pick of the best if he wants."

He pulled into an alleyway. In the sudden dark Cira tightened her hold on the pistol, pulse quickening. After five or six meters, they emerged into a small courtyard. Venner shut down the engine.

Cira pushed open the door and stepped out onto neatly-dressed flagstones. A row of arches had been cut into the ground level wall of the large prefab box that served as the foundation of the house. Above, the house was brick; slender columns supported a sloping roof that shielded a second-story arcade. The walkway let onto a parapet over the tunnel. The walls of the tunnel were also brick, as was the wall opposite the main house. Another prefab, directly across from the tunnel, seemed outfitted as a garage. Cira looked up past the enclosing wall and saw more of the city, mounting higher toward the rim.

"Are all those empty?" she asked.

"A lot of them."

Venner had opened another storage compartment and hauled out a pair of valises. The lid over Cira's pack and rifle stood open. She regarded him across the roof of his transport.

"Why are you helping me?"

Venner cocked his eyebrows speculatively. "If you'd tried entering Crag Nook on your own, what do you think would've happened?"

"I'm not saying I don't appreciate what you've done. I just want to know why."

He came around the transport, a valise in each hand. "Let's eat." He walked on, through an arch, into the house.

Cira looked back at the tunnel. She stared at it for a long time, sorting her options. Finally, she pulled out her backpack and the broken rifle, slammed the lid, and followed Venner into the house.

The entrance opened into a room that ran the length of the prefab. The white floor was mosaiced in dirt. Far against the wall to her right lay a chair with two legs broken off. The sound of her footsteps made the room seem larger than it was.

Double doors let into the main sections. They passed through a large common room, off which other, smaller rooms opened, all empty of furniture until she came to the kitchen. A table and an assortment of mismatched chairs stood near the refrigerator. A faintly sour odor tinged the air.

She heard Venner upstairs. She stepped away from the kitchen, fished out a food bar, and looked for the stairs. Venner was coming down as she found it, in a room whose bare walls showed the traces where pictures had once hung.

"There're plenty of rooms up there," he said, heading back toward the kitchen. "Pick one that's open and come on down to eat."

Cira considered opening out her bivouac in this room, or better yet in the first room with the broken chair. But it was obvious that Venner left few signs on the ground floor of habitation. She took the stair to the second floor and found herself in a long corridor with doors on either side.

Most stood open. Two rooms were filled with broken furniture. Two more were empty. One contained a thickly-padded highbacked chair and a small table. Two were closed. She listened intently for Venner, then tried each door. One was locked. One contained a bed, a desk and chair with a portable polycom, and a commline receiver on the floor in the corner. The valises stood beside the bed.

She took the room with the chair. She set down the pack and leaned the rifle against it, removed the hat and coat and placed them on the chair, and then took out her handscan and checked for any other life signs in the house. Only one trace—Venner.

Cira opened the back of the scanner and took out one of the stored remotes, then returned the scanner to her pack. She checked her pistol and stepped into the corridor. Her pulse raced as she listened for footsteps or breathing or any of the other few score sounds that betray someone's presence. She pulled the door closed and went directly to Venner's room.

She lifted the polycom gently and found the access panel. Her hands shook and she almost dropped the remote and the polycom. A second later, though, she had placed the device inside and set the polycom down. She stood at the top of the stair a extra few seconds to calm down. Taking a deep breath, she went to the kitchen.

Cira stopped in the doorway and watched Venner, now dressed in a loose white shirt and baggy black pants and sandals, move from place to place on the cooker. He had set up a pair of fields around different sections, one to grill the meat, which smoked within its isolated column, the other for the sliced potatoes, which danced suspended in roiling oil just above the surface. Rich aromas permeated the air. He was carving a loaf of bread that looked very much like the kind Cira remembered from home—dark brown, not a smooth patch on the whole oblong thing—when he glanced at her.

"Hungry?"

"Now I am."

He studied her. "*Thought* you were Armada. The coat was a good idea, if anybody'd seen you out in just your flightsuit you'd 've been dead."

"I didn't bring a change of clothes."

"Easily gotten." He set the plate of bread on the table then checked the meat. He smiled and touched a contact on the cooker. The field dissipated and the smoke wafted immediately away, except for the delicate wisps coming off the meat itself. He picked up a long fork and deftly speared a slice of potato. He studied it for a second, then nibbled an edge. His eyebrows bobbed once and he ate the slice. "Another minute."

He scooped the meat onto a plate and set it on the table, then poured two cups of coffee. He entered a more complicated series of instructions into the cooker—eight or nine touches on the contacts—and the oil was siphoned off from the potatoes, which slowly fell into the bowl he set below them.

"Let's eat." He sat down and picked up a fork.

"I'd like an explanation now."

He gestured at the plates. "Vrim veal and local grown spuds. The coffee is imported, but I'm not sure from where, it was in the house system when I moved in."

"Why are you helping me?"

"I'm not."

Cira raised her eyebrows skeptically.

"Well," he said, "I *am*, certainly, but none of this is free. I expect compensation."

"In what way?"

Venner smiled. "Not exactly from you." He pointed at the plate before the empty chair. "Please. Before it gets cold."

When Cira continued to hesitate, Venner sighed. "I can understand you being suspicious. I'd be. But if you're not going to trust
me, why did you come with me?"

"What were my options?"

"Limited." He shrugged. "I'm hungry. I've been on the road
since late last night. By the way, that was a hell of a show you all put
on. It was almost too low in the south to see, but out on the plains,
away from any city lights, it was spectacular."

Furious and confused, Cira watched him begin to eat. Now
that the question had been asked, she realized how few options she
really had. Forage in the field—but though she knew what was
locally available she had no idea how to go about obtaining it;
enter Crag Nook alone—but Venner had correctly pointed out the
risks, which were very high; or rely on local aid until the Armada
returned—which was essentially what regulations dictated. But
those regulations assumed more than one survivor and a team of
Armada pilots possessed a very different set of potentials. Three
or four might forage effectively, build shelter, or manage to infiltrate a questionable enclave, and through it all provide cover and
back-up for each other. The regs did not assume one person in
the field. The regs implicitly maintained that this did not happen,
which seemed to Cira an absurd presumption.

But it was consistent with Armada history. The fact remained, after she sifted through all the possibilities, no one had
envisioned an Armada task force failing. Pilots either won in
combat or died in space, and if they managed to get to ground
then historical fact indicated that such ground would be friendly
ground. The historical concept "Behind enemy lines" was no
more than that—a concept. Until the seti had been encountered and the borders represented an actual separation of humanity from something else, rather than merely a marker showing how far they had come to date, there was no enemy in a
position to have territory constituting a line that one could be
behind. It was a startling realization, but Cira quickly accepted
it: the Armada did not believe that this could have happened.
By all the authorities the Armada held sacred, Cira should not
be standing in a stranger's kitchen "behind enemy lines" wondering if she ought to trust him.

Confusion dissipated. She was left dependent on her own resources. Already the teachings of childhood had gone by the wayside—never accept gifts from strangers—and she had done everything by what regs there were and exhausted their advice.

The only things left were to run or bide her time and see where the situation might lead.

She pulled out the chair and sat down.

Venner filled the big tub with cold water, then dropped the thermolyte in. He thought wistfully about repairing the water heater and again dismissed the idea: too much work, too time-consuming, especially when he did not know how long he would still be on Finders. In a few seconds a stream of bubbles rose from the ten-centimeter-long tube. Within a minute steam wafted off the surface. He reached down with the tongs and pulled the stick from the bottom and dropped it into the vacuum container. After adding some oil and a healthy dollop of fragrance from Pan Pollux, he stripped and stepped into the now-hot water. Venner winced—he had almost left the thermolyte in too long—but he eased himself down until he was up to his chin in the milky bath. He moaned pleasantly. He glanced to the ledge on his right, checking that his pistol was there, in reach.

The pilot had finally gone to her room. Venner had entertained her, graciously and uninformatively, for hours, waiting for her to give up prodding him and retire for the night. She had been equally unforthcoming, but with a stoic resistance to conversation that first amused then irritated Venner, as if she were afraid that to say anything at all would lead to an inevitable gush of information. She was in shock, that was obvious, and therefore unpredictable. In a few days that should pass and he might find her useful. He had found that the best pay-offs came from the highest risks, and picking her up had been a very risky gesture.

For now, though, he only wanted to let go, enjoy his bath, think about nothing. It had been four days since he had been able to relax like this.

It was short-lived. The commline in the next room beeped insistently. Venner ignored it for most of an hour. As the water cooled perceptibly, he sighed and stood. Better than nothing, he thought, though not perfect. He toweled off and padded in to work.

Two signals. He pulled on a robe, sat down, and keyed one. On the platform, a woman appeared briefly. Venner winced inwardly.

"Co Harias," he greeted.

"Co Cambion has been wishing to speak with you for nearly a day," she said.

"I've only just got in," he said. "Errands." He smiled at her. "Is it too late? I can—"

"Stand by, please." She vanished.

A moment later Maxwell Cambion appeared.

"Hil," he said. His voice sounded jovial, as usual a complete mismatch to his facial expression, which was blank.

"Co Cambion. I just got back to Crag Nook."

"Yes, you went to Emorick. How are things there?"

"Crazy. I think we can deal with Jonner Liss better than with Uri Govanchi. Govanchi's a purist, interested only in supporting the entire rebellion. He sees you and the Pan as two versions of the same thing, won't consider working with you. Liss is more practical. Anything to keep Finders from falling back into Panner hands. The problem is, Govanchi's got the larger quarter of Emorick. Specifically, he controls the port."

"Hmm. For the time being we can use Downer's Cove, but eventually we'll have to secure Emorick. All right, I'll send some agents to negotiate with Liss. I have a question about the handling of Alexan's retrieval."

Venner frowned. "Yes…?"

"Did you instruct your teams to take anyone else?"

"No. Just your son."

"Just Alexan."

"Yes. Just Alexan. Why?"

"Others are missing. I'm wondering…never mind."

"I'll talk to my people, find out if someone is freelancing, but my instructions—"

"I'm sure were perfectly acceptable, Hil. I'd appreciate a discreet inquiry, though."

"Sure."

"You'll be in Crag Nook for the time being?"

"As far as I know."

Maxwell nodded. "Let me know what you find. We're going ahead with Alexan's synaptic restructure. As soon as it's complete we'll send him up the line to you. I'll let you know exactly when. I want him placed where he won't be any trouble."

Venner nodded, his fingers clawing. Why not just kill the poor soul? he wondered. "I'll see to it."

The image winked out. Venner stared at the empty space, drumming his fingers on the edge of the desk. "Perfectly acceptable..." That was as close to a compliment as Venner ever received from Maxwell. But what was all that about others missing? Venner mentally ran down his list of operatives, wondering if anyone might be doing business on the side.

He cleared the channel and accepted the other comm. He grinned at the older man who appeared.

"Sean!"

"Hi. What are you doing?"

"Sitting in my manse in Crag Nook preparing for the firing squad."

"Getting your spiritual house in order?"

"That, too."

Sean shook his head, grinning. "I have to leave Finders. I'm heading out to Skat, then back inward. Anything you want me to take along?"

Venner briefly thought about Cira. "No. Have you gotten any word on when the next task force is due to arrive?"

"Some, no minutes and seconds. You've got seven days."

"Who are they sending in?"

"Don't know that. I *do* know the Vohec are being forced to pull back. This time is likely to be messy. I expect Finders will be in Armada hands in ten days. Crag Nook might not be a place you want to be."

"Finders is a place I'd rather not be. Cambion's sending me Alexan, though, sometime soon."

Sean frowned. "Is *that* what happened? Nic was asking me some odd questions." He cocked his head to one side. "He's sending him to you *as* Alexan?"

"Hell, no! The steel-faced fuck is wiping him first. What about Nic? What does he know?"

"Nothing specific. But the kidnapping is general knowledge, just not the identity of the victim. I'm wondering if Nic knows about Alex."

"Ask him."

"It would be nice to be so simple and straightforward, wouldn't it? Alas, the life of a double agent…"

"Double! Hell, you've got it easy. Try slicing four ways."

"Just keep track of your loyalties, Hil. That's the only way to know for sure when you've made a fatal error."

"My loyalties are quite in order. I and myself, in that order. At the end of this fiasco I ought to be able to retire, open that little station on Tabit I told you about. All I need to do is keep my skin on till then. When are you pulling out?"

"In fifteen hours. If you think of anything else you want or need, you've got that long."

"Thanks. Safe journey, co."

Sean nodded and vanished.

Venner leaned back in his chair and stared at the ceiling. As always, he felt certain Sean Merrick—partner, confidante, colleague, sometime friend—was not telling him everything. Few of the coes Venner dealt with ever did, but it only bothered him personally with Sean. They had worked together for almost six years and Venner had never quite grown comfortable with the man.

Double agent, triple agent, quadruple agent—four-way split, keep the loyalties clear. Pan, secessionist, independent mercantilists, and Maxwell Cambion—those were the factions. Venner worked for Armada security—first and always, supposedly—and Maxwell Cambion. But he had made deals with both warlords in Emorick and, through Sean Merrick, with the independent spacers who were the communications and logistical network of this so-called revolution.

Options. They were necessary, valuable commodities, but it was possible to have too many. Now he had an Armada pilot under his roof. He had no idea what to do with her, how to use her—if at all—to best advantage. He should, technically, just get her back to the Armada so she could dutifully report. But how much had she seen and what would she say that might affect *his* situation?

And Sean was heading out, away from Finders, leaving him to work alone. He sighed wearily. It would have been so helpful to have been provided clear instructions. "Keep situation fluid and destabilized" was interesting but not very direct. How much of a mess did the Armada want when it finally secured the system?

The soft click of the door jerked him out of his chair. Cira stood just inside the threshold, pistol leveled at him. He glanced toward the bathroom door, remembering his own pistol on the bathtub ledge. Her eyes were narrowed, her mouth set, shifting slightly as she ground her teeth. She did not quaver, did not avoid his direct look. Venner raised his hands slowly from his sides, palms out.

"Was it the coffee?" he asked. "I made it too strong, didn't I?"

"Sit down."

He reached for the chair and turned it, facing her. Carefully he lowered himself onto the seat.

"Hands underneath," she said.

He tucked him hands, palms down, beneath his thighs.

"Can we discuss this?" he asked.

"That's why I'm here."

He remembered all the different ways to disarm someone, all the techniques to overcome an opponent who has the advantage. He remembered, too, all the times none of those ways had been useful—nearly every time.

The end of the pistol came even with his mouth, less than twenty centimeters away.

"What do you know about Alexan Cambion?"

"Who?"

Her face seemed to flex, almost like a spasm, for an instant. Then he was staring at his bed, a sharp, cold numbness slowly turning to hot pain spreading over the left side of his face. He blinked, aware that consciousness had skipped a beat, and that it had to do with the bitter taste of blood in his mouth. A hand took his hair and yanked his head around to face the woman, the Armada pilot—no, he amended, the Armada soldier, combat veteran, warrior; the upset, make that angry, Armada warrior. The cold was gone now, the entire left side of his face prickly hot, and the end of the pistol was nearer.

"I listened *in* on your comm," she said tightly.

Venner nodded. Of course, why else would she be here? Black pinpricks danced at the edges of his vision. Warm liquid ran down his neck and a spot just above his cheekbone began to throb. When had she had a chance to bug his room? He had sent her up to find herself a room, alone. Stupid, he thought, he had thought her too shocked to think that clearly, that efficiently. Assumptions will kill you…

"Rude," he said.

She pulled back and jerked, her fist impacting him in the diaphragm. His chest seized up as if trying to suck itself inside out. He gasped and thought how wrong this was, how completely out of control this whole thing had become.

And what a tremendous punch she had.

"What do you know about Alexan Cambion?"

He focussed on her face. "Not much—Maxwell's…son…"

"Where *is* he?"

"Maxwell has him."

"Where?"

"South, at the mines."

"Distance?"

"'Nother hundred k, hundred ten, twenty." He swallowed. He could not keep his left eye open. The throbbing had spread while he talked, encompassed his cheekbone, the orbit of the eye, a line down to his molars.

"What did that mean about his synaptic restructure?"

Her voice shook slightly. Good, Venner thought, maybe she's losing control. Fine. If she loses enough control maybe I can overpower her, maybe she'll start shaking and drop her pistol. Or maybe she'll just kill me.

"It's…memory alteration." He tried to wave his hand for emphasis, but it did not move. Oh, yes, he remembered, sitting my on hands.

"Like a mindwipe?"

"Something like…sure…"

Several seconds of silence went by and Venner thought for a moment she had left. The side of his head was a field of pain now and it was hard to care about anything else.

"Why?" she whispered. He was not even sure she had spoken until she said it again, slightly louder. "Why?"

Venner shrugged. "Maxwell...always has reasons..." He winced and looked up at her. "Do you know Alexan?"

"How do I get to the Cambion mines?"

He would have laughed, but the moment the muscles in his face began to contract the pain changed his intent.

"You could get a job, I s'pose."

"What about you? Could you get me in there?"

"No."

"He said he was delivering Alexan to you. How?"

"Pipeline...tramway..."

"And Alexan becomes your responsibility then? You're supposed to place him where he won't do any harm?"

"My option."

He heard footsteps recede, return. She paced. Venner struggled against the pain. She stopped before him again and he braced himself as best he could for another blow.

"You're going to place him with me," she said.

"Fine," he said, nodding slightly. "Help me."

A hardness prodded his neck, shifted to beneath his jaw: the pistol. "You'll take delivery and turn Alexan over to me, spy. Understand?"

"Fine, fine...help..."

She walked away, out of the room, then came back. He felt hands under his arms.

"Come on."

He heaved to his feet, shoved forward, bringing his arms out and around to embrace. The entire motion was unconscious, thoughtless, a hindbrain attempt to overpower. He almost had her. Had his eyes been open, he might have managed it, or so he reasoned later.

Instead, she ducked low, caught his weight on her shoulder, and he felt himself pivot in mid-air and come down, and Venner collided—face first—with a wall or maybe the floor.

He rolled, forced an eye open, and kicked at the shape above him. He missed and rolled again, trying to get to his feet. He managed it precariously, turned, and punched at the form that danced before him.

I can do this, he thought, and stepped forward to engage her. Then her fist caught him in the left side, snapping a rib. Her boot slammed onto his right foot, just missing the ankle, and she cracked him in the head once more. He screamed sharply. She tripped him and he landed face down on the floor. He then felt a weight land on his back.

"Damnit! Damnit! Damnit!" she shouted, and with each shout she hit him, solid body blows to shoulders, mid-back, sides, and a final one to the head that shut off his consciousness.

Alexan opened his eyes. He had been alone when he had drifted off into sleep. His eyes burned; he remembered crying. He sat up.

Two beings—seti, nonhumans—stood nearby, watching him. One was tall, soft-furred, with large amber eyes, and a delicate web-structure on its throat, just above the collar of its floor-length blue robe. The other was nearly human, red-skinned with dark green eyes—no whites, just green from corner to corner—and a straight lipless slit for a mouth. He—it seemed male—wore a midnight blue tunic and pants that gave a distinctly military impression.

"What is the worst part?" the furred one asked, its voice like three separate voices in harmony.

"What—?" Alexan began, confused.

"What is the worst part," the other snapped. "Simple question."

Alexan's pulse began to slow as he stared at the two seti. "I know you," he said.

The red-skinned one grunted. "That is the worst part? That you know us?"

"Of course not," the other said. "He's frightened, he's trying to find something to balance with. He knows us, that is a statement needing confirmation."

"Odd. Of course you know us. I am Lovander Mipelon, this is Ambassador Tan-Kovis."

Uncertainly, Alexan stood and approached the pair. "Mipes."

Mipelon closed his eyes, giving a good impression of human exasperation. Tan-Kovis's eyes seemed to ripple gleefully. "He remembers now," Tan-Kovis said.

"Kovy," Alexan said, tentatively reaching out to touch the ambassador. He grinned. "Why are you here?"

"To ask you questions," Mipelon said. "The first being, for some reason I cannot understand, 'what is the worst part?'"

"The worst part of what?"

"Your situation," Tan-Kovis said.

"Listen, Kovy, Maxwell won't talk to me. I need to explain to him, tell him why I did what I did, but he won't come here, he won't get on a commline with me. Maybe—do you think you—?"

"No," Tan-Kovis said. "Maxwell has made up his mind. Unless he changes it, so it will remain."

"Is that the worst part?" Mipelon asked. "That your parent won't talk to you?"

"No... Mipes, I'm in trouble. Stop quizzing me and help me."

"Is that the worst part?" Tan-Kovis asked. "That you're in trouble?"

"I don't know what the worst part is! It's all bad!"

"Does it hurt to know this?" Mipelon asked.

"Of course it does."

"It would be better if you did not?" Tan-Kovis asked.

"Doesn't that follow?" Mipelon asked his companion.

"Not necessarily," Tan-Kovis said. "Humans seem very much at home with the Rahalen convention of speaking in single propositional states that do not have direct oppositional corollaries."

Mipelon blew a short breath. "Philosophy," he said with disgust. He looked at Alexan narrowly. "Would it be better if you did not have these things to know?"

"What things?" Tan-Kovis asked.

"The things that are all bad!" Mipelon snapped. "What are we discussing after all?"

"That is what I intended to discover. I do not think he truthfully means everything is bad. Do you?"

"No," Alexan said. "No, I suppose not. I don't count knowing you two as bad."

"There," Tan-Kovis said. "You see? When I asked 'what things' it was not rhetorical. Specificity is important. It has nothing to do with philosophy."

Mipelon nodded.

"Do either of you," Alexan asked, "have any idea how long Maxwell's going to keep me here?"

"Not long," Tan-Kovis said.

"Do you know when I can leave?"

"You can't," Mipelon said.

The chamber door opened and Michen came in. He looked Mipelon and Tan-Kovis over unhappily, then glanced at Alexan before going to his collection of instruments. Mipelon turned to watch him.

"The worst part," Tan-Kovis said quietly, almost a whisper.

"About being me, you mean," Alexan said, suddenly certain that this was what the seti wanted.

Tan-Kovis nodded.

Alexan wet his lips with the tip of his tongue and stared, transfixed, at Michen as he moved from board to board. "I never dream," he said. "When I sleep, there's nothing."

"How do you know about them," Mipelon asked, "if you have never done it?"

"People talk about it all the time," Alexan said lamely. In truth, he did not know why he missed dreaming. He knew others did it, but—

"It's time," Michen said abruptly, without looking up.

Mipelon turned back to Alexan. "Good-bye."

"You never explained the *qonteth* to me," Alexan said, remembering the Vohec shrine far south of the equator.

"It would take longer than we have," Mipelon said.

Tan-Kovis reached out and laid a hand on Alexan's shoulder. "Everything happens in the mind," the seti said. "Good-bye."

Alexan watched them leave the chamber and ached to run after them. He tried to remember when he had met them and could not think of a time when they were absent. Mipelon the Vohec projection, Tan-Kovis the Ranonan ambassador. All Ranonans were ambassadors, so he had heard. He rubbed his shoulder where Tan-Kovis had touched him, suddenly puzzled by the simultaneous certainties that he would never see the Ranonan again and that this had not been the last time they would converse. He turned toward the door and stopped when he saw Michen watching him.

"What was that about?" Michen asked.

"What?"

"That stuff about a 'kawn-teth'?"

Alexan shook his head. "Nothing."

Michen shrugged. "No matter. Come here."

Alexan took three steps automatically, then stopped himself. Michen scowled impatiently and touched a contact on the console. A few seconds later the cell door opened again and four men entered.

"Alexan, come here," Michen said.

Hesitantly, Alexan obeyed, eyeing the four men who stood near the door, watching him, waiting. They had the solid, grainy look of miners, thick wrists, broad shoulders, feet set wide. Born and raised on Finders, half their lives spent digging for ores in the high gravity.

Michen took his forearm and pulled it toward him. Alexan watched anxiously as Michen placed an injector on the inside of his elbow and released the solution. The spot was red and tingly.

"What was that?" Alexan asked.

"Go sit down," Michen said. He set the injector back in a rack with five others. "I'll tell you exactly what it is because it doesn't matter now. Go sit down. Go. Sit."

Alexan returned to the cot. He resented being ordered around, but he had never found a way to refuse command. It had always seemed safer to do what he was told than rebel. Maybe, he thought, it's just a lack of imagination—what would I do otherwise?

Michen nodded at the four miners, who filed out of the chamber as quietly as they had entered.

"Memory is like a map," Michen said. "You can follow its trails and discover its destinations along the way. The map changes over time, becomes more complex, layered, side roads twist this way and that, detours spin off. The synaptic pathways are the roads themselves, the electrochemical signals are the vehicles. The vehicles themselves contain passengers that debark when they arrive at their destination and contribute to the nature of the visit."

He came out from behind his consoles, hands clasped before him. "The pathways serve multiple functions—they aren't always and everytime a roadway for a memory—but they always return to their original function when secondary and tertiary functions cease. In this way, we can make a detailed map of the entire functioning landscape of the brain." He smiled at Alexan. "We can always reroute the pathways."

Alexan shivered slightly. This was familiar. He had heard all this before, somewhere, but...

"The deeper coded memories tend to resist rerouting. We don't worry about that, then, we just send different signals—different 'visitors', if you will—to those destinations. We do all this with a virus, which I've just given you. The virus is designed to trace a certain kind of signal and alter the receptor at the other end, to either impede reception or, barring that, alter the type of information the receptor will accept. Now as soon as this starts to happen, the brain reacts. New connections are formed, and as they are, the virus itself undergoes a slight alteration in response to the new landscape it finds itself in. It can't adapt *too* well, though, and ultimately it dies. But not before it reinforces the new pathways. It does this because it seeks itself out after it has altered. Sort of searching for a companion of like type to try to regain its original nature. It facilitates pathway construction and reception. Builds new roads, bridges, sideroads. Now, don't worry, Alex, you won't be a gibbering idiot. Those functions that constitute what you might call a fundamental persona are hardly impaired at all. You'll still know how to eat, use hygiene cubicles, walk, pat your head, and rub your belly at the same time. You just won't remember having done anything for the last, say, fifteen years. You won't remember exotic things, like those two seti bastards who just left. You won't remember serving with the Armada, fighting at the battle of Finders, or this conversation. A lot of other things. Some of the really deep memories—relating to identity and so forth—well, I tailored a special virus to go after those. We already had a map of those, know exactly where they are—or were, since by the time I finish explaining this, you probably won't know who the hell I am—and we couldn't exactly let you go blabbing all that stuff to whoever might ask you."

He sat down on the cot and patted Alexan on the shoulder, an almost fatherly gesture, and sighed. "There are benefits. You get to become a whole new somebody. You won't have to actually deal with the fact that you are not Maxwell Cambion's son, at least not anymore. All this unfortunate disappointment of the last few days won't bother you. And you get to stay alive, which otherwise might not have been an option. Maxwell doesn't keep useless things around and you've got to admit—if you still can—that you made yourself pretty damn useless."

Michen stood. "There isn't time to redo you as Alexan Cambion into anything we can work with. The Armada is already on its way with a second task force. I think this one will do the job. That's another benefit. You don't have to deal with the awful fact that your precious Armada hung you out here to be a martyr. But I think they're about to do the job right. Finders is about to get really thumped and I, for one, don't plan on being here when it happens. But I'm getting off the point. If we had a month, maybe two, I might be able to fine tune you so that we could have returned you to the Armada and *this* time seen you do what you were *supposed* to do in the first place." He shrugged. "No time. This is a quick and dirty fix for an unpleasant circumstance. You won't remember, though, and that is, after all, for the best." He leaned forward. "Alex? Alexan? Hm. I'll never get over just how fast that works sometimes."

Thayer-Cambion Mines rose between two massive slabs of mountain, a three-columned tower supporting a wide disk. At the base of the tower, a small compound of service buildings clustered, and the access road shot out eastward a few hundred meters to meet the junction of the Tameurla Road, the Eastering Road, and the southbound Champ Du Terre. In the wedge formed by the Eastering Road and Champ Du Terre lay the unfinished earthworks of Cambion Mines own spaceport. Fifteen shuttle pits, a half-finished maintenance corridor, a pair of warehouses, one complete, the other roofless and weatherworn, and the overturned dirt that showed where the rest of the field would go when they got around to finishing it after the war.

Even with only fifteen pits, a considerable amount of material shipped through this port. It was less than half the size of the one at Downer's Cove just on the other side of the Hobics, and Emorick's port, with seventy-five pits, dwarfed it. Maxwell intended eventually to have fifty pits and ship all Cambion product out through it, but that would be a while yet.

Heavy machinery rumbled constantly around the port. Trucks and transports moved between the pits and service building. Others traveled back and forth from the tower. As Nicolan drove away from the shuttle pit toward Thayer-Cambion Mines he thought how impossible it was to defend a surface facility from an Armada strike.

If the orbital defenses failed, nothing on the ground would hold for long. The choice was surrender, abandonment, or destruction. The Armada might just destroy this facility in any case. Emorick was the important base, Downer's Cove less so.

He shifted in the seat, trying to find a comfortable position. He had been in space for three weeks, preparing for the assault, supervising clean-up afterward. It amazed and disturbed him how quickly he had adjusted to the lesser g, how long it seemed to take to readjust to his homeworld's higher gravity; he wanted to believe himself more adaptable. Also, it did not seem worth the effort this time; he had to leave again in a few days.

He looked up at the tower as he neared. The columns were thick, wider at the base to take the weight. It was a ridiculously delicate-looking piece of engineering for all its exaggerated size, a work of sheer denial. Finder's gravity was twenty percent greater than terran normal. Landing wrong from a short jump broke ankles, ruptured knees. Architecture tended to hug the ground, or huddle against a sturdy mountain wall. If the mineral content of the crust was more contaminated or harder to get to or simply *less*, Finders would not be worth living on. But Maxwell raised this tower just to deny Finders its practical limits. One major earthquake would probably bring it down. In spite of the illogic—or perhaps because of it—it was impressive.

He entered an elliptical courtyard. Ramps led off to the various buildings and the road itself continued into a declivity, disappearing within the mountain. Nicolan parked near the base of one leg, grabbed his pack, and eased out of the transport. He stretched, drew in a lungful of dry air, and walked to the wide doors. Out of the corner of his eye he saw a brief bluish flash—the somatic ID scans. Skin texture, hair density, profile, mass, and reflexive reactions matched a continually updated template. Everything aligned and a section of the doors opened for him. He stepped into cooler air and kinder light. He rubbed his eyes as the lift took him up.

The lift let him out on the executive level. Privacy shields turned the wide plaza into a maze of opaque and semi-opaque walls. Nicolan made his way toward the center and the only solid structure on the entire level. Setting his pack down against the wall, he placed his right hand against the door, waited for the scan to flash green, and pushed through into Maxwell's office.

Maxwell sat behind his desk, hands steepled with index fingers tapping his lips lightly, the expanse of windows behind him opaqued. Michen's image stood on the commline plate. The conversation was private: Nicolan could see Michen's lips move, but he heard nothing. As the door closed Maxwell glanced his way and dropped his hands. Michen stopped speaking, scowled, and the image evaporated. Maxwell stood and rounded the desk. His eyes glistened and Nicolan sensed the smile Maxwell wished to show. They came together in the center of the big office and embraced.

Maxwell pushed away and squeezed Nicolan's shoulders once before stepping back. Nicolan felt a surge of emotion—love, pride, giddy joy—and, in that instant of communion, nearly said so.

"I'm glad to see you," Maxwell said. He turned away then and went back to his desk.

The moment passed. Nicolan tried to recover, jarred into a brief awkward hesitance by the backwash.

"Has Casm heard anything?"

"Yes." Nicolan's voice was rough. He cleared his throat. "Unfortunately, the Vohec have to withdraw."

Maxwell nodded. "Has Sean Merrick left?"

"Yes. He's taking a long orbit out and he'll transmit his scans before going translight. I've already positioned squadrons as sentries, so we should know as soon as the Armada makes an appearance."

"And the remanufacture?"

"The last fifty ships are being completed now. Then the tender must pull out." Nicolan sighed. "I'm not encouraged. I don't think we'll have as easy a fight this time."

"We won't. In fact, you and I won't even be here. I want you to arrange with Casm to transport us out."

"To what purpose?" Nicolan asked, surprised.

Maxwell looked up. "Think it through. Finders can't be defended from the ground. When the Armada comes back this time it will be with a sense of mission—revenge. We embarrassed them, bled them a little. When they get through—"

"When?"

"When, yes, you don't think we can fight an effective action without the Vohec control platforms to coordinate, do you? When they get through they'll try to reduce the surface to powder. We can't very well fight a rebellion if we're dead."

"But if we leave don't we relinquish claim?"

"We never had a claim. We have an agreement with the Vohec _Qonoth_ to exploit the mineral rights in exchange for acting as caretakers of the system. If I read the charter correctly, the Vohec may well be back once the Armada takes it."

"Why not just stand down then? I mean, we've six hundred fighters in-system."

"We can't. That's in the charter. We must be seen to do everything we can as caretakers. If we withdraw all our forces, as sensible as that may be under the circumstances, we are in violation of the charter and the Vohec will do nothing."

"So if we sacrifice all those coes, the Vohec will deem us suitably responsible? That's a hell of a price. That doesn't take into consideration all the coes on the ground."

"Cambion tunnels go deep. I think there's a fair chance most of our people will survive."

Nicolan fell into one of the couches. He glanced at the commline plate.

"How's Michen doing?" Nicolan asked.

"He's nervous. Understandable."

Nicolan nodded. "I saw all the activity. You expected this."

"One of several possible outcomes, yes."

"I'm not comfortable dicing with lives this way."

"And you think I am?"

"You're not showing any doubts."

"Don't confuse decisiveness with pleasure. Self-castigation earns nothing, costs time."

Nicolan closed his eyes. Verbal fencing with his father wore him down. "Casm also informed me that if the Armada secures Finders, the Vohec may declare war on the Pan Humana. If they do, the Rahalen Coingulate will censure them, possibly intervene."

"Then it's all the more necessary that we be with them. War between the Seven Reaches or any of its members and the Pan is the last thing I want. We'd gain nothing."

Nicolan nodded. That made sense to him. Maxwell rarely had a single reason for any of his actions, but Nicolan often found most of his reasons shallow, unsupportable. Except the strategic ones.

"How long since you slept?" Maxwell asked.

"I don't know. Thirty hours, forty..."

"Then go sleep. I have work to tend to. I'll have dinner with you later."

Nicolan pushed himself to his feet. "I'll call you when I wake up."

"Did you find anything more out about those abducted prisoners?"

Nicolan stopped by the door. "No. I traced them to a shuttle, the shuttle has disappeared."

"Are you continuing the investigation?"

"I've got a couple people on. Right now it's not high on my list. If we lose Finders it's a moot issue."

"It's important to be able to trust your people."

Nicolan nodded, pushed out the door. His heart pounded.

A number of the privacy shields had been reconfigured since he had entered Maxwell's office; new meetings, new arrangements. Nicolan retrieved his pack and wound a path through them to the lifts.

He descended two levels and dropped his pack off in his room. He then continued down to the sublevels. The lift opened on a wide platform that overlooked a broad staging area. Three main tunnels angled off, separated by roughly thirty degrees. Small transports with clear carapaces, called moles, were emerging from the southernmost tunnel. Other moles were parked alongside the much larger diggers. Nacelles of various sizes were stacked about. At the foot of the platform, huddling against the north wall, was the On-Site Coordinating Area. A few coes sat at the big control board. One looked up and waved to Nicolan.

Nicolan pulled a helmet from its niche in the wall beside the lift door and went down to the OSCA. The display above the console showed the webwork of Cambion tunnels. Radiating out and down from the Cambion compound through the mountains, the network was like a very old hive. Major tunnels split off into secondary shafts, small connecting tunnels laddered among them. Halfway through the mountain range—about one hundred eighty kilometers—the web ended, cut off abruptly. Only two tunnels continued on to the opposite side of the range, the west tunnel going all the way to Downer's Cove. A third tunnel reach north along the eastern edge of the Hobics to Crag Nook.

As he stood there, Nicolan glimpsed the man who had waved to him touching a contact with a casual negligence, like scratching an itch on his face. No one seemed to notice; the man leaned back and gave an exaggerated stretch and a loud yawn.

"What's that?" one of the others asked, pointing at the screen.

A red light had appeared in one of the small connecting corridors.

"Don't know," the yawner said and reached for the console again. He frowned as he worked. Finally he turned and looked out across the chamber and scowled. "Probably just a sensor glitch. Damn, everyone's gone already. I'll go check."

"Mind if I go along?" Nicolan asked.

"Patrician's privilege," he said grumpily as he brushed by. He jogged across the staging area to a mole.

"Sorry," one of the other workers said. "It's been a bad shift."

Nicolan shook his head and loped off after him.

The mole lurched out of its niche as Nicolan reached it. He grabbed the roll bar and swung into the passenger seat. The driver sped toward the western tunnel, swerved to the right as a pair of moles emerged, then raced downward. Bluish lightstrips ran ahead of them to a vanishing point that soon became a fork.

"Are we in a hurry, Kee?" Nicolan asked.

"Wouldn't do to waste time around the boss, would it?" Kee returned and flashed a grin.

"Some reason to be this private?"

Kee glanced down at the panel and flicked the commline off. He looked over at Nicolan and nodded slowly, a finger to his lips.

Kee wound his way through the narrowing tunnels till Nicolan thought he would go all the way to Downer's Cove. At last, he turned into a rough-finished connecting corridor, barely wide enough for the mole. He stopped about fifty meters in and motioned for Nicolan to get out. Nicolan followed him another twenty meters, to a junction box from which thick cables dropped to the floor and trailed away in both directions.

Kee opened the box and pulled out a small device. He dropped it into his pocket and sat down, back to the rock.

"Your abduction victim was brought straight to Michen," Kee said. "From there, I have no idea where he went. There was only one and Leon Rike was the team leader and Harias went along."

Nicolan squatted down against the wall opposite Kee. Leon Rike was one of Maxwell's personal security people.

"There was complete access cleared for them on the way up and back down," Kee went on. "This wasn't loyalists."

Nicolan nodded. "No, I suspected this was all Maxwell. Why, though? And what's Michen doing with him?"

"That's a little out of my depth."

"It's all right. I'm not asking for more. Thanks, Kee. This was...this was great."

"As to the privacy, though...I attracted some attention this time."

"Leon?"

"No, I don't think so. When I accessed the security records to do the match on incoming and outgoing personnel, shuttle launches, who was where and when, that sort of stuff, I discovered that someone else had been trying to break into the system. I tried to trace the access, but it faded out too quickly, scattered in a thousand directions. So I continued my research. When I finished, I noticed that *my* survey was being accessed. Someone ended up with the same data I'd just gotten. I have no idea who, but I've been noticing a few new faces down here since."

"Anyone with polycom clearance?"

"No one that's not supposed to have it. But...it's more a feeling than anything else, but I think a new security team has been brought in, one I don't even think Leon knows about."

"Maxwell's security-conscious almost to the point of paranoia, but..."

Kee shrugged. "Keep alert, boss, that's all. There're new eyes around and I don't know what they're looking for."

"Point out the new faces to me. Let me see what I can find out."

Kee nodded. "So when do you think the Armada will be back?"

"You expect them to be back?"

"Absolutely. I used to *be* Armada, remember?"

"I remember. Well...I'm hoping we have a good six days left."

"Then we probably have three." Kee stood, pulled the device out of his pocket and tossed it across to Nicolan. "That was our sensor malfunction. Better you hang onto it."

They returned to the mole and Kee backed out of the tunnel, then headed back. They did not speak till Kee drove into the staging area. He parked the mole and got out.

"Absolutely," he said loudly as he strode back to the OSCA. "I'll make another damn check of the system, yes, boss! Like I got nothing better to do than chase ghosts in the system!"

"I don't want any 'ghosts' causing anyone to get hurt," Nicolan snapped. "We've got a safety tradition to maintain—"

"Oh, abso*lute*ly, a tradition! I'll get *right* on it!"

People had stopped to watch. Nicolan turned around slowly, locking eyes with each one and each one in turn looked away.

But one was slow, held Nicolan's gaze a second longer than the others, and when he did turn away it seemed more to imitate the others than a natural response.

Nicolan walked purposefully back to the lift platform, replaced his helmet, and summoned a lift. As the door opened, he located that co again, took a long look, then stepped into the lift.

He closed his eyes and leaned against the wall. The lift rose out of the mines.

Chapter Four

Venner heard the intruders the moment they forced the door. The lock gave way with a sharp click, like a thin bone snapping, and a second later came the muffled sounds of hushed voices. He listened as intently as he could and counted three of them. One mounted the stairs.

Up to that point Venner had been annoyed. He could not move with the neural blocks Cira had placed on his neck. Two of them, secretion pads leaking tailored neurotoxins through his skin; far too much, but she had mistimed the first one and he had nearly thrown it off before she realized it. With two, his dreams came heavy and laced with chaos; his brain chemistry was being altered, but he had been locked in place before he could tell her. Stupid, she had no idea about the potency of neural blocks. It was better to stay awake, but he was beginning to have trouble telling the difference. He could open his eyes, at least, but it helped little. He thought he should be hungry, certainly thirsty. She had let him urinate before she left, but even so surely something remained in his bladder. The blocks kept him from feeling that, too, so it did not really matter. Until now.

He lay stretched out on his bed, hands at his sides, staring up at the ceiling. People were going through his house uninvited, *she* was gone, and he was immobile. As he heard the softly ascending tread, his annoyance turned to anxiousness.

Almost three days now since she had slapped on the double pads and left the house. He thought it was three days, but it might only have been two. Or one. His time sense was severely skewed by the chemicals oozing through him. Three, two, one, it mattered little, it was too long. His injuries were not so severe that his life was threatened, though Cira had broken a couple of bones and bruised him badly. Until he got to someplace more civilized he would have a scar covering his right cheek and jaw; she had knocked a couple of teeth out with her first blow. To her credit she had stopped short of killing him. At least with the neural blocks he could not feel his broken rib.

Before, she let him free of the blocks when he had to eat or void waste. She kept him on a short leash then, always armed, alert. Venner wondered how long she could maintain her hyperaware readiness. He was impressed despite his anger at being held captive. But the helplessness wore on him. He almost felt the erosion in his mind, a slippage that worsened when he tried to resist it, aided no doubt by the chemicals seeping into his system. He had never been successfully betrayed before. People had tried but he had always seen it, always managed to compensate, turn it to his advantage. Now that it had happened—now that he felt abandoned and had been rendered immobile, a perfect victim—he did not so much chafe at it as break down, layers of self sloughing off like dead skin. Slippage. Yes, that was a good term for it, that's exactly what it felt like.

The footsteps stopped at the top of the stair. Venner forced his breathing to remain calm, even.

"Hey, Shuller!" someone called from downstairs.

"Shut up!" the one at the top of the stair—Shuller—snapped.

"Hey," the other voice came back, quieter. "We got a fucking feast here. You got to *see* the fucking pantry!"

"So cook me something and be quiet. I ha'n't checked the rest of the fucking house."

Venner closed his eyes as the footsteps began again. A floor panel creaked sharply. There were some security traps, but Cira knew nothing about them and there was no way he could activate them in his condition.

A door opened. Distantly, he heard the clink of pots and pans. Shuller came back into the hallway. In the last two days he had heard his commline queue sound four times. There was a backlog of messages for him, which, if they remained unanswered, would certainly bring someone around to see what was wrong. He always left a response code to let everyone know he was gone. Another door opened. Above all else Venner felt deeply embarrassed.

"Well, well. Someone *is* home."

Venner kept his eyes closed and stopped breathing. The neural block had relaxed all his muscles to the point where he was sure he looked like a corpse.

"You don't stink yet," Shuller said, stepping closer. "'Course, I may just be inured to it all by now. Are you really dead, co?"

The bed was bumped. Suddenly Shuller brought his fist down on Venner's chest. Venner felt it, of course, but it was as if he had been struck through a thick pillow. He controlled his breath—barely—and kept his eyes shut.

"Hm. Maybe you are." He chuckled. "I only know one good way to find out."

Venner would have shuddered if he could, imagining—because he had seen it before, often—what the "one good way" was. Cira had managed to kill him after all. He listened for the sound of a weapon being drawn, the delicate rustles of plastic and metal against flesh.

Instead there was the sound of a seal being peeled open. Then the spatter of liquid striking cloth in a tight stream. His belly warmed a bit.

"Well, I am," Shuller said after a time. "Must be dead. Nobody lays still to be pissed on." He laughed again, then turned away and explored the room. "Nice gear," he said. "We may just be here a bit." He laughed again and left the room.

Venner felt the slippage quicken.

Cira leaned against the edge of the kiosk and nibbled the oat patty she had just purchased. She had never dealt in loose scrip before and the values fluctuated daily, making it maddeningly confusing to plan how many of the small slips of paper or stamped metal coins she would need. The patty cost five tagents today, but yesterday they had been three. The pants and baggy blouse she had bought the morning after she had arrived, five days ago, had cost half a tagent and still could be bought for less than a tagent. Power cells for any purpose ranged from twenty to a hundred; a rifle cost ten tagents on average, but the ammunition was fifty tagents for a box of twenty cartridges. Cira could not figure out the basis for these prices, but she went along, pretending none of it surprised her, grateful Venner had a considerable amount of scrip in the house.

The street angled up, making the tightly-packed buildings seem to lean as if against a high wind. A number of vendors had set up temporary booths in between the more permanent kiosks to hawk goods and services. Since she had been here Cira had not been inside a normal shop; business seemed to be conducted exclusively on the streets, except for those few who from time to time were invited into one of the closed-up shops. What was transacted within she did not know, but she doubted it had anything to do with ordinary needs. Everything a co required was available on the streets— food, clothes, weapons, survival equipment for Finders, knick-knacks, assorted odds-and-ends that had value before the Secession but now represented the detritus left behind by Panner civilization. It was just as impossible to tell who had moved into vacuums created when others had been moved out of former niches—who had been invested or vested, owners and occupants and legal users, or who had been transient, disinvested, fringe players on the rough interface between Pan and frontier; neither group could be distinguished. Possibly the former had been killed if they had not managed to get out before Secession. They were all jumbled together now, mixed and blended, made a seamless whole.

Through the locally-manufactured corrective glasses she now wore, the dominant color of that seamless whole was green. A few of the long overcoats that proliferated throughout Crag Nook, and, she presumed, everywhere else on Finders, were blue or gold or maroon, but most were green, a wide variety of green, which in the harsh uncorrected orange light of Diphda appeared various shades of black or charcoal grey, as did the wide-brimmed hats.

As she watched, the throngs began moving in the same direction, spontaneously caught up in a flow. Cira finished the oat patty and let its cheap wrapper fall to the street with all the other litter. She stepped away from the kiosk and fell into step with the increasing traffic heading downward, toward the center of town. Within twenty paces she found herself carried along in the midst of them.

No one spoke loudly, only in whispers which barely rose above the sound of thousands of feet. The street joined a larger thoroughfare that took them off to the right, descending. Cira glanced back. Crag Nook mounted against the rock in layers. Through every crack she saw people moving along.

The wide street veered to the left, and as she came around the turn she looked down into the large amphitheater at the heart of Crag Nook. People poured in from other avenues, filling the tiers of seats. The stage was occupied by several people seated in highbacked chairs, a podium, a smaller raised dais, and a big desk with an old portable polycom hulking on one corner. Many of the coes on stage wore long white robes with black sashes hung around their necks.

Cira looked for a way out of the mob, but the group she had joined carried her down the long steps all the way to the rows of seats nearest the stage. Reluctant to make herself conspicuous, she shuffled into the third row and sat as far from anyone else as she could. It was a futile attempt as the amphitheater filled and people crowded close and pressed into any empty space available. She glanced at her watch; she had been gone from the house for nearly three hours.

The man behind the desk, an older co with thinning white hair, stood ponderously. He touched the polycom.

"We start in one minute," his voice thundered out, the echoes splashing back. "Find a place to stay still, and be still."

Cira craned her head around. People crowded the lip of the arena, began filtering down the steps and filling them up. There was no easy way out now. It looked as if everyone in town were present. She turned back to the stage.

"All right," the old man said. "I am Justice Evan Nance, as you all ought by now to know. I declare these hearings formally seated and in session. Any disturbances or disruptions will be duly re-corded—"he patted the polycom—"and accordingly dealt with later. I expect quiet and respectful attention. Everyone sit."

Justice Nance took his seat as it grew quiet. He stared unblink-ing at the polycom, his hands palms down on the desk. One of the unrobed coes leaned close to whisper to him. Nance nodded and looked toward the far side of the stage.

"Insofar as the normal practice of law has been rendered tem-porarily untenable," Justice Nance said, "it falls to those of us who purport to represent the idea of the law to do what we can to assure the survival of its fundamental integrity till the time a system can and shall be reinstated for and by the protection of the rights and privi-leges of the commonweal. That said, everyone gathered here must understand that the judgments we make here and now may one day be the foundations of such a system and that if we err in the name of vengeance, vindictiveness, or vituperation we may have a system in time that will mête out a similarly worthless service to all of us. In

short, our judgments stand. There will be no mob supercession of
our prerogatives. Anybody who disagrees with this court's decision
is more than welcome to take it up with me or any other officer of
the court, but you will all damn well leave the decision stand in word
and in fact." He glared out at the gathered audience, then gestured
to the co who had whispered to him. "Bring out the accused."

Four men brought a fifth person up to the stage from below.
Cira shuddered. The prisoner was taken to the raised dais and placed
there. Her wrists were bound behind her. The left side of her face
was swollen, purple bruises beginning to fade to sickly green and
yellow at the edges. Her uniform was torn at the shoulder and one
leg was ripped. She stood stiffly, the one open eye blinking rapidly,
fixed on a point far over the heads of the audience. Cira pressed
her lips together tightly and glanced left and right.

"Will the prisoner state her name and rank?" Justice Nance requested.

The prisoner opened her mouth slightly and a thin line of blood
ran down her chin. She paused and swallowed with difficulty.

"Mila Salasin, sub lieutenant, Armada Carrier *Castille.*"

Cira closed her eyes. Alexan must have reinstated her at the last
minute. At least she was alive. Cira did not know about the two
pilots she had ordered to stand down—she did not know if the
Castille had survived. The few rumors she had heard contradicted
each other.

Justice Nance heaved himself out of his seat and thumped across
the stage to Mila. He took her hand and she winced visibly. He said
something to her quietly and she seemed to calm down, then stepped
off the dais. Nance touched her face lightly, felt her glands, then
pressed her ribs. She almost fell into his arms then. The guards
caught her. More blood spilled from her mouth. Nance shook his
head, his lips drawn inward in an angry expression, and he returned
to his desk.

"The prisoner has been beaten recently," he said. "She was captured two days ago and I saw her then. She was not in this condition."
He slapped the desk. "I will not tolerate abuse of prisoners. Just
because they represent the enemy does not cancel the fact that they are
human beings! Take her to an infirmary and see to her injuries. This
trial is postponed till the health of the prisoner improves."

"Fucking hell it is!" someone in the audience shouted.

A rifle shot split the quiet. Mila jerked, grunted, kept her feet under her. She shook her head, dismayed. The pair of guards near her stepped clear, crouching, and another shot sounded. Her chest exploded and she dropped to her back like a sack.

Nance pounded on the desk with the flat of his hand, spittle streaming down his chin. "You ignorant bastards!"

Another shot took Nance in the shoulder and flung him backward. Suddenly the stage was full of armed coes, aiming energy weapons into the audience.

"Damn!" someone near her hissed. People stood, overcoats opened, and weapons appeared.

Cira touched her own pistol, heart racing, and stood.

"Settle down!" The co at the edge of the stage spoke into a portable amplifier, her voice ringing across the amphitheater. "You all know me! You know damn well I'll just burn the next section a shot comes from!"

"Fucking Panner!"

A shot ricocheted off the stage, near her feet. She took a step back and glared. For a moment Cira thought she would order a fusillade into the audience. But the moment passed, became seconds, and she did nothing. It was a mistake. The crowd grew noisy and more shots were fired. The guards on the stage backed away.

"Damn—" the woman said and pointed.

Three guards raised their weapons and fired. The bright pulses of energy lanced far to Cira's left. She heard the thunderous crack of air filling in the vacuum behind the bolts, joined seamlessly with an eruption in the amphitheater. That was the second mistake.

The mob surged as one. Cira was knocked to one side, then the other. She jammed her hands outward, felt a gratifying impact on each palm, and hopped up on the seat. She looked toward the rim of the amphitheater. Puffs of smoke drifted across a dizzying confusion of people in motion. A few clots fought toward the exits, but there was still no clear passage. Cira turned again. The stage was empty but for a couple of bodies.

Cira jumped onto the shoulder of a big co in front of her. She pushed off before he could grab her and made another shoulder. She slipped off, though, and pitched forward, very fast, and slapped the floor. Her wind left in a numbing burst. Her ankle throbbed slightly. She pushed herself up against the high gravity and looked around. A man watched her and shrugged, giving her a wide, amused grin. Reflexively, she smiled back, then leapt for the stage.

Rifle shots sounded constantly now, a loud background static. A few struck around her, raising puffs of dust, as she sprinted across the stage.

One of the bodies was a guard. His energy rifle lay nearby; Cira snatched it up, checked the action, then surveyed the amphitheater. The riot was now full-blown in all the grotesque grandeur of riots. Patches of unoccupied seats appeared as groups pulled and pushed apart. They exchanged shots among each other, taking up sides according to some indecipherable local standard.

She went to the other body. Mila. Cira crouched over her. The first shot had struck her in the hip, a small hole that barely bled. The second shot had burst her chest. Mila stared skyward from one open eye.

Cira turned the body on its side and patted the left wrist, found the ID bracelet, and removed it. She slipped it into a deep pocket inside the overcoat and stood.

Three coes stood around her. One was the big man who had grinned at her. The other two—a man and a woman—kept wary watch on the amphitheater, rifles in hand.

"Mess, a'n't she?" the big man said.

The others nodded, made a stroking motion across their foreheads, then glanced back at the riot.

Cira hesitated. When none of them moved to restrain her or harm her, she sprinted for the rear of the stage.

Her chest ached dully with each breath. She quickly probed her ribcage but found nothing that seemed broken. Her ankle was growing worse, though.

Wide stairs led downward from the stage, narrowing to funnel through an archway. Cira sprinted down the stairs, the impact on her ankle increasing the pain with each step.

At the archway she stopped and peered up the corridor. At the far end another archway let into a larger room, artificially lit. Cira saw no one and hurried on. She looked cautiously into the room, then noticed that the three locals had followed her.

A conference table dominated it, surrounded by highbacked chairs. Several more chairs lined the walls, all unoccupied. Here, the sound of the riot was barely audible, a muffled susurrus.

Three more doors led off the room. Cira guessed and headed for the one to the right. The others followed, treading lightly. Cira glanced impatiently back at them. The big one with the grin smiled again, nodding as if to say "you're doing fine, lead on." She wanted to tell them to leave on their own, she did not wish to be their leader or rescuer.

She reached the door, turned—

A rifle butt impacted her shoulder, spun her around. She staggered, caught her balance, and tried to turn completely to bring her rifle to bear. The move torqued her ankle just enough. Pain lanced up her leg and she caught her breath.

The guard stepped from the doorway just as the big man reached him. He swung the stock of his rifle—Cira noticed for the first time that it was one of the ornate ones, long and heavy— in a tight arc that connected sharply with the guard's jaw, dropping him heavily to the floor.

Cira stumbled against the wall and leaned there, easing off her right foot.

"Thanks," she said.

"No mind," he said and looked at her leg. He handed his rifle to the other man and stepped alongside Cira. "I'm Rollo, Hersted Family. This is Olin and Becca."

Cira nodded to each of them. "I'm Cira."

"Pleased," Rollo said. He wrapped an arm around her back, caught his hand beneath her left arm, and lifted. "You just do the shooting, I'll walk you."

The corridor ran about twenty meters and led to another vacant chamber that Cira recognized as a guard room. Couches, chairs, an old polycom, folding tables containing the remnants of meals, a couple of games spread out and half-played.

A young guard was stretched out on a couch. One leg draped over the end, foot planted firmly on the floor, his left arm raised so his fingers rested lightly on the bridge of his nose. His rifle lay on the floor. He looked pale, perhaps injured.

As they entered, he looked around at them instantly and grew paler still. There was a space of time where they regarded each

other, a static tableau between decisions. Cira thought she understood the look he gave them. He did not want to fight, did not
want to be hurt or give hurt anymore. When it passed, all he did was
point to the exit and turn his face away.

"Co Cambion."

Nicolan opened his eyes, the dream dissipating instantly. Snatches
of it danced away—faces, tall plants, a broken-walled fortress—
and left him staring at the troll standing alongside his bed. He squeezed
his eyes shut and rolled over.

"Co Cambion."

"What?"

"Maxwell has left the compound."

"To where?"

"Downer's Cove."

Nicolan rolled over again and blinked at the unlovely device.
The room was dark and in the dimness it seemed both larger and
less substantial. The Vohec trolls were much more elegant. "Downer's
Cove?"

"Yes."

"When?"

"He left twenty minutes ago. He said not to wake you till your
usual time."

"Very considerate of him. I could have used a few extra hours
of sleep. Why did he go?"

"A report came in that an explosion has occurred there, at the
Cambion offices. Some damage to the tunnels is also suspected."

"And he went there himself?"

"Yes."

"Hell." Nicolan sat up stiffly and rubbed his eyes. He hated it
when Maxwell did something like this. Cambion Mines employed
people who were trained to deal with this sort of thing. But Maxwell
still treated it like a floundering start-up operation, small and
underfunded, where the owner had to do more work than anyone
else. "Did the report say anything about the cause of the explosion?"

"No."

He stood and stretched. His back ached dully. "All right. I
want—what's the name of the on-site supervisor?"

"Bel Ollic."

"Bel Ollic, yes—I want him on comm in ten minutes. Also get me the on-site chief engineer. I want a description and a good guess as to cause. I'll take both in Maxwell's office. Ten minutes."

The troll scooted out of the room. Nicolan rinsed and dressed quickly and hurried up to the executive level.

As he walked out of the lift he squinted into the full light of sunrise washing eastward from behind the mountains. In the distance the Orca Mountains were a pale line beneath a stream of smoke drifting from Mt. Stable.

Few people were on the floor this early and fewer privacy shields. Nicolan surveyed the unoccupied desks across the now-enormous space. Those present nodded respectfully to him as he went to Maxwell's office.

It seemed odd to enter and not find Maxwell. Nicolan had been told occasionally that one day it would be his to run, but in all other things Maxwell made his own death seem so unlikely an event that Nicolan never thought about it. Like most people on the frontier, in the Distals, Maxwell had begun a family early—he was only thirty-two when Nicolan was born—but unlike most when Nicolan's mother had died in a mining accident Maxwell had companioned with no one else. Maxwell was only fifty-five now and death seemed far away.

Unless the Secession killed him. Nicolan suspected his father was on some Armada security list as a prime insurgent. Maxwell Cambion had refused to leave when the evacuations occurred, had refused to give an explanation to the Forum agent on the scene, and had left his home and offices in Emorick to hole up at the Mine after emptying his polycoms of all data. Maxwell Cambion was one of three people on Finders who commanded the respect and resources sufficient to form a government and it was Maxwell Cambion who had initiated negotiations with the Vohec for arms and support. Maxwell had thrown himself into the Secession, just as he had thrown himself into building his business. He was a rebel and it had cost him. More than sixty percent of his traffic had been with the Pan Humana. Nicolan had seen him gamble before, risking enormous losses on the prospect of enormous benefits. This was one of his gambles, certainly, but it would only pay off if the Secession was a success. Nicolan kept his reservations to himself, but he had serious doubts that the Pan would allow a dozen colonies to simply withdraw.

He sat down behind Maxwell's desk and punched for the filters on the windows. The bright morning sun dimmed and he opened the commline. No one appeared on the plate.

Nicolan drummed his fingers, then touched a contact. "Station One, I expected a commlink to Bel Ollic."

"Co Ollic has not responded, Co Cambion."

"All right, what about the chief engineer?"

"Co Haral Tallard. Let me check."

Nicolan looked out toward the port as he waited. Pale against the rising sun, a shuttle was making a descent. The bright white flare of its heat shields flickered wildly through the agrav field that brought it down slower and slower.

"Co Cambion?"

A short, wide-faced woman stood on the plate. She wore stained blue worktogs and dark circles under her eyes. "Co Tallard?"

"No, I'm Engineer Fisher, Co Tallard's assistant. She's at the damaged site right now."

"Where's Bel Ollic?"

"Dead."

Nicolan blinked, stared.

"We've got riots here, Co Cambion. They started shortly after the explosion. We're a little busy—"

"I want a report. The explosion, what caused it, what's going on."

She sighed impatiently, closed her eyes, and nodded. "All right. Early this morning there was an explosion four hundred meters down the transit shaft connecting us to the compound. Five minutes later was another one in the main shaft from the mining offices. Both explosions brought down rock, closed both bores completely, but did not start repeating fault collapses."

"Both?"

"Both. Very professional. We got diggers in immediately, shouldn't have been a difficult job, and then the riots started. First in town, then at the mine. A mob attacked the digger crews at the transit tunnel. We had to pull crew away from the main shaft to help there. Co Ollic went in immediately to try to impose order and was shot. The riots are out of control in the town, but we've got a perimeter around the offices and the main shaft and some of our people are helping the local constabulary hold the transit tunnel. Three more explosions have gone off, one at the town administrative offices, one in the community power plant and one at the shuttle port."

Nicolan's fingers squeezed into fists. "Instigators?"

"No idea, Co Cambion. But we've heard riots broke out in Crag Nook last night. We've heard some grumbling the last several days that Maxwell Cambion is working secretly for the Pan Humana and intends handing Finders right back to them, but nothing to suggest this kind of action."

"My father—Maxwell Cambion is on his way there."

"We haven't got the transit tunnel open yet. He won't get through."

"Have someone—Co Tallard if possible—send him back if he does get through. I—"

A flash of light caught his attention. He looked out across the plain to the port. The shuttle hovered over a landing pit, a bright spark throwing the entire field into brilliant relief. It abruptly blossomed into flame. Black smoke seeped through the red and orange fire and the burning twisted shards rained across the port.

"Never mind," he said. Two other pits burst upward. "Tell him we're under attack, too."

Nicolan cut the connection. A moment later the alarm sounded. Within minutes crews were at their stations; the executive level staff poured onto the floor. Nicolan activated all the screens in the office. Every wall panel became a display. He watched the magnified view of the port.

Heavy black smoke boiled off the field. Through the grimy pall, damage control vehicles crowded around the two blazing pits and the wreckage of the shuttle. Foam suppressant sprayed from nozzles. Between these machines the flat panels of energy soaks glowed dimly. The heat still rolled from the fires like dry water, washing across the port in suffocating waves. The smaller shapes of people moved in and out of visibility, some running, others moving carefully.

Shuttles still waited in other pits, unable to lift off. Pits three, eight, and eleven were damaged; the remains of a shuttle in pit three. Wreckage sprawled from the pit's broken lip to the southeast. Twisted metal, polyceramo shards, burnt and melted forms. To the south the two other damaged pits bled smoke, the one—number eight— much less than the other. Energy soaks moved out north as the fire in pit eleven came under control.

A man appeared on the commline plate. He was short and broadshouldered, his clothes soot-smeared. He wore a breather mask.

"Co Cambion!"

"Padig?" Padig was the port engineer.

"We're being shot at, Co Cambion! From the northwest."

"What...?"

He increased magnification on one of the displays and saw a puff of dust spitting up from the polycrete. Another burst up a few meters away. Solid projectile small arms fire.

"The autotracks are taking them out," Padig explained. "But the targets are small and there's a lot of them. The system can't take them all."

"How many injured do you have?"

"Five dead, nineteen wounded."

"Get me a visual inside the operations center."

A screen opposite the plate changed from a view of the port to inside a wide room. Bedrolls, sheets, pillows, and blankets had been laid out on the floor, on which lay wounded coes. A couple of port personnel moved among them with handscanners and first aid kits. Bandages on forearms, healant patches on scalps, shoulders. One had her right pant leg cut open and a compress on her thigh. None of them had plasm sacks or metabolic monitors. They all seemed relatively calm—sleeping or staring ceilingward or watching the med techs, waiting. Nicolan saw no frantic faces or death pallors. He nodded.

"I see twelve. You said nineteen."

"The bad ones are in the infirmary. Please—we need help."

Five dead... "Do you have any weapons?"

"Some e.p. sidearms, no rifles. The shields are designed for meteorites, falling debris, heat absorption. We can't stop a missile."

"I know, I know—" Another person—staff—appeared along-side Padig. "Yes?"

"We've got incoming tracks out of the northeast," she said.

Nicolan looked at the screen displaying a grid map. Three bright points moved toward the port out of the upper righthand corner. A display at the bottom of the screen gave the speed and time till impact—twenty-six seconds.

"Are the defensive bunkers armed and up?"

"On automatic."

"Lock them on the tracks, fire soonest."

It took five seconds for the big energy pulse guns to reprogram and lock on. The three tracks vanished a few seconds later.

"Full report," Nicolan snapped. He stood and left the office.

In the center of the floor, people huddled around the holo projector. Nicolan worked his way through. Displayed on the wide, meter-high oblong table was a representation of the whole area, corresponding to roughly thirty square kilometers. The mountains, the Cambion compound, the port. Smoke rose out of the damaged pits. As Nicolan neared he saw white grid markers superimposed over the scene and red lines connecting the port to the mountains.

The woman who had broken into his comm with Padig looked up at him. "The s.p. fire is from at least three positions in the mountains, two north—" she pointed—"and one south. We haven't pinpointed the source of the missiles yet, but they all came from the northeast. Our scans show nothing. No trace from the last several hours of surveillance shows anything."

"Mobile platforms, good camouflage," Nicolan said. "Any ideas who?" Everyone around the table exchanged dubious looks, suggesting they had opinions but none strong enough to voice. Nicolan grunted. "I might hazard a guess at Govanchi."

"I didn't think his reach was this long," someone said.

"Favors, bought and owed. They might be any group, even a recovery mission out of Crag Nook, but Govanchi is the mover." He shrugged. "The question is where did they get the missiles and where did they acquire the camouflage. They got into position without leaving a security trace, visual imprint, satellite track, nothing. We can't just blow them out of their positions in the mountains because they're right over a major trunk off the Crag Nook link."

"Incoming," someone said tightly.

In the projection the phosphorescent trace of four missiles appeared, hugging the ground and moving very fast out of the northeast.

"Backtrack that!" Nicolan ordered. "Fire when in range."

"They *turn*," a technician complained.

As Nicolan watched, the traces diverged, following different courses, then moving back toward each other. At five hundred meters four pulses of energy shot out from the tower and touched each missile, bursting them in flight.

Nicolan went to another console and peered over the tech's shoulder.

"Just probabilities again," the tech said.

"Heat traces, damnit," Nicolan said.

The tech pointed at a large area on one screen. "They're in there. Before they launch that entire volume is flooded with heat from random sources. Against that temperature the missile's track is invisible."

"And visual?"

"Heat mirages from the same sources. The missiles themselves are camouflaged, we're only tracking them once they emerge from the circle."

"We're not really equipped to deal with this," Nicolan muttered. "Get me an uplink to the tender." He moved to another console. The tech worked quickly and a screen cleared, then displayed a menu. Nicolan touched the path for Lovander Casm.

The Vohec appeared a second later. "Co Cambion?"

"Lovander Casm. I require assistance. Will you receive data?"

"Yes."

Nicolan glanced toward the group around the holo. "Transmit everything through this link."

"In a few seconds," Nicolan continued to Casm, "you will be receiving a situation packet. Our port is under attack. We do not have the resources to effectively counter—"

Casm held up a hand. "A moment. I am receiving now." He looked to one side for a time. Then he shook his head. "I am afraid we cannot assist you. We have been restrained by the authority of the Rahalen Coingulate. We cannot interfere."

"I understand that, Lovander Casm. I am not asking for intervention, just better telemetry. Can you scan through the heat that's shielding the launch vehicles?"

"Under the interdiction, that constitutes military intervention. It would be participating in a military action. I apologize."

Nicolan sighed.

"This is embarrassing for us, Co Cambion," Casm continued. "Yes, we can accomplish what you ask. We are kept from doing so. I wish there was some way—"

"There is. The satellites—you sold them to us, correct?"

"Yes."

"Are you not obligated to assure us of their continued function, at least until you leave?"

"Of course. It was agreed that we would provide maintenance—"

"Excellent. Then provide it. Recalibrate and test, using your own sensors as a match, and report their performance to me. I want to know what they will scan and what they will not scan."

Casm stared at him for several seconds. Then: "Of course. We will use as a test target what appears to be an aberrant heat mirage some one-hundred-fifty kilometers northeast of your position. Allow us a few moments to run the appropriate tests."

"Thank you, Lovander Casm."

He grinned at those around him. They grinned back.

"Two more," a tech said, and on the holo table a pair of lines traced the path of a pair of missiles coming at the port.

"Co Cambion?" Lovander Casm was again on the screen. "We have run the tests on your surveillance satellites. It seems we sold you substandard merchandise. The resolution on all three is quite fine for normal atmospheric interference. They can, for example, see clearly the five pockets of personnel in the mountains that are directing small arms fire toward you. However, they cannot resolve the six mobile launchers and ten support vehicles moving in a southerly direction and currently—" Casm glanced briefly to one side "—one-hundred-forty-two kilometers northeast of you. Nor are they capable of detecting the convoy of twenty-five vehicles coming north. I suspect we have delivered you the wrong satellites. We're terribly embarrassed about this oversight."

Nicolan felt a chill cross the back of his scalp. "Can you verify these tests? I want to see the two scans, if you don't mind."

"Certainly. Downloading now."

"Shit," someone breathed.

"Govanchi can't mount anything like this," Nicolan said.

On a pair of screens alongside Casm's image the two displays came up. The one—showing what the satellites "saw"—showed the port, the smoke, the mountains, and pinpoints locating the snipers. The other showed the two convoys. Both moved very fast. It was a pincer move, clearly, and just as clearly it was expensive and professional.

"Thank you very much, Lovander Casm. Will you see to compensating us for the inconvenience this error has caused?"

"Of course. I would like to extend the hospitality of my personal invitation to you and your father. Is this acceptable?"

"Certainly. We'll be in touch. Thank you, Co Casm."

"Then we shall not withdraw from the system until such compensation is possible." The Vohec nodded and the screen blanked.

"We've got tracks on them."

"Project their position, start firing at the convoy," Nicolan said. "We need to get the rest of those shuttles off the ground. Find me Co Rike."

A second later Rike appeared. "Yes, Co Cambion?"

"I'm sending you telemetry," Nicolan said. "Prepare teams. We have snipers on the mountain north of us. They're over major tunnels, we can't blast. Also, I want the entire compound on alert. We are under attack."

"Partisans?" Rike asked, frowning.

"No, it looks like Armada commandos."

"Oh. I'll see to it."

The screen blanked. "Send him the telemetry."

Everyone was looking at him now. He felt it the instant he said the words, "Armada commandos." He ignored the stares and studied the tactical display. There was no other explanation. The only question he had was how long had they been on the ground.

"Co Cambion," the commtech said. "Comm from Lovander Casm."

"Yes?"

Casm reappeared on the screen. "I thought it prudent to inform you that your satellites are being interfered with. There are ten distinct wave patterns being generated at numerous points throughout their orbital corridor that are blocking their input."

"Can you compensate?"

"Only by exceeding the designed parameters of the satellites."

"In other words, by intervening."

Casm nodded and, although the Vohec's face did not change, Nicolan sensed the seti's impatience. "My sincerest apologies," Casm said. "Were it up to me—"

"I understand completely. I don't hold you responsible. Would you link me to Commander Shinnick?"

Casm's face was replaced a few seconds later by a woman with severe, pulled-back grey hair and deep-set blue eyes. "Nic."

"Ann, how many fighters do you have still with the tender?"

She smirked. "Ten. Remanufacture was completed yesterday and I dispatched everything else for perimeter duty with the rest. I held ten for courier duty."

Nicolan nodded and kept his annoyance to himself. They had argued the deployment of ships. Ann Shinnick insisted that if the Armada got through to Finders the battle would be over. Best to deploy where they could do the most good—out at the edge of the system. Nicolan had deferred, especially after the first engagement with the Valico task force. He had been troubled then, but had been unable to identify why. Now it was clear. No one had expected infiltration.

"Fine. You've got the datafeed from Casm?"

"I've been watching. I've already prepped the pilots. The ships are standing by."

"We need the missile launchers taken."

"Five minutes, Nic."

"Incoming," a tech said.

On the holo table three tracks raced toward the port.

The tram slowed and finally stopped. Maxwell pulled down the release lever on the hatch and pushed the door open. The air outside in the tunnel was gritty, the light bad. He stepped down onto a siding and looked back the way they had come. The tunnel stretched away to a pinpoint, the strips of light bright. He walked around to the nose of the tram.

Through the haze of dust hanging in the air, stirred into eddies by the tram, he saw a wall of cracked, broken stone collapsed in their path.

"Shit," Rhonson hissed, stepping up behind Maxwell. Rhonson, one of Maxwell's favorite engineers, advanced to the edge of the debris as if expecting the rock to pull back from him. "Thought I felt something." He sniffed loudly. "This was blasted."

Rhonson returned to the tram and emerged a minute later with a small kit. He opened it and pulled out a handscanner, which he linked to the gear in the kit. For the next few minutes he walked back and forth across the face of the cave-in, poking the scanner closer here and there, finally returning to the kit.

Meanwhile the rest of the passengers stepped from the tram. Maxwell had brought a small team—Rhonson and his assistant, a dwarfish Founder named Kolit, and six security officers, who now ranged out around the tram, surveying for their own signs. Maxwell coughed lightly. The ventilators immediately around the debris no longer worked.

"We've got about eighteen meters of debris," Rhonson announced. "There's activity on the other side, so I think they're working at punching through. We're still a good six hundred meters from the mouth of the tunnel, though." He studied his instruments quietly. "I'd say at least three different charges were set to bring this down and its purpose was purely to close it off."

"What about the diggers in the tram?" Maxwell said. "Can we cut through with them?"

"It'd take several hours to do it right." Rhonson closed up his kit and straightened. "There's a spur about half a k back that links to one of the exploratory shafts."

"Safe?"

"With breathers, sure. Let me see if I can pull the schematic." He went back inside the tram. A second later he leaned out. "Max, we have a problem."

Maxwell jumped into the tram and followed Rhonson to the small control blister in the nose. Rhonson pointed to the panel. A red light winked every few seconds. Above it a screen showed a schematic of the transit tunnel, with their location marked in blue, stationery. Far back along the tunnel another tram was coming toward them, marked in green.

"It's unmanned, just moving along. Speed's picking up."

Maxwell stared at it for a moment. "Get this thing reversed." He went back to the hatch and leaned out. "Everybody on board! Move! Now!"

As his team scampered back on board the tram, Maxwell told Rhonson, "Stop us at the spur, then set the tram on automatic and send it back."

"It'll be close, Max."

The hatch sealed and the tram started moving.

"When we stop," Maxwell said, "everyone out, fast. Get your breathers on, have whatever you're bringing with you ready, and get into the spur as quickly as possible."

"Three seconds," Rhonson called. The tram slowed down again.

Maxwell opened the hatch before they stopped rolling. "Out!" He pushed them as they crowded into the hatch. "Come on, Rhonson!"

"All right, all right, give me a second..." The engineer worked at the console, then turned. He grabbed his kit and a mask and in three strides was out the hatch.

Maxwell pulled a mask out of its compartment and jumped just as the tram began to accelerate back down the track.

He landed, staggering, on the platform before the entrance to the spur. Rhonson was already opening the heavy composite door. Maxwell looked down the tunnel at the receding tram. He slipped the mask over his head; the seals tightened up against his skin while he closed the earplugs. He tapped the throatpiece lightly and the comm came on.

"In!" Rhonson commanded.

The team hurried into the smaller tunnel. It was wide enough for four people shoulder-to-shoulder, and seven meters high. Just within the entrance an emergency locker had been set into the stone, next to a commline and a duplicate set of door controls. Rhonson began closing the door and Maxwell punched in his access code to the commline.

The door swung inward. When it was less than a meter to closed, a deep, metallic rumble coursed up the main tunnel, muffled by the earplugs, followed immediately by the sharper concussion of an explosion. A big one. Maxwell felt a chill at the sound, surprised he could hear it at all.

The door stopped, still open.

The power light on the commline went out.

"Down the tunnel!" Maxwell shouted.

Suddenly stones, a dense cloud of dust and grit, driven by a fast, loud wind blew through the open door, bounced off the opposite wall, and pelted them. Maxwell dropped to the floor and covered his head. The pressure wave passed then, slamming the door shut and cutting off nearly all sound. Maxwell scrambled forward, putting distance between himself and the entrance. He lay there for a long time, waiting for his pulse to slow and his breath to come easily.

He rolled over and pushed himself up on his elbows. The only sound now, coming sharply through the commlink, was a chorus of mismatched breathing. The only light source was a pale grey-green light panel set high on the wall. Around him he saw the vague shadow-shapes of the others sitting or lying against the walls.

"Everyone here?" he asked.

"Solig's gone," one of the security people said.

"Where?" Maxwell asked, standing. "Light. We need more light." Emergency lights winked on and Maxwell saw Rhonson by the big breaker panel near the door. Maxwell froze.

Caught between the frame and the massive door itself, half of a crushed body hung limply.

"Happened too fast..." Kolit said.

"Main power's out," Rhonson said. He stood and went to the locker. There was a loud click and the sound of a metal door falling open and banging against rock.

Bright white light flooded the tunnel from a handlamp. Rhonson dialed it down and fished around in the locker. Maxwell stared at the body in the harsh wash of the handlamp, then turned away.

"Lamps, rations, breathers," Rhonson muttered the inventory. "This'll get us through."

"Through to where?" Kolit asked.

"Well," Rhonson stepped back and looked down the spur, though all that was visible were the ever dimmer light panels that trailed away. "This joins the main shaft about three kilometers on. From there we ought to make it to the offices in Downer's Cove."

"If nothing else caves in," Kolit complained.

Maxwell reached into the locker and pulled out a handlamp. "I'm not worried about cave-ins." He went to the door and shined the light into the tunnel beyond. The hurricane created by the explosion had left loose debris everywhere. About fifteen meters along, he found more of Solig's body, bloodied and torn.

Maxwell returned to the others. "Let's go."

Silently, then, they sorted through the supplies, divided them up, and started down the spur. Maxwell brought up the rear and kept glancing back toward the entrance.

"Wasn't just a collision," Rhonson whispered.

Maxwell started. He had not noticed the engineer drop back.

"No," he said. Even without the sound of the explosion, the velocity of the wind and its draw indicated a sizeable device. Maxwell shook his head slightly and touched his lips. Rhonson nodded and moved forward again.

Maxwell looked back. One dead was too many already.

Some of the light panels had gone out, their chemical reactions exhausted, creating spaces of total darkness along the passage. One of the group would switch on a handlamp through these dark sections. At one time the spur was scheduled for widening into a regular tram corridor, but it seemed unlikely in the foreseeable future. Other details demanded Maxwell's attention.

As they neared the end of the spur, the mountain around them seemed to vibrate with distant thunder. At the mouth fine dust filled the air. Maxwell pushed to the head of the group.

The exit opened onto a wide platform bordered on the other side by a short stair leading to another, larger, doorway. Newer light panels set the dust-filled air aglow. A sharp explosion lit the opposite doorway and more dust blew into the chamber.

Maxwell descended the stair and peered through the door.

The main shaft was a vertical hole twenty meters across, rimmed by catwalks at six meter intervals connected with lifts and staircases. Workstations and offices had been carved out of the side of the rock wall. A huge tube normally hung in the center of the shaft, the conveyor for raw materials. Now, the conveyor tube rested against the wall, gaping cracks all along its length. The catwalks had been busted up and torn down in several places, and most of the workstations were dark. One just above and opposite Maxwell was a blackened hole, wider than it should have been. Looking up, Maxwell saw that the roof had been shattered. Jagged sections still hung from the lip—part of the conveyor tube dangled precariously against the side—and beyond the sky, streaked by fast-moving black smoke, was visible.

Maxwell stared, stunned. Details resolved—holes in the wall where weaponfire had impacted, charred sections of catwalks, girders and cables hanging from the offices, bodies...the bodies did not look like bodies, did not look like people, but ragged clumps of fabric and meat, organic debris.

Another explosion echoed through the shaft and Maxwell withdrew.

"Max!"

Rhonson was at the far end of the chamber, by a trio of doors. One stood open.

"We still have some power," Rhonson said.

Maxwell hesitated. It might be simpler to go back down the spur, wait for the shooting to stop. He was not afraid of the fighting, or personal harm, but he was not sure he wanted to see what was above, in Downer's Cove. A moment passed and he hurried to the lift.

The lift door let them out in open air. Smoke drifted across the plaza. The on-site offices to their left burned, a smoking pit. Black soot smeared the polycrete all the way to the lip of the shaft. To the right stood the receiving station, a big polycrete warehouse that formed a horseshoe around the shaft. A single hole had been punched in the wall, though the impact of several more hits had blown chunks out. Crates, nacelles, sandbags, and corpses formed a defensive wall from the western end of the station south, almost to the service road that bounded the office. People in worktogs and personal clothes huddled behind this makeshift fortress wall, rifles resting in small holes or on top, aimed outward.

Maxwell sprinted to the service road.

Below, Downer's Cove was ablaze. To the north, the government buildings still stood, but heavy energy pulse fire licked at the walls, crackling in the air. The constant, oddly-delicate sound of solid projectile fire punctuated the seamless crackle and roar of fire from the center of town. Black smoke poured up from the residential districts and the warehouses just below the mines.

A hand closed on Maxwell's arm and jerked him off his feet. He rolled, prepared to shout angrily, and came up sitting with his back to the barricade.

"Damnit—!" he began.

A gloved hand—he assumed it was the same hand that had grabbed him—pointed, cutting him off.

Rhonson was crawling away quickly, slapping at his burning pant leg. Three mine workers surrounded him and one draped a blanket over the leg, smothering the fire.

Where they had been standing Maxwell now saw nothing but charred black and red piles that still smoldered.

Maxwell closed his eyes, sitting very still for several seconds. Finally, he said, quietly, "Thank you."

His rescuer grunted. When he looked, Maxwell saw a line of defenders tending to their weapons, returning fire. Explosions rocked the ground. Maxwell crouched and looked through a gap in the wall.

Through the smoke above Downer's Cove a trio of black silhouettes flew a neat V formation, turned, and fired down into the inferno.

"Where's Ollic?" he shouted.

"Dead," someone shouted back.

"What about Tallard?"

The nearest defender turned to him. She was a broad-faced woman, soot smearing her skin. "Tallard took a crew to the tramline tunnel to try to clear the debris. Haven't heard anything since. I'm Fisher, Tallard's assistant. Who the hell are you?"

Maxwell pulled his breather off then. "Your employer."

Fisher gazed at him for a long pause, then grunted again. "Not till this is done you aren't."

"Who's in charge of defense?"

"Tallard was, after Co Ollic died. She handed it off to me, but it's not a situation requiring a leader. Only a matter of time before they reduce this place to slag."

"What's keeping them from doing that immediately?"

Fisher grinned. "We strung sheets of reflective myranar on the other side. Energy pulse dissipates." The grinned faded. "But solid projectile works fine."

Maxwell grunted. "Then we need to do something about it."

"Hm. You know something to do?"

Maxwell nodded. "That's why I'm still your boss. Let's get to the warehouse, see what's in inventory."

Fisher chuckled and nodded. "Yes, Co Cambion. I'd like to see this."

"You do realize what's happening, don't you?"

"We got a fucking insurrection, that's what's happening!"

Maxwell shook his head. "That's Armada out there."

The block wore off in time, but Venner did not recall how long a time. He did not know how long sensation had been returning before he noticed it, first in his fingertips, then his stomach, next across his shoulders. The tingling did not last long enough before it turned to pain. When he understood what was happening he became impatient.

The intruders were wrecking his house. He heard them in other rooms, breaking furniture, knocking things over, *disturbing* his environment. True, he told himself, trying to keep the anger and embarrassment at a distance, it was not exactly *his* house, but he had taken it over shortly after the evacuations and he had grown fond of it. He had rearranged, brought in new things, made it comfortable. They were wrecking it.

Each of the three had taken turns coming into the bedroom and doing something. One had urinated on him again, then, realizing that the first one—Shuller—had already done that, defecated alongside the bed. Venner had wanted to call him a coward for not having gall enough to shit *on* him, but he held his tongue. The third one had brought a pan of eggs up and cracked them open, one by one, and dropped the shells onto Venner. Now, hours later, the mingled odors of piss, shit, and rotting eggs clawed at Venner's throat.

Not one of them had bothered to do a scan to see if he really was dead. They had not even turned him over, otherwise they would have found the neural blocks. Amateurs, he thought bitterly. Fucking bottom-feeding juiceless amateurs.

Cira was long overdue and he had listened to the gunfire outside for days. It seemed like days. Had to be, but his brain had stopped keeping track. Night, day, what difference did it make when the air smelled so bad? Venner figured that a riot had broken out, like the one shortly after the evacuation. There had been some local authorities then to quell it, but that had slowly dissolved before the rawer, uglier force of the vigilante groups and the strengthening nationalists. Likely as not, the nationalists themselves had started this one and Venner expected it to rage for days. Riots made excellent opportunities for purges. Cira was probably dead, he decided.

The house was quiet. The intruders were still, their destruction suspended for the moment. Venner bit his lip as feeling returned joint by joint, followed by cramps and burning tendons. Patience, he cautioned himself; time will hand you everything. He had never before noticed how much pleasure was contained in the contemplation of revenge.

When he could feel the length of his legs he slowly tried to sit up. His back screamed. He swung his legs out and set his feet on the floor. As he pushed himself up his left leg slithered straight forward across the floor and he flailed wildly to catch himself on the edge of the bed. Eggshells fell delicately. His arms, his stomach, his thighs all erupted in surges of pain. He closed his eyes and waited.

He blinked and looked down. He had stepped in the pile of feces. His lip curled reflexively as he stood. Stretching helped slightly, though it hurt, too.

After a couple of minutes, he reached to the back of his neck and peeled off the exhausted tabs. He was dizzy for a few seconds, then the pain focused him again. Carefully, he crossed to the bathroom.

The tub still contained water. He dipped his right hand in— cold, as he expected, but it felt oddly comforting—then eased himself in. The chill water ate at the pain, supplanting it with its own persistent feel. Venner wiped his hands over his chest and stomach, his thighs, pushed across the flesh as if pushing off an old, dead skin. He pulled a rag from the edge of the tub and bent far over to wipe at his soiled foot.

As he dried himself, shivering slightly, he smiled. He could feel his bruises again, the ones Cira had given him. The broken rib throbbed wonderfully.

He pulled on a pair of pants and a loose shirt, but decided to remain barefoot; he walked more quietly that way. His pistol was on the table beside the polycom. He tucked it into his waistband, then went to the door.

Venner stopped just within the threshold, a tingle across his scalp, and a second later one of them came before him. The man stopped abruptly, his pale eyes widening slightly. He raised up on the balls of his feet as his muscles tensed from startlement, his mouth beginning to open, hands moving out from his sides for balance.

Venner jammed his right thumb straight at the man's throat, just below the Adam's apple, a swift, deep jab that elicited a small, fragile gasp. He brought his other hand to the back of the intruder's head, held it firmly, then brought his free hand across the man's jaw, snapping his head around and breaking his neck.

Venner caught the body, brought it into the bedroom, and laid it gently in the smeared shit.

He heard the others laughing from the kitchen as he descended the stairs. Only the kitchen lights were on, spilling into the hallway. Venner padded silently to the door.

Both of them sat at the table, feet propped, chairs tilted back. Shuller was grinning while the other still laughed, face red and eyes watering. He shook his head as if at the unlikeliness of the joke he had just been told. Venner smiled with them, though he could not say why.

He pulled the pistol from his waistband, aimed at the laughing intruder, and shot him in the head. The body slammed back against the wall, blood splashing in bright patterns, and fell from the chair.

Shuller kicked back as Venner shifted aim. Venner missed, the shot punching out a large piece of the stonework. Shuller somersaulted, came up to a crouch with a small pistol in his hand. Venner dropped, aimed, and shot Shuller in the right knee.

Shuller screamed and fell to his side, the pistol clattering across the floor.

Venner crossed the distance quickly and kicked the weapon further away. Shuller tried to roll, but Venner kicked down on the wounded knee and Shuller screamed again. Venner kicked him across the face. Shuller sprawled backward, sliding up against the cabinet. Venner aimed at his left eye.

"Oh, fuck!" Shuller exclaimed, his skin waxy-pale and sweaty. "No, co, no! We work for you! We're Armada!"

Venner hesitated, frowned. "What?"

Shuller swallowed. "Truth! We're Armada. I—oh, fuck, my knee, shit—my ID is in my jacket..."

"Armada?"

Shuller nodded frantically.

"Then, why did you treat me this way?"

"Thought you were dead..."

"You didn't bother to check."

Shuller closed his eyes, shook his head. "Please...my knee...*hurts*!"

"I imagine. What I've been hearing—a riot?"

"Yes. All over. We had units in place before the task force arrived...supposed to coordinate...riots in Emorick, Crag Nook, Downer's Cove, everywhere..."

"So why are you here instead of coordinating?"

"I...we didn't mean anything...didn't know...shit, my knee..."

"You think I'm a secessionist."

"No! I—"

"You were told to come here to secure this station, weren't you?"

For a few seconds Shuller did not answer. Venner stepped close and kicked the knee.

"Agh! Yes! Secure station...against..."

"No, that's all right, you don't have to tell me the rest. You were waiting to see who else I was in contact with. I know how the procedure works."

Venner saw the network that had betrayed him with a clarity he realized was irrational. But its truth pushed what remained of his loyalist reference aside. The slippage rushed on, suddenly, and, watching, Venner felt himself turn. No going back now, he thought, no little shop on a safe, inner Pan station, no pension...

"Please...my knee..."

"Does it hurt?"

"Yes."

"Do you want me to make the pain go away?"

Shuller nodded.

"You know—just so you know, in your heart, deep down—I wasn't a secessionist. Really. Not till this."

Venner pulled the trigger.

Chapter Five

Cira hobbled along, her ankle collared in pain. Rollo Hersted casually braced her as she ate from a small paper cup. The stew was thick with rice and noodles and local cheese. Vendors conducted business even while fighting raged on streets right in front of them. The prices had risen tenfold from earlier in the afternoon.

Crag Nook crackled with s.p. fire, burning, clusters of desperate, enraged people running. The cloud cover above them glowed dirty orange; Cira guessed that maybe a third of the town was ablaze. The riot had spread from the amphitheater so fast that she could only believe it was planned. The implications troubled her, but for now she gave them little thought; priorities reduced to simple choices, one at a time. She needed to get back to Venner's house, then she needed to find Alexan. After that—well, if her deductions about the riot were correct, after that would take care of itself.

The riot burned into the night. Cira and the Hersteds worked from street to street. Smoke filled many narrow passages, but people wore breathers, carried them under their overcoats as a matter of course. Cira saw no human faces, only masks, the eyes oil-slick-surfaced sensor plates. She pulled her own goggles on and the town transformed into bas-relief green and grey background with demon-bright actors scurrying through the improvised drama. As her ankle worsened, the Hersteds broke into a boarded-up shop and let her rest, packing her from calf to instep in compresses till the swelling went down. It was not broken, only sprained, but already it had darkened against her copper-brown skin. There were no anæsthetic patches—too hard to come by, too expensive—but the compress eased most of the ache.

Lying in the dark, she listened as the fighting danced around the shop. Reduced to sound alone, it did not seem so bad. She had been to carnivals that had been louder, more raucous. This was different, though—she jumped at each unexpected sound, her heart racing.

The rattle of fighting and burning seemed further away by morning. Olin wrapped Cira's ankle—the swelling much reduced—in a new compress and helped her pull on her boot. He strapped it with a belt and cinched it tightly. Cira bit down against the pain and managed to walk fairly straight to the door. Rollo stayed close to her while Becca and Olin stepped out in a crouch, rifles ready.

Three buildings across the street had burned to the ground. Ghostly wisps of smoke hovered above the blackened debris; embers gathered brightness, dimmed, flickered. Through the ruin the north end of Crag Nook was visible. Halfway up the side of the hill from the amphitheater, which was lit now by brilliant cold white floodlights, one whole section was fiercely burning. The flames leapt and surged, eating the houses, filling the streets and alleys. All around it, though, the edges seemed brighter, a white-hot circumscription. Sparks drifted toward it, spattered into the brightness along with tongues of fire, and Cira realized that the blaze was contained within heatsoaks. The energy was not being drained out to kill the blaze; the soaks were only holding it in, keeping it from neighboring sections. Groups roved the streets, visible by the clusters of handlamps. West of the amphitheater a large blockhouse structure was burning.

"What's that?" Cira asked, pointing to it.

"Old civic center," Becca said. "Processing center now. Was. A'n't no more."

"Where now?" Rollo asked.

"South," Cira said automatically. Then she asked, "Where's the station for the tunnel from Cambion Mines?"

Rollo raised a hand. "South."

Cira nodded and started off. The further south they went the less damage they found. Fewer gangs roamed these streets. Instead people, alone or in twos and threes, huddled close to doorways, in gangways; some looked down from upper floor windows, rifles and pistols resting on sills, ready. They came into a brighter-lit street with vendors selling food, water, ammunition, and they all ate.

The softer orange of sunrise began to ease the hellish fireglow on the clouds as they started up the street to Venner's house. They kept to the shadows all the way and Cira pulled out her pistol as she started down the short corridor into the courtyard.

Lights burned in the first floor windows. She studied each place where a weapon might appear, but saw nothing. The neural block must have worn off hours before; she had expected to be back long ago. She glanced up at Rollo.

"Cover," she said.

He nodded and Cira started across the pavement. With each step she expected a shot. By the time she reached the door she was sweating freely, ankle protesting. She touched the jamb, then turned and motioned for the Hersteds.

They ranged out quickly, always keeping an eye on the upper floors, checking each others' back. As they came up to her, she opened the door and pushed through.

Light spilled from the kitchen across the floor. There was a slight metallic tang in the air. Cira stood in the hall and listened to the house. Silently, the Hersteds came in behind her. Olin went to the staircase and pressed against the wall so he could watch both the stair and the room. Becca stayed at the entrance, watching the courtyard.

Cira went toward the kitchen, Rollo a step or two back and to her right. She peered cautiously around the edge and jerked back at the sight of two men sitting at the table at the far end. Rollo shifted his rifle and jumped to the opposite side. Silence stretched from seconds to a minute. Rollo shrugged and Cira looked again. Neither man had moved. She raised her pistol and stepped into the kitchen. In four paces she made out their wounds.

She did not recognize the men. Their eyes locked fixedly on nothing, dull and curiously artificial. One had been shot in the kneecap as well as the forehead. Cira used her handscanner to verify it, but there was no doubt they were both dead.

"No one else," Rollo said.

"Check upstairs," Cira said. "Carefully."

Rollo left the kitchen. Cira bent over one of the corpses and tried to close its eyes, but the lids stubbornly refused to slide down.

A pair of chits lay on the table between them. Cira picked one up and turned it over. Featureless charcoal grey, standard issue. She popped it into the reader slot of her handscanner and keyed it. Immediately a request for an authorized access code scrolled across the small screen. She did not possess the code, but she recognized the protocol: Armada security.

"Another body up there," Rollo said from the door.

She limped upstairs to the room where she had left Venner. The air stank, partly of shit, partly of spoiled meat. The bed was empty and several components of the polycom and commlink equipment were missing. The third body was in the bathtub, already starting to bloat. Unsurprisingly, she did not know this one, either.

She sighed and sat down on the edge of the bed.

"What now?" Rollo asked.

"Hm? Oh." She wondered at what point she had become their leader. Perhaps from the moment she had led them from the amphitheater, though it was more that they had led her. She had fallen into command easily enough, though, so perhaps it was her assumption as much as theirs. "Check the rest of the house, then rest. We can stay here." She forced herself to her feet. She was suddenly core-weary. "Let me scan the larder. He's well-stocked, but he might have poisoned it."

"If you like, I can do that," Rollo said. "Least, Olin can, he's got med. Kept us alive so far."

Cira nodded as she staggered toward the door. She pulled out her handscanner and shoved it at Rollo. "Use this, it's probably more accurate than Olin's kit."

She made it across to the room Venner had given her. She fell into the bed and slept.

He was sitting in the corner, repeating his name quietly under his breath ("My name is Alex...Alex...my name...Alex...is Alex..."), when the lights went out. For a few minutes he sat still, only vaguely aware that something was different.

Lights flared through a doorway, roved over the consoles and monitors, followed by quick footsteps.

"Damnit!" someone hissed.

Alex placed his hands carefully on the floor, palms flat, preparing to jump up and run. The lanterns shifted, explored, one of them finally shined directly on him, making him squint.

"What about him?"

"I don't—damnit, get him to the tramline and send him to Crag Nook."

"We had reports of riot in Crag Nook just before—"

"You *asked* what to do! I just told you! If you don't like it, do something else!"

The voices were familiar but Alex could not remember from where. The light moved off of him, back to exploring the equipment on the opposite side of the chamber. After a time it seemed they had all lost interest in him.

Quietly, he pushed himself up to his feet and pressed his back against the wall. He moved sideways toward the door, pausing for a moment, remembering that a barrier stood between his half of the chamber and the other. But the power was off, he reasoned, so the transparency had to be off as well. He continued on.

Suddenly his hand went through the open doorway. Adrenaline surged through him. He watched the lamp beams trace paths over the machinery, listened to the quiet whispers, then stepped around the edge of the door, into—

The lights were out everywhere. Alex blinked hard several times, but his eyes did not adjust. He stayed against the wall and moved along.

The wall trembled and a moment later the corridor filled with thunder. As that sound died, Alex heard running. It came nearer and he looked left and right into the darkness. Finally a cross corridor bloomed with light as a group of people hurried along, handlamps glowing in their midst. Alex followed.

He rounded the corner and ran as quietly as he could till he caught up with them. He hung back, just outside the sphere of illumination. None of them spoke. It thundered again and they quickened their pace.

At another intersection they encountered a different group. Everyone stopped, lamps mingling. Alex moved in among them.

"Where—?"

"—power's down all through the complex—"

"What about the trams?"

"Down there—"

"—Armada attack, has to be—"

"—trams! Damnit, we need to get out from under all this rock—"

"Don't panic! Last thing we need is a stampede in the dark!"

"—which way?"

The now-larger group moved off down the lefthand corridor. Alex stayed with them, well inside their ranks. No one paid him any attention. They looked, their eyes peering, wide and aggressive, but they did not see. Alex shivered, recognizing their stark panic. He had seen the look before, the fear of people desperately denying the likelihood of death, but he could not remember where.

Ahead came a sound like running water. Alex craned his neck to see. The corridor ran straight to an archway filled with light. As they neared it the sound resolved into the sound of hundreds of shouting voices.

He was suddenly reluctant to go on. He looked behind him to see if he could drop back again, but the group pressed forward and carried him along, under the archway, into the mob that crowded the tram station.

Portable generators ran the banks of floodlights shining down on the scene. The huge cavern floor was filled with people, who shifted like waves of water, pulling, pushing, trying to work forward to the edge of the platform. Each time the thunder came, the shouting increased and everyone tried to surge closer to the edge, to be nearer to the next tram.

"Everyone please be calm and wait your turn," an amplified voice echoed above them. "We are moving extra trams out as quickly as possible. Please be calm. The walls of the cavern are quite safe. The only danger is from panic. Please be calm. We are moving extra trams out as quickly as possible."

If anyone paid attention, it was impossible to tell. Alex was jostled and squeezed constantly. He was beginning to think he should have stayed where he was. But this was what those people had intended to do with him, put him on a tram and send him to Crag Nook. He assumed the trams all ran to Crag Nook.

Something struck the side of his head. He winced against the blow, shook his head, and he was struck again. He staggered, unable to fall in the close press. He blinked and tried to turn. He saw a face, wild-eyed with fright, staring at him, teeth clenched, a string of spittle traced down the chin. The man swung his arm up as if to fend Alex off and Alex knew this was the man who had hit him. Alex reached up calmly and seized his ear. He pulled down, hard, then rammed his arm straight. The ear tore, the face twisted in agony, and Alex let go. Alex wiped his hand on his togs, feeling suddenly confident, and worked his way through a brief opening in the crowd before him.

The right side of his head was numb. A warm, moist trickle ran down his neck. His right ear started ringing. He touched his scalp and his fingers came away wet with blood.

He saw other beatings going on around him. People were fighting for position, dragging others away from the edge of the platform, knocking them down, pushing and shoving and hitting. He stumbled over a body on the floor.

The trams were visible now above the heads of the mob. He was close. He pushed between two men and both grabbed him and pulled him back. He kicked down at the knee of the one on his right and the hand let go. Momentum sent him spinning backward, toward the man on his left. He lost balance for a moment, tried to recover, but a fist caught his left cheek and a boot came up hard into his stomach.

He dropped to his knees, his entire torso heaving. Each breath caused a spasm that forced the air back out before he felt he had taken a breath. People crowded around him, stepped on his fingers, scooted him along. He reached up and grabbed fabric, pulled himself to his feet, and let the new surge carry him forward.

Abruptly he was within centimeters of a tram door. People jumped ahead of him, inside. Those already within held out hands to some, pushed others out. Alex was dizzy, black dots dancing across his vision. He steadied himself the best he could, picked a spot, and jumped into the quickly filling tram. Someone snagged his collar and tried to hurl him back out, but he reached around and gripped the wrist and dug his thumb deep into the tendons. The hand opened, Alex let go, and he fell deeper into the car.

He wanted nothing better than to sit down and recover. The seats were buried under people, standing, sitting, squatting. Dazed, he turned in time to see the doors slide shut. The tram began to move and in a few moments the faces beyond blurred.

"You!"

The big man had grabbed his togs and pulled him around.

"You *fuck*! My partner didn't make it on! *You* took his space, you fuck!"

Alex raised his hand, intending to jam his thumb into the man's eye. Too quickly, though, the man hit him in the jaw. His head snapped around. Another blow snapped it around the other way. The black spots began to join up now. He did not feel the third punch.

The fighters came out of the clouds and slid gracefully through a long arc that brought them level about twenty meters over the ground. Nicolan watched, enthralled, as they went after their hidden prey.

"Closing," a tech said. "Another couple seconds... "

Everything shut down at once. Nicolan blinked, still staring after the fighters, and frowned at the sudden brightness through the windows. Then he turned and found everyone staring in stunned amazement at their suddenly lifeless consoles.

Distant explosions brought his attention back around. Several kilometers away the ground was on fire, black smoke beginning to billow into the sky. A few seconds later the five fighters came streaking back by, heading northeast to the other targets.

"Yes!" Nicolan hissed.

The control tower at the edge of the landing field erupted in flame. Two more pits blew, the shuttles within them scattering into a million hot arcs. The remaining shuttles began to lift, one by one. At about a hundred meters one of them exploded. The rest surged upward, out of the now useless ruin of the port.

"Where are the damn fighters?" he whispered to himself.

Ten ships dropped out of the clouds. Nicolan started and stared at them. Shinnick had said only five...

They flew northeast. As they became pinpoints in the distance, Nicolan recognized them.

"Abandon the complex!" he shouted.

For a moment no one moved. Then it was as if a switch had been thrown. Everyone headed for the exits.

"Do we have any comm at all?" he demanded.

One tech had remained at his post. "No, Co Cambion. Everything just...*went*."

"The lifts don't work!"

"Power is out," Nicolan shouted back. He looked out the windows again. For the moment everything was still. "Pry the doors open! We'll have to climb down the service ladders!"

At the far end of the room, two people on each side began to pull the big doors apart. Nicolan watched anxiously till they were open.

"Will they stand open?" he asked.

"Yes," several people replied.

"All right, *move*! It's a long climb, we need to be down at the base."

One by one, they let themselves down over the edge, found footholds, then handholds, and disappeared into the lift shaft. Six, seven, eight of them...four to go, including himself.

He glanced out the windows. Several black pinpoints ranged out across the horizon, bobbing at various elevations, moving very fast. Nicolan opened his mouth to tell the others to hurry.

The north end of the room disintegrated into countless fragments. The concussion knocked him off his feet. Automatically he scrambled for cover, clawing his way across the floor. His body slammed into a desk and overturned it: he crawled behind it.

The explosions came in fast succession now, maybe six, so close together he could not count them. Glass, plastic, polycor, steel, aluminum—the air was suddenly a sea of shards. Nicolan felt heat, heard the hammering against the underside of the desk. Then the desk was picked up and thrown against him, and he was carried with it, back against the wall. His ribs erupted in pain, the desk fell away, and he dropped onto a pile of hot debris. He jerked his hands up, then tried to stand, but he had to put his hands back into the heat to push himself up. He staggered back, brushing burning fragments from his hands.

The roaring all around him was like a loud wind. He looked toward the windows and sucked in his breath. Half the floor was gone, sheared off. Beams, burnt carpet, sheets of flooring, cables all hung out in open air, like protruding bones and veins from an open wound. The windows were gone. Small fires crackled everywhere. Furniture had been thrown, twisted out of recognition, against the interior wall.

Nicolan stumbled to the edge and looked down. The port was completely enveloped in flame and smoke. The road was chewed up with craters and the gates were gone. The roaring grew louder and he looked up. Black winged shapes streaked through the sky, half a dozen of them turning about to make another strafing run at the complex. Armada fighters.

He hurried to the lift. The doors still stood open, the shaft housing apparently intact. He dropped to his hands and knees and started to swing his legs over the side to climb down and stopped. Below, the shaft was bent sharply, and wisps of smoke trailed up from below. A gaping hole in the shaft wall let light on where a body lay at the crook of the bend, twisted and bloody.

He gulped air for a second, then looked back at the approaching fighters. This was the only way down. The ladder seemed still attached to the shaft wall, at least at this end. He let himself over the side.

His hands stung with each new grip. The skin was tender, blackened where it did not bleed.

He missed a rung, caught himself, and looked. There was no rung to miss. He let himself further down to next rung and continued on.

At the bend, he pointedly did not look at the body. He sat beside it and searched the walls for handholds. The rip in the wall came close to him. The metal was curled inward, charred. He touched it gingerly, found it had cooled, then let himself out over the chasm, balancing against the edge of the hole.

The entire wall had been crumpled severely below the hole, like a giant fist had punched into it. He listened for a few seconds to the rushing sound—where were the fighters, what was their approach?—then carefully set his feet on a deep fold.

He was still hanging on to the edge of the hole when the next series of explosions thundered throughout the tower. He closed his eyes and hung on, the metal vibrating heavily in his hands. He lost his footing, swung out, and came back against the wall. He gasped at the pain in his ribs and nearly lost his grip. He screamed and forced his fingers to remain locked around their precarious hold till the shaking stopped.

The ladder took up again five meters further down. The shaft had been pierced in several places, but nothing as severe as the bend. At ground level the double doors stood open, but the lift was gone and he continued climbing down, into the mines. Explosions rattled the tower again. Loose debris clattered past him and landed noisily below. Ten meters down he encountered twisted wreckage. He pushed it away from the ladder with his feet until he could not stay on the ladder. Then he climbed down through the beams, struts, and plating.

He touched bottom finally—as close to bottom as he could get, an uneven tangle he could no longer work through—and he looked up. He estimated he was about twenty-five meters down. In the dim light he studied the walls and found another set of doors just a meter or so above him, partly open. He worked his shoulder between them and pushed against one. It slid back with a slight grinding noise. When he stepped back it did not slide shut again. He pulled himself through.

It was much darker here. Evidently power throughout the complex had been shut down. Even if the initial outage had been confined to certain areas, the bombardment was completing the job. He felt along the walls until he found a locker. Within he discovered a handlamp, a pair of utilities, a medkit, and a pistol— an s.p. and a belt with three pouches of ammunition. He strapped on the belt, holstered the weapon, and opened the medkit. While more explosions shook the ground, he applied antiseptic gel to his burnt, aching hands. He stepped into the utilities and zipped them up over the gunbelt. Medkit and lamp in hand, he went through the next door.

He emerged onto a gantry that ran around the wall of the OSCA. A portable generator powered one set of floodlights aimed across the floor. Crews were sorting out provisions from the big lockers. Several moles were missing and most of the diggers. Nicolan saw light spilling from the mouths of the main tunnels.

He worked his way around the gantry to a stair and descended to the floor. As he neared the assembly of crew, several of them turned toward him with raised weapons.

"Wait, it's Nicolan Cambion," he said.

For several seconds no one spoke. Nicolan started to worry.

"Hey, boss."

Kee stepped through the rank of miners and grinned at him. Nicolan sighed in relief and laughed.

"It's the boss, coes," Kee said. "Rest easy, we're all safe now."

Uneasy laughter rippled through the crowd. Weapons were lowered and Kee stepped toward him.

"Good to see you, boss," he said. "I was sure no one upstairs survived."

"Did anyone get down?"

"Didn't see a-one."

Nicolan's legs began to shake. Kee reached out and steadied him, then caught one of Nicolan's hands and looked at it. He hissed.

"Malgo," Kee called, "got a burn here."

"It's all right," Nicolan said, stupidly he thought. Of course it's not all right.

"Shit, boss," Kee groused.

"What's going on?" Nicolan asked.

"Divvying up the supplies and preparing to leave."

A woman stepped up to him, took his hands, and shook her head. "Over by the lights," she said and shoved him along.

"Leaving for where?" Nicolan asked.

Nicolan sat down with his back to the wall near the floodlights. Malgo squatted next to him and opened a larger med kit and went to work on his hands. Kee looked back at the miners.

"Don't know really," he said, "but we a'n't staying here. Problems, though. The trams to Crag Nook are all taken by support personnel, families, office staff, and the maintenance staff. They sealed this section off. The tunnel to Downer's Cove has been closed."

"What? Maxwell's there."

"Hate to tell you, boss, but the odds are good Maxwell's dead. Not only was the far end collapsed by an explosion, someone sent a tram loaded with thermotin up Maxwell's ass. It collapsed the tunnel in the middle."

Nicolan let his head fall back against the stone. He was vaguely aware of Malgo spraying healant on his hands, wrapping them, slipping hygienic gloves on. Kee squeezed his shoulder briefly.

"Sorry, boss."

Nicolan looked at him. The man seemed embarrassed more than anything else. Nicolan shook his head.

"So where *are* you going?"

Kee sighed, clearly relieved to discuss something else. "We can work through the secondary tunnels and link up with the tunnels from the Downer's Cove operation. Some are going there, they've got family. The rest of us are figuring on taking the southern tunnel all the way to the other side and heading south along the coast."

"To the old Thayer smelting works?"

Kee shrugged, then nodded. "It's a place to start."

"We could get to the Champ Du Terre road from there." Nicolan nodded. "Good. How many?"

"Maybe eighty of us."

Nicolan looked at Kee. "What about our initial problem?"

"Still don't have that taken care of, boss."

"Someone closed down all our systems."

Kee nodded.

"Where's Rike?"

"No word since he took his people out to take care of the snipers."

"Would he know to head south?"

Kee shrugged. "You know Rike better than I do."

Malgo slammed her kit shut. "Tomorrow I'll change the bandages," she said. "Don't take off the gloves till I say."

Nicolan nodded, then pushed himself to his feet. "Kee, you stay with me. Looks like we're going south."

A rumble drew everyone's attention toward the ceiling. It passed and a minute later everyone resumed talking.

Nicolan looked at the tunnel to Downer's Cove. Maxwell dead. Maybe, he amended. It would be best, though, he decided, to assume that he was. There was no one to fall back on for decisions in any case.

"Maybe you should've evacuated when you had the chance," Kee said. "You know, go with the other Panner loyalists?"

Nicolan looked at him strangely. "Why? This is home." He shook his head and walked toward the miners.

Sunlight set the window aglow with dull orange. Cira stared at it, for a long time not recognizing the light, the window, or her own thoughts. It was a pleasant way to be, unmoved by anything other than the sensual quality of the light and the brief dissociation from self. The state passed almost as soon as she noticed it.

The next thing she became aware of was the stillness. She sat up and listened intently: no shots, no crackling of fire, no distant shouting…quiet.

Cira rubbed her eyes with the heels of her hands. She had slept in her clothes. She stretched against the stiffness in her joints. Her ankle throbbed, but not as badly as the night before. She turned on the bedding and looked up.

Rollo, Becca, and Olin sat on the floor around her. Becca rested against the door, Olin in the opposite corner. Rollo was directly across from her. On the floor in front of him lay her handscanner and e.p. and goggles.

"Morning," he said.

"Morning," she replied.

He gestured at the equipment. "Nice stuff. Top quality."

Cira nodded slowly, her mouth dry. Her bladder ached dully.

"Armada issue," Rollo said and sighed.

Cira nodded again.

"You?" he asked.

Cira worked her tongue until she could swallow, then licked her lips. "Lt. Cira Kalinge, Wing Leader, Valico Task Force."

"Pilot," Becca said. There was a surprising touch of admiration in her voice. When Cira looked at her, she blushed slightly.

Rollo sighed again. "Hersteds have no luck left." He looked at her narrowly, clearly weighing choices. "We came down from Emorick after the first riots. Govanchi and Liss divvied up the city between them, said everybody has to choose one or the other, Mater Ghasa said that's shit, Hersteds are leaving. Getting out was as hard as staying. Hersteds had property in Emorick, concessions on the port, good estate. Twelve of us left, others stayed. Olin's pater stayed, said it di'n't scan to give up our holdings on account the Armada would be back and Govanchi and Liss both would be bad memories after. Well, maybe. We got ambushed on the Tameurla Road. Mater Ghasa was hurt, my brother Jallik was killed. Mater Ghasa died by the time we reached Crag Nook. Seven of us walked in here. Two up and left one day, we don't know where to, and two of us died in idiot fights."

He shifted slightly and cleared his throat. "We been getting by since, looking for a way. We talked about joining another family and that still looks viable. For all I know the ones who stayed in Emorick are together and doing fine and still Hersteds. Becca and Olin been arguing against us losing the name, but it a'n't been easy keeping

together with no place, no trade. We talked about going back to
Emorick, but we could as easy die on the way as die when we get
there. Options get fewer."

"Why'd you stay with me?" Cira asked.

Olin grunted. "We got a natural revulsion to riots."

Rollo nodded. "You jumped up there to help, it occurred to all
of us at about the same time that maybe you were crazy or maybe
you were just brave. Anyway, you weren't going with the rest of the
mob. It followed if you could act apart maybe you were like us. If
so, I figured that maybe you di'n't like being without family, just like
us. It was a gamble."

"And now?"

"Well," Becca said, laughing nervously, "you surely a'n't like us in
some ways."

"Now…" Rollo said quietly. He picked up the e.p. "We talked
about evacuation, back when it was called. Mater Ghasa said it was
a good idea for people with nothing to hold them here, but Hersteds
are—were—landed. It was her idea to hold out till the borders
were settled, then try to remain loyalist. Some in the family thought
that was wrong. *I* thought it was wrong. Pan wanted us to leave
everything just because some Vested paranoids di'n't like setis. Give
in now, I told her, and we end up with no room to go outward, no
room to trade free, no room to *think* like we want."

"I remember that night," Olin said, smiling thinly. "Mater Ghasa
told him he was shitfull, that all he was saying was secessionist propaganda that was as bad as the loyalists saying seti eat human young
and poison planets with hostile microfauna. Then she said—" He
laughed. "Go on, Becca, you do Mater Ghasa better than I."

Becca lowered her voice in imitation of someone much older
and more cautious. "Rollo, *think* with your head, don't just use it
for your hat. What is the Pan going to do way out here? The cost
of a war then the cost of the patrols, the borders will be as open
as they ever were, you see. Hersteds sit here and wait till it's all
over and we will be just the way we always have been. Listen to
one side or the other and you panic and run and leave everything
worthwhile behind."

Rollo smiled and nodded. "That was before Govanchi and Liss
and the riots."

"Who—" Cira's voice cracked and she coughed lightly. "Who are they?"

"Fearless leaders," Olin snorted.

"Jonner Liss," Rollo said, "was commander of the police garrison. Uri Govanchi was the city comptroller. They disagreed over who controlled the port. Liss occupied it almost immediately after the provisional government declared Finders in secession. Govanchi organized a deputized mob to oust Governor Cowan and his committee, which they did quickly enough, but then Liss wouldn't relinquish control of the port. One thing after another, shots were fired, people chose sides." He shrugged.

"What happened to Governor Cowan?"

"Hung," Becca said.

"If you di'n't declare loyalties," Rollo went on, "your property was seized. If you declared wrong, same thing plus you like as not ended up dead. Even if you declared right you had to surrender use to one or the other. Mater Ghasa finally said the hell with both."

He placed her pistol carefully on the floor again and laced his fingers together. "You saw us through a bad night last night. Brought us safe here, saw we had food, shelter."

"Where are you from?" Becca asked.

"Homestead."

The three Hersteds looked at each other.

"Then," Roll said, "you know about family."

Cira pushed herself back on the mat, against the wall. "Sure," she said, frowning.

Rollo noticed. "Oh. You have family already. I can see if you don't want to give up a name or share a heritage."

The other two looked disappointed. "No, it's—" Cira felt confused, torn by conflicting realizations. "I need food. Coffee."

"Damn," Olin said. "Sorry." He jumped up and crossed the room.

"Wait," Rollo said, grabbing his pant leg. "We need to settle something."

Olin leaned back against the wall, looking chagrined.

"Armada's coming back," Rollo said. "That much everyone knew after the first assault." He looked at Cira. "We want to attach to you. Hersteds were and always have been loyalist. We don't want to end up in some realignment camp, nameless and homeless."

"Then why didn't you evacuate?"

"Why—? Because Finders is home. Pan has an argument with the Seven Reaches, fine, but why should we leave our home because politicians can't agree?"

Good question, Cira thought, but then how do you show loyalty except by obedience? She thought of her father, the look on his face when she announced that she was joining the Armada. She shook her head. Too complicated right now. She was still fuzzy from waking up.

"So what is it exactly that you want from me?" she asked.

"We—" Rollo began, then glanced at the others.

"We want you to be Hersted," Becca said. "Be family."

Cira stared at her for a long time. Even through the uncertainty she felt faintly pleased. "A little sudden, isn't it? I mean we've only spent one night together."

Rollo gaped in surprise, then laughed. Olin and Becca grinned.

"I felt safe with you," Cira said. "If I intended ever to join a family I'd give Hersteds a good look. But like you say, I already have family, on Homestead."

Rollo reached out and ran a finger over the barrel of her e.p. Cira watched, fascinated and terrified. So, too, she noticed, did Olin and Becca. Finally Rollo pushed the gun across the floor, toward her.

"Won't gain anything to harm you," he said. "Besides, you did good by us last night."

Cira leaned forward and picked up the pistol. She set it on the bed and looked up at them.

"I'll vouch for you," she said. "I'll see to it everything is all right." They visibly relaxed. "Now," she added, "I'm hungry."

The tram station was in chaos. Venner eased his way around the periphery of the crowds pushing against the fence and to the stairs leading up to one of the traffic control offices. Eight people, rifles raised skyward and sidearms displayed beneath open overcoats, guarded the bottom of the stair. He studied each of them briefly, picked the one most likely to be in charge, and stopped before him.

"What?" the man barked.

Venner smiled, opened his palm. The guard looked at the small ID disk resting there, looked hard at Venner, then nodded. He gestured to the others and they let Venner pass.

As he mounted the stairs he felt self-satisfied. He had just verified his suspicions about what was happening. At the top he looked back down at the thirty-meter stretch of fence and the diverse crowd pressed against it. From here he could see more armed coes on the opposite side of the fence, facing the mob. The small strip of plaza between the fence and the row of arched gateways that led to the tram platforms was empty but for them. Beyond he saw a tram unloading. More guards were herding the arrivals into thin lines through another set of gates. People were being let into Crag Nook, no one was leaving.

Crag Nook burned. Large sections of it anyway. The civic center that had, till yesterday, been a *de facto* prison for Panner loyalists, was a smoldering ruin. As far as Venner had been able to learn no one had been released before it was torched. There had been a pitched battle fought around it.

Venner pushed through the door into the office. Tables lined both walls down its length with polycoms and commlinks set up, operators busy at them. The room was crowded with people. Venner moved by them, easing past with small muttered apologies. His left eye was aching again; he was convinced his cheek had a hairline crack near his nose, not enough to incapacitate him, only remind him, along with the dull ache along his left side, that he had been badly treated.

As he approached the door at the far end, it opened and three people emerged. Venner recognized two of them and stopped, startled, at the same time they noticed him.

The woman's face froze. The nearer man seemed puzzled for a second, then surprised. The man Venner did not recognize raised an eyebrow and seemed to try to watch all of them at once. He was definitely off-world—slightly Asian features, short white hair.

Venner smiled at the woman. "Co Harias, what a surprise!"

"Venner...?" the man said hesitantly.

"And Captain Laros," Venner continued, stepping toward them. "Just the man I wanted to see."

"Uh..." Laros hesitated a second longer, then turned to the stranger. "Co Shirabe, would you excuse us? Co Harias." He went back through the door.

Venner gestured to Harias. "After you."

She narrowed her eyes stonily, then followed Laros.

The stranger—Co Shirabe?—gave Venner a quizzical look.

"Family matter," Venner said and went through the door.

More people crowded a slightly larger room. Laros and Harias were heading straight for the back of the room and another door. Venner quickened his step to catch up and managed to squeeze through with Harias. He palmed his small e.p. and pulled the door closed behind him.

They were alone now, in a cramped private office with an oversized desk dominated by a portable field polycom. Four ominous-looking e.p. rifles leaned against the wall to the left of the desk. A large flatscreen hung on the opposite wall displaying a topographic map of the northern hemisphere of the continent.

Laros reached the desk and whirled on Venner.

"What the hell are you thinking, coming here like this?"

"Save the pique," Venner said and pulled his left hand from his overcoat pocket. He handed Harias the three ID disks. "Read these, then tell me what you think."

Harias frowned, took them to the desk and inserted them into a handreader. She gave him a puzzled look and handed the reader to Laros.

Venner watched his expression carefully. The anger faded into suspicion, then ill-ease.

"Friends of yours?" Venner asked. "Don't bother explaining or denying. They came, they hurt me, they're dead."

Laros flared. "Those were *our* agents!"

"Not anymore." He looked at Harias. "I always thought Maxwell had a leak in his security. I had no idea it was so highly placed."

"There are a lot of things you don't know, Co Venner," she said.

"True. But then there are a lot of things I don't need to know. There *are* some things *you* need to know, though. I'll tell you a few of them, let you worry about the rest."

He crossed the room to Laros, grabbed his shirt, and brought his knee up sharply. Laros convulsed, groaned. Venner stepped back and drew the e.p. and aimed it at Harias. He held the pistol on her for several seconds, then lowered it.

Laros was ashen and looked up at Venner with hate-filled eyes.

"Don't speak," Venner said. He pulled Laros away from the desk and moved him into a chair. "Sit on his lap," he told Harias. When she did, Venner went behind the desk and quickly inventoried what was there. He touched the interface plate briefly, let the menu load into his memory, then started selecting. "I'm very good at this," he said casually while he worked. "You develop a talent eventually for riding the line, half in, half out of the system." He finished and stepped back. "I may have just released a virus into your databases, I may not have. In any case, I have what I want."

He came close to Laros and Harias. He waved the pistol slightly.

"I'll tell you something you need to know. I no longer work for the Armada or the Pan Humana. I'm not working for Maxwell Cambion, either, in case that's a question. You also need to know that I intend to kill you, Laros. Both of you." He smiled quickly at Harias. "You didn't trust me. You sent three agents to kill me. That's unacceptable."

"You're a double agent," Laros said tightly. "How does anyone trust you?"

"I'll concede that it's a worthy ethical problem. I imagine it's one of those things you have to learn to take on faith."

He straightened, rocked briefly on the balls of his feet. "Given the manner in which I have just done this, I expect you understand that I'm not entirely well anymore."

He brought the butt of the pistol across Harias's forehead. She spun out of Laros's lap and hit the floor heavily. Laros pushed backward against the wall, seeming to try to climb through it to get away from Venner. Venner caught a handful of his hair and dragged him across the room to his desk. Laros flailed his arms, off-balance. Venner felt him nearly recover enough to make some resistance. Too late. Venner slammed Laros's forehead against the edge of the desk. Laros rolled away and sat down, back against the desk. His forehead was bright red, beginning to purple. Laros raised his hands to his temples, his eyes squeezed shut.

"I'll see myself out," Venner said.

His heart skipped along, driving the pace of his actions. He stepped into the operations room. No one gave him a second look. He did not return the way he had come, but went through a back door that led to a flight of stairs descending into the maintenance shops and storerooms.

Few coes were around, and he walked confidently, his entire posture set on a goal that was *elsewhere* and brooked no interference.

He had been through this facility a score of times, a number of them clandestinely. He made his way easily onto the loading docks that opened inside the tunnel, near the mouth.

The long tube of the tram filled the bore hole. Ramps extended from wide doors to the apron of the dock. Nacelles and crates were being loaded on board. Passengers that had ridden in the cargo holds were queued up and escorted to the main receiving area.

Venner strolled purposefully to a group of people standing at the rail separating the main dock from the control area. They regarded him with reserve, eyes slightly narrowed. Venner picked out the commander and stopped in front of him.

"O.I.C.?" he asked, knowing immediately that this was the officer in charge.

"Yes."

Venner showed his ID.

The officer straightened and his overcoat opened slightly, revealing the dark grey tunic of the Armada.

"I'm Commander Camil," he said. "How can we be of service?"

Venner gestured casually at the loading. "Materiél for Emorick?"

Camil nodded.

"I'm to accompany it. I've been in negotiation with the two faction leaders fighting in Emorick. One of them gets part of this shipment, the other...well, you understand."

Camil allowed a thin smile. "Of course. We can arrange a private room—"

"No. I'm riding in cargo, with the shipments. I don't want my arrival advertised in any way."

"I should comm the Emorick O.I.C.—"

"I said no." He looked toward the line of passengers. "Who are they?"

"From the Thayer-Cambion complex. We don't know if they're partisans or patriots, so we're taking no chances. All of them are being interred. We can sort it all out later."

Venner nodded slowly, then glanced at the loading. "Which one has the combustibles? I'd feel better not riding in that car."

They all laughed.

"All the combustibles are being loaded from that car—" Camil pointed "—back. Take any of the others. You're sure you don't want a cabin?"

"Hmm? Who else is traveling this tram?"

"I have a contingent of marines and a party of loyalist guerrillas. No one else."

"Keep one section between cargo and passenger clear. I may change my mind mid-trip."

Camil grinned. "As you wish." He turned to an aide. "See to it."

Venner walked smartly away from them, crossed the dock, and went up a ramp into the cool interior of the cargo hold. A residual stench of human bodies sweating in fear teased his nostrils. He smiled to himself. A few days from now, he knew, this would be impossible, security would strangle all access in its ridiculous grip. For now, though, the net was loose, things slipped through. The Armada was back, but only partly—they did not have Finders yet.

Nacelles stacked against the bulkheads made a narrow passage down the center. Venner stepped out of the way as the last robot left the hold. The ramp folded up against the door. As it sealed, Venner went to the rear and accessed the joining door.

The loading was nearly complete. He moved back from section to section until he came to a chilled hold containing volatiles. He tapped the lading readout on one: nitrogen compounds, intended to be diluted and mixed for fertilizer. He checked the others and found largely the same, with three nacelles packed with polymethanols used in the same process. In the next section he found the same thing and in the next. The last car contained cases of s.p. rifles and ammunition, all, he knew, intended for arming one side or the other in the territorial dispute in Emorick.

Venner pulled out a detonator from an inside pocket. He opened one of the ammunition cases, set the charge for two hours, and placed it inside. He retraced his steps to the first hold of combustibles and placed two more, one in a nacelle of nitrogen compounds, the other against a polymethanol nacelle, both set for two hours.

He worked his way forward then. When he came to an empty passenger section, he checked out the window. This section was outside the cargo dock, against the outer area. People with rifles gathered in small groups watching the last of the queue marched out.

Venner palmed his ID and stepped onto the platform. Immediately three guards approached him. He held up his palm and they hesitated, then gestured for someone else to come forward. A woman walked up, glanced at the ID, at him, then nodded.

"Let him through," she said and turned away.

"Thanks, coes," Venner said.

He passed through the archways, into the narrow strip separating them from the main gates. Armed coes were dispersing the crowds now, pushing and shoving. Shouts punctuated the steady grumble of the mob, but it seemed they were moving back.

Venner stepped from the gate and headed left, in the general direction of the amphitheater.

He gave the offices one last look. From the balcony the white-haired man, Co Shirabe, stared down at the scene. For a moment he did not see Venner, but then his eyes shifted and Venner knew he was spotted. He slipped his hand inside his coat, felt the pistol, and kept walking. Co Shirabe, though, did nothing. He watched, that was all. Venner turned away then and continued on.

He did not remember crawling into the corner, only that it seemed like a safe enough place, away from the close-packed legs and the occasional kicks that had followed him, driven him to seek another spot to be. Tucked behind the last bench at the rear of the tram section—too tight a squeeze, really, but by bunching his shoulders forward he could push himself back against the wall—the packed throng eventually forgot him and left him alone.

The air grew rank. Too many people in too small a space. When the tram had left the station the babble had been constant. Now no one spoke. The only sound beside the steady drone of the tram itself rushing up its tunnel was the arrhythmic susurrus of breathing becoming more labored.

The man who had beaten him up had disappeared among the others. Alex searched the new faces that came into view as people shifted position looking for friends or family, but he did not see him. The CO_2 rich air combined with his injuries and the exhaustion left in the wake of adrenaline rush, so eventually he stopped caring. He stopped caring about the man and the beating and all these others around him and why he was on an overcrowded tram. Stopped caring about where he had been or where he was going and how unclear so much of it was, with names unattached to faces and nameless faces. He wondered, briefly, if "Alex" was really his name or just a convenience that he had latched onto. Then he stopped caring about that. Caring took effort and he did not have the energy.

"What is the worst part?"

He glanced around, but the words had come from within. A memory. The worst part of what? he wondered, and settled back.

He dozed and when he woke up he had a headache. It was easier to sleep, so he dozed off again. The rhythm of the tram and the breathing should have lulled him, but deep sleep refused to come. Small incongruous sounds interrupted the steady background, odd smells wafted by, and a general ill feeling grew that kept him on the edge of alertness.

It seemed that the trip was taking far too long. The third time he awoke he was annoyed that the tram still moved. The fourth time he tried to get to his feet to find someone to whom to complain, but he could not get his shoulders past the top edge of the seat. He sat back down and tried to sleep once more. When he came awake again and found the tram still moving he became afraid. They had missed the stop, plunging on into another tunnel. The air would not hold out. He would, along with everyone else, die. He swung an arm up and cracked his wrist against the seat. The pain made him suck in his breath and he choked. His throat was dry and he hacked painfully until, drained, he let his head fall back. He stared at the ceiling and toyed with the pitiful notion that it would be his last sight.

"Cira," he whispered. That name came with a face: dark, wide through the cheekbones, long eyes, mouth pulled into a perpetual moue that could, with a twitch, express amusement or displeasure. Who was she? The name—Cira...something "K"—evoked the face, a sense of pleasure, of welcome, but nothing else. Alex closed his eyes and chased the memory.

The tram lurched, the sound changed, going deeper, grinding, and he opened his eyes. They were stopping, arriving. The memory vanished.

People started pushing to their feet, stumbling, their voices first tentative, then plaintive, then demanding. Suddenly the doors, on the opposite side from Alex, opened. Bright daylight flooded in. The crowd surged forward, then balked and came back like water rebounding from a wall. A few people shouted angrily in dry voices.

"One at a time!"

Alex jumped at that voice. It was deep, loud, and denied argument. He *knew* that voice—that kind of voice—understood its implicit authority. The words were not important. Alex wanted to obey. He managed to get to his feet and sidle out from behind the seat.

"Quiet!" the voice commanded.

Most people stopped talking immediately.

"Who the fuck are you?" someone demanded. Alex was startled that anyone could muster the ego to challenge that voice.

"Quiet! You will all leave the car one at a time! Remain in single file! Do not deviate! You will—"

"We'll shit! Let us out!"

There was a prolonged stillness. Then the crowded shifted and Alex was buffeted as people pressed back.

"Hey—!"

A distinct crack cut the air. Feet shifted, a sound like a log falling on thick grass, then a brief, harsh ripping noise accompanied by a high, thin squeal. Through all this Alex did not breathe; he listened, as, he felt, did everyone near him.

"Now," the voice said, quietly, almost gently. "Once more. One at a time, single file. Move."

The car began to empty in orderly fashion. Piece by piece, the space around Alex grew. People shuffled forward, the air became more breathable. The back of his neck cooled and he closed his eyes for a moment. He looked up with a start and saw that he stood alone. A small clot of people gathered near the door. He pushed off from the wall toward them.

He stopped abruptly. On the floor in the aisle lay a body. The head pointed back at Alex, neck bent and eyes open. A small pink crescent of tongue extruded between his lips and his arms were flung wide. From sternum to groin his belly lay open, his coveralls soaked in red-black blood. Blood pooled beneath him, but the heart was still and did not pump.

Alex stared, fixed by the familiarity of the body. He tried to fit the conviction that he had seen this before—or at least part of it—with what he remembered.

"Hey."

He looked up. A short, thick-set man in an ill-fitting ankle-length grey-green overcoat stood in the tram door, watching him. A sergeant—Alex could think of no better title—he regarded Alex with a patient, ancient expression that jarred Alex. Alex stepped carefully, shakily, around the body.

He glanced back once. Right-side up, the face clicked into place: the man who had beaten him up.

"Come on," the sergeant said.

Alex stepped down the ramp. A pair of men carrying e.p. rifles stood on either side. Behind the one on the right Alex saw a stack of weapons of all types. The sergeant grabbed his collar from behind and held him while the man on the left ran a handscanner over him. He nodded once and the sergeant guided him the rest of the way onto the platform and to the end of the row of passengers.

More people in grey-green overcoats faced them, all armed with rifles, a few with e.p.s, most with s.p.s. The ones with the energy pulse weapons all wore an expression of calm purpose, faces betraying no thought beyond the task at hand, no feeling besides alertness. The others were less controlled, uncertain to varying degrees, but unwilling to break rank and question events. They gave the calm ones furtive glances, clearly troubled by the mix of feelings.

Beyond the guards was a row of wide archways and beyond these he saw high metal gates closed against a press of people who faced their own collection of guards. To his right, the tram emerged from a tunnel in the face of a sheer rock wall. The platform extended into the tunnel. Under the canopy of rock machines moved cargo nacelles into tram cars.

"All right!" the sergeant was in front of them now, walking slowly down the line. "We have a problem to solve. Finders is being damaged by riot. This has to stop. However, the people responsible look just like you, talk like you, act like you—at least until they start destroying everything around them. That's when they are no longer like you."

He had reached the far end of the line and turned sharply. "Our problem, then: we've got to sort you all out. That takes time and right now we don't have a lot of time. So we're going to keep you all together until we *do* have the time. We'll start immediately, of course, but you're all going to have to be patient."

He stopped a few coes away from Alex. "So I want you all to go through that gate—" he pointed back the way he had just come. "Just like you left the tram. Quietly. Single file." He smiled. It had a shockingly pleasant effect on his face, and Alex almost laughed. "Go on, now. Through the gate. We have a lot of work to do."

The incongruity of the scene struck Alex with its simple elegance. A pleasant request made after a brutal killing, backed up with armed threat. There was no question of disobeying, yet that did not matter. It was *reasonable*, everyone was willing to cooperate. Still, Alex did not believe him.

He turned obediently in the indicated direction and waited for the line to move. The sound of walking feet—out of step, which Alex expected the sergeant to be angry about—grew as the line lurched forward. Finally the man in front of him stepped away. Alex raised his foot—

—and stopped against the flat of a long knife. He jerked back and the knife fell. The sergeant stepped in front of him.

"You look like hell, co."

Alex nodded, unsure what to say. He thought: already...?

"Why don't you come on along with me and tell me how you got hurt so bad."

The sergeant stepped back and gestured with the knife back toward the cargo dock. Alex frowned, the back of his scalp and neck tingling. He pointed toward the receding line.

"I ought to go," he said.

"What's your name?"

"Alex."

"Alex what?"

"I—" He stared at the sergeant for several seconds, then shook his head. "Don't know, sergeant."

For an instant the man looked startled. He frowned, then nodded. "It's all right, co. We can help you remember that, too."

Chapter Six

The second phase of the Armada Operation to retake the Diphda System began five days after the disaster that saw Task Force Valico routed by local Secessionist forces. Now, with a sober appreciation for the strength and skill of their opponents, Task Force Micheson and the survivors of Task Force Valico—a few carriers and their escorts—have struck surgically, the operation proceeding with cautious efficiency.

The ships deployed by Finders are clearly of seti design, compact, fast, and maneuverable, with a surprising punch. Valico Task Force was taken completely unprepared in the first engagement. This time there was no frontal assault. Instead, small units penetrated the perimeter, drawing fire. Once engaged, a superior Armada force attacked, crippling that section and drawing other Founders from other points to shore the breach. Section by section, over the course of several hours, the sphere of defenders was weakened.

Through the gaps created by this tactic, hundreds of small landers were sent through to Finders carrying marine counterinsurgency units. Grounding at the isolated town of Orchard Crest, far out in the plains of the continent of Whale, this reporter observed the operations of Marine Sergeant Palker's group.

The three landers touched down at equidistant points around the town. Each released its contingent of seventy marines, four troop carriers with weapons array, and three assault tanks. Their entry into Orchard Crest was met with sporadic small arms fire. Within thirty minutes the town of fifteen thousand (pre-evacuation census) was under Armada control.

Loyalist partisans were quickly identified and assigned garrison duty. Family members of the partisans were conscripted to accompany the marines to assure loyalty. Security measures ensued—arrests and internment in the town's civic center, seizure of all public information nodes, control of all communications systems—upon arrival of the command staff.

The next morning commenced a multi-front guerrilla action against the key strongholds of the Secessionists—Emorick, Crag Nook, and, far south, the Thayer-Cambion complex. By luck, this reporter remained attached to Sergeant Palker, who was assigned the task of infiltrating and destabilizing Crag Nook.

Tory looked up from his notebook and contemplated changing the phrase "a few carriers and their escorts" to something more accurate. After all, Task Force Valico had only *had* a few carriers to begin with and none of them had been lost. But carriers were useless without fighters and they *had* lost all of those. Tory wondered if it was worth destroying the flow of the piece for an accuracy that few would appreciate anyway.

Another tramload of refugees lined up on the platform below. He watched while Palker delivered his lecture—the third time today and each time spoken with conviction—and the refugees stared at him, stunned and dazed. When he finished, marines moved down the line and herded them into the holding pens adjacent to the station.

Palker stopped the last man in line. Even from this distance it was clear he had been severely beaten; his face was swollen and bruised, he limped, and blood caked around his mouth. Palker spoke with him quietly, then gestured for a pair of marines to escort him away, in the opposite direction, into the cargo docks. Palker stared after him for a few moments, then followed, resheathing the big knife he had been carrying since Orchard Crest.

Tory flexed his fingers on the railing. He wanted to follow them, try to find out what was special about this one refugee that he alone out of three tramloads was separated out.

He hesitated. Someone stepped from one of the now empty tram cars. Tory watched him look at the last of the refugees, then in the direction of the docks, then upward, toward the offices. He stopped and locked eyes with Tory and Tory recognized him. He had come in earlier, interrupted his conversation with Laros and Harrias. What was he doing now? For a moment he considered going down and asking him who he was, but he froze. There was an unapproachable quality to the man. The moment passed and the stranger walked on, to the archways. He flashed an ID and was let through.

He decided to see if Laros was free again. The man was very good at evasive answers, but Tory believed himself even better at wheedling information. Tory switched the notebook off and slipped it into its pouch.

He stepped into ops to find everyone standing and staring in the direction of Laros's offices. Shouts came from the far end, the heavy tread of running boots.

"What's happening?" he asked the co nearest the door.

She blinked at him dazedly. "I don't know. Someone said Laros has been shot."

Tory hurried forward.

Two marines stepped out of Laros's office and took positions on either side of the door. Tory stopped short. Within, Laros was sitting behind his desk, a med tech pressing a bandage to his forehead. Harrias sat on the floor nearby staring fixedly at the ceiling. She blinked, and only in that instant Tory knew she was still alive.

Boots clattered noisily behind him. Tory looked around and saw Sergeant Palker at the head of five more marines bearing down on the office. Palker glanced in at the scene and scowled.

"I'll fill you in later, co," he said quietly to Tory. "Better you aren't around just now, though."

Palker and two of his troops entered the office and the door closed.

Tory had come to respect Palker in the last few days. He knew the sergeant was holding back a lot of data, but he was truthful with what he did reveal. This was all very new to Tory. Wars did not happen these days, not like this. Space was wide, even though translight travel times made conflict theoretically possible. The Pan was generally too comfortable a place for anyone to spark a war.

At least, he thought, that's the line. He had believed it, too, until he watched Palker and his marines. Though Tory had come to admire the skill of these soldiers, he had to wonder from where they had gotten it. Their training had been good, the best, but such confidence only came with actual experience. There were rumors, of course, like Millennium, but Tory had never seen any hard evidence to support the accusations that civil oppressions occurred within the Pan, that the Armada had been involved in actions against colonies before, and that perhaps the entire Secession was as a result justified. Rumors.

He backed away and strolled toward the front door again. Along the way he asked a few people questions about what had happened just before the alarm.

Tory returned to the balcony. He leaned on the railing and looked down at the now empty platform. The tram was still there. If this was like the last one, soon a company of marines, reinforced by local loyalists, would board and head northward, to Emorick, where similar actions were under way.

The action—the term the marines used—had consisted of starting a riot. The local loyalists had not been sure who these troops were at first—vigilantes from Emorick or a civil garrison from Orchard Crest or Downer's Cove. Communications with every other town had been severed, there was no way to check. But they knew now. It was clear in their faces, an uneasy mixture of fear and relief. The Armada was back and the locals could only hope distinctions would be made between loyalist and secessionist.

The riots were finally under control, at least. A third of the town was in ruin, another third damaged. Smoke still rose, wraith-like, to hover over everything. The smell was sharp and old at the same time, death and ash. Who would count the bodies, he wondered, and who would tell the survivors?

He expected at any moment to be tapped on the shoulder and escorted off-planet and out-system. He suspected Task Commander Palada had a lot to do with his presence here. For the most part, the Armada personnel ignored him. A few—officers—were evidently uncomfortable with a journalist in their midst. They did not know what to do with him—what to tell him, what not to, what to let him see, or not see—so answered almost none of his questions and shepherded him gently away from things they might later discover they should have kept from him.

Like the holding pens adjacent to the station, slowly filling with refugees.

He descended the stairs and strolled out onto the platform. A couple of locals stepped in his direction, hesitated, and looked toward the marines for guidance. The marines gave slight head shakes and the locals backed off.

Which way? he wondered, glancing right and left. The odds were good he would be stopped at the gate to the holding areas. He went left, into the cargo docks.

A grotto had been carved out of the side of the mountain. It stretched back in a series of tiers. Cranes tracked across the high ceiling. Cargo nacelles, crates, and tractors of various sizes occupied the tiers. Robots moved to and from, several still plugged into their cradles against the wall just within the mouth of the tunnel.

Tory spotted a pair of marines guarding a small door on the third tier. No other door was being guarded.

Loading was almost finished. Tram doors slid shut with sharp metallic echoes. Robots moved back to their niches as each completed its assigned tasks. Most of the matériel being shipped north had come from Crag Nook warehouses—private property, in ordinary circumstances, now seized by the Armada—and the rest had come out of Orchard Crest, which was now the main grounding point for the operation.

He mounted the metal steps at the first tier, then ascended to the next. As he reached the third tier and approached the marines, his pulse quickened. He nodded to the pair.

"Coes," he greeted them. "I'm Tory Shirabe, Ares-Epsilon NewsNet." They nodded politely. "I'd like to ask you some questions—"

The one on the right frowned. "Questions?"

Tory smiled. "Yes. You know the kind of thing, life on the front, barrack detail, your feelings on things. Frankly, you two are the first ones I've seen standing still long enough to say anything to." That got a slight nod, almost a smile. "But I've been wanting—*hoping*—to be able to talk to someone besides officers and noncoms. I've been *wanting* to interview the coes doing the actual work." That *did* get a smile, from both of them. "I suppose you two are busy, though."

"We're assigned," the one on the left said. "Doesn't mean we're particularly busy."

"Oh. Then, you don't mind if I talk to you?"

"Stand back to two meters," the one on the right said. "That's regulation. Then go ahead."

Tory turned to move back and switched on his recorder. He stopped at two meters and faced them, smiling.

"So, let's start with an easy one. Where are you from?"

He kept them talking and chuckling for half an hour, moving gradually from the mundane into areas of more interest. One marine was from Nine Rivers, the other from Eurasia. The only interest they held in common was a fascination with ancient spacecraft, which had initially led them to the Armada. Both had entertained ambitions in engineering; the one from Eurasia still did, but the one from Nine Rivers no longer knew what he wanted to do. Perhaps a career in the Armada. Neither was sure how they had gotten into the marine branch since both had wanted ship duty, possibly a try at Officer Training School. Something about the opportunity for quick advancement had brought them into the marines, something about the Riot that had triggered an urge to go armed *personally* to the defense of the Pan. The marines seemed a fast track to someplace. Nothing learned in the marines was of any use to the Eurasian, but on Nine Rivers there was always law enforcement work on the rivers, which could get pretty wild. They had done garrison work on Earth, a fact both were proud of and saw as plusses for the future. As soon as the Distals began withdrawing from the Forum and declaring independence in the wake of the Riot, both had been assigned to Task Force Micheson and found themselves heading for the frontier. So far duty had been fairly routine, nothing terribly dangerous— not nearly as risky as the streets of any Earth city just after the Riot—and a great deal terribly dull.

"Like standing guard over an empty room?" Tory suggested, grinning.

"Oh, hardly empty," Nine Rivers said expansively, mockingly.

Tory cocked an eyebrow questioningly. Eurasia suddenly looked less comfortable.

Nine Rivers grunted, his hand drifted to his waist for a key.

"Hardly empty at all," Sergeant Palker's voice intoned.

Both marines jerked to attention, their eyes abruptly distant, devoid of any admission. Below, the tram began to move out, on its way north.

Palker smiled at Tory and patted him on the shoulder.

"Go ahead," he said to Nine Rivers. "Let him see."

Frowning, the marine placed the key against the access panel. The door slid open. Palker motioned for Tory to precede him into the small cell.

For a mad instant Tory imagined the door closing behind him, locking, and Palker informing him that he had violated an arcane military code. The instant passed as Palker stepped into the cell with him. Tory relaxed then and looked at the lone occupant, stretched out on a cot, a field medunit riding on his chest, cables and tubes connected to various parts of the prisoner's body.

Tory stepped closer, avoiding looking at the face until the last moment. When he did he winced. Half of it was a swollen bruise, the eye closed and pus-filled, the lips turned inward around caked blood. The other half—

Tory started. "Lieutenant Cambion?"

"You know him?" Palker demanded.

"He was a wing leader on board the *Castille*. Lieutenant Alexan Cambion."

Palker pulled a handslate from his belt and entered the name. A moment later he sucked air between his teeth and turned to the two marines.

"Get a medical transport down here and get this man to the infirmary. *Now!*"

The marines ducked out of the cell.

"I thought there was something about him," Palker said.

"I saw you separate him from the last group."

Palker grunted, a sound that seemed almost an approval. "As bad as he is, someone gave him a hell of a beating. Anyone that unpopular with the locals might be worthwhile to us. I hadn't counted on this." After a thoughtful pause, he wondered, "Where the hell has he been?"

"Where have you been, Co Merrick?"

Sean Merrick smiled mildly at the officer, a Lt. Commander Litch. "The job is rather peripatetic."

"Of course. It's only that you've been out of contact for the last thirty-nine days. We were beginning to worry." Litch glanced at the screen that displayed part of the report Merrick had turned in. "But I think the detail here explains a lot of it."

Merrick nodded noncommittally and looked over at the pair of marines lounging near the hatch a half-dozen meters away.

"Well," Litch said, switching the screen off and retrieving the disk from the reader. He slipped it back into its case and placed that into a security pouch. "Corporal."

One of the marines came to attention then strode quickly up to them. The officer handed him the pouch.

"Deliver this to the bridge, Task Commander only."

The marine nodded once, then left on his errand.

Merrick made himself smile again, wondering when he would be cleared to leave. He felt closed in, surrounded.

"Where to now?"

"Oh, I 'm headed back in," Merrick said.

Litch nodded. "I suppose we won't be needing the intelligence corps much longer. This insurrection should be cleared up in a matter of weeks, then we can get back to normal footing."

Merrick suppressed a laugh, gazing in amazement at the officer, trying to imagine what kind of "intelligence" the man had been looking at that might lead to that conclusion. Certainly not Merrick's. He included just enough raw fact to show that the Secession was not a temporary or minor aberration, that more than likely the Secant would become a permanent fact, separating the Pan from its lost colonies and the vaster seti Reaches.

"Well," Litch went on, "I can clear you for immediate departure if you like. I couldn't interest you in dinner tonight...?"

"Thank you, co, but I'm on a fairly tight schedule. After all, as you pointed out, I've been out of contact for thirty-nine days. I've got some making up to do."

"Of course. Just a thought."

"I appreciate it. Maybe if I get back through this way and you 're all still here—"

"Not likely, but the invitation is open."

Merrick shrugged. Litch punched data into his console, then motioned for the other marine.

"Escort Commander Merrick back to his ship. Dock Nineteen."

"Thank you again, co." He glanced at the package on the officer's desk, then turned away and followed the marine. He kept waiting for the day he encountered someone too honest to accept contraband—a "gift" from over the border, seti in origin, illicit and in high demand—and foul up Merrick's carefully constructed web of favors and blackmail. As yet, after twenty-eight years, he had not found such a co. Still, one day he expected to step on board an Armada ship and not be let back off.

The marine rode in the shunt with him. Merrick made a couple of attempts at conversation, but the marine was silent and taciturn. Perhaps he resented the bribery he had just witnessed. As long as he only makes trouble for his superior, Merrick thought, and not me.

The shunt left them off on a broad catwalk above the auxiliary docking bays. Below, most of the bays were filled with small robot transport ships and stacks of supply nacelles, ready for delivery into combat areas. Bay nineteen was cluttered with odds and ends. A multipurpose airlock had been installed in the big cargo hatch. Merrick slid down the ladder to the bay deck. He looked up and saw the marine still on the catwalk watching him.

"Thanks for the company, co," Merrick said.

The marine walked away, unresponsive.

Merrick punched his ID code into the panel on the lock. The door cycled open and he stepped through. The second door cycled and he pulled himself, suddenly weightless, down the umbilical to the airlock of the *Solo*.

He had left the gravity off on board. He swam into the lock, sealed the hatches, and activated the ship's g. He gradually drifted to the deck, weight returning easily to about eighty percent Earth normal.

Merrick went quickly to his bridge, dropped into the command couch, and completed disengagement procedures. As the green lights winked on one after the other, his pulse increased slightly. One might wink red and he would have to wait while a snafu unraveled and delayed or cancelled his departure—

All green. He laughed loudly and initiated egress. *Solo* drifted away from the belly of the enormous carrier, orienting itself in relation to the fleet around them. *Solo* found the best open lane out and accelerated.

He watched the ships on his monitors as he fell past them. Hundreds of ships, all sizes. Carriers, tenders, cruisers, shuttles, troop transports, couriers—Task Force Micheson was many times larger than Valico had been. Already Finders had been invaded, the perimeter defenses of the system breached, the days of its secession numbered. The only way Cambion could hold the system was with seti intervention. Any guerilla action on the surface would be insignificant, ineffective. Merrick had heard remarks from Founders that they would fight until the Armada was gone or they were dead. He did not doubt their sincerity, only their reason. Numbers favored the Armada and Merrick did not believe in the assumed superiority of just causes and valor. In war, numbers mattered more than anything: number of ships, number of troops, number of casualties, amount of firepower, amount of available supply, amount of reserves. Finders had been heavily evacuated just after the Riot. Less than a million people remained and a good number of those were effectively useless in combat because they were needed for other things—agriculture, manufacturing, transportation, maintenance—or were simply incompetent in a fight. All the Armada had to do was kill ten percent of the combatants and Finders would fold. That was not so large a number. It would not be difficult once the spaceborne elements were eliminated. For good measure, the Armada might kill twenty percent.

Solo shot out of the cloud of ships and Merrick closed his eyes. He told himself that nothing he had done mattered; he had given the Armada no information that might have made the outcome more inevitable than it was.

The console chimed. He sighed and opened his eyes. *Solo* requested a course. Merrick punched up the numbers he had plotted several days ago. Less than a minute later, *Solo* accelerated to transition speed, formed its envelope, and fell into translight.

Merrick pushed himself up from his couch and walked down the short ramp into the common room. He ordered a drink from his bar and took it to a couch. He sipped from the glass, then set it on a low round table. The trip would take two days along the course he had plotted—a long curve, dipping deep into the Pan, then swinging back out across the Secant into the Distals—two days till another duplicitous meeting. He wondered how it would be to simply choose a side and go with the choice. At times he lost sight of his goal in the complications of multiple agendas.

Right now, though, his goal was necessarily personal. He had been awake for nearly sixty-five hours, half of it on stims. His hand trembled slightly as he picked up the glass and took another drink. He set it down, lay back on the couch, stretched out, and slept.

The alarm shrieked through his dreams and jerked him awake. He fell off the couch, knocked the glass from the table as he groped for balance.

"Shut up!" he yelled as he stumbled up the ramp onto the bridge. The shriek ended. Merrick fell against the command couch and blinked at the console. His head pounded from lack of sleep, the accumulated toxins, and the sudden waking.

A ship was alongside *Solo*. The main screen showed the image of a long black ship, the contours visible only in sensor-enhancement. It was easily five times the size of *Solo* and he did not recognize the configuration. Seti, yes, but which? Then he noticed that both ships were moving well below light speed and the back of his neck tingled coldly.

Merrick sat down and tried to sort out his thoughts. Seti; obviously he had been tracked out of the Diphda system; they must know who he was; they were powerful enough to effectively eliminate almost all his options. He drew a deep breath and touched the contact that sent a recognition signal.

"Sean Benjamin Merrick."

He started at the voice that came over his comm system.

"Yes."

"We wish to confer."

"Who are you?"

"Ranonan Ambassador Tan-Kovis."

Merrick grunted. "That's not a Ranonan ship."

"Nor is it Rahalen, Menkan, Cursian, Distanti, Coro, or Sirisian."

Merrick waited for more, then frowned at the silence. "Do you wish to confer on my ship or yours?"

"Which would facilitate your comfort?"

"I suppose I'd feel better on my own ship—"

"Of course."

Suddenly the seti ship expanded, filling the screen. Merrick caught his breath, pushed himself back into his couch. The *Solo's* momentum had dropped to zero according to the instruments and a limitless black suffused the screen.

"May we come aboard?"

Merrick swallowed thickly, then stood. "Sure. I'll be right there."
He gave the console a last look and saw that a slightly denser but
compatible atmosphere now enveloped *Solo*.

In the lock he initiated the cycle and waited, drumming his fingers anxiously on the edge of the console. First one, then a second
seti climbed down to his deck.

The first was a Ranonan, tall, golden-furred with very large,
liquid eyes. It wore blue-striped black robes belted at the waist and
soft boots. The second was a Vohec projection, seemingly human
except for the solid green eyes. His midnight blue tunic and pants
possessed a distinctly military cut.

"The ship's Vohec," Merrick said.

"Yes," the projection said.

"I," the Ranonan said, "am Ambassador Tan-Kovi. This is my
associate and advisor, Lovander Mipelon."

"I'm Sean Merrick. May I offer hospitality?"

Both setis bowed slightly and Merrick led them to the common
room.

"Coffee," he told his kitchen, "extra strong, black." He turned to
his "guests." "My system is programmed for a number of refresh-
ments from the *Sev N'Raicha*," he said, taking care to pronounce the
word properly, the collective cognate by which the seti races were
generally known and which humans had corrupted to "Seven Reaches."

"Nothing for me," the Vohec said.

Tan-Kovi stared at its companion for a long moment, then said,
"Do you have *Skleal?*"

Merrick smiled faintly and gave the order. Half a minute later
the bar presented the coffee and the tall glass of green-blue foam
the Ranonan had requested. Merrick brought them over, set the
Skleal before Tan-Kovi, and sat down with his coffee. He gulped
two mouthfuls, wincing at the temperature, feeling immediately more
alert, whether from pain or caffeine he did not care.

Tan-Kovi lifted the glass to its mouth. A third of the foam
disappeared. A gauzy membrane slid up over its eyes, then back
down, and the Ranonan nodded.

"We are here to discuss Finders with you," Tan-Kovi said.

"Oh?"

"What are the Armada's intentions?" Lovander Mipelon asked.

Tan-Kovi touched the Vohec's leg lightly. "Mipelon..."

"You were aboard the manufacturing platform," the Vohec continued, "apparently as a sympathizer to the Secessionist cause, and an acquaintance to Nicolan Cambion. Then you were on board one of the primary ships of the Armada task force now besieging Finders."

Merrick raised his eyebrows. "And now—"

"And now you're within *my* ship."

Merrick drained his cup and refilled it. "Courtesy, coes."

"Of course," Tan-Kovi said. The Vohec shot the Ranonan a clearly irritated look. "We have an interest ourselves. We would appreciate knowing the Armada's full plan."

Merrick laughed shortly. "I don't know their full plan. I can guess."

"Do so," Lovander Mipelon said.

Merrick glared at the Vohec. "You know, up to this point I've been very impressed by this demonstration. You followed me through translight, latched on somehow and slowed me down before my ship could let me know what was happening, then swallowed me inside your ship just to have a talk. But I only impress so far and you're pushing the limits."

"Mipelon," Tan-Kovi said. "The law of courtesy—"

"Does not apply to spies and traitors."

"I beg to differ," Merrick said. "It must above all apply to spies. We provide the information on which all policy is made and we can severely damage policy if we're not treated right." A lie, Merrick knew, at least among humans—more often than not, reports from field operatives like himself were ignored—but perhaps not among the seti...

The Vohec stared at Merrick. Small flexings across its face suggested uncertainty, impatience, anger—difficult to tell and Merrick cautioned himself against reading human signs into seti expression. Finally, the Vohec shuddered and snapped, "Humans!"

Merrick leaned back. His heart raced and he worked to control a slight tremor in his hands, but suddenly he felt a great deal more confident. He smiled indulgently.

"No matter. War is not conducive to good manners. But we have to try whenever we can. Do you agree, Ambassador?"

"Of course," Tan-Kovi said.

"Will the seti intercede if Finders is in danger of falling?"

"The Rahalen Coingulate has expressly forbidden all intervention," Tan-Kovi said.

"Then why are you asking for this information? If you can't do anything, what difference can it make?"

"We have concerns."

Merrick stood. "Then let's talk about our concerns and see where they might intersect. More *Skleal*, Ambassador?"

The air shimmered with heat, even through the smoke that boiled off the still-standing sections of Downer's Cove. Maxwell hurried along under cover of the myranar shielding, experiencing the wash of energy even through the thick piles of dirt around which the reflective film draped. The big electron drills required an hour to recover from thirty minutes' use. At the moment only two of them could fire.

Eventually they've got to give up, he thought.

They had nearly lost ground before the electron drills were brought out of the warehouse and activated. Maxwell still could not manage his reaction to the initial barrage. The invisible wash of hard particles poured across the slope below. No screams, hardly any sound at all, only the sudden brilliant release of energy as the highly-charged fragments of matter touched—

He squeezed his eyes closed for a second, then kept moving. A huddle of people sprawled against the barricade firing down into the murk of the burning town. The drill bulked over them, a collection of boxes and rods culminating in a thick extrusion of darkening composite material. Maxwell studied the heat scoring, like gangrene creeping back toward the mount, and recognized that the barrel had only a couple hours of useful life left.

He fell against the earthen breastworks. Rhonson lay below the drill barrel, magnifiers to his face. Maxwell called to him, his voice growing harsh from shouting over the noise of combat. Rhonson looked at him, scowling, then pushed back from the edge.

"We've about pushed them back!" Rhonson shouted. "They've stopped trying to ascend the slope!"

Maxwell took the magnifiers and climbed up.

Directly below the earthen wall, past the edge of the mirrored sheeting that after four days was dented, torn, and punctured, the ground lay churned up and broken, black and orange and clay red, for about twenty-five meters. From that point on, in thickening fingers that came together, the uneven terrain smoothed out, contours softened beneath a glazed finish that caught the light sharply. It was impossible to tell what the small mounds once were—vehicles, weapons, perhaps the molten carcasses of personal armor—but the compressed, hardened finish continued into Downer's Cove where it had cut new streets through entire sections of town. Through the heavy smoke Maxwell could see swaths cut by the drills, matter pushed aside and down, smeared into a viscous uniformity and frozen in time.

Several of Maxwell's people had left the wall, refusing to continue after they saw the effect of the drills. At first, Maxwell had been outraged. Now, he sympathized. It was hard to look at what he had done, hard to convince himself of its necessity. In fact, he could not.

But they kept coming and the drills were the only real weapons he had. Is that my fault? he wondered.

He slid back down and gave Rhonson the magnifiers.

"Another day," Rhonson said, nodding. "They'll pull back. It can't be worth this."

Maxwell nodded. He started to say something about the life of the barrels when a new sound snagged his attention. Rhonson frowned and looked up.

For a few moments the sounds of battle faded as firing stopped along the wall. Maxwell crawled back up to the edge and looked down, but the plain below was empty of movement.

Then he glanced skyward.

"Shit!"

The first bolt struck the base of the wall an instant later. Heat and debris erupted. A man staggered away, his clothes afire, followed by three companions who wrestled him to the ground and tried to smother the flames.

Maxwell felt himself pulled away. He could not take his eyes from the squadron of fighters now firing steadily into their position.

Two of the drills being worked on burst apart. Hot fragments and screams filled the air. Rhonson dragged Maxwell away until Maxwell shrugged himself free.

"Get to the shafts!" he shouted.

Rhonson nodded and spoke into a commlink at his throat.

People scattered. The grotto walls rained rock and metal. The fighters poured fire into the mining installation.

Maxwell turned in time to see the rest of the drills shatter.

"It took too long," he said. "We took too long."

Then he was running with the others, hurrying back into the recesses of the grotto, toward the new shafts he had ordered cut. The fighters veered off and for several seconds they had a respite.

The wounded were carried on gurneys or by companions. They moved as fast as they could and Maxwell was surprised and pleased at the relative orderliness of the retreat. They all knew the way to the shafts, they all knew they had to get there. None of them doubted the rightness of abandoning their positions now and Maxwell did not have to reinforce the order to withdraw. He had little use for the kind of bravery that accomplishes nothing and he had made sure all his people understood that.

But, as they reached the staging areas for the new shafts, he wondered at the cost. They had been killing their neighbors for the last four days. Now they had lost, because the Armada was early, because they were not enough, because—

Worry about that later, he told himself, it's time to get everyone out, to safety.

The fighters started hitting them again. Maxwell looked up at the roof of the grotto.

What took them so long to get here? he wondered. Surely the counterinsurgents in Downers Cove had been comming them for a strike since Maxwell had brought the drills up, but only now...

"Where are we going?" Rhonson asked, suddenly at his side.

"The north caverns," he said automatically. "That's the only place we can go."

"Can we get there from here?"

Maxwell blinked at him. "We'll have to."

Rhonson started to argue, but clamped his mouth shut and nodded.

The explosions drowned all further conversation.

Nicolan...they've hit the complex, certainly. Nicolan...

Then he was getting into a mole and descending into the pit.

The Thayer smelting works jutted up out of the gravelly slope like mushrooms. Old sealant softened all the edges of windows and doors, oozed down walls. No one had used these facilities in over twenty years. The slag pile ran downslope toward the bay three kilometers west. Nicolan had seen vids of the operation in its heyday, processing tons of ore and turning out the pours of steel, aluminum, and titanium that had gone into building the Cambion complex, Crag Nook, the port at Emorick, a good portion of Emorick itself, and later the tramlines. Once the transit station had become fully functional and orbital smelters were built, the cost of doing the work planetside shut the Thayer works down. By then Houston Thayer, Maxwell Cambion's partner, was dead, his family had left for the inner Pan, and Cambion was one of the wealthiest families on the Finders.

Nicolan sat on the roof of a mole and surveyed the compound. His hands itched. Behind him the rest of the convoy was spread out on both sides of the old service road.

Kee stood a few meters ahead of the mole. He kicked a piece of tailing. "Do you think anything still works?"

Nicolan looked to his left, up the slope to the mountains towering above. The sky was a ragged curtain of yellow-grey clouds. His entire body ached from the last four days' work. All he wanted to do was lie down somewhere and sleep for a week.

He sighed and slid to the hood, then jumped to the ground. His legs complained; he stretched and ignored the pain. "Find the garages, we have to get these vehicles out of sight."

Kee studied a handslate, then pointed to a long low structure about twenty-five meters away. Nicolan strode up the slippery gravel till he came to a smooth level stretch. He looked back at the convoy anxiously. They had emerged from the tunnels in the middle of the night and while night was worthless as cover he had still felt less exposed.

Close up, the sealant was a pasty brown, black, and greenish tar smeared around the seams of all the accesses. Down the length of the building Nicolan counted twenty six-by-six meter doors, interspersed by standard size entrances.

Kee sprayed a fine mist on the sealant of the door at the north end. Nicolan looked at him questioningly and he held up the sprayer. "Recombinant microfauna," he explained. "Changes the molecular structure. Should work fairly soon... "

The goo began to run. First in small streams, then bigger clumps dissolved and oozed downward. In a few minutes the sealant was a stream of brackish liquid running into the drain trough at the base of the wall.

Kee stabbed at the lock and the door lurched open. Nicolan curled his lips at the stale gust escaping.

"Well," Kee said apologetically, "it *has* been twenty years." He pulled on his breather and goggles and stepped through.

Nicolan slipped on his own mask and followed.

The light from the door spilled warmly across the dusty floor and onto a metal desk. Nicolan moved out of the light and stood still while his eyes adjusted to the gloom. To his right, in the shadows, Kee rummaged. Then an inner door slid open and Nicolan stood alone for a few moments.

Lights flared and Nicolan squinted. Dust lay thick on everything in the office. Kee's footprints were clear all the way to the door at the far end. A few seconds later Kee reappeared.

"Looks like the generators still work, boss."

"Good. Get the bays unsealed and everyone inside. Then see if there's anything like a shield we can get up."

Nicolan pushed himself away from the wall. Still no time to think about Maxwell.

He had yet to come to terms with Maxwell's death. Constant movement, organization, details, all had pushed any other considerations far to the side. Even now, he realized, he was thinking about the viability of using the Thayer compound for a base. It was exposed and anyone with access to a halfway complete history of Finders would know what it was. All in all it was an impractical stronghold. But they needed something and Nicolan felt it was worth the gamble to give it to them at least for a short time. It was within reach of the Vohec artifact. Though he did not know what the structure was, Nicolan suspected—believed— they would not permit it to be damaged. It was a slim possibility at best, but he was grasping.

In the next office he found an old, bulky polycom console. He wiped the dust from the screens and the keyboard and punched the power switch. The main screen winked on, a calm sky blue. Nicolan typed in a query for a menu.

System limited, the screen informed him, *major memory cores inaccessible.*

Meaning, Nicolan thought, they were dumped when the compound was abandoned. He finished typing and waited.

Base schematic available. Please Wait.

A diagram of the complex scrolled onto the screen with a bright red dot pulsing to show where Nicolan was.

Through the empty halls the grinding of huge doors riding up on long unused rails echoed. He followed Kee's footprints down a corridor into the loading bays. The convoy of moles trundled inside. Soon the silence was banished by human voices and machinery being reawakened from a twenty year sleep.

"I want cleaning details formed first," Nicolan called. "Find the living quarters, straighten them out, then report to Kee for further instructions!"

"Yes, mother," someone replied.

Nicolan grinned as others laughed.

He returned to the polycom and continued searching. Finally he found a map of the continent. He toyed with the cursor, enlarging and studying sections, until he stopped at one area. Almost directly east, just over the mountains, out on the plains of Whale, south of the point where the Eastering Road turned northward, lay the seti shrine.

Or whatever it was. He had never heard a satisfactory explanation of the big domed structure. The contract drawn up initially simply set that region aside, never to be exploited by humans or any of their agents. The agreement was fundamentally suspicious, but the first generation of colonists had been interested in securing the system first. Like all such arrangements humans entered into, they probably thought they could work something out later, after they were already too entrenched to be moved. Privately, Nicolan felt they had been overly optimistic and unrealistic. He knew many setis, a few fairly well. Nothing led him to believe they could be manipulated in the ways humans had always been used to manipulating each other.

Diphda was at the edge of the Vohec *Qonoth*, so the first agreements necessarily and directly involved them. The shrine was theirs, Nicolan knew, but they had never once claimed that Finders had ever been theirs. As time passed he grew convinced that their aid hinged on that structure, in spite of what the Rahalen Coingulate might decide.

Perhaps their intervention did as well. Nicolan stared at the map and smiled.

After the fires died out, the smoke gathered in the air over Crag Nook, seemingly trapped by the deep alcove. It would bleed away in time, but for now gloom would be constant. Cira and Rollo walked toward the tram station through streets eerily quiet after the recent violence. Most of the stalls were gone, closed down, leaving longer, slower lines for those that remained. Armed coes stood at the intersections, randomly checking IDs, occasionally hassling anyone that seemed argumentative or vulnerable. Cira had been stopped a couple of times, but she wore only her Armada field utilities now, sufficient passport for most of the new bullies.

The attitude in the streets was different. She did not notice when it changed, only that one day it was dangerous to go out, the next it was dangerous in a new way. Two days passed before she realized that the Armada had arrived. She waited one more to see if it was permanent, then took Rollo with her.

In Cira's opinion Rollo Hersted possessed an admirable ability: he kept all doubt and worry from his face at will. She had learned to recognize the signs in other ways. He held his rifle tighter when uncertain; the otherwise casual manner with which he surveyed the street became sharper, constant. The other two relied on him tremendously. If in fact Mater Hersted was more capable, more reliable than Rollo, Cira decided she did not want to meet the woman. That kind of power was a little frightening to contemplate.

The tram station came into sight at the end of a street. The arched main gate was guarded by eight coes in local overcoats and s.p. rifles—except one, she noticed, who carried an e.p. They did not talk among themselves, but sauntered back and forth before the gate, alert and waiting. Cira's shoulder pressed against the wall of a hostel, under an eave. She watched the guards. Rollo silently stood behind her, rifle ready, covering their rear. She did not know what she expected to see by more careful inspection, only that it seemed like a good idea not to rush up to the gate.

Finally, she pushed away from the wall. Her ankle throbbed once, reminding her that she was not yet fully healed. She winced, then turned to speak to Rollo, and stopped. Bright red graffiti stood out from the sooty wall.

"The anvil of day forges the metal of night!"

"Come on," she said and took a step toward the gate.

Rollo touched her shoulder. She looked up at him.

"You're sure this will be fine?" he asked quietly.

"Sure. I'll see to it you're taken care of. You helped me, that will go a long way."

Rollo nodded, for the first time a slight frown showing his doubt.

The locals started forward as they approached. Then the one with the e.p. gave a short order and strode toward her.

Cira stopped ten meters from the gate and let him approach the rest of the way.

"This better be real," he said, scowling at her uniform.

Cira extended her left hand, holding her ID chit between thumb and middle finger. His eyes on Rollo, he snatched the disk, shoved into the reader at his belt then pulled the reader out and glanced at the screen. His expression softened.

"Come with me, Lieutenant."

Cira jerked a thumb at Rollo. "Him, too."

"He's not—"

"Him, too!"

The marine nodded and led the way through the gates.

As she followed him into the station proper, Cira felt incrementally better. The orderly stamp of the military was evident all around, a comforting gestalt. By the time she reached the top of the stairs to the station offices she felt confident and safe.

"He waits here," the marine said as they stopped outside the door, where two more marines stood guard.

Rollo stared at them, clearly uneasy.

"Rollo. I have to report in. You can wait here. I'll see to it everything's all right."

He nodded slowly and stepped back against the wall.

Cira walked through the next door into a busy operations center. It was a welcome, almost homey sight.

The marine knocked twice on the door, waited for the barked command from beyond, and opened it for Cira.

The man behind the desk looked up from one eye. The other was shut within a thick purple and green bruise. A square bandage covered that side of his forehead.

"Yes?"

"Lt. Cira Kalinge, Wing Leader, Valico Task Force, reporting."

He blinked at her for a few seconds. "Another one...?" He looked at the marine. "Get that journalist."

The marine left.

"I'm Lt. Commander Laros, Micheson Task Force. Your task commander...?"

"Palada."

"Commander Palada is with Micheson now, along with the remainder of his own task force."

The door opened again. Cira looked over her shoulder. Tory Shirabe started and broke into a wide grin.

"Lt. Kalinge!"

"Co Shirabe..."

"Fine, that'll do for now," Laros said. "Please wait outside, Co Shirabe."

Cira watched him leave, then turned back to Laros.

"Commanders Micheson and Palada will want a full report of everything that's happened to you from initial contact with the enemy on. Until that report is completed, you will have no further contact with anyone."

"Sir, I brought with me a local who was instrumental in saving my life. He and his family—"

"Family!"

"Three people in total, Commander. The Hersteds."

"But you only brought one?"

"The others are waiting on word."

Laros folded his hands. "Word on what?"

"I promised to see that they were taken care of. They were of considerable aid to me—"

Laros waved a hand. "I'll see to it, Lieutenant. We can use more local militia."

Cira wanted to protest, uncertain if the Hersteds were willing to act as soldiers against their own. "Thank you, Commander," she said.

"You'll be escorted to a private room with a recorder. Have you eaten recently?"

"This morning. Also—" She opened her shoulder pack and pulled out a block of data chits. "These are all the records I could find in the data base of a local *agent provocateur* named Venner. I believe security will be very interested in what they contain…"

Laros jumped up and came around the desk. He took the block in his hands, one good eye wide.

"I'm…sure, Lieutenant…yes…"

He placed the block on his desk and stared at it. Abruptly, he straightened and looked at her as if he just remembered her.

"Uh—please go with Corporal Gemik and begin your report. I'll contact Commander Palada as soon as I can." He touched a contact on the desk. The door opened and the marine stepped back in. "Escort Lt. Kalinge to the interrogation room. See that she has a recorder and is not disturbed."

Cira stepped toward the door. Beyond, halfway down the length of the operations room, she saw Tory Shirabe watching her.

"Lieutenant?"

She looked back at Laros.

"Welcome back, Lieutenant," he said.

"Thank you."

#

Tory Shirabe watched Lt. Kalinge escorted away, to the interrogation room. It might be hours before she finished, days before he might talk to her, if at all.

Two people, Lt. Kalinge and Lt. Cambion. No other survivors from the Valico fighter wings had been found. He had heard talk that a good deal of the debris was missing, too, though there had hardly been time to do a thorough survey of the entire system. There was rumor of a large seti vessel in-system, but he could get no confirmation. Tory had tried to talk to Lt. Cambion, but all he discovered was how much the man did not remember. Alexan Cambion did not remember the battle, the task force, how he had come to be on Finders, or what had happened to him since grounding. He did not recognize Tory. At least Lt. Kalinge had recognized him.

Sergeant Palker came down the hallway. He gave Tory a nod then entered Laros's office. A few minutes later he emerged, spoke briefly to a marine, who left, then approached Tory.

"I'm taking a patrol into town, secure and recover job. He didn't say *not* to ask, so I'm assuming it'd be all right for you to come along."

Tory smiled. "Thank you, sergeant."

Palker nodded toward the outside door. "Local out there name of Hersted. He's taking us. Wait with him, we'll be around." He spun around and walked off.

Tory switched on his recorder. In the small room between the inner and outer door he found a pair of marines and a big man with a long-barreled s.p. wearing a mottled, ankle-length overcoat that had been patched a couple of times. He stood with his legs apart, back against the wall, at an angle that let him watch both doors, the marines, and now Tory.

"Hello. I'm Tory Shirabe, with the Ares-Epsilon Newsnet."

After a long pause, the man nodded once. "Saw your work. The piece on the Etacti terraforming breakdown."

Tory blinked. That had been one he had almost forgotten himself, it had been so arcane. He wondered why that piece would stick in a Founder's mind. "Thanks."

"You're here for the war?"

Tory nodded. "I came in with the first task force."

"Mmm. Shame about all those people."

"All right," Palker said, stepping through the door. "You're Hersted?"

"Rollo Hersted."

"I'm Sergeant Palker. I'd appreciate it if you'd take me back to where you and Lt. Kalinge have been staying. We can bring in your other family members."

Hersted studied Palker. "That's not all you want."

"No. The rest is our concern."

The Founder seemed to weigh all this cautiously. At last, he nodded. "Let's go."

A squad of six marines waited at the foot of the stairs. Palker gave a quick series of hand signals to them and they fell into a loose formation, fanning out to right and left behind Palker, Hersted, and Tory.

The streets looked unfinished, work in progress with pieces missing, piles of material lying about, and almost no people. The multiplicity of bootsteps reverberated sharply back and forth. Tory studied the scene in silence, questions just below expressability. Crag Nook was not a town anymore, but a collection of structures. The living element was shattered, dysfunctional. They rounded a corner and found a line of people stretching from a stall beneath a grimy fabric awning. Smoke wafted from behind the counter. One by one, people left the stall with a small bowl of steaming food and disappeared. A group of local militia stood nearby, watching. No one, except the militia, looked at the marines.

The house Hersted brought them to was an impressive structure with a courtyard behind a solid wall.

"Stay sharp," Palker said.

Hersted frowned at the sergeant.

Tory stayed abreast of Palker following the big Founder to the main entrance. Hersted pushed open the door and stepped through.

"Olin! Becca!"

They stood in the long foyer and waited for a reply. Hersted looked ceilingward and called the names again.

"How many?" Palker asked quietly.

"Just two…"

Palker motioned to the marines and they moved into the house, quick and alert. Tory listened intently but a few seconds after they left the foyer he could not hear the marines.

Hersted went through the next door. A staircase to the right ascended to the second floor and another door opened into a kitchen to the left.

Palker's comm beeped and he snatched it from his belt. "Yes?"

"Second floor, third door on left, Sergeant."

Palker took the stairs two at a time, Hersted close behind. Tory sprinted after them.

Two marines stood in the hallway, looking through the open door. Palker glanced in, then gave Hersted a startled look. The Founder leaned in, then entered.

A man had been clamped against the wall upside down. Blood ran from his nose and mouth, smearing his forehead. Tory felt his lips draw back against the pungent smell. A dark stain spread from the man's crotch down over his clothes.

Hersted stared at him, unable, it seemed, to say or do anything more. One of the marines shifted his weight minutely and attracted his attention, then pointed to the opposite wall.

A young woman sat on the bed, her eyes fixed on the mounted man. At first glance there seemed to be nothing wrong with her. Then Tory noticed that her arms ended in cauterized stumps.

On the bed before her, in a bloodsoaked pile, lay her hands, arranged to gently cup a set of genitals.

Then Tory realized that they were both still alive.

At least he felt better now. He no longer ached and was not frightened all the time. Where they had placed him was comfortable and he sensed that the device surrounding him was healing him. He trusted the attendants. They wore uniforms he dimly recognized, spoke in familiar cadences, moved with reassuring efficiency.

He had been told that his name was Alexan, but he was not sure. Since he remembered no other name, that would do for the time being. He remembered little from before the tram ride on which he had been beaten. Nothing clearly, not even his dreams.

Now he was being moved.

The heaviness of familiarity was an urge that would not complete, a threshold sensation, sourceless and constant. Everything he saw, everyone he heard, reaffirmed his mounting conviction that he must know all this. A surplus of intimacy suffused each waking minute, apprehensive and inconsummate.

It was best when things were happening; the distraction of detail alleviated his frustration. Eventually, he thought, there would be no new detail and either he would remember or the frustration would destroy him.

He had spoken with the journalist for over an hour once it became clear that the man knew him. They moved Alexan from the cell to a comfortable bed and his automated healers and he had not seen the journalist since. The man had insisted they had known one another and Alex was inclined to believe him, even more now that he was gone. Three days had passed since arriving here in the tram and now he was to move once more. Attendants, some with weapons, wheeled him down corridors, then out into the open air.

The sky was dirty, a grimy yellow-white, and he smelled burning. He was not outside for long. They pushed him up a short ramp into a close space that resembled a tram. His gurney was hooked into a wall and most of his escort left. A medtech leaned over him, smiled, and told him the journey would be brief, then he would be on his way home. That sounded wrong. He had assumed all along that he *was* home. No one had given him any reason till now to question that assumption.

So where was "home"?

The entire closed space lurched, then settled down. Alexan dozed off.

When he opened his eyes he was again being wheeled down a corridor, but this one was very different. No stone, all metal and plastic and composites, all functional, all cold and efficient.

At last he was alone in a room all to himself. It was pleasant and comfortable and the monitors and healers were still attached and working on him. He felt safe. He was leaving home. Again.

Chapter Seven

Until she stepped off the courier onto Homestead Transit Station, Cira had not realized how much she resented going home. The walk down the ramp from the ship, across the bridge to debarkation, became an exercise in discipline. Her reluctance turned physical—a profound urge to turn and leave, a weakness to be overcome. She felt queasy, legs rubbery, by the time she reached the immigration desk and handed over her ID chit.

"Welcome home, Lieutenant," the officer said, smiling. "Hope you have a pleasant leave."

"Thank you."

Cira looked across the debarkation hall. Columns designed as amalgams of major architectural traditions and resembling none of them lined the walls. From between those against the interior wall, light rayed over the occupants, striking sharp shadows. Cira found the whole thing shallow—fake drama, a heavy layer of the heroic implicit in the classical motifs, the impression being that just visiting here would make one better.

More than half the hundred-odd people waiting in the high-backed, richly-upholstered chairs—chairs that made conversation with the person on either side uncomfortable at best—were tourists. The heady mixture of colors and fabrics—faces fat and thin, austere and jubilant; hair long, short, thick, sculpted, unnaturally colored; body parts decorated with tatoos, jewelry, organic modifications; clothing gaudy, spare, heavy, luxurious, and ascetic—assaulted her. For over four years she had seen little of the Pan beyond Armada ships, stations, and the data feeds over public access networks. It was very different to see society at large on a popular journal and to be confronted with it in the flesh. The Pan Humana was a vulgar complexity of nearly a hundred settled worlds, thousands of city-sized stations, and nearly half a trillion individuals adhering to billions of customs and served by millions of institutions. The monetary value of the trade that daily crossed from star to star, not to mention

planet to planet, moon to moon, station to station, and every combination thereof, had long since passed beyond meaningful calcula-
tion. But within the diaphanous boundary that gave shape to the
Pan Humana, no one went hungry except by choice. That one fact
seemed more than adequate to dismiss any criticism.

They had, these people from Faron and Eurasia, Nine Rivers
and Neighbors, Tabit and Procyon, Aqual and Zephyr, Toliman Station and Cooper's Rock, been told that the war now waged in the
Distals was to defend that value, to keep the unthinkable from happening, that violence and hunger should return to humanity and its
civilization.

She collected her duffel from the inspection desk and took a
shunt deep into the station. She stepped off at random—circuit
twenty, segment fifty-nine—and joined a dense flow of humanity.
The circuit was fifteen meters wide and lined with every sort of
shop, nightclutch, sleepover, omnirec, restaurant, and service stop
available to the citizen of the Pan. Cira let herself be carried along
until the eddies washed her into a narrow espresso shop. She ordered a cup of cocoa and asked about a good hotel.

Unless she wanted to go all the way to the opposite side of
circuit twenty, the best hotel nearby was on circuit twenty-one—the
Tanner-Morrisel.

The room she took offered a view over several acres of parkland
contained in its own circuit with a isolated gravity envelope. She
could look directly "down" on pleasant contours of sculpted terrain, watch kites bob in artificial breezes, observe people playing as
if she were flying over them in a slow-moving ship. She stripped
off her uniform, showered, and sat before the window until
nightcycle darkened the park. She ate in her room and drank half a
bottle of Nine Rivers ale. She slept dreamlessly and woke with a
mild headache.

She showered again, then opened her duffel and spread out her
clothes on the bed. Cira stared at them, hands on hips, hair dripping
down her shoulders and back, and tried to remember the last time
she had worn civilian clothes. Since arriving at officer's school she
had worn uniforms. Even during leaves she had chosen to remain
uniformed, though she had bought these clothes she now examined,
thinking to wear them one day after graduation, on leave as a fully

rated Armada officer when she imagined herself inured to the specialness of being in uniform. That day had not arrived, though she was faced with *a* day that in every other respect qualified. The clothes looked strange and she could not imagine herself in them. Finally she put them back in her duffel and pulled on a casual blue-grey shortsleeved uniform.

She studied her reflection in the mirror briefly, nodded, and left the room.

After breakfast in the hotel restaurant she went down to the parkland and wandered the walkways. When she looked up all she saw was sky and cloud, an illusion generated on a thin sheet of material suspended between this circuit and the next. The sky was the blue of Earth skies.

People noticed her, pointed her out, but no one came up to speak to her. As nightcycle came on she returned to circuit twenty-one, wandered till late, and went back to her room. She finished the bottle of ale and slept fitfully.

Cira drifted. She made no plans, followed no pattern, except the nightly bottle and the morning discomfort. She had never handled intoxicants well and used to wonder why people indulged them. She believed she understood now, but she did not examine this new knowledge closely. Her leave was open-ended, with a minimum ten days required. Ten days. The Armada had decided that was the necessary time for her to center herself, regain any confidence, stability, and composure lost at Finders. She was not certain what she had lost at Finders but she did not see how time off could help her recover it. If she had lost it at Finders then it was at Finders she should look for it.

She was surprised on the sixth day when a man came up to her table at breakfast. She had grown accustomed to being left alone; the uniform kept people at bay. Not this one. He was slim, pale, and dressed neatly in a red pullover and white baggy pants.

"Lieutenant Kalinge?"

She frowned and nodded.

"May I join you?"

"Do I know you?"

"No." He pulled out the chair and sat across from her. He motioned for the servor. When the device stopped at the table he ordered coffee. It floated away and a few seconds later returned with a steaming cup. "My name is Jamer."

"You already know mine."

He sipped his coffee and nodded. "Of course." He pulled an ID chit from his waistband and slid it across the table. The emblem of Armada security was etched onto it.

Cira flicked it back. It shot off the table and Jamer caught it neatly and returned it to his waistband. "What can I do for you?" Cira asked. "My report was as complete as I could make it—"

He grinned affably. "Oh, this has nothing to do with your report, Lieutenant. I'm here only to see how you're doing."

"How I'm doing?"

"Yes. You've been here for six days now. Are you enjoying the hotel?"

Cira shrugged. "It's nice enough. I'd prefer returning to duty."

"I can understand that. Civilian life…lacks meaning after a tour in the military. A certain *frisson* is missing."

Cira nodded, waiting.

"Do you intend to go planetside?" he asked.

"Actually, no."

"Really? I understand you're a native of Homestead."

"Have you been planetside?"

"Yes."

"Then you know why I'm not really interested in going down."

Jamer laughed. "I found it a charming place. It's one of the more Earthlike colonies."

"I'm happy for you."

Jamer studied her while drinking his coffee. He set the empty cup down and laced his long fingers over his stomach. "You're intending to spend your entire leave on the station?"

Cira nodded. "Four days after today. Frankly I can't wait to get back to duty."

"Ten days is the minimum, Lieutenant. You might take longer."

"Ten days is plenty for me."

"Ten days is the Armada's minimum. If necessary you'll get more."

Something in his tone told her this was more than a suggestion. "How much more?" she asked.

"As much as the Armada thinks is necessary." He signaled for another cup. "You're sure you don't want to visit planetside? Take the opportunity to go home, see your family—"

"If I do, then perhaps the Armada will consider the minimum sufficient?"

"Oh, I wouldn't try to second guess those kinds of decisions. It couldn't hurt, though."

Cira sighed wearily, looked across the restaurant to the giant window strip that looked down on the parklands. "I suppose a trip to Ozma City wouldn't be such a bad idea—"

"No. Go home, Lieutenant. Visit your family."

Jamer fixed her with a steady gaze, all trace of good humor and cordiality gone.

"Is there some reason the Armada feels such a visit is necessary?" she asked.

"The Armada always has reasons."

"Yes, sir," she said tightly.

He smiled then. He lifted his cup. "They serve good coffee here."

Tory glared at the man on the other side of the room. "There has to be a way," he said much more evenly than he felt. "You're my redactor, Jon, you're supposed to be good at getting things. Here's your chance to prove how good. Get me back on Finders."

Jon Buson pursed his heavy lips and shook his head. He looked sad, which made him appear older than he was. "Sorry, Tor, not possible. The Armada has declared Diphda completely off limits to all media."

"Last time I checked the Pan was a free autocracy. What happened?"

Jon shrugged. "Maybe the Pan is, but the Distals aren't. It's not just Diphda, I'm having trouble getting people anywhere on the front." He folded his thick arms across his chest and looked out the panoramic window.

Tory did the same, unable to continue glaring at the man and unwilling to soften his resentment. The city of Charic spread below up to the edge of the Confluences where three rivers came together. The sky of Nine Rivers was a dazzling metallic blue. The city was a jumble of crowded construction, shoved between the docks on the rivers and the spaceport. The vibrancy, the self-evident affluence, the commercial cheeriness of the city worked on Tory in odd ways, leaving him discomfited, uneasy. Finally, he looked away.

Jon's office contained a small polycom station and a bar. He had a desk somewhere that he never used. Chairs, sofas, and pillows were scattered across the floor in no particular pattern. Tory went to the bar and poured a glass of wine.

"I'm sorry, Tor, I really am."

"I bet you are."

"I *am*, damn you! You were sending good work back! Our market share was up! You think it pleases me that the Armada has shut journalists out?"

Tory looked around at Jon. "Yes, actually, I think it does. Gives you an excuse to browbeat the government, take trips to Sol to attend Forum sessions, and editorialize extemporaneously without fear of having your leash yanked by the shareholders."

Jon burst into laughter. When he finished he drew a deep, dramatic breath. "So: what are you going to do?"

Tory shrugged, leaned back against the bar. "Eventually I'll find a way to get back to Finders. For now...there are a few things I could follow up."

"Such as?"

"Well, such as Lt. Cambion and Lt. Kalinge."

"Mm."

"Cambion is in a hospital on Toliman Station. Kalinge is on leave visiting her homeworld. They both left before I did and I didn't get a chance to talk to them much."

"Then why are you here instead?"

"I wanted to talk to you before I did anything."

Jon grunted. "You never listen to anything I say any other time. What's different?"

"The situation. We've never been at war before. At least, not that we've ever admitted."

"Yes, I read your stuff, whether you believe that or not. I've already assigned a couple people to find out where else the Armada might have gotten combat experience."

"Turn up anything yet?"

"No. Well, yes, a lot of evasion on the part of the Armada, more than necessary if something weren't being hidden. All this is strictly off the official agenda, mind you."

"Sure. That's why I'm taking a leave of absence." He paused, then asked, "Did you ask about Millennium?"

"Directly? Do I look insane?"

"Well…"

"No, I didn't. And you won't either, unless you want to end up unaccounted for."

"Permanent guest of Armada security? Just the fact that you're talking like this means there's something to it."

"Of course there is. And maybe I've got people looking into it and maybe I don't. For you, though, Millennium is off limits."

"Hey, I'm on vacation, remember?"

"Good for you. A rest, that's just what you need."

"I think I might go to Toliman Station and see if I can find out how Lt. Cambion's doing. How did you manage with his service records?"

"They're classified, of course. The disk on the bar behind you."

Tory picked up the data chit and slipped it into his pocket. "I don't know how long this one will take, Jon."

"Do I look like I care?"

"As a matter of fact—"

Jon raised a hand and Tory fell silent. "Already got you booked on a liner to Toliman Station, tomorrow. We're advancing you discretionary credit—you need the rest, you really do—and I'm having our station chief at Toliman meet you and take you to a good hotel." He jabbed a finger in Tory's direction. "If it looks like you're stirring trouble for yourself, leave. You won't do me a bit of good in detention for the duration of the war."

"I'm so glad you care."

Jon looked at him with an expression that unsettled Tory. The eyes, old and brown and filled with intent, seemed infinitely sad.

"The shit's getting thick," he said. "We could all drown in it. Take care, Tor."

Tory took the lift down to the ground floor and walked out onto the boulevard. He watched the traffic for a time until he realized that he was trying to justify two incompatible images—Charic and Crag Nook.

The med techs had managed to reattach the girl's hands, but the last time he had seen her she had been sitting on a cot staring at them as if they were alien. The man had died before they could get him stabilized. When Palker had informed him that he was being shipped out-system—sorry, Co Shirabe, orders, nothing to be done—the girl still had not told anyone what had happened. Tory woke abruptly now and then, shaking, hands tentatively touching himself.

The battle in space had been quick and efficient, combat between machines. He knew people had piloted those machines, but everything had happened so fast, was so final and so indisputable that the horror was intellectual. A disemboweled fighter was not a terrifying sight. On Finders, though, days of fighting had resolved nothing. Victory was an accumulation of steps that required a brutality unfamiliar to Tory. He understood them, could see why and to what purpose each step was taken—the intellect was not horrified— instead it became a sanctuary against the pulsing cold revulsion each step triggered in the rest of him.

Lifted out of it, put on a courier, and ushered back into the deep parts of civilization, he was left with a paralyzing ambivalence. He had been on Nine Rivers Transit Station for three days before contacting Jon. He had sat in a small private room with a bottle of aqual and an inhaler, waging a different kind of battle. At the end he had won and left the room without having ingested either substance. He felt validated, but *for* what and *against* what he could not say.

He recounted the facts as he saw them:

The Pan Humana was waging war;

The purpose of the war was to close the borders and prevent further contact with nonhuman civilizations;

The war was being waged on humans who disagreed with the isolationist policy and were attempting to separate themselves from the Pan.

He laughed wryly. Easily stated facts. The reality behind them was a confusing mess. Tory's head roiled with ambiguities, uncertainties, dilemmas, and paradoxes, not least of which was the question of his own part in all this rippling history. He needed to explore the situation to find the answers to settle his doubts. The problem was, the Armada had effectively shut him out of the theater of exploration.

So, he thought as he walked back to his hotel, that leaves the nosebleed seats.

He had checked into a resort hotel near the docks. The smell of the rivers permeated the air. It was warm and humid and the coolness of the hotel lobby felt good.

"Someone has been waiting to see you, Co Shirabe," the desk informed him.

"Oh?"

A light over the counter pulsed, then indicated a direction, toward the lobby bar, and a holo appeared above it of a woman with a wide face and intensely red hair. Tory frowned at the image.

"Did she say what she wanted?"

"She mentioned that she wished to converse with a colleague."

Tory grunted. "Thank you."

She waited in a booth, running a fingertip around the rim of a tall glass of violet liqueur. Tory slid in across from her. She smiled briefly, but Tory kept his expression neutral. Already he felt an anxious twist somewhere between her face and the back of his brain.

"Co Shirabe."

"Co Marlin. What can I do for you?"

"I've been following your material. I'm impressed."

"Unique situation, it's not that difficult to make it interesting."

"Not to most coes, but to another journalist?"

"I'm not usually modest. You should enjoy this while it lasts. What do you want, Jesa?"

Her eyebrows lifted slightly and the set of her jaw changed. Tory silently congratulated himself on how fast he had shifted her approach.

"I understand you've been banned from the Front."

"So has every other journalist."

"But you were there, on Finders." He nodded. She sighed tiredly. "Don't be an ass, Tory. I'd like to help you get back there."

"Really? For what? Half credit on the reports?"

"Why not, if I do half the work?"

"If you do half the work. I can manage my own return, thanks."

"Why are you so against working together?"

"We did once, remember?"

"Are you still angry about that?" She shook her head. "That wasn't me, Tory, that was my manager. What happened before was all—"

"I don't care. Sure, I believe you. But there's a problem. I work for Ares-Epsilon, you work for Interpan. Conflict of interest. We're contractually obligated to fuck each other over. I don't blame you for stealing my stories, not you personally, but you represent the people who did. To me that amounts to the same thing. If I were you I'd have the same attitude about me."

"I do. That's why I'm suggesting we set up an independent corporation and syndicate everything."

"I'm already syndicated." Tory shook his head and stood. "This is a waste of time, Jesa."

"You're going to tell me that Buson can actually get you back to Finders?"

"No. I'm not going to tell you anything."

"I can guarantee you transport."

"Your price is too high."

"What price? Damnit, Tory—"

"No." He frowned, studying her face. She seemed genuinely puzzled. For a moment he felt himself slide toward an explanation, which, he knew, would lead to accusation, protestations, a series of counterarguments, and ultimately an attempt at reconciliation. He stepped away from the table. "No, Jesa. Not again. It was bad enough last time." He walked away.

When she did not follow, Tory felt relieved. Jesa Marlin was not the first to approach him since his return—there had been four other requests for interviews already, but journalists interviewing journalists had always struck him wrong—and he expected more. So far he had brushed them all aside without hesitation. Jesa brought more credit to the negotiation, though. A part of him wanted very much to work with her again. Not only work, but everything else that had then become a part of their relationship. It always startled him to look back and see how natural it had felt. He believed her that the appropriated bylines, unshared leads, and pilfered stories were the demands of her contract, but he had thought—hoped—that their relationship would become privileged. When it did not, Tory found ways to break with her. They were professionals, it should never have grown personal. The break was the right thing to do. Keeping his distance now was the only thing to do.

But by the time he reached his room he felt less confident. He busied himself packing, checking the reservations for his trip, and cleaning up some articles to be fed over to Buson. Out of curiosity he requested information on travel options to the Distals—Skat, Maron, and Etacti specifically—and in each case he was told that all passages to these points had been suspended till further notice.

He requested confirmation of Jesa Marlin's personal address code, then filed the number in his notebook, dropped it in his travel pack, and stretched out for a nap.

The view out the window was pleasant. Alex liked to sit and read novels beside the window so he could look out now and then at the sweep of green lawn, the brilliant lake, the haze-softened mountains on the other side of the water. He remembered that the view was artificial, that in fact the hospital was within the body of an enormous transit station, but that did not diminish the beauty of the scene. Someone had been very thoughtful in placing it outside his window. He had told himself—and no one had contradicted him—that it was *his* landscape, just for him. It looked nothing like home, not even a projection of what home might one day be, but that did not matter.

By the time he had arrived here his physical injuries were healed. The bones had been repaired, the scarring was gone, and when he looked in the mirror in the hygiene cubicle he approved of the smooth skin and human symmetry. If anything he felt he looked better than before.

The room was wonderful. It changed at a thought. He had first discovered this by accident and it had frightened him. He had been dreaming and then awoke to find the environs of the dream all around him. That first time it was space, hard vacuum, the numberless stars all around, and a planet near enough to be a sharp disk. He stared and gasped for air. He could not breathe, but somehow he did anyway, and suddenly he was back in his hospital room, in his bed, gripping the sheets from the abrupt sensation of falling...

He began playing with it, a few minutes each day, until he understood how the room functioned. The image he wanted reproduced had to be very powerful for him, deeply felt and intimately envisioned. Then he let himself drift, his mind floating free of identity. He found this easy to do once he learned the trick, almost like napping lightly while listening to music and being absorbed wholly by the music. The room could get through then and reproduce what he imagined. Maintaining the illusion took concentration, a skill which improved with use. He spent more time in space because it pleased him. He felt comfortable in the void. But there were other images that drew him as potently.

There was one, a single chamber, dimly lit. A cot and hygienic cubicle on one side facing a mass of equipment on the other. Despite the actual spaciousness of the room it seemed cramped and stifling. Alex did not like it, but found himself there more and more, usually after waking from vivid dreams. At first he left it quickly. After the fifth time he found himself in it, though, he began to explore.

The cot was bolted to the wall. The walls were glass-smooth stone, veined and mottled under a glaze. The one door was heavy; his hand pressed to its plate did not open it. The equipment was all medical gear of one kind or another and a pair of dedicated polycoms. He knew this place. He tried to access the information in the polycoms, but the screens displayed kaleidoscopic patterns that made no sense.

The strongest impressions came when he stretched out on the cot. The room seemed to close in on him then, squeeze him with implications and nascent meaning.

A man stood behind the main console. Alex sat up and stared at him. He was old, hair thick and grey at the temples, thinning over his scalp, and a harsh expression over his wide face. The old man's hands moved as if he were playing a musical instrument.

"Who are you?" Alex asked.

"You know very well who I am," the old man said, "even if you do not."

Alex crossed the room and leaned on the console. The old man gazed back evenly.

"M-mmm—"

"Say it!"

Alex flinched. "Michen?"

"Told you. Now go lay down, I have work to do before you undo yourself."

"Where's my father?"

"Dead. Now lay down."

Alex felt panicked. "No, he's not dead. He's outside that door!"

"No."

"Don't tell me no!"

"All right."

The door opened and another man stepped in. Tall, fine features carved in an expressionless, thin face, black hair...

"Father...?"

He shook his head slowly. "He's dead."

"No, you're my father."

"I'm Maxwell. I'm not your father."

Alex looked back at Michen. "What—?"

"Go lay down, we're not through."

"Go lay down," Maxwell said.

"Who are these people, Alex?"

He turned at the new voice. A woman stood behind him. She was slim, compact, yellow hair pulled back from a square face. She stood with her arms folded over her chest, legs apart, and an expression of intent curiosity.

"I—" Alex began, then hesitated. He felt compelled to answer her question, but he did not know what to say. The two men he thought he knew waited quietly, Michen still moving his hands over the console. "I'm not sure. This one is Michen, our family physician. This one is...Maxwell...I thought he was my father, but he says no... "

"It's all right, Alex. It's not important who they say they are, but who you think they are."

He nodded, sensing that she was in some way correct, though he could not see how.

"You say Michen is the physician?" she asked.

"Yes." He looked up at Michen. "You are, aren't you?"

Michen nodded.

"So," Alex went on, "who is *he*?"

"He's Maxwell," Michen said

"He's not my father?"

"No."

"Who is my father?"

"Houston Thayer."

Alex blinked furiously, as if a swarm of gnats had just flown into his face. "Who is Houston Thayer?"

"Your father," Michen replied.

"But who is he?"

"Not 'is', Alex," Michen said. "Was. He's dead."

"Who was he?"

"Your father," Michen said.

"Then—" He looked at Maxwell, who still stood watching him, impassive and silent. "Who is *he*?"

"That's Maxwell. Do we have to go through this again?"

"He's not my father?"

Michen sighed. "Hopeless, useless, worthless, witless. Go lay down, Alex, we have work to do."

Alex stumbled backward until his legs caught the edge of the cot. He sat down, still blinking, his head tight. He knew this place. This was where he had been changed. He knew these men, they had changed him. But who was Houston Thayer and what did he have to do with all this?

The woman blocked his view then, leaning over him. Gently she pushed him back down onto the cot and laid a hand on his forehead. Instantly he slept.

He awoke in his hospital room, gazing out the window at the pleasant scene he knew was not really there.

From the road the stead looked the same as the day Cira had left it. The white towers of the processing plant lined up to the left of the long, low equipment shed. Far to the right were the livestock pens, stables, and barns. Between the two sets of structures stood the main house, a collection of prefab domes and towers joined by jury-rigged native-wood construction. Beyond lay the fields of newheat, corn, ramshorn, soy, and greenspit, thickly-cultivated fields that rose and fell in graceful contours, like a vast ocean frozen in mid swell. Scattered across them, biomonitors blinked blue, carefully measuring the acidity and alkalinity of the soil, moisture, the growth of the reworms that fixed minerals and released nutrients and controlled local phages, and the ripeness of the crops.

Almost thirty people lived in the main house, sometimes swelling to fifty during harvests—temporary workers, permanent staff, and Cira's family. She had grown up with a constantly changing cast of people orbiting around the core members of the household.

That people left had seemed to her natural, and she had spent her childhood patiently waiting to take her turn. It had never occurred to her then that her decision to leave might cause a negative reaction. She had spent many hours since going over the bitterness her departure had created. Time and energy and what she had come to believe was a finite reserve of emotion were consumed in trying to understand. Instead of support, her family offered outrage; instead of sympathy, they called her ungrateful, a traitor, worthless...worse; instead of wishing her luck and success, they closed her out. When she finally gave up and put the issue away, she sealed it with resentment, convinced that she would never have to deal with it again. To do so meant to go back and it seemed that the Armada would keep her safely away. That had proved to be a false assumption.

Her legs trembled slightly. In five years she had gotten one letter, from Moriana, her younger sister. That one had been troubled, full of anxiety and hints at unexpressed tensions, barely a year after Cira had left. Her own letters, few as they were, all bounced back unaccepted. She stopped writing.

She walked down the ocher road toward the stead. After twenty paces her legs felt firmer. She gripped the strap of her knapsack and straightened slightly. For the occasion she wore her formal uniform, a sleek midnight blue tunic with sapphire and gold piping at the collar and wrists, sky blue pants and black boots. Her black garrison cap was cocked far to the left side of her head, the small Armada medallion and the blood-red Valico pin flashing in the yellow light of Tau Ceti.

Someone stepped onto the veranda. He stopped when he saw her, then hurried back inside. Cira wet her lips lightly and stared at the door, wondering if anyone else would come out. She made it to the porch first.

From a distance the main house looked small. Close up, it assumed its true scale, looming like a displaced hill or an ancient castle. The compound was enormous. From here Cira's family cultivated and harvested nearly twelve thousand acres. The Kalinge Stead was not the largest on Homestead, but it was far from the smallest.

The click of her bootheels resounded under the porch eaves. At the door she pushed the bell plate and waited. A faint breeze passed along the length of the veranda. She looked toward the equipment shed. The garage bays were all open, but she could see nothing in the deep shadows within.

She frowned and pressed the bell plate again. After a few minutes she set her knapsack down against the wall and walked to the lefthand end of the veranda.

The various smells of the place brought a cascade of familiarity. The earth here possessed a damp loamy odor that was surprisingly like a certain beer from Etacti. Then there were machine oil, ozone, stale, wet fur, fresh cut wood and straw, hot plastics, animal musks, water. It all mixed together into a thick amalgam out of which Cira found she could still identify each one and each one still evoked memories, good and bad, faded and sharp.

She stepped off the veranda, felt the yield of the ground under her tread, and shuddered pleasantly. Suddenly she wanted to leave because she found that she wanted to stay.

People broke from the shadows of the equipment shed, striding toward her. They wore varicolored worktogs, dungarees, worn boots, heavy shirts, wide-brimmed shapeless hats. Cira froze in place. They moved fast, some carried tools, and she saw no one familiar. With nowhere to go, she faced them straight on, feet apart and hands on hips. Her heart raced as they surrounded her.

Faces jostled before her. Browned, etched by sun and weather and work and worry, deep eyes. Temporaries. They kept about a meter away from her. She could reach them at a meter, but it would be difficult and give most of them time to react. She remembered wager fights when she was little, coes stripped to the waist and faced off, bets made all around. A lot of it had been graceless brawling, but some had been almost beautiful to watch.

"If you got business here," a sharp, nasal voice said loudly, "state it neat and leave."

Cira turned and looked up at the man standing on the end of the veranda. He seemed smaller, less thick through the chest than when she had left, but the face was still proud and solid. The grey that had been only a trick of the light five years ago now spattered his close-cropped hair. His hands were on his hips in unconscious mirroring of her own stance.

"Hello, faitha," she said quietly.

For a moment it did not seem he had heard her. Then he frowned, a slight tightening of the mouth, and his hands fell to his sides.

"God," he breathed. He made a gesture with his right hand and the crowd around her drew back. He stepped off the veranda, came up to her, and wrapped his arms around her.

In that instant, smothered in the warmth of him, she nearly broke. She had left this and for a long time had been glad. She knew this feeling was momentary, that it would end at the first unkind word, the next ambivalent response, but the gesture itself mattered more than what surrounded it, past or future. This cost him.

"Welcome home, daughter," he said and she felt his voice against her face.

He stepped back and looked at the temporaries. "This is Cira, my daughter. She belongs here." He nodded once, definitively. "Go on back to your work."

They turned away and sauntered back toward the shed. In a few seconds Cira was alone with her father. She looked at him. She had gained a little height in five years and she could very nearly look him straight on.

"In front of them," he said, "we're family." He turned and walked back to the door. "Mori!" he called, his voice thunderous. "Your sister Cira's home! See to her room!" He kept on walking to the far end and disappeared around the corner.

Where were you, she wondered, when I rang the bell...?

A skinny girl with a wide face and a thick braid swinging behind her sprang from the door. She grinned widely and ran toward Cira. In her wake came Riv, her younger brother, and Saysheen, her aunt.

"Cira!" Moriana screamed and jumped to the ground. She wrapped her long arms around Cira's neck, laughing, and Cira staggered.

"Cira..." Saysheen smiled.

Riv seemed uncertain, thumbs hooked in his belt. Saysheen elbowed him.

"Welcome home, Cira," he said.

Cira regarded him. When she had left he had not yet entered puberty, only thirty-eight hundred days old. Now he appeared nearly grown, shoulders broadening, arms sinewy, face serious.

"Thank you," Cira said. "Saysheen, how are you?"

"Not bad, considering. God, it's good to see you. Why—?"

"Why've I come back?" She shrugged. "I'm on leave. What else do you expect me to do?"

"Marel wasn't too happy, though?" Saysheen guessed.

"Faitha was faitha."

Moriana shook her head. "He'll get over it. Let me take you to your room. *My* room! We can share!"

Cira smiled at her. "Well..."

She stepped onto the veranda. Saysheen stopped her with a gentle touch on the shoulder. She moved her hand to Cira's face.

"It's been too long," she said. "And I really expected it to be a hell of a lot longer."

"How long would that be?"

Saysheen shrugged. "Maybe as long as it takes for Marel to pass on."

"I never thought things were that bad."

Saysheen gave her a skeptical look. "Oh, of *course* you didn't. That's why it's been five years, because things aren't that bad. Well, *I'm* happier than I can tell you that you're back."

"It's not for long, Saysheen."

"It doesn't have to be." She squeezed Cira's hand. "Now let's let Mori overdo the welcome and get you settled in. We can talk later."

Moriana grabbed the knapsack and nearly skipped ahead into the house.

"Everybody!" Saysheen called. "Cira's home!" The main hall was empty and her voice echoed dully between the high walls.

"Cira, god, it's so good to *see* you!" Moriana half-whispered. Saysheen gave her an indulgent smile. "Were you at the front?"

Cira nodded, her eyes surveying the hall. Light flooded from the translucent skylight. To the right an archway led to a great room where, she remembered, all family meals were held, parties, readings, music played. Further along a staircase opened. Two more stairs broke the lefthand wall and another archway led to the kitchens and the bunkrooms for the temporaries. From this central place the house recomplicated into a branching labyrinth.

"We have a guest room over the common—" Saysheen began.

"I thought—" Moriana blurted. "But she can stay with me."

Saysheen shook her head. "I think Cira would prefer a room of her own. It might be better."

Moriana looked betrayed, then shrugged. "All right."

Cira squeezed Moriana's upper arm gently. "We'll talk. I've got a few days."

"Here." Moriana handed over Cira's knapsack and strode off, disappearing up the nearest lefthand stair.

Riv grunted.

"What—?" Cira started to ask.

Saysheen held up a hand. "This way, Cira." She led the way up the righthand stair.

At the top they stepped onto a balcony overlooking the great room. Cira looked down at the pair of big tables, half rings that faced each other. She had played along this balcony when she was small, though it was forbidden. Along here were the guest quarters. Saysheen opened one and Cira stepped in behind her. Everything looked smaller now. Bed, desk, reading chair, a polycom terminal.

"So you really were at the front?" Saysheen asked, turning the blankets down and fluffing the pillows.

"I can do that," Cira protested, dropping the knapsack. "Yes, I was. Finders."

"Finders!" Riv said.

Cira turned. He leaned against the door jamb, thumbs still hooked casually in his belt. Now, though, his eyes were wide. She nodded.

"I thought everybody was killed there," he said.

"Evidently not," Cira said. "Actually, most of the task force got away. It was the fighter wings that took the worst of it. Of us there were only two survivors." She winced at the memory of Mila Salassin.

"Riv, I doubt she wants to talk about that right now," Saysheen said. "Leave is for healing. Now, why don't you go down to the kitchens and see if there's anything for your sister to eat."

Riv scowled, but left.

"It probably wasn't the smartest thing to do," Saysheen said. "Coming back here, I mean."

"I wasn't given a choice."

Saysheen frowned uncertainly. "I'm sorry about the reception you got. We've had recruiters up and down the major steads since this started. Marel decided the next would be met with less hospitality than the last."

"Where is everyone? I expected more than just four people."

"Kenan and Tryshel are in the ramshorn fields checking the soil saturation—we've had excessive rainfall this season—and Bricia is away at school."

"Hester? Luec? Stacy? Reg?"

Saysheen sat down on the edge of the bed and waved a hand dismissively. "Around."

"Who saw me coming?"

"Ezrem."

Saysheen looked up and for several seconds did not look away. In her quietly aging expression Cira saw how much had not changed. She saw how disappointed Saysheen was that the others had not come to greet their sister and cousin. Cira studied all that Saysheen let her see, on a face that was achingly close to that of Cira's mother. Maitha was a decade dead and Saysheen had done her best for five years to fill the role her sister had left. When Cira had left, Saysheen alone of the older members of the family had not condemned her. Saysheen had taken her to Ozma City, to the terminal to catch the shuttle up to the station for the first leg of her journey to her new life.

Saysheen closed her eyes.

"I'll try to be as little trouble as possible," Cira said.

"Don't be silly! You go ahead and be the biggest pain in the ass you can!" Saysheen caught her breath and stood. She drew Cira into a long hug and kissed her face. "I'm so glad to see you." She went to the door. "Get some rest. I'll see about that snack Riv was supposed to be getting. He probably got lost. We can talk later."

"Don't wait too long, Say. When I leave this time I doubt I'll be back again."

The door closed. Cira stretched out on the bed. She twirled her garrison cap around a finger and stared at the ceiling.

Toliman Station orbited the poles of Alpha Centauri Prime, perpendicular to the orbit of its bright orange companion star. The system possessed no planets, only broken debris kept jumbled by the conflicting gravitational tides the two stars created. The system was too close to Sol to leave ungarrisoned, but outposts tend to grow in time and Toliman Station became enormous: at eight hundred fifty septillion metric tons it was easily the largest station in the Pan Humana, outmassing even the older Mars-Earth Transit Station.

Alpha Centauri B was a brilliant orange spot over the horizon of Prime. Solward, the much smaller third star of the system, Proxima, was in flare time, and burned a hot hellish red. The wall length panorama in the restaurant compressed the views, showing both stars in the same field of vision and filling the dining room with the mixed lights of the three suns.

Tory shifted his gaze from the display to the restaurant entrance to his watch. Human waiters—an ostentatious sign of a truly elite restaurant—moved professionally between tables. He sighed impatiently. The great lie about journalism, he had discovered, was that he would get used to waiting on people. He was patient as long as he was engaged. Being made to wait bled patience off like an air leak in hard vacuum. He was on his third drink; he cautioned himself to have no more until he ate, but the glass was down by half and he had yet to order. His stomach felt slightly acid from the alcohol and breadsticks.

Then she came into the room. Tall, very slender, face almost gaunt, but made striking by long, thick eyebrows. Tory sat up straighter; so did several other people, he noted. She had presence. The maitre d' brought her to Tory's table. Tory stood and nodded politely.

"Co Albinez?"

"Co Shirabe. I've listened to your work." She gave him a pleasant smile and sat down. "Have you ordered yet?"

"No," he raised his glass. "Just killing time."

"Everything here is good, but I recommend the Cetian glover steak."

Tory cocked an eyebrow. "I had my eye on the Beef Wellington. It's been years since I was this close to Earth, I thought I'd indulge an old habit."

She lifted a finger and the waiter came over. She ordered for them both—Beef Wellington for two.

"Now, Co Shirabe," she said. "You indicated that you know one of my cases."

"If you're the one who has Lieutenant Alexan Cambion."

Her eyes narrowed. "You know him?"

"Knew him. I was with Task Force Valico when it entered Diphda System. He was helpful in orienting me and providing data feeds. I thought he'd died with everyone else, but..."

"Hmm." The waiter set a drink in front of her. "What would you like in return for any assistance I might render in this case? More 'datafeeds'?"

Tory hesitated. "May I ask first how you came to be handling his case? It was my understanding that the Armada intended to keep this strictly within the family, as it were."

"Your understanding is accurate except in one regard. The Armada often contracts out work, especially if it's not the usual."

"Lt. Cambion isn't the usual?"

"No." She sipped her drink.

"Your specialty is in cerebrotropic overlays."

"'Mindwipes' in the vulgate. Yes and no. My specialty is in memory. CTOs obviously enter into any study of memory."

"Is that what you think has happened to Lt. Cambion?"

"There's no question of that, which is why the Armada contracted me." She sat back and smiled. "You're very good, Co Shirabe."

"Excuse me?"

"We have no agreement yet on a working relationship and you're managing to extract information from me. Not much, but still..."

"My apologies, Co Albinez, I didn't—"

She waved a hand. "Don't. Apologies are irrelevant. It's your job. However, before we go any further, let's come to some terms."

Two hours later Tory stared at Alexan Cambion through a wall-sized transparency. The young lieutenant lay in a medunit in a small room. His physical wounds were healed, at least those that had been visible. According to the monitors he was in a CTO coma. As Tory understood it, Cambion was dreaming vividly, so vividly that he likely did not know it.

Tory wondered if he was, too. He looked over at Claye Albinez and wondered what her priorities were. Dinner was excellent, the conversation after their negotiation varied across many topics, and he found himself affected by her. The deal he had made seemed innocuous enough—she was to preview anything he wrote about whatever she told him and in return she promised to answer all his questions as honestly as possible as long as the answers violated no Armada security restrictions—but Claye seemed far from innocuous. She worked him as well as he had ever worked an interview and when she was through and invited him to come see Lt. Cambion, he was not sure what, if anything, he had revealed or surrendered that he might regret later.

She was by reputation one of the best, perhaps *the* best, in her field. The trouble, Tory admitted silently, was that he did not quite understand the limits of her field. She had written papers on gene therapy, viral induction restructuring, cerebrotropic overlay, cortical reorganization, and information theory. Tory comprehended how it all related, but it gave no name to Claye Albinez's expertise. Quite simply, he did not know what she *did*.

"Why the coma?" he asked.

Claye Albinez glanced up from a console. "I'm putting him through self analysis." Tory waited. She touched the interface plate briefly, then joined him at the transparency. "In this state, he has a direct connection with the sense-response generators. It's all feedback loops, just current passing through his brain, but it enables him to construct extremely vivid dreamscapes for himself. He doesn't know he's in a coma. He doesn't even know he's here, he was delivered in this condition."

"What's the point if he's been mindwiped?"

"Well, that's the misconception about CTO. Nothing's actually been wiped out, as in destroyed. Selective blocks reroute memory pathways. In response, the brain makes new ones. Or, in elaborate procedures, new ones are put in their place."

"Hence the Overlay part."

"Right."

"So Lt. Cambion has been given what? A *very* good overlay?"

"More than one."

"How's that?"

'I 've found traces of at least three overlays. Lt. Cambion is not, from everything I 've been able to discover, who he ever thought he was. "

"Can you tell how old these overlays are? "

'Not to the hour, but the first one was done when he was about twenty-two hundred days old—roughly six years Earth standard. The second was done when he was about fifty-seven, fifty-eight hundred days. That one was much deeper, of course, and the path map matches what his ID scan was when he entered the Armada. The last one is less than a hundred days old, so it probably happened when he was on Finders. The interesting thing about *that* one is that it 's incomplete. Existing pathways have been blocked, clearly in preparation for a new overlay, but although the synaptic anchors are in place, no new overlay has been introduced. "

"So they didn 't finish the job. "

"So it seems. "

'Does that mean you can recover what 's been blocked? "

'Possibly. Once blocks are put in place the brain begins to try to find ways around them. New pathways are created in the attempt, but usually what you get is new personality construction. No memories, but emotional and aesthetic artifacts that try to fill in for memory. Eventually daily experience provides enough memory for the new pathways to make something with, and that obscures what was blocked. It gets tricky to decide which pathways to trim away, which ones will open up old ones, and which ones will just do more damage. "

Tory digested all this while watching the monitors. He nodded. 'That 's the purpose of the CTO coma? "

"Exactly. We 'll let *him* do the digging. We keep him in there until we get a breakthrough. "

"Then what? "

'There 's a program that allows me to enter his dreamstate, a sort of neutral ground where we can talk. It 's right on the surface of his dreamstate and doesn 't intrude into the actual process. " She frowned thoughtfully, fold her arms. "Actually that 's not entirely true. I can go deeper. There 's a danger, though, of intruding into something important and destroying the validity of the process. Once in a while I have to in order to assess what 's going on. He *can* be hurt in this condition. "

"Hurt. You mean psychologically?"

"Oh, no. His entire brain-body system is engaged by this process. It has to be for it to seem real for him. That means his autonomic systems are engaged, too. He can die in there."

"Don't misunderstand me, Co Albinez, but can you—"

"I'm very good at this, Co Shirabe."

"All right. So how long before you know what happened to him? Or should I say *how* it happened to him?"

She smiled indulgently. "That would be more accurate." She shrugged. "That depends on him, how fast he can rebuild the old pathways, how much he has to cut through to get to them. And how willing he is to do it. He may just not want to know."

"I think I can understand that. And how long has the Armada given you?"

"The Armada doesn't set my schedule."

"They don't set mine, either, but they certainly can interfere with it."

"They haven't interfered with me yet. I did get the impression that sooner would be better than later. But as I said, this can't be rushed." She looked at Cambion silently for a time. "There's one other thing about him that's odd. Physically he's been overlaid."

"How do you mean?"

"A series of passive viruses has gone through him to rebuild his basic genetic structure."

"So…"

"He's probably not actually related to anyone else named Cambion. Traces of two incompatible genetic codes are visible, one overlaying the other. I've got a trace on the non-Cambion code, that was one of our breakthroughs. Cambion's partner, Houston Thayer, contributed the basic material; it's a good bet that he's Alex's actual father. Alex doesn't accept that, though. Thayer appears from time to time, but Alex rejects the relation. It's a sophisticated job, I'm impressed. Good enough to identify him as Alexan Cambion, son of Maxwell Cambion of Finders, Diphda System, at least to the Armada scans."

"This sounds like an awful lot of trouble for someone to go through just to slip an impostor who doesn't know he's an impostor into the Armada."

"Interesting problem, isn't it? I would very much like to know who did the actual reconstruction surgery, who tailored the virus, and why."

"If I ever find out, Co Albinez, you'll be one of the first I tell." Tory stared at the comatose man. "Would it be possible for me to enter that neutral state you mentioned and talk to him?"

Cira awoke before dawn and left the house. Bright blue-white lights pierced the dark from the corners of all the buildings. To the north she saw robot tenders in one of the fields, gliding between the rows. From the west came the heady memory-rich odor of newheat.

She headed east at a jog, down the narrow service road.

The steady impact, shoe to ground, pace perfectly metered, jarred through her body, shoved the breath from her nostrils in faint wisps in the cool air. She warmed to the run as the road gradually slanted uphill, toward a ridge now visible against a brightening sky.

Twenty minutes from the compound to the crest. Cira danced in place and grinned into the coming daybreak: five minutes faster than the last time she had run this trail, a few days before reporting for duty. She blew air from her mouth, hands on hips, and walked along the ridge.

Tau Ceti peeled aside the curtain of sky from the horizon, spilled buttery yellow across the rippled valleys all carved up into steads as far as she could see. Six narrow rivers cut through the landscape. Somewhere far south they joined the great Altheus River that spanned the breadth of the continent.

Cira squatted, rocking slightly on her toes, and stared out at the land. Home. Hectares of tall trees huddled in isolated islands, separated by cultivated fields. Sunlight picked out structures—transplanted manifestations of change, objects of humankind, small compared to the environment they were meant to dominate. Small and powerful. Home.

She spoke the word aloud, played with it in her mind, imposed it on what she saw, and waited for a stab of meaning. Nothing came. Home. A planet, a place. Born here, left here. Memories crowded around all the names, many even pleasant, like this one, running to the ridge before dawn to watch the sunrise. But—where others spoke of bonds and roots, ties of emotion to a particular world, city, house, Cira *only* saw a world, a city, a house. Too many years wanting to leave and the fierce, almost brutal rejection of her goals had deadened the connection. But she wondered now if it had ever meant to her what it obviously meant to her family.

Disappointed, she started back.

People moved about in the main house. She trotted around to the rear, spotted a team of temporaries heading out to the newheat fields.

The rear door let her into a short hallway between the kitchen and the family storeroom. The kitchen door stood open and as she walked by she saw Saysheen programming the chefs.

"Good morning."

Saysheen grinned brightly. "Well! I thought you'd sleep in." Then she nodded. "So, you went up to the ridge."

Cira stepped into the kitchen. "Need help?"

"No, I'm nearly done. You get your shower. Breakfast in fifteen minutes."

"Is, uh... "

"Marel always eats with the family. Go on. You'll be late."

Cira went back to her room. She dropped to the floor and pumped through thirty push-ups, then stripped and showered.

Clothes hung in the closet. Not hers, but they looked like they would fit. She hesitated. She had considered wearing Armada utilities or her dress uniforms all during her stay, but that reeked of vindictiveness. She grabbed a pair of baggy work pants and a loose pull-over shirt.

As she descended to the main level, the sound of voices grew. Family filled the kitchen.

"Cira!"

Mori and Saysheen spoke at once. Saysheen smiled indulgently at the young girl, then shrugged at Cira. Saysheen pointed at the long table where the others jostled for place, talked, argued, and now, one by one, looked around at Cira.

"Sit," Saysheen said. "Breakfast is nearly ready. I thought I'd maybe have to send it up to you this morning. We all hear how the Armada spoils its people, but I didn't think breakfast in bed was regulation."

Cira met each gaze evenly in the silence. Mori, grinning, noisily pulled a chair next to her, then waved Cira to take it.

Bacon, wheatcakes, seasoned rice, syrup, and coffee filled the table.

Marel looked around, frowning. "Did everyone forget how to speak?" he asked quietly.

Cira smiled and walked toward the chair beside Mori. She nodded at the faces that watched her. Riv, opposite Mori, looked sullen. Kenan and Tryshel beside him, twin round expressions of surprise, their thick shoulders hunched around wide plates filled with food. Hester—Cira noted, startled, that his hair was receding, making his already wide forehead deeper still above large, cautious eyes—stared at her as if at a piece of machinery that would not function. On Mori's side of the table Luec, Saysheen's oldest son, grinned suddenly. Cira patted his shoulder.

As Cira sat down, Stacy and Reg came in from outside, arguing about something, and stopped abruptly when they saw her.

"God, I heard, but—" Reg started.

"Heard true," Stacy said.

Reg and Stacy were adopted, orphans from Tabit who Ezrem, Marel's brother, had brought back with him when he came to Homestead to give up merchanting and settle down.

Ezrem pushed in behind the two and looked sharply at Cira.

"Shit," he said. He gave Reg and Stacy and gentle push. "Sit, eat. Time to stare during." He took a chair at the end of the table, beside Hester. "You got arrogance, Cira, I give you that."

Cira glanced at Marel, caught a brief expression of dismay before he looked down at his plate.

Reg and Stacy took seats on Cira's right, and Saysheen set more food on the table, then took her own chair at the opposite end from Marel.

Cira spooned rice onto her plate. Kenan poured her a cup of coffee.

"Ramshorn's got a blight," Ezrem said. "Might have to burn it all."

Marel started. "I thought we were rid of that."

"So did I. Looks like we got it still. Must be in the soil. Last year's treatment didn't work."

"All right. I ll go out there with you after breakfast. Anything else?"

"Irrigation pump in section nine isn't right,"Tryshel said. "Down to thirty percent."

"Sediment?" Marel asked.

Tryshel shrugged. "Haven't had a chance to look. Last week, it was at eighty-two percent."

"Hm."

"Why don't you take Cira,"Saysheen said, "let her have a look?"

Tryshel looked at Saysheen, startled, then glanced at Marel. Marel looked uncomfortable but said nothing. Tryshel nodded.

"Are we going to town today, Saysheen?"Mori asked. "I thought we'd take Cira."

"Not today. We have to go over the market indexes, remember?"

"Oh," Mori said glumly.

"Maybe tomorrow,"Saysheen said. "And Riv can come with us."

Riv scowled and shook his head. "I have things to do."

Cira ate quietly, listening to the conversations. In a few minutes Cira felt invisible, absent. They talked about necessary matters concerning the stead. Business, a briefing, assignments sorted and handed out. Then, as plates were emptied, they filed out of the kitchen, on to their chores. Marel finished his coffee standing, waiting on Ezrem, who patted the air with one hand and sopped up syrup with a biscuit in his other hand.

"Ready?"Tryshel asked suddenly, standing.

Cira nodded.

They followed their own long shadows to the garage. Tryshel took out an agrav sled. Cira strapped into one of the two seats just behind the pilot's chair and Tryshel shot off south.

Wind roared in Cira's ears. So close to the ground, tall crops on either side blurred by speed, her stomach tingled.

Five kilometers south of the compound, Tryshel turned west, crossed a low ridge, and Cira looked down a long sloping wedge of land broken at the base by a thin snaking stream. Tryshel turned to follow the stream, northwest, through a cleft in a rocky hillock. The stream fed into a small lake. On the opposite shore stood the pumping station. Tryshel parked the sled in the shade of a caril tree.

The station was stained green and yellow with age and molds.

"I checked the intakes," Tryshel said. "No clog, so it has to be internal."

Cira opened the door and peered in. One bare light flickered reluctantly over the machinery within.

"Did you bring lamps?" she asked.

Tryshel nodded and went back to the sled.

They worked almost wordlessly. Cira ran the diagnostic program contained in the station maintenance monitor, but the only thing it indicated was a temperature malfunction. Something was getting too hot.

By midmorning she had pulled apart the pump assembly.

"Bearings," she announced, wiping grease from her hands.

"Damn," Tryshel said. "Have to order a set. Could take a month."

"Why?"

He shook his head. "Don't know. Doesn't make sense. It's not that parts are unavailable, it's that they won't release them till Armada approval comes through. In case *they* need the part, you understand, and our order might interfere."

Cira frowned. She studied the bearings for a few minutes. "I can rebuild these. Let's pull them and take them back."

"You're sure?"

"Absolutely."

Tryshel and Cira wrestled the parts out. Old bolts, seals that did not yield, metal and plastic and composite that had grown together almost organically over the decades resisted them at every step. They had to trick it as much as bully it, improvising constantly just to get it apart. Cira pulled and grunted, sweating in the close, uncooled confines of the station, in concert with her stepbrother in a wordless performance. They got the faulty bearings onto the sled just after noontime. Cira dropped to the ground, sweat-soaked, every muscle tight, the blood throbbing in her temples. Tryshel sat down on the edge of the sled and stripped off his shirt to wipe his face and under his arms.

"I hope you weren't just boasting," he said.

Cira laughed dryly. "If I was, believe me I'd learn how to fix them after all that."

Tryshel handed her a canteen.

"It's good to see you," he said.

She took a long drink. "Thanks. It's good to see you, too."

"I didn't think you'd come back."

"Neither did I." She swallowed more water and handed the canteen back. "What's everyone doing? Did anyone leave?"

"Bricia left. She's in university. She never lets us know, she just arrives for a ten-day or a season, then leaves just as abruptly. Hester left for a while. Faitha turned into a real ass after you left and Hester couldn't stand him. I thought Ezrem would, too."

"You mean Faitha improved?"

"Some." He shrugged. "The stead means everything to him. This war brought him back to it."

"How do you mean?"

"We get told things about it. You don't know what's true, what's propaganda. You stick with what you know just to keep balance. I guess the idea that you were out there, in it somewhere—he didn't want to think about that, so he thought about this place."

"So it brought him back to the way he was?"

"No. But he's not an ass anymore." He grinned.

"Do you ever think about leaving?"

"What, the stead?"

"Homestead."

"Like you?"

"Well, maybe not joining the Armada…"

"I thought about it once. I got over it."

"Why?"

"I could ask why you didn't."

Cira shrugged. "I just didn't."

"Well. I just did."

Cira swung playfully, slapped his arm. He laughed.

"Let's get this thing back," he said, standing. "I want to go out and check the other stations, see if we can reroute some of the flow to compensate."

Cira pushed to her feet. "It's not going to take me that long to fix this. Assuming the shop is as good as I left it."

The machineshop was much as Cira remembered, with a couple of new items. Tryshel moved the bearings onto a bench, slapped Cira's shoulder.

"You could start on them tomorrow if you like," he said.

"Thanks. I want to check over the tools."

She stripped off her damp shirt and wiped her face, then went to a locker in the corner. An old faded set of once-white utilities hung there. Cira smiled and took them down. She stepped out of her pants and into the soft, familiar work clothes.

She keyed for the shop log and went down the list of tools available. She remembered creating this manifest and entering most of the listings. It pleased her that nothing was different, that the lists and the codes and the commands were all mostly as she had left them. Someone had taken care to maintain the shop and make a few upgrades. She selected the tools and the stock she wanted, then, without consciously deciding to, started to work on the bearings.

The repair was simple, but time-consuming and laborious. Cira worked methodically, falling into pace with the necessities of the task. Dismantling, grinding, shaping new parts, resurfacing, replacing worn components. The machinery was old, perhaps had never been replaced since the station was built. Cira tore it down and made it new, following the trail of wear and collapse. She tightened down the carapace on the outside, dropped the wrench on the bench, and stepped back. Done. She blinked, mildly surprised. With a quiet laugh she ran one final series of tests and confirmed the success of all her work.

She stripped off the utilities, now smeared and grimy, and tossed them into the cleaner beside the locker. Her own clothes were dry, though still dirty, but she needed a shower. She pulled on her pants, draped the shirt over her shoulders, and stepped outside.

Both moons shone down from directly overhead. Cira stared at them, confused. She looked at the house—lights filled the ground floor—and thought, no one came to get me...? Pleasure mingled with vague disappointment. Cira shrugged impatiently, unwilling to let anything blunt her good feelings, and strode to the back door.

Laughter came from the great room. She stood in the hallway between kitchen and storeroom and listened. The laughter made her homesick.

She went quietly up to her room.

The door opened and two people came into the room. Alex smiled at the woman, Dr. Albinez. She had brought a man with her this time and Alex had the immediate impression that they had met before. He was slightly shorter than Dr. Albinez and his short hair was white.

"How are you today, Alex?" Dr. Albinez asked. She bent over his monitors, studied them for a moment, then smiled at him. "I've brought a visitor. Do you recognize him?"

"I—he's familiar…"

"Tory Shirabe, Alex," the man said. "Remember?"

"Tory Shirabe…" He toyed with the name in his head. Yes, he did know it, but the memory was vague.

"Do you remember Palada?"

Alex blinked at Tory Shirabe. "Palada…" That name—if it was a name—was also familiar, but it caused uneasiness. "What do you want?"

"Co Shirabe wants to ask you some questions, Alex," Dr. Albinez said. "About before."

Alex nodded.

"Do you remember the battle, Alex?" Tory Shirabe asked.

"No. Dr. Albinez has mentioned that, but I don't remember."

"Do you remember Finders?"

"Yes, I was born there."

"To whom?"

"You mean my parents? Maxwell and Patricia Cambion."

"Did you spend a lot of time with them? With your parents?"

"No, not really. Patricia died when I was very young, so I don't remember her at all. I was away at school a lot. Maxwell runs the largest industrial complex in the system. Maybe in the Distals."

"The Thayer-Cambion Corporation, right?"

"Yes."

"Who was Thayer?"

"Houston Thayer, Maxwell's partner. That was before I was born. I don't remember Houston Thayer. Maxwell was my father."

"Of course. Did you always know you were going to enter the Armada?"

"It was something Maxwell and I talked about a lot, ever since I can remember. He said he'd be proud of me if—" He looked up at Dr. Albinez, suddenly very depressed. It was as if a chemical had been injected at that moment to change his entire mood. In a few seconds it changed again, into bitterness, then self-loathing. He wanted her to see this, to notice his torment, so she could take it away. It occurred and recurred, round and around, usually after one of his dreams. She narrowed her eyes at him and his mood lifted slightly. She *had* noticed. "I wanted him to be proud. He—"

"What's wrong?" Tory Shirabe asked.

Dr. Albinez studied the monitors. "Breakthrough, maybe. Alex, why isn't Maxwell proud of you?"

No, he thought, don't ask that, you're supposed to help me, make me feel better, if you ask that I have to face—

"Because I went home," he said, his voice cracking. He felt his face pulling into a pained mask, tears at hand. "Because I didn't do what he wanted me to do."

"What did he want you to do?"

"He wanted me to be important."

"Aren't you?"

He shook his head, afraid to speak further.

"Why aren't you important, Alex?" Tory Shirabe asked.

Pain lanced through his skull from the crown of his head downward. Don't ask, he thought, shaking his head slowly so his neck would not cramp.

"Because he failed."

Alex jerked up in bed and looked at the door. Maxwell stood there, staring at him, his face as expressionless as ever, but his eyes full of anger. Tory and Dr. Albinez stepped aside.

"What's this?" Tory asked.

"I—"

"He," Maxwell said, pointing at Alex, "was supposed to be in fleet command, an attaché, someone useful. *He*," the finger stabbed the air again, "came back in a fighter craft and got shot down just like all the rest. Fodder. Worthless."

Alex chewed his lip till he tasted blood.

"Why torment him now?" From behind Maxwell a tall creature, soft-furred with large, glistening eyes, stepped into the room. Both Shirabe and Dr. Albinez drew back.

Maxwell turned on the seti. "He's my creation, I'll do what I want."

"But he's his own person," the seti—a Ranonan, Alex remembered—insisted.

"Never," Maxwell said.

"He *is*," the Ranonan pressed. "We made sure of it. While you tried to shape him for yourself, we introduced variables. We wanted to see who he would become on his own."

Maxwell stared at the seti, his fingers clenching and unclenching. "You ruined everything I wanted to do."

"You wanted to build a goal-directed consciousness. We wished to see that succeed."

"Then why did you meddle?"

"It was more interesting if he chose his own goals."

"He's *mine!*"

Alex closed his eyes. He heard a scream, then realized it was his own. When he opened his eyes the room was empty. His breathing slowed and he wiped his face. His hand came away wet, but the moisture evaporated quickly.

This is all a dream, he thought, and instantly knew it was true.

Still, the view from his window was pleasant.

Chapter Eight

The digger churned in the darkness beyond the edge of the flood-lights. Nicolan squatted, listening to the grinding, the sporadic surges as soft pockets in the earth surprised the motors, and the heavy/soft impact of ground-up dirt as it struck the floor of the tunnel, like rain on canvas. Suddenly a shaft of light, broken by falling soil, speared down onto the insectoid shape of the digger, and a voice in his earpiece said, "We're through, boss."

Nicolan straightened to his full height, then hunched his shoulders unconsciously even though the tunnel was large enough for the moles and diggers. His knees popped and his thighs ached. He wanted to get back into space and every planetside inconvenience reminded him.

Two people jogged toward him from the worksite. Behind them the shaft of light widened as the hole was enlarged.

"Enough, Kee," Nicolan said, "keep it minimal. We need to check outside first."

"Right, boss." The digger wound down. The cascade of dirt slowed till only a few chunks spattered down. A cool, heavy quiet filled the tunnel.

Nicolan tapped the fabric along his jaw, switching comm channels. "Fio, send up the probes."

A woman jogged by him dragging a small cart. She stopped near the digger, which now stood motionless in the pool of light. She bent over the cart and worked within, then lifted a small sphere out and raised it toward the opening. The sphere shot upward. She repeated the process four times, then knelt beside the cart and peered into it.

Nicolan drew a deep breath and slowly paced the width of the tunnel. He looked back the way they had come, at the long straight pipeline cut from the Thayer Smelter to here, almost five hundred kilometers east of the Hobic Mountains. Nicolan had been astonished to find ten working electron drills stored at the old works.

Without them it would have taken months to dig this much tunnel. Still, compared to the older tunnels that laced through the Hobics north of them, this was a crude wound under the skin of the world, rough-walled and dank. Probably dangerous, too, he reflected, but they would have to find time later to brace the weak points, seal the cracks, and make it safe and livable.

"All clear," Fio's voice interrupted his thoughts.

"Great," he said and tapped his jaw again, expanding the channel. "All right, we've got some time. I want the canopy in place before we open the hole to full size. Joller, send word back down the line that we're through and to start expanding the two new bases. I want to be prepared to abandon the smelter works in two days at most. Miriel, I want your team ready to move out in one hour, as soon as the canopy is deployed." He clapped his hands dramatically, the sound sharp and resonant. "Everybody has a job, let's do it."

The tableau that had formed while the digger worked dissolved. Equipment needed shuffling. Six coes hurried forward with a heavy bundle between them. The snap and scraping of field gear, weapons, and groups reforming echoed through the hollowness. Comm babble crowded his earpiece as everyone coordinated. Nicolan smiled and tapped his comm patch; the chatter died out and he returned to his mole.

The polycom link flickered intermittently. The signal was jumbled to keep the possibility of traces to a minimum, but it was annoying to have to wait for the entire message to load before accessing it. Soon, he told himself, soon we'll have cable laid, direct conduit, shielded and secured. And proper plumbing, too, he added wryly. He sat before the unit, fingers laced over his belly, and waited for the ready light. Finally the green dot winked on and Nicolan punched up his access to the backlog of data from his observers.

He sat motionless as the reports scrolled up the screen. The Armada was sitting in the spaceport proper at Emorick and holding half a dozen partisan groups at bay, occasionally striking out unpredictably at one or another section of the city. The partisans themselves fought each other as often as they fought the Armada. No estimate on casualties, but three-fifths of the city was battle scarred, entire neighborhoods, commercial sectors, and public places reduced to ruin by the incessant skirmishing. The Armada claimed to be shipping refugees offworld, twenty shuttles a day, but Nicolan's observers claimed only one or two shuttles came or went daily and they had found no evidence that refugees were loaded onto any of them. It was unclear if the tram tunnel from Crag Nook to Emorick had been reopened. The explosion that had collapsed it had left an enormous crater and the aftershocks had weakened the tunnel twenty kilometers in either direction. That was seventeen days ago and since then sabotage of Armada units and installations had been a daily problem in Crag Nook. Martial law remained in force there, but someone, Nicolan did not know who, was running a very effective guerilla operation. The garrison at Orchard Crest had been attacked three times and the last one had taken out the Armada commander. Roving bands—Nicolan hesitated to ennoble them by calling them partisans, they were mostly thieves and sociopaths taking advantage of the anarchy—harassed travelers on the Tameurla Road, requiring regular Armada patrols. One unconfirmed report claimed that the north coast town of Terralaq had been abandoned entirely. The Armada had garrisoned it twice since the occupation and both times had suffered high casualties from snipers and random assaults on underdefended areas. Still no word from Downer's Cove, except that the Armada had sent in another company of marines. With all the scattered guerilla activity, the Armada's time and attention were thoroughly occupied. As a result, Nicolan's people had built this tunnel unmolested.

The benefit was nearly negated by the drawbacks. None of these attacks were coordinated; there simply existed no central command around which the disparate partisans might cohere, so all the flailing and vehemence accomplished little strategically. In fact, it cost too much. The Armada took too many prisoners, who were then shipped...somewhere. The net effect was little more than annoyance for the Armada and a steady diminution of Finders' resources. There was nothing yet the Founders could do to push them out of the system, and until that was done the Armada controlled Diphda, Finders, the future.

Nicolan switched off the terminal, leaned back, and rubbed his eyes. His hands still itched a little, but the new skin was beginning to lose its pink and develop calluses.

"Hey, boss."

Kee leaned through the hatch, grinning.

"Yes?"

"The canopy's open and functioning. Want to see?"

Nicolan followed Kee to the hole. The digger hulked now under a gauzy light. Scaffolding mounted to the lip. Nicolan climbed up into the open air.

The canopy covered the hole and the area around it to a diameter of two-hundred-fifty meters, about seven meters off the ground. A hundred meters out it began to curve down till it met the ground, forming a low dome. From the outside it looked like the terrain around it; within, it was about seventy percent transparent. Unless sensors looked very closely and directly at it, the canopy provided effective cover. Nicolan doubted they would receive much scrutiny: the hole opened four hundred meters from the Vohec *qonteth*.

He turned to Kee, nodding. "I want this egress finished. We need to be able to get our equipment in and out quickly, so a lift needs to be installed."

"Already tearing one out of Thayer," Kee said.

"Good..." They had gone over this several times already, but it felt right to do it again now that they were on site. Besides, new ideas cropped up with repetition. "I want a cap, too, something to slide in and out, just in case."

"Tricky. As long as we got the time..."

"Sure." Nicolan started walking in the direction of the *qonteth*. He glanced at Kee. "Want to take a look?"

Kee nodded, grinning, and fell into step alongside Nicolan.

Miriel's team ranged out along the perimeter where the canopy peeled back like a big tent flap. Four groups of three people each worked between the perimeter and the Vohec site installing long-range field sensors. The equipment was very sophisticated and sensitive, adapted from mining survey scanners, capable of defining micro fractures in solid rock to a thickness of ten kilometers and generating partial extrapolations on strength, shock effects, and ancillary reactions around a bore hole.

The *qonteth* rose out of the ground to the east, an enormous pedestal upon which grew a low dome, like a blister, that caught the light dully in its coppery surface.

"So just what is it?" Kee asked softly.

"Why are you whispering?" Nicolan smiled at Kee's startled expression, then shrugged. "I don't know. Believe me, I've asked. The only answer I ever got, other than it's important to the Vohec, is that it's a problem."

"A problem? For who?"

Nicolan remembered the conversation with Lovander Casm, and the impression of reluctance on the Vohec's part to discuss the *qonteth*, compounded by a reluctance to disappoint Nicolan. The interchange had been frustrating. He had sensed an opportunity slipping like mud through his fingers. Every turn the discussion took led into apparently impossible language barriers, conceptual irresolution, and simple misunderstanding. After a few hours, both gave up, making polite excuses and half-promises to try again later. But on this point Nicolan's interpretations had been clearer. The *qonteth* represented a problem in every possible use of the word and many more that the equivalent Vohec word—*teth*—encompassed. Not a problem *for* anyone, at least not only that.

Nicolan said, "I don't know. They didn't say."

"Hm. Setis are strange."

Nicolan looked up at the sky. Bright melon-orange clouds streaked overhead. He sighed and nodded. "So are we."

Kee looked at him curiously, then back at the *qonteth*. "So do we go have a look inside?"

"No. I don't want anybody entering it."

"Then..."

"We just enter and leave nearby, I don't intend to use the *qonteth* for anything else."

Kee grunted. "I wonder if the Armada will understand that."

Nicolan smiled. "Probably not."

Bright flashes silhouetted the northern sections of Emorick. Venner sat cross-legged beneath the metal sheet he had pulled over the ruins of two close-set walls. The small space had once housed a hygienic cubicle, but that was gone along with the rest of the building. Even much of the rubble was missing, hauled off by locals to reinforce other parts of the city, or pulverized in another sweep by Armada urban pacifiers. That two walls still stood amazed Venner.

Venner scraped the sides of the can with his spoon, mining the last smears of field rations. He licked the protein rich goo from the bowl of the spoon and flicked the empty container away. He lifted his canteen and took a mouthful of water, held it, and slipped the spoon in between his lips. He swished the water around, swallowed, then wiped the spoon dry and returned it to its sheath in his mess kit. The night blazed again. He drank deeply.

The sound took almost three seconds to reach him. When it came it was a low thrum he felt at the base of his spine and in his belly. A very heavy pounding. Ten kilometers away, he mused, a little less. Venner almost pitied whoever was beneath it.

A small beep sounded in his left ear. He glanced down at the device to his right, a notebook displaying a grid of the surrounding area. A white dot of light indicated the position of the warning signal just tripped. He nodded slightly to himself. They were right on time. He lifted the e.p. rifle into his lap and watched the darkness off to the right, about two o'clock.

He saw them finally, silhouetted briefly in a horizon-wide flash, four people spaced a couple meters apart from each other, picking their way carefully over the rubble. Venner checked the notebook again; no other alarms showed. He switched it off and slid it quietly into its pouch on his backpack, then gently shifted the rifle in their direction.

Three of the four stopped about fifteen meters out while one came forward.

"Stop," Venner said quietly.

"Co Venner?"

Female, Venner noted. "You're from Liss?"

"My name is—"

"I don't care what your name is. Are you from Jonner Liss?"

Venner listened carefully to the small shiftings in the darkness: she tightened her grip on her weapon, took a step back, another forward, relaxed slowly. He anticipated each motion and felt vaguely pleased as each occurred. She wrestled with the insult and finally decided not to challenge him.

"Yes," she said.

He waited a long time before answering, until she took another step forward.

"I'm Hil Venner." He stood. "Take me to Liss." She remained motionless now, silent. Venner smiled. "Please," he added. "This way."

Half a kilometer to the northeast buildings still stood. Pale light panels tacked to broken walls gave a bleak lambency to the tattered structures. Nothing was straight, all the vertical planes leaned at angles to each other. Windows and doorways opened into unyielding black.

His escort ranged out around him, covering four points and moving silently. Venner recalled his last visit to Liss and how impressed he had been with the secessionist's troops. The constant skirmishing with Armada marines had made them even better.

He nearly missed the first guard post. The emplacement seemed no more than a tighter pile of wreckage in an intersection. Venner almost started when he noticed the people within, long barrels of heavy e.p. guns protruding over the dark stone. Immediately after, he saw the braces on the lower walls of the buildings, sheets of metal filling in the windows, a less shattered look to the street. Then more people, in small groups, all armed, all dressed in dirty grey.

Liss's headquarters were in the basement of a hostelry that lacked its top three or four floors. Venner was led into the barely illuminated stairwell and down a long passageway to a thick drape. His guide—he assumed the female—pushed aside the fabric, letting thick buttery light blind Venner for a few moments.

"Come in, Co Venner, we're all waiting for you. Leave your rifle, please. Rasal, take Co Venner's rifle."

Venner hesitated, then handed his rifle to the woman. He stepped into the room.

A big table dominated the center of the room, propped on large polycrete blocks. A grid of Emorick lay over the surface, certain buildings marked with bricks or pieces of wood or empty cans or discarded machine parts. No one paid any attention to it. At least five tight clusters of people carried on conversations in different parts of the basement while Jonner Liss sat on the edge of an old metal desk reading from a handpad, a field polycom beside him. Other equipment was stacked against the walls, interspersed with collections of arms. Far in the back, cots lined the wall, some occupied, one being used for something other than sleeping. No one paid attention to that, either.

Jonner Liss was a skinny man with large, perpetually sad green eyes. He wore black utilities and an oversized blue jacket. His eyes jerked back and forth as he read. When he finished he tossed the handpad on the desk and looked sharply at Venner.

"Did you know Govanchi is dead?" he asked.

Venner nodded, though in fact he had not known.

"The Armada tried to make a deal with him," Liss continued. "Idiot refused, they killed him before he left the meeting. They invited me to the same meeting. I didn't go."

"Would you have made a deal?"

"Of course, if they'd been sincere. Killing Govanchi doesn't inspire confidence in their sincerity."

"I thought you didn't like Govanchi."

"I didn't, but I respected him. If he gave you a promise he kept it. If he could." He narrowed his eyes at Venner. "So what can I do for you, spy?"

"It seems I'm currently unemployed."

Liss's laugh was a short loud bark. "I don't doubt it! Blowing up a tramload of Armada supplies and the Emorick tunnel at the same time could get anyone dismissed!"

"You knew that was me?"

"I do now." He laughed again. "You want a job? Why come to me?"

"I thought..."

"I'm not hiring. Did you know Task Commander Palada has been recalled?"

Venner's eyebrows went up.

"You *didn't!* I'm surprised, Venner—you, I'd have thought, would keep track of such things."

"I've been on the road," Venner said, irritated. "What do you mean Palada's been recalled? What for?"

"Two days ago, to answer charges of negligence. Armada command wants to know how he managed to lose all his fighters in less than ten minutes."

"Which leaves Micheson. He's a fool."

"How so?"

"Palada would never have killed Uri Govanchi. Micheson would. It's his special brand of myopia."

Liss crossed his arms and studied Venner. "You mean, if he can't come to terms with a problem he simply kills the source."

"Something like that."

Liss shrugged. "It has the charm of economy, you must admit."

"Stupidity has no charm. Govanchi was a secessionist to the core, he had followers. Now he's a martyr. That will make it even more difficult for anyone to deal with the Armada in future."

"Hmm." Liss hopped from the desk and walked around behind it. "I thought you had a working relationship with Cambion." He cast about amid papers on the desk.

Venner was mildly surprised that Liss knew about that, but after a moment's reflection decided that it was not so odd. Liss was well connected. Venner had suspected that Maxwell Cambion, probably through his security specialist Rike, had contacts with Liss. Perhaps even with Govanchi, certainly with several of the smaller partisan leaders. Venner had been a different sort of tool for Maxwell.

"Haven't *you* heard," Venner said slowly, "Maxwell Cambion's dead?"

Liss hesitated in his search.

Venner smiled. "You didn't know, did you?"

"The reports have never been confirmed."

"A perfectly political answer, phrased with military confidence. True, but no word at all has come out of Downer's Cove except that the shooting stopped eight days ago. I think we all would have known if Maxwell Cambion had survived."

Liss straightened and looked wistful. "It must've been a hell of a fight." He shook his head, looked at Venner. "So you don't know if you have a future here."

"I know I'm at liberty to make my own associations."

Liss stared at the table with the city grid. Venner watched him work the possibilities, weigh the alternatives, the risks, and enjoyed the sensation of immanence. The negotiations were over now; Venner wondered if anyone else in the room who had been listening understood that—or even that negotiations had been taking place. Venner glanced around. Everyone seemed occupied, unaware of Liss or Venner. Venner sensed, though, that he and Liss were the center of attention.

He surveyed the room again, feeling that he had missed something. An old man sat cross-legged with two others, handing a handpad back and forth and discussing it in low, tense voices. His white hair was close-cropped now, but Venner pictured him with a full fluffy head and then knew how Liss had known of his association with Cambion.

Liss sighed deeply. "I need to know what other groups I can depend on. The problem is," he jabbed a finger toward the table, "the damn Armada is squatting on the port, encased in their defenses, arbitrarily hammering sections of Emorick, and I don't have the resources to get them out."

"Those kind of resources aren't on Finders."

"Depends on how they're deployed. Strength can be used for negotiation as well as assault."

"You'd negotiate?"

"Only an idiot would think we could throw them out."

Venner nodded. "So what are you asking me to do? Contact as many independent groups as I can and see if they'd be willing to form an alliance under your command?"

"Perhaps be a little persuasive while you're at it." Liss grinned. "And you can confirm Maxwell Cambion's alleged death while you're at it. In fact, I'd appreciate it if you'd make certain he's dead."

"Oh?"

"At this stage Cambion could only complicate the situation."

"Meaning you want complete control."

"Meaning without it the Armada might find it expedient to simply eradicate everyone on Finders."

"I'll need letters of authority, provisions, a vehicle. I lost mine. Had to leave it behind in Crag Nook."

"Tomorrow night you'll have everything you need. Tonight you can sleep in a clean room. Rasal, take Co Venner to a room, see he has food and is not disturbed. Oh, and give him his rifle back."

Venner stood. "Thank you, Co Liss."

Liss nodded absently, already reading another handpad.

Venner glanced at the old man again then followed Rasal from the basement, pleased with himself. As long as Liss kept his word, Venner would have everything he wanted.

Rasal led him a short way down the street to another broken building and down into another basement. This one, though, had been rebuilt below ground into a series of small private rooms, much like the cabins on a liner. Venner thought about traveling and for a moment felt isolated and burdened, cut off from everything important to him.

"I'll come back in the morning," Rasal said, pushing open a door. She leaned into the room and switched on a light. When she looked at him half her face was lit in wan yellow light, the other half gone in shadow. "Are you hungry?"

"No."

"Would you like company?"

He started, surprised, then frowned. "No."

She shrugged. "Suit yourself."

"I have a question. Do you have a staff med? I...have a problem I'd like looked at."

"You can go to the infirmary like the rest of us—"

"I think not. Really, I'd rather see the best, if you don't mind."

Rasal regarded him mutely for several seconds, then shrugged again. "I'll see if he's got time."

He watched her walk back up the corridor, into the darkness, then listened till the sound of her boots dwindled to nothing. He stepped into the room.

A mattress lay on the floor, blankets rolled up at the bottom. A folding chair, a box with a pitcher of water and a glass on it, and a field toilet. A single light panel was bolted to the ceiling, above the small sink to the left of the door. Venner closed the door and set his rifle against the wall beside the mattress.

He stripped off his overcoat, loosened his tunic collar, and unstrapped his holster. Carefully, he hung the belt on the chair with the butt of his pistol clearly visible from the door. He fished out his other handgun from his overcoat and lay it beside him on the mattress. Legs folded, back against the wall, he waited, listening to the sounds of the building.

Venner had never understood how the chill in brick and stone made noises clearer, brought them closer. The barrack transmitted a faint cacophony to all its parts, breathing, murmuring, the delicate drip of water, a brief laugh quickly hushed. With eyes closed it was like being at a party where he could hear everything but conversation.

Steps approached. He opened his eyes and watched his door. The pistol was a small pressure under his thigh. The steps stopped and knuckles rapped at the door.

"Come in."

The old man stepped into the suddenly cramped room. He looked grumpy, displeased to be here, but he carried a small medkit in his left hand.

"So what's *so* wrong that you've got to have the chief med—"

"Close the door, Michen, and sit down. We should talk."

The old man—Michen—froze in place, eyes narrowed and fixed on Venner. Venner smiled, granting Michen a modicum of respect for not showing immediate fear. Instead he was appraising Venner.

"Please," Venner added.

Michen pulled the door to and set his kit on the sink.

"Do I know you?"

"We both had the same employer for a time."

"Couldn't imagine who you might mean."

"Maxwell."

"Hmm." After a moment, he shrugged. "All right, so what?"

"I wanted to talk to you about some things that never quite made sense while I worked for him. Please, sit down, Michen."

"I think not."

"Why?"

"Can't see as I have anything to say about those days that would interest you. Co Venner was it? You're a double agent."

"I have a little more talent than that." He smiled but Michen remained stony. "I'd like to talk to you about Alexan."

Michen shook his head slowly. "I have nothing to say about that."

"Oh, come on, Michen! The world's falling apart! What use are secrets between former coes?"

Michen straightened and picked up his medkit.

"Where are you going?" Venner asked.

"You don't need me. I have other things to do."

Venner lifted his pistol. "Don't. I really have nothing to lose if I shoot you."

Michen looked at him steadily. "Neither do I." He reached for the door.

Venner shot to his feet and jammed the barrel into Michen's ribs. The old man winced, backed up a step, and Venner wrapped his fingers around his throat. The flesh was thick. Michen stumbled backward and Venner steered him against the wall and down onto the mattress. He snatched the medkit out of Michen's hand and stepped back.

"I think we have a lot to talk about," Venner said.

Merrick drifted around the station in a wide orbit, waiting for the port authority clearance and the guide beacon to bring him to a berth. The station appeared as if in the intermediate stages of construction. Whole sections gaped open to vacuum, structural beams and struts tracing out the skeleton shape of what would be there. Six months ago, the last time he had visited Etacti, the station had been complete, fully operational. He came around the planetward side; the holes were ragged and burnt.

Etacti was an oversized world with almost no atmosphere, good for little more than the minerals mined from its crust. For all that, it was an easier environment than Finders. People lived on it—or in it, as the case may be, cities carved deep into the surface, warrens as extensive as those on Mars a hundred light years away. Eta Ceti burned across it, a K3 calcium-rich star attended by its lone solid planet and three gas giants that were also elementally generous and heavily mined.

It was the station that made Etacti important. Plans had been to construct a shipyard here, far from the control of Istanbul, the Forum, and the Primary Vested of the Pan Humana. For almost fifty years, since the settlement was established, an agonizing game had played out between Etacti and the Pan over needed technologies, machinery, licenses, expertise; a carrot-and-stick travesty that kept Etacti constantly short of its goal and the station stalled, only the first phase complete.

"*Solo*, you are cleared for docking," the station announced. "Your beacon is open."

"Thank you much, Etacti Transit," Merrick said and checked the docking pilot. A blue light was on now, indicating the link to the station. He initiated the docking sequence and leaned back in his couch.

Solo followed the beacon into a cradle which retracted down a tube. Merrick watched the service lights wink on as the station maintenance and comm umbilicals connected up. When the all secured light came on, he pushed out of the couch and headed for the lock.

He descended to the bay deck on a cargo lift, holding onto the naked framework casually. Three people waited before the arched exit. They looked military, though none wore a uniform. The way they stood, their posture and evident readiness, said more than a uniform could. The cavernous bay echoed the faint grinding of the machinery, the dull clunk as the lift touched down, and the small ticks of his boots.

One of the three stood a pace in advance of the other two. She was shorter than Merrick, but seemed to look him straight on. Her hair was light brown and close-cropped, a thick queue flowing from her crown to the base of her neck. Her deepset eyes seemed colorless in the flat functional light of the bay. The other two were young men—boys, really, barely out of adolescence. Both wore sidearms in plain sight.

"ID," the woman said, extending her right hand.

Merrick handed over his chits. She slid them into a handreader and checked them quickly, then pocketed the reader and the chits.

"Am I being arrested?" Merrick asked.

"Detained. Come with me, Co Merrick."

"May I ask—"

"No. Please come with me." She turned and gestured toward the exit. The boys stepped apart.

Merrick shrugged and smiled.

Beyond the bay entrance they boarded a shunt. The boys sat front and back and stared at him while the woman pulled out her own sidearm and checked it over. After a five minute ride the car let them out in a wide circuit. The light was low and gloomy and they were the only people walking down the broad way.

Across from the shunt station a low archway opened into a densely-equipped communications center. People talked in hushed voices. The trio led Merrick through the maze of consoles to the back, then through a connecting door into a smaller office.

Six people stood or sat around a large tactical display. They all looked at Merrick as he came in. The officer handed his ID chits over to a man who stood at the edge of the display.

He was tall and heavy. He nodded and smiled, then looked at Merrick. Merrick smiled back.

"Simon."

"Sean. Welcome to Etacti. You're in solid shit, my friend."

"As bad as that?"

Simon motioned for him to come closer. Merrick approached the broad table. Projected down onto the surface was a display of the Distal Front. Denebola marked the boundary—the Secant, as it was called—with the Pan Humana. Then came Diphda, Beta Fornax, Gamma Ceti, Skat, Gamma Aquarii, Kappa Pegasus, Markab, Etacti, and Gamma Hydras. The display was three dimensional and extended "below" the surface of the table. Gamma Hydras, a small colony called Holdkeep, was the farthest "down," while Kappa Pegasus floated "above" the rest. This was the main theatre of the war, where the Armada was concentrating its efforts at crushing the Secession. Red flags floated among the star points to indicate Armada fleets. The one at Finders was bright and prominent—they knew where that one was—and two more were just as solidly at Beta Fornax and Holdkeep. But they were less certain about the others, in between systems. One was apparently heading for Markab, currently the capital of the Secession; another danced at the outskirts of Skat. Two more were outbound from Denebola, targets still tentative, but projected to be Kappa Pegasus and Etacti.

"What do you think?" Simon asked abruptly.

"About what?"

Simon waved at the display. "How accurate are we?"

"How should I know?"

"Because you just came back from the Pan."

Merrick shook his head. "No. Normally you'd be right, Simon, but not this time. I never got back to the Pan."

Simon cocked his eyebrows. "Really? Then where've you been for the last ten days? It *was* ten days ago you left Finders."

"Was it?"

Simon grunted. "There's one fleet missing in this, the one that hit us."

"What happened to it?"

"A *lot* of it…" Simon laughed deeply, briefly. "A lot of it is being used to repair the damage the rest of it did to us. I don't know where the survivors are." He looked at Merrick significantly.

"I didn't detect anything on my way in."

"Hmm." He glanced at the others, then jerked his head to Merrick. "Come on."

Merrick followed him past the display, back further still to another door, and into an even smaller office—slightly larger than a closet, barely able to contain the desk and polycom and the pair of chairs and the autobar, to which Simon went immediately.

"Close the door," he said, punching instructions into the machine. "I propose we drink each others' health until we have no inhibitions left. Then maybe we can learn truth."

"I'm being honest with you. But I won't turn down a drink."

Simon laughed as he turned, a glass in each hand. "Thought not." He handed one to Merrick then sat behind the desk. "Truth is viscous."

"Isn't that 'vicious'?"

"Sit down. I had eight thousand two hundred and fifty one casualties in the course of the Armada siege. Four days, I didn't think the bastards would ever leave."

"Why did they?"

"We beat their ass."

"Bullshit, Simon. Etacti's impressive, but there's nothing out here that can stop an Armada task force from taking what it wants."

"Finders proved that wrong."

"Finders was a fluke."

"Whatever it takes."

"Palada's task force stumbled in there expecting nothing more strenuous than simulated maneuvers, practice runs. They got surprised. Micheson's didn't make that mistake, which is why Finders in under Armada control now."

"In our case, they didn't expect us to take out their flagship." Merrick stared at him and Simon nodded. "I'm telling the truth. The *Erin Go Bragh* burst open like a bug on a hot grill. It only cost us eight thousand plus casualties to do it. The rest of the fleet dissipated."

"They'll be back."

"That depends."

"On what?"

"How we do at Finders."

"We?"

Simon grinned and knocked back his drink. "Where've you been for ten days, Sean?"

"Conferring."

"With the Vohec?"

"If you can ask that, you don't need an answer."

Simon leaned back in his chair and studied Merrick down the length of his long, straight nose. "We're fencing. That's no good."

Merrick set his glass on the desk with a sharp crack. Liquor sloshed over the rim. "I didn't come here to talk to you, much as I might like your banter. I'm here to meet someone. Now what the hell do you want? Am I under arrest for something or not? If you want me to tell you what I know—about *anything*—you're going to have to stop playing games with me."

Simon laughed and spread his hands. "All right, all right. There's a Vohec ship in one of our docks right now."

"Which one?"

"Hell, I can't pronounce any of their names, except the commander's. Lovander Casm. Do you know him?"

Merrick sat back. "He was liaison at Finders. What's he doing here?"

"He says he's waiting for you." Simon smiled wryly. "Not the one you were expecting?"

"So when can I see him? Have you even told him I'm here?"

Simon waved a finger. "Of course, we have, Sean. I'm not about to irritate the Vohec. This rebellion works, we'll be living with these setis." He came forward. "But I want to be in on whatever meeting you have with Casm."

"That's up to Casm."

"Ask."

Merrick smiled. "What did you mean about Finders?"

Simon shrugged. "You can read a tactical display. You figure it out."

Merrick thought about what he had seen in the display. Finders was under Armada control, Etacti was not—but a fleet might be on its way to reinforce the one Simon claimed to have beaten. Finders and Etacti were two anchors of a triangle, the third point of which was Markab. There was something there, but...

"Now who's fencing?" Merrick snapped impatiently. "So when do I meet with Casm?"

"Tomorrow. I've got you all to myself for now."

Merrick lifted his glass and took a drink. "And what do you want to do with me 'for now'?"

"I want to see if I can't make you choose sides for once."

Merrick laughed. "Simon, I choose sides every time I make a run." He set his glass down again. "No, what you want is for me to commit myself exclusively to you—"

"To the Secession."

"Whatever! The problem is you don't know if I have or haven't. For all you know I may be more committed to this than you are. But you want a guarantee."

"What's wrong with that?"

"Everything. Now when do I get to see Casm?"

"When I say you do."

Merrick leaned on the desk and scowled at Simon. "I'm sorry you lost eight thousand people. When I left Finders the death toll had topped fifteen thousand and not even half of those were caused by the Armada. Beta Fornax was shut down completely, I have no idea how many dead, but there *were* forty-one thousand people there. Cennevil on Skat slaughtered eleven thousand Pan loyalists, did you know about that? No, I didn't think so. When this is all over that son-of-a-bitch is going to be a Hero of the Secession. The Armada has sealed off all nonmilitary communications on and from Holdkeep and the last word I got from there was about killing pits where secessionists were being systematically butchered. When this is all over who do you think is going to be lauded and who condemned? Now unless you want to feel responsible for more of this shit, let me talk to Casm."

Merrick watched Simon try to stare him down, but gradually Simon broke eye contact. His mouth twisted briefly into a childish pout. He sighed tiredly and touched his intercom.

"Lenda, please inform Lovander Casm that Sean Merrick is ready to see him."

Merrick smiled. "When I see him I'll ask that you be informed of everything that goes on."

"Sean, if I find out that you're conducting negotiations with the Vohec without authority—"

"Stop it. You know, Simon, you've done a hell of job since Freda died, but the fact remains *she* was governor of Etacti, not you. Your position as Stationmaster bestowed you with the lieutenant governorship, but let's be honest: skills at managing cargoes, shipping schedules, docking facilities, and station maintenance don't necessarily make you equal to the task of interstellar diplomat."

"Are you through venting?"

"Are you through fucking with me?"

Simon's face reddened.

"I said I'll see you get informed. *I* don't even know what Casm wants."

The intercom beeped. Simon slapped the switch. "Yes?"

"Lovander Casm is ready to see Co Merrick."

"Thanks, Lenda. Have an escort ready for Co Merrick." He waved toward the door. "Go on."

Merrick studied the man for a moment. "You're not coming along?"

"What for?"

"Well, if Casm's in a receptive mood…come on, Simon. Might be your lucky day for diplomacy."

Uncertainly, Simon stood. After a few more awkward moments he gestured to the exit and fell into step with Sean.

The Vohec ship was docked nearby. A spindle met them at the lock. Merrick stepped closer.

"The generosity of Lovander Casm is recognized," he said. "I am Sean Merrick."

"You are expected," the spindle acknowledged and began to drift away.

"If you please," Merrick called.

The spindle stopped.

"May I request an indulgence?"

"Proceed."

"Please welcome the presence of Stationmaster Simon Kaskemon."

"Denied."

Merrick looked back and saw Simon glower, embarrassed. He shrugged and mouthed *"Sorry."* Simon shook his head and waved him on, then turned and walked away.

Merrick followed the spindle down corridors that seemed insubstantial, as though made from thick cloth or dense smoke, to an area that appeared infinitely large. Cloudlike approximations drifted overhead, writhing darkly in and out of each other.

Lovander Casm sat in the center of a broken circle of low consoles and tables; cushions lay about. Casm was tall and painfully thin, his head appearing too large for his body. He wore a midnight blue bodysuit and a light blue jacket.

"Co Merrick."

"Lovander."

"Sit with me. Food, drink."

A tray appeared on one of the console, filled with small dishes and an assortment of bottles. Merrick chose a couple of treats he thought he recognized and poured from a bottle of pale violet liquid. The aroma reminded him of honeysuckle.

"Your generosity is recognized," Merrick said and lowered himself to a thick cushion.

"I must first ask the nature of your request to bring Co Kaskemon to our congress."

"Political. He was being difficult. I made a gesture to assuage his suspicions."

Casm nodded slowly. *"Co Kaskemon has been in contact with Armada elements. It is my opinion that he is a Pan loyalist. The engagement in which the Armada flagship was neutralized exhibited questionable circumstances. The tally of organic debris in the aftermath did not match the personnel complement that ought to have been aboard the Erin Go Bragh. Prudence dictates that you refuse to trust him."*

Merrick nodded glumly. *"I'd expected something like this."*

"Why?"

"I think he was responsible for Governor Choskers' death."

"He probably knows you suspect. Well. You were contacted by Lovander Mipelon and the Ranonan ambassador Tan-Kovis."

Merrick fished a chit from inside his jacket and handed it to the Vohec. Slender fingers accepted it.

"Do you know the contents?" Casm asked.

"I scanned it. It's a report on the situation on Finders. A couple of sections don't make a lot of sense to me, some stuff about an encoding experiment...?"

"What is your assessment of the situation at Finders?"

"The Armada has control of the system itself. I'd say they could stabilize their hold on the planet in under forty days."

"The Rahalen Coingulate has ordered us to remove our support from Finders. We have petitioned for exception, but it is doubtful we will receive one."

"And if you don't?"

"It is not acceptable that Finders fall into the Pan Humana."

"That's inevitable now, unless the Secession succeeds."

"No, it is not inevitable. It is likely that the Pan Humana will simply eliminate the human presence on Finders and retreat back beyond Denebola. It may be to our advantage to wait and see. It would certainly not be to anyone's advantage for war to break out between the Vohec *Qonoth* and the Rahalen Coingulate."

"So what will you do?"

Casm poured himself a glass of clear liquid and drank. "You and I shall talk a while. Perhaps we can arrive at a solution together."

Nicolan switched off the comm and slouched back in the uncomfortable folding chair. He glanced at the handslate on the desk beside him and winced. The inventory of equipment and materiél was grimly accurate and allowed no other conclusion than that any campaign against the Armada would fail. The Founders had lost support from the Vohec; all the major cities were occupied; the roads were patrolled by air and on the ground; and the transit station was denied them. He had no idea what had become of the construction platform—or any of the humans on board it. Nicolan's resources permitted him to be an irritant that might be squashed at any time. Nothing he did militarily would be decisive.

So what was left? He had a list that he constantly reshuffled into new priorities: make preparations for a long siege; try to reopen the mines and cannibalize the Cambion towers; slip off-planet somehow and make his way to a different part of the Front; contact other elements of Founder resistance and forge some kind of communications network; find his father's body.

Other things, smaller details. The last teased his conscience. There was no overall advantage to be gained from it. He had played with the justifications for hours and none of them proved sufficient. Downer's Cove possessed a small spaceport, but since no word had come out of there it was a reasonable assumption that the Armada had secured it. Even if in the long run retaking Downer's Cove proved possible and worthwhile, other factors had to be tended to first. For instance the liberation of Terralaq. The scant intelligence he had received suggested some sort of internment camp had been established there. A single road connected the two cities. Seizing one without the other would be inadvisable.

For that matter Emorick and Terralaq were connected by one road. The three supported each other very neatly. Since the tramline between Crag Nook and Emorick had been broken, only the Tameurla Road offered possibilities...

It would be safest to try to retake Orchard Crest, out in the middle of nowhere, connected only by a spur road. It was an impossible tactical situation. He could not take any of them without taking all of them and right now—the inventory caught his eye again— he could take none of them.

Air surveys had overflown them already. He was sure the Armada knew about the base, but its proximity to the seti structure protected them from attack. For now. Kee was establishing a ground perimeter about ten kilometers out. Earlier in the morning he had dispatched a team back to the Cambion compound.

Nicolan had given up trying to find out who the infiltrator was. For all he knew, that co was dead or had left to rejoin the Armada. He found it impossible to operate suspecting everyone. If something blew up in his face and the only explanation was betrayal, then he would know. Until then, he needed to trust his people.

He rubbed his eyes. Too much to do, too much to think about, too much to know that he did not know.

He filed the last communiqué and stood. His back hurt. He stretched and left the command vehicle—a digger fitted with the best communications and polycom gear they could adapt—and strolled toward the Hole. Guards played a game of dice at the foot of the lift. They nodded at him in recognition and he rose to the surface.

Finders had no moon, so the night sky was illuminated only by the wash of stars. Nicolan stood at the edge of the bubble and looked up at them, for a moment forgetting where he was and why. Humanity had come out here more than two centuries ago. Not to fight a war, he thought, surely not. Wars were ever available at home, on Earth. No, people came because they—some of them—stood on clear evenings and looked at the dome of night and thought, *I want to go there!* The impossibility of that dream taunted them all the more. Light was the fastest thing they knew and all the numbers said it could not be beaten. And certainly it could not, on its own terms, but the universe itself was pliant. A bargain could be made, a deal to overlook a nip and a tuck in the fabric of space-time, so a ship might slip between the rules, unnoticed. It was a solution only a dreamer might conceive and only a committed dreamer might make real. But it had to be, Nicolan thought, no other course would have been acceptable; we had to come.

Nicolan recalled that the first colony ship had been built before the theoretical models of the translight envelope generator were developed, built to go to the stars at sublight, a huge generation ship that was to travel for decades, maybe centuries. They were going to come, one way or the other.

But not to fight wars. Not that, again, after all that had been learned and all that had been argued and all that had been decided. Humanity had reworked itself, reshaped its ideas of governance and living to make wars—not impossible, no; after all, the Armada existed, had existed for a long time—too much trouble, too much bother. When people are comfortable war is simply not worthwhile.

Then they found the seti realms. Aliens, nonhumans. Fear makes people uncomfortable and, he supposed, that made war worth considering.

But on their own kind?

Of course, he thought grimly. Setis were bad enough, but humans who wanted to mingle, to learn from them, to trade, traffic, and truck with them were worse. Race traitors, the Outsiders within, the aberrant strain. So the fear became pathological. People seemed incapable of tolerating extreme differences. Not enough to simply let the Distals secede and close the borders. No, the mutants must be exterminated. Cut off an arm and cremate it in order to save the organism.

The only chance the Distal colonies had was to make it too damn expensive to finish the cremation. Surely they could not win a toe-to-toe war with the Pan Humana.

Nicolan let his gaze fall to the *qonteth*. The palest outline was visible in the starlight, a milk-and-ivory nimbus that arched long and low from horizon line to horizon line.

He was halfway there before he realized he had made a decision to go.

The ground was hard beneath his feet; occasionally he stepped on a small patch of dried out grape-lichen, making a faint crunch. A cool breeze tickled his face from the southeast.

In the darkness, the size of the *qonteth* deceived. He was on it before he expected to be, his hands pressed against the cold sandstone. He shuddered, viscerally aware of transgression. He ought not to be this close. He must not enter. But no one had ever said that. The warnings had been inferred, not implied. Or was this more justification, so he could do *one* thing he wanted to that was ill-advised?

Nicolan felt his way along the wall with his left hand brushing the surface of the alien dome. Out to his right the plains gave back dim, patchy light from the stars. This close the dome was black. If he took his hand away and stood still he felt disembodied. He kept his left hand against the wall and occasionally looked skyward. Before him the lightless pitch danced behind his eyes as his mind searched for sight. He walked on, tracing his path against the wall, and came around the dome.

He looked right and saw blackness. Nicolan stopped and looked left—blackness—forward—blackness. He swallowed, hard, his heart picking up speed. Pressure increased against his ribs, on his lungs. He looked up and the stars were gone.

His legs trembled slightly with each step. Silly, he told himself, a trick of the night. Keep going and come around to the starting point again. He walked on.

Light increased. It was a somber greenish-blue and he only became aware of it gradually. He looked up and saw a single strip aglow down the center of the ceiling. He let his hand fall. Somehow the light diminished his anxiety a little. He shook himself, flexed his hands, and walked on.

The brightness never grew beyond a murky twilight. After a time it seemed that the corridor spiraled inward, but Nicolan could discern no visible curve ahead.

Abruptly, the passage ended.

Nicolan stood at the rim of a large amphitheater. A dozen rows of seats descended, encircling a central stage. The seats were wide and deep, with troughs cut where armrests would have been for humans. At the base of each seat, cut into the floor, was a circular depression.

Nicolan jumped from tier to tier, down to the first row. The space above the stage was filled with a display. He sat down and watched.

At the center shone the ruddy orange ball of Diphda. Finders moved in orbit, along with the gas giants. Another planet circled closer in that did not exist in the actual system. Or perhaps at one time it had. Two large stations floated within the system, one midway between Finders and the unknown inner planet, the other near the perimeter of the system. Ships scattered throughout. Nicolan identified three fleets moving in formation. One was high above the pole of the sun, moving downward toward Finders— "downward" from Nicolan's perspective—and containing easily a thousand ships. A second fleet, also containing perhaps a thousand ships, came in from outside the system in a trajectory that would intercept the perimeter station. The third fleet was near the larger gas giant and was in the process of dividing its forces, each to meet one of the other fleets. This third fleet contained far fewer ships to begin with; divided, the defending forces were massively outnumbered. Also, Nicolan understood as he watched, neither force could reach its opponent before the others reached their apparent targets.

Then he saw the fourth fleet, far "below" the system. Three thousand ships, more, watching, poised to divide and attack or launch straight in, covering most of the approaches to the system from beyond, so even if there was a relief fleet on its way—and Nicolan saw none—such a fleet had limited access to the theater of action. The assaulting fleets could easily change course, regroup, redirect. The lone ships scattered throughout the system numbered less than two hundred, and they were occupied with robot probes released by the attackers.

He wondered for a moment where the tactical details came from, how he knew the numbers. But then the drama unfolded and Nicolan watched, rapt, as battle was met.

Sean sat in the darkened room, nursing a hot cup of *seraic*, and staring at a display of the action against the Armada task force Simon Kaskemon bragged about. The *seraic*, a Rahalen drink, tasted of curry and butter and almonds and chocolate and other things for which he had no name.

Lovander Casm had provided the room and the recording and the drink. The recording was his, a "gift" from the Vohec, along with copies of all Simon's communications with the Armada. Sean did not know what he would do with any of it yet. He did not look forward to the next few days. Part of him wished he could remain on board Casm's ship indefinitely. He offered sanctuary for the time being. Sean had viewed the recording five times now and with each viewing he grew more convinced that Simon probably would not let him leave if he could help it. The engagement had been incredibly easy for the station forces. Sean remembered the *Erin Go Bragh*. A very old ship, ready to be recycled for its materials, on the list for replacement with a newer ship. The Secession had summoned her once more into battle, undoubtedly for the last time, and it was something of a shame that she had been sacrificed so coldly. He felt a pang of regret for the few people who had been on board when the ridiculous assault force from Etacti Transit had attacked and ripped her apart.

Where is the real fleet? he wondered. He sipped his *seraic* and closed his eyes.

"Co Merrick?"

He opened his eyes, blinked. "Yes, Lovander?"

"I have the comm prepared that you requested."

"I'll be right there, Lovander."

He gulped the rest of the *seraic*, stinging his throat. He hurried from the room, down the short corridor, into Lovander Casm's presence.

The Vohec patted a seat beside him. Sean bowed slightly and sat down.

As he looked up he saw several people seated around him. The link was perfect, giving an impression that he could touch each of them if he wanted.

"Greetings, fellow revolutionaries," he said.

A couple of them winced, a few others smiled. Kol Janacek, chairman pro tem of the Secessionist council, merely looked impatient. Sean suppressed a scowl at Valen Cennevil, who chuckled dryly.

"What do you have for us, Co Merrick?" one of them—Terrance Gholan of Skat—asked.

"A tactical update, other matters. The situation on Finders is deteriorating. The Secessionist effort there has been reduced to guerilla action. Maxwell Cambion is more than likely dead, but that remains unconfirmed. Etacti is secured for the moment, but it seems to me that Simon Kaskemon is prepared to betray the system. I don't know how, but he certainly repulsed the Armada task force too easily. I have come here from Beta Fornax. The situation there is stalemate, neither the Armada nor the Secessionists able to move effectively against the other. I don't expect that to remain unchanged. Once Finders is secured, Micheson will be redeployed to Beta Fornax."

"Unless something keeps him at Finders," another of the group said.

"I have conferred with the Vohec," Sean continued. "We have some options to consider. The Rahalen Coingulate has requested that they remove themselves from the situation at Finders. They are prepared to do so assuming the Armada simply ends its action and leaves. However, the situations at Beta Fornax and here at Etacti suggest that the Armada could establish a new boundary for the Pan Humana."

"In which case the Armada won't leave?"

"In which case they won't leave. Now, you can continue to fight a guerilla action against them, gamble on one major assault, or simply retreat into the Reaches."

"Without seti aid we can't risk an assault."

"And an ongoing guerilla action would drain us."

"Retreat," Gholan said, "is unacceptable."

"It may be inevitable."

Sean listened while the conversation devolved into small disputes over endless details. Occasionally one of them asked him a question and he gave short, economic answers. The truth, he reflected, could not be contained in such an interrogation, so he did not even try. He glanced at Lovander Casm from time to time, but he knew better than to think he could read a Vohec by expression, or any seti, for that matter. Still, he looked for a reaction—any reaction—to the debate. The future of this part of space was being discussed. Sean wondered if that meant anything to the seti who had always lived here, roamed here, trafficked here.

"So we're agreed?"

Sean blinked, looked around.

"Yes, I think so," Kol Janacek said. "Let Etacti go. Maybe it'll distract them from other parts, like Markab. If they need reinforcements to hold Etacti, then they won't have enough to send elsewhere."

Sean frowned. "What? Excuse me, but you've got half a million people on Etacti."

"The Armada won't harm them once the combat units are dealt with. They'll be repatriated."

"You can't seriously believe that!" Sean snapped.

Gholan fidgeted. "We can't see any way to reinforce Etacti without jeopardizing some other system." He glanced at the others, clearly unhappy with the decision. "Without seti support, this sacrifice is…necessary…"

"But—"

"There's another possibility," Cennevil said. "We could detonate fusion devices on both Finders and Etacti. That would make both worlds essentially worthless."

The others stared at him with mutual disbelief. Finally he shrugged.

"Just a thought. Never mind."

Kol Janacek cleared his throat. "It's decided. Let Kaskemon yield the system if he intends to. The fact is we can't risk support units. Finders is already lost, Etacti is obviously next."

"After what I told you about Beta Fornax," Sean said, "you can't believe these people will receive humane treatment."

"The loyalists will," Janacek said.

Gholan glared at him, then shrugged. "Resources dictate this course, Co Merrick. Perhaps at a future date…"

"Right," Sean said.

"Thank you for your report, Co Merrick," Janacek said.

"At your service, co."

One by one the members of the council vanished.

"You are not pleased," Lovander Casm said.

"How could you guess?"

"What will you do?"

Sean sighed. "I've already watched friends die on Finders. Max Cambion was a member of this council and I didn't hear a word in his memory."

"War does not support sentimentality until it is finished."

"Mmm. I think for now I'll go back to my ship, if I can."

"I will provide an escort."

"No. I don't want Simon to know I suspect him."

"I ask again, what will you do?"

Sean turned to him. "All right, here's the way it lies. Finders may well fall, in which case you may be correct that the Armada will remove the loyalists, sweep the system clean, and leave. Your honor is served, no risks taken. But if Etacti falls, then the Armada might assume they have a chance at reclaiming a good portion of the Distals for the Pan Humana, including Finders. They won't leave. With Etacti, Finders, and Beta Fornax secured, they might well move deeper into the Distals. Everything you wanted by way of human contact, every thing the Coingulate wanted, everything any seti out here wanted, will be shot down with an invasion. The Secant will be pushed back and you'll be forced either to fight or withdraw, but in no way will you derive the benefit you expected. The Vohec *Qonoth* has already risked a great deal to help humans retain our colonies out here. You didn't do that out of any altruism, or I've misunderstood you completely. You expected something in return. You're not going to get it if what this council just decided goes forward."

"What do you propose?"

Sean blew out a long, loud breath. "I don't know. But you have to be prepared to come into this, one way or the other. There's an Armada task force somewhere outside this system probably waiting for a signal to come in." Sean stood. "You figure it out."

He walked out of the chamber. He did not know if he had misread the seti, or if his analysis meant anything to them. He was angry and he felt reckless. Things were flying apart. How they came back together...well, maybe he had read them right.

He left the Vohec ship and strolled to the shunt. A pair of human guards waited. Sean wished he had stayed for one more cup of *seraic*.

He rode the shunt with them in silence, listening to the hum of the machinery all around them. Such a vast place, enormous and complex and expensive...tossed out like bait, a die gambled against what seemed to Sean a small chance.

The shunt stopped and he got out. Lenda, the officer who had first met him and escorted him to Simon, waited.

"I 'll take him," she said to the escort.

The pair left. Merrick blinked at Lenda.

"Come on," she said. "Co Kaskemon is waiting."

Merrick looked past her. For the moment they were alone.

"Wait," he said. "You 're taking me straight back to Simon?"

She nodded.

"If you do, maybe you should know that I 'm going to kill him."

Her eyebrows drew together in an expression of curiosity.

Merrick swallowed and continued. "I believe he killed Governor Choskers and I know he's an Armada contact. In fact, he's just waiting for an opportunity to hand the station over."

"But the *Erin Go Bragh*—"

Merrick shook his head. "Do you honestly think that was real?" He pulled the disks from his jacket. "These contain evidence to support my accusations. Go over them before you make a decision." She took the disks, held them gingerly between thumb and middle finger. He watched her work through that for a few seconds. "Anyway, you have a choice. Take me to my ship directly or back to Simon."

"I could kill you here, now."

"And what would Simon think? He 'd wonder why and you 'd have to lie to him. Or risk what I just said being true." He sighed heavily. "This is an ugly time, co. It 's going to get worse. These may be the last honest words a stranger says to you for a long time."

"Why tell me?"

"Someone 's got to pick up the pieces when Simon 's dead. And I still need to get to my ship."

He watched her and wondered how many illusions he had just finished destroying. But it did not take as long as it might have. She nodded.

"Come on, Co Merrick. Simon 's waiting for you."

Chapter Nine

Tory's head felt tight, as if just released from a too-small container after a long period of storage. He blinked constantly, dazzled, as though everything he saw was new and unique.

He was led through close, bright white corridors to a series of locks, then into a receiving area. A woman stood by the single desk and looked up when he entered. She finished entering data on a handheld keypad and came toward him.

"Tory?"

He smiled—too widely, he felt, but he was having difficulty controlling his reactions—and said, "Hmm?"

"It's Jesa, Tory," she said.

"Right."

"You're being released to my custody. Is that all right with you?"

"Oh, sure." He thought: released?

She—Jesa—took his left hand in her right and tugged him gently along. More doors, uniformed guards—Armada?—and finally a shunt platform. They waited alone on the long, coldly-lit apron. Jesa paced anxiously, glanced at her watch, the chronometer on the wall, the door from which they had emerged. Finally the shunt rolled up, the door opened, and she ushered him inside.

The shunt rolled out of the station and suddenly Jesa was in front of him. He jerked back, startled, as she placed a small device on his forehead. She pushed his left sleeve up and slapped something else onto his forearm, another box, only this one pricked him. He hissed and tried to rise, but Jesa deftly held him back with her fingers pressed into the hollow of his clavicle. After a few seconds, she removed both objects, slipped them back into her kit, and took out one more device that Tory recognized as a hypodermic. She shoved it against his arm and fired it. Tory jumped aside from the sharp bite. Angry, he knocked her hand away and stood. She lost her balance and sat down gracelessly in the aisle. He stomped away from her, spun, and raised his hand, finger out to underline his words—

'Shit!"he hissed. The glow vanished from everything and the tight-
ness under his skull became momentarily unbearable. He closed his eyes
and sparks danced across the inside of his eyelids. His lungs heaved.

When he opened his eyes he was on hands and knees, a pool of
chalky white vomit on the floor beneath him.

Jesa helped him up. He trembled, and slipped once, but she got
him into a seat, then, to his amazement, she was on the floor cleaning
up his mess.

"I underestimated your feelings toward me," he said, his voice
harsh and gravelly.

"Shut up, Tory," she snapped. "When we arrive, don't say anything. Smile and follow me." She stood. "Clear?"

He wanted to ask why, but the way she glared at him he decided
to wait. He nodded.

"Get some sleep," she said. "We've got about a half-hour ride."

He nodded again and closed his eyes. It was the easiest thing to
do and the hardest thing to keep doing. The mob of images that
crowded forward behind his eyes tumbled in his head, bewildering,
maddening, and damning. He remembered clearly the pair of Armada security officers approaching him after he had left Claye
Albinez's lab, presenting their IDs, asking him to accompany them.
After his arrival at their station offices, details fell apart, jumbled
together, vanished.

"What did they do?"he sobbed. He opened his eyes then, once,
and saw Jesa sitting across the aisle, watching him fearfully, her hands
clutching the kit in her lap. He closed his eyes again and willed sleep,
till, mercifully, the shunt ride ended.

They stepped off together onto a crowded platform. He
found it easy to smile because he had missed people, missed crowds
and human voices and closeness. Jesa led him by the hand and he
grinned drunkenly all the way out of the station, up to another
level, and into a private car. He stared out the window at the
passing cityscape—widely-spaced structures, separated by lush gar-
den areas. In the distance he saw lone towers, graceful spires,
domes, delicate architecture.

"Where are we?"he asked.

"Pollux."

"What...?"

"Yes, it surprised me, too. The idea that the most secure prison in the Pan Humana is underneath the most decadent pleasure city in the Pan Humana—well, most coes would be shocked."

"They wouldn't believe it."

"How much do you remember?"

"I—right now, too much. It's all getting in the way." He looked across at Jesa. "Thank you."

"You're welcome. Of course, this might cost me my career."

"Then why?"

"Oh, I want something."

"What?"

She shrugged. "Your gratitude was a good start."

"Now, wait—"

"Yes, let's wait. We can talk when we get where we're going. In the meantime, concentrate on remembering. I want details."

He looked back out the window. "No, you don't."

The transport left the city proper and went airborne. It arced in a lazy trajectory down into the center of a resort complex. They landed on the broad plaza before a tower of amethyst and cerulean steel pylons. Jesa took him up to the eightieth floor.

In the middle of the penthouse six people surrounded a data platform. Flatscreens were everywhere and all the displays on the platform were filled. It resembled a tactical center, like those Tory had seen on board Armada ships, but these were not Armada.

Jon Buson rose to his feet, smiled, and hurried around the table to Tory.

"She did it!" he said. He patted Jesa's shoulder. "By damn, she did it! Thank you!"

Jesa folded her arms and nodded mutely.

"What's all this?" Tory asked, waving at the scene.

"This," Jon said expansively, "is what we hope will tear open the war and get at the truth." He laughed harshly. "This is part of the defense team for Task Commander Palada."

"Defense…?"

"He's being court-martialed for negligence and breach of authority."

Tory approached the work station. "I don't get it. How long have I been in custody?"

"Eighteen days," Jesa said. "We've been trying to pry you loose for ten. You've been subpoenaed for the defense, but the Armada was able to delay your release."

"Then how did I get out?"

Jesa tapped her chest. "Me. I pulled a lot of favors. We wouldn't have gotten anywhere without the subpoena, though, so we spent a lot of time setting this up with the defense."

Tory sat down. "Palada...court martial? But—that's cold. He lost most of his command and they're court-martialing him over it."

"There's some evidence that he sacrificed them to make a statement," one of the advocates said. She cleared her throat. "He'd made several complaints in the year preceding Finders to the effect that Valico Task Force was not up to par, could not handle such an action, other things relating to Valico's preparedness. Questions have been raised about how he knew Valico could not manage, and if he exercised poor judgement in committing his forces."

Tory laughed. "He had orders—!"

"That's what we thought," Jon said. "Turns out there's a little known, seldom used regulation that requires officers of the Armada to disobey in instances where the orders are clearly inadequate, illegal, or immoral. Palada had a choice. The charges have been brought against him based firmly on Armada regulations."

"But disobedience would have gotten him reprimanded, probably relieved of his command, and the next poor idiot would have gone in." Tory stood. "I can't think right now."

"Co Shirabe," another advocate said. "We need your testimony, on the record, of your assessment of Valico and the quality of Palada's leadership."

"How am I supposed to testify to that? Maybe I might make a guess about how good a combat unit Valico was, but I don't know Palada."

"We'll work with you, Co Shirabe. We'll find out what you do know and if any of it will help and in what way."

Tory looked from the advocates to Jon to Jesa. "Fine. Right now, I've just returned from the dead. If you'll excuse me, I need sleep."

"Sure, Tor, go right ahead," Jon said. "Sorry to start in right off like this. We can talk later."

"Sure."

He went to one of the bedrooms that surrounded the main room. Without turning on a light, he stripped out of his clothes and lay on the edge of the bed. For a long time he was afraid to close his eyes. He did not want to see what waited in sleep.

"Alex?"

The room was still dark, only the shapes of its furnishings visible. "Yes?"

"How do you feel?"

"With your hands." He suppressed a chuckle; it was a joke fast becoming old between them, but it still made him laugh.

"Have you spoken with your father lately?"

"No."

"Alex..."

"No!"

"Shall I check the log?"

"No. I talked to him day before yesterday."

"What about?"

"Nothing important." He felt himself waking, and aging as he did.

"Everything's important, Alex."

"Why?"

"Because it concerns who you are."

"Do you know who I am?"

"Not yet. But we're getting closer. Now, would you like to tell me what you spoke to your father about?"

"Not really. It's boring."

"Alex..."

"All right." He pushed himself up in bed, still refusing to open his eyes. He did not want the night to be gone yet. Some of the dreams had been especially vivid, particularly pleasant.

"Alex."

He opened his eyes. She sat across the room, near the door. She was dressed in a shapeless blue coverall today. He preferred watching her when she appeared in something that revealed her figure or some part of her body that she normally kept hidden. Lately, though, she had grown reticent, more conservative. They shared fewer jokes,

too, and their conversations were much more formal. Sometimes
he got the impression that she was being watched, but the only others ever in the room were his phantoms.

"Hi," he said.

"Good morning. Sleep well? Ready to start?"

"Have I eaten already?"

"Yes."

"We must be in a hurry today. So, what do you want to talk
about?"

"Let's review your last conversation with your father."

Alex sighed and nodded. He shifted his gaze to the opposite
side of the room.

A man appeared that he did not recognize.

"Who's that?" she asked.

"I don't know. Who are you?"

The man opened his mouth, shaped words soundlessly.

Alex shook his head impatiently. "Where's my father? I want to
speak with my father."

The stranger continued to mouth things.

"What's he saying?" she asked.

"Nothing." Alex closed his eyes, concentrated. When he opened
them again Maxwell stood where the stranger had been.

"Yes?" Maxwell said.

"Father…"

"Yes?"

"What we talked about the other day."

"What about it?"

"I want to go over it again."

"To what end? Didn't you hear enough?"

"Why do you—?" Alex coughed, swallowed.

"Hate you?" Maxwell finished. "I don't. Hate requires energy,
has a purpose. I don't hate you. I don't feel anything toward you.
You disappointed me. I have no regard for you."

"But—"

The stranger reappeared beside Maxwell. Maxwell appeared
not to notice.

"You're not worth hating," Maxwell continued. "This is pointless, dull, and a waste of time. We've been over this. We went over

this before you left for service in the Armada, we went over this when you returned, disgraced, defeated, for all intents dead, at least to me."

"Why are you tormenting him?" the stranger asked.

"He keeps asking me to. What am I supposed to do, refuse my son?"

"No. But he's not your son."

"What do you mean?" Maxwell turned to face the stranger. He was taller, leaner, altogether more imposing. "Of course he's my son. I made him everything he is."

"You remade him into everything he is."

"The same thing."

"Including a failure, by your estimate."

"So? I take responsibility for that. I made him, he failed, it's my fault. Why should I keep going over this?"

"Maybe you shouldn't. Maybe you should let me go over it with him."

"You? What can you do that his own father couldn't?"

"Since I was killed when he was an infant, maybe not much. But it might be worth seeing what his real father *might* have done."

Maxwell turned away again. "You're not his real father. You just supplied the raw material, the initial genetic soup. I raised him, I trained him, I shaped him, I gave him a name, a home, a purpose—"

"Which he failed."

"That's my responsibility, too."

"Maybe not. Maybe it was never your responsibility. That's why you failed."

"Nature over nurture? Old argument, absurd, meaningless."

"Perhaps. But he keeps asking for answers from his father, you keep talking to him, he never feels satisfied. I might agree that nurture is more important than nature, but there has to *be* some nurture for that to be true. Seems to me you haven't provided either."

Alex listened, stunned, and watched as the stranger changed. The softness of his features diminished, lines appeared in his face, the hair solidified. He gained height, though he remained shorter than Maxwell. Alex still did not recognize him, but he seemed more familiar.

"If," Maxwell snapped, "you think you can provide better answers, go ahead. Talk. I'm fascinated."

"Thank you." The stranger approached Alex's bed. He rested his hands tentatively on the railing and smiled at Alex. "Hello."

"Hello," Alex said. "Who are you?"

"Your father."

"But Maxwell—"

"Is not."

"What's your name?"

The stranger shrugged. "What's in a name?"

"It's how you know who you are, isn't it?"

"Maybe. But when you forget your name and you still are, then how important can it be?" He smiled wryly. "Sorry. Cheap philosophy. It's in the wiring. Your friend has been trying to tease me out."

Alex glanced at the doctor, still sitting by the door, watching. She smiled at him and nodded.

"Evidently," the stranger continued, "you're a very layered organism. I'm essentially the basic template on which Maxwell overlaid his own structure. He's right, he made you. Literally."

"How am I supposed to find out who you are if you don't know?"

"I don't know. But I'd like to try to help you find out who *you* are. Do you really think knowing my name will do that?"

"It's a start."

The stranger nodded thoughtfully. "Let me ask some questions first."

"All right."

"Why did you deviate from Maxwell's intentions for your career?"

"I don't know. It just didn't seem sufficient."

"How do you mean?"

"Well…" Maxwell stood stiffly where he had appeared, his head turned sharply away. "When I arrived at Armada OTS several people came to me and offered their services. It became obvious pretty quickly that I was being handed an easy track. After two years I saw all the open doors, saw where they led. It would have been nothing to walk through them and end up in Armada security or supreme command. General staff, that's where Maxwell wanted me to be, and all these people were willing to pass me through the system and place me there."

"Why not take it?"

"It was a gift. Maxwell told me all my life that things worth while have to be earned. It wasn't that I didn't want the positions offered, but I wanted to earn them. I wanted to know that I deserved to be there. The only track not being handed to me without effort was line duty."

"And that was exactly what Maxwell didn't want."

"So I discovered. I still don't understand why. I'm a good pilot!"

"You were shot down," Maxwell said, "in your first real action."

"That's not true!" Alex snapped. "I saw action on Earth, during the Riot!"

"That wasn't action," Maxwell said, "that was slaughter."

"I thought you were staying out of this?" the stranger said.

Alex looked at his face. The shape was clearer still and the sense of familiarity almost overwhelming.

"Go on," the stranger said.

"I don't know what else to say. I did what I thought I had to."

"Why did you think you had to?" Maxwell demanded.

"Because—it was expected—you wanted me to earn everything, I couldn't just accept a position, and I knew you wanted me to be in the general staff eventually—"

"Eventually! Didn't you *listen!* I wanted you in the general staff as soon as possible!"

"Unearned?"

"I earned it! Can't you understand that? You never earned anything! *I* earned it! You wasted *my* efforts!"

The stranger turned. "Will you shut up? Nobody cares about your aspirations."

"My aspirations are *his* aspirations! I built them in!"

"Not well enough, evidently."

"You have nothing to do with this! You contributed nothing to what I tried to do!"

"True enough. But I may be the only thing he has left that's all his."

"I don't want to talk about this anymore," Alex said.

"Fine," Maxwell said and vanished.

The stranger remained. "I'm not really a memory. I'm an abstraction. You don't have to be afraid of me, but I might hurt you."

"That might not be so bad."

The stranger smiled and patted Alex's foot. "You remembered me once. You're sure you don't now?"

Alex stared at him for a long time, then nodded. "You're Houston Thayer."

"That's right."

"You're my father?"

"As they used to say in ancient times, you're from the seed of my loins. However..." He gave Alex's ankle a last pleasant squeeze. "We'll talk again." He winked out.

Alex looked at the doctor. "Did you do that?"

"I've been working on an enabling program to create something out of the underlying code in your make-up. I wasn't sure it would work. I provided the stage, you might say, and you put on the show. Do you have any idea who that might have been?"

"No..."

"How do you feel about Maxwell now?"

"He's not my father."

"Did you really think he was?"

"Yes."

"You never talk about your mother."

"She died. I was very small."

"Didn't Maxwell talk about her?"

"No. He never talked about things that didn't exist."

"An odd thing for a father, not to ever mention his mate. Dead or not, there's a responsibility—"

"Maxwell did what—he did—" He shook his head impatiently. "Maxwell had reasons."

"I'm sure. I have to go collate this data, Alex. I'll be back tomorrow. Sooner if you want me. All right?"

Alex nodded and looked out the window. He felt her leave. It was his clearest sense, knowing when people left.

Cira roused a couple of temporaries to help her replace the bearings. As dawn lightened the eastern sky she piloted the sled out to the pumping station, smiling at the wind-muffled curses of the two men as they clenched the safety bars.

At the site, she gave them short, precise instructions, worked with them through the better part of the morning, and ran the tests herself while they sprawled in the shade.

The station needed more than new bearings and Cira made numerous adjustments, trying to bring it into alignment with its own specifications. It was nearly noon when she finally finished.

The two men watched her as she stripped her shirt and toweled herself. She ignored them and looked across the small lake.

"It's true, you're Armada?" one of the temporaries asked suddenly.

"Yes."

He nodded. "Had an uncle once was Armada."

She waited for more. "And?"

"Nothing. Just saying."

She pulled on a fresh shirt and loaded the tools back into the sled. The two men stood.

"You been to the Front?" the other asked.

"Yes." She slammed the lid. "Finders."

She did not recognize the look they gave her then. A combination of incredulity, pity, and maybe disgust; an alloy of all three, a new emotional substance. It approximated cautious respect and Cira took it as such.

"Thanks for your help, coes," she said. "Let's get back."

"Uh—slower this time, co?"

She smiled. "All right."

She drove back at a gentler pace. Tryshel and Hester stood before the workshop as she pulled up. Riv watched from the back door of the main house.

Cira powered down the sled on the garage apron and thanked the temporaries again. They hurried back toward their barrack, passing Hester who strode toward Cira. Tryshel remained where he was, hands on hips and head slightly lowered.

"What did you do?" Hester asked.

Cira began pushing the sled into the garage. "I reinstalled the bearings in the pumping station."

"Were they fixed?"

"Of course." She connected the sled to its charger and started up the power transfer. Then she pulled the tool box from the back and took it to the shop. Hester followed.

Saysheen leaned past Riv. "Cira! Mori and I are going into Creighton, do you want to come?"

"I need a shower."

"Fifteen minutes." Saysheen ducked inside.

Cira replaced the tools, finished the requisition log, and closed down the file. Hester stood in the shop doorway, glaring at her.

"Do we have a problem?" she asked.

"Maybe they do things different in the Armada, but you should check with somebody before you go do something like that."

"If you'd like, I'll go back out and pull them again so you can bench test them and install them yourself. That doesn't seem very sensible, though, so unless you have a reason to think I did a bad job—"

"That's not the point, Cira!"

"You might try saying 'Thank you' instead of—"

"Don't tell me how to behave!"

Cira sighed heavily. "The water transfer is near optimum spec. I adjusted the sensors and the conduit relays, so in flood season they'll shut it down before the overflow tears up the bearings, which is probably what happened. Nobody's done a full maintenance survey on that equipment in a long time. The bearings will probably give you another five seasons, but they will need to be replaced. They can't be fixed next time." She stepped up to the door. "I'm going to shower and go into Creighton with Saysheen."

Hester worked his mouth as if he needed to spit. He was a full head taller than Cira and nearly filled the doorway. With mild surprise Cira realized she had already lined up all the proper strike points and decided on how best to take him down. She kept her expression neutral, though, and waited until he stepped aside.

She grew angrier as she neared the house. Riv still stood in the door, watching.

The shower seemed to help. Saysheen and Mori waited on the front porch.

Mori talked incessantly all during the ride into Creighton, but Cira heard none of it. She replayed the events with Hester, taking each aspect apart and studying it. What happened there? Hester was enraged, but over what? The bearings? Hester, she remembered, had always been quiet and stoic and proud of his reasonableness. She had learned to hold back with him, not to overreact or respond to the wrong thing. She remembered Finders, then, and her reaction to the spy, Venner. Overreaction, certainly. After surviving that battle, it seemed she had lost an edge, the ability to reserve action until appropriate. Maybe Hester had lost it, too. She did not know what had happened here since her departure. Tryshel said Faitha had turned into an ass, maybe others had changed, too.

"We're in Creighton," Saysheen announced, "where are you?"

"Hm? Oh, sorry."

The cab let them off on the upper deck of a multileveled town mall. Cira went to the railing at one end and looked down into the center of Creighton.

In five years very little had changed. The terminal where Saysheen and she had caught the transport to Ozma wore a new façade and, opposite the terminal, the police station supported a new comm tower, a military design, obviously to link them to the garrison at Ozma and the transit station. The government center was the same as she remembered, as was the civic auditorium, the advocacy hall, the ecological study center, the district resource management building, and the smallish bubble of the Pan Forum representative's local office. Around this civic core she glimpsed theaters, shops, data centers, omnirecs, arcades, the athletics arena. Cira recalled days coming here with her brothers, sometimes twice a month. What they had done then blurred together in her mind into a kind of archetypal experience—surely they could not have done *so* much all in one day—but few details stood out. The haze of memory and later, sharper disappointments set childhood in nostalgic amber.

The same. Static. She tried to imagine this place in riot, like Crag Nook. How was it necessary, she wondered, that to keep Creighton unchanged, untouched, that Crag Nook had to happen? She traced the threads of justification to find one that was strong enough to explain and the only one that seemed in any way self-consistent was that in order for Creighton and the tens of thousands of Creightons throughout the Pan to remain as they were there must be no alternatives.

That anyone would want to leave home and sever the ties could only imply that home was flawed, imperfect, and unsatisfactory. Therefore secession represented the ultimate criticism. To permit it would be to admit the validity of the criticism, which would inevitably necessitate change. Nothing could remain as it was, as it had always been.

Cira blinked, surprised at herself, her reasoning. She pushed away from the railing and turned to find Saysheen and Mori reading a public notice board near the lifts. Mori waved to her.

Saysheen smiled at her. "What do you think?"

"Hasn't changed, has it?"

"Not much. Not on the surface anyway. So, where to first?"

"I want to go to the data arcade," Mori said. "I keep up on everything that's happening at the Front."

"Why?" Cira asked. She shook her head. "I'd like to see a play myself or just wander around."

Mori seemed disappointed, but Cira did not feel inclined to humor her. She did not know how to tell Mori that the data feeds in the public arcades gave virtually no useful information and Cira did not care to listen to half-truths and complete lies.

"Well," Saysheen said, "I'm hungry and I've been wanting to have some of Algar's steamed skutchon."

"Algar's still here?"

"Of course."

"I'm on for that."

"Okay," Mori said. "Then after?"

"I'll take you to the arcade," Saysheen said. "Let Cira wander if she wants. She's been away."

Algar was a smallish man, an immigrant from Nine Rivers who still possessed some of the lilt of Nine Rivers langish. He effused delight to have Cira back in his restaurant and gave them the best table, near a broad window that looked out over a strip of parkland. He had just received a fresh shipment of skutchons that morning and, for Cira, he would prepare them personally.

The hand-sized sea creatures were shaped vaguely like ancient shields. When properly prepared—and Algar was a master—they were delicate, like cake, with a rich, buttery flavor cut by a unique spiciness. Cira had not realized how hungry she was until the platters arrived.

Saysheen took Mori to the arcade, but they caught up with Cira within the hour; Mori had wanted Cira there, to add more to the datafeeds. They wandered the shops afterward, till evening, then took a cab back out to the stead. Cira felt warm in Saysheen's company and Mori seemed content to laugh and talk and simply *be* with Cira. By the time they returned, Cira was weary. Her muscles ached from the morning and the walking, her belly was full of rich food, and she went straight to bed.

In the morning Ezrem and Reg asked her to accompany them back to Creighton to receive a shipment of field monitors. Reg said little—he had always been shy—and Ezrem talked about the workings of the stead, market prices, problems of shipping, storage, endless details that flowed from him as if they comprised a kind of mystery story. Cira helped him inspect the new equipment, then oversee its loading into the stead carryall. They spent the balance of the day programming them.

The next day she helped Stacy and Reg disperse them in the ramshorn and newheat fields. She traced the glitches that erupted in field conditions, made adjustments, and ended up reprogramming the entire cadre. The temporaries put on a party in their barracks that night and Cira attended, ostensibly to chaperon Mori and Riv. Riv did not go, though, and Mori quickly vanished from sight. Cira danced, was persuaded to sing, and drank far too much mash.

Conversation was almost exclusively local. It was an easy rhythm. She worked hard, contributed her talents and knowledge, which, to her surprise, were remarkably transferable from military equipment to farm equipment, and found herself drifting into the comfortable pattern of stead life.

With plenty to do, the days ran together. She rarely saw Marel, and did not speak to Hester after their encounter in the tool shed.

On the seventh day it ended. Late in the morning a courier arrived in a sleek Armada floater and handed her a disk, saluted, and left. The disk bore the official Armada seal. Her ears warmed.

"What is it?" Saysheen asked.

"Orders."

"Oh."

She slipped the disk into her hand reader. "Report back to the garrison in Ozma tomorrow. A transport will pick me up here at ten hundred."

"Hardly gives you enough time to say good-bye."

Cira did not want to smile in front of Saysheen. She shrugged, turned off the reader. "That's the Armada. You're on their time."

"I'm not," Saysheen snapped and left the room.

Cira went to her room and packed. Then she went up to the ridge again and sat looking out over the land.

Seven days. If she concentrated she remembered everything she did, in sequence, but it tended to jumble together. Each day overflowed with details, but the whole formed a muzzy sameness.

When the shadows began to grow long she returned to house. Cooking smells filled the air. She showered, pulled on her off-duty utilities—which she had not worn since arriving seven days earlier—and went down to dinner when it was called.

The conversation lapsed briefly as everyone took in her uniform. When talk resumed it was not the smooth banter she had grown used to over the last few days, but guarded, selective. Saysheen said nothing, Mori was clearly confused, Riv kept giving her accusing glances, and Marel ate in stony silence.

When she came into the great room afterward it sparked surprised looks.

Ezrem poured brandy, Hester lit a fire in the big hearth. A few old jokes were told, eliciting quiet, companionable laughter.

When the second glass was poured, Cira stood.

"I'm leaving in the morning."

The only look of dismay she did not expect was Marel's. He opened his mouth to say something, then snapped it shut.

"Why?" Mori asked.

"Orders," Saysheen said.

Cira nodded. "My orders came this morning."

"I thought you had ten days," Tryshel said.

"Something's changed."

Hester grunted. "You don't seem very upset."

"I'm not. To tell you the truth, I can't wait."

Marel frowned at her. "Then why didn't you leave this morning?"

"I wondered about that myself, this morning. About an hour ago I realized that I wanted to have a talk with you all."

"What about?" Ezrem asked, looking significantly at Marel.

"The thing that's been on everyone's mind since I've been back—probably since I left—and no one's been willing to bring up. I don't know, maybe you thought if no one said anything then I'd resign my commission and stay."

"You mean why you left in the first place?" Ezrem said. "And why we seem to've resented it?"

Marel glared at his brother, but Ezrem ignored him.

"Something like that," Cira said. "But before I start I'd like to know if anyone here has any questions."

Riv stood and headed for the door. Cira moved laterally and caught his arm. He jerked loose and looked at her hatefully.

"You first," Cira said.

Riv tried to find a way around her, but she deftly blocked him. He glared around at the others before he fixed his gaze on Cira. He looked as if he had a mouthful of extremely sour bile.

"Go on," Cira said. "This is your chance."

"Why are you alive?" he shouted.

"Well," Cira said, blinking. "I didn't expect that one. Do you mind clarifying that?"

"Everyone was killed at Finders! But not you! Why?"

Cira shook her head. "I don't—"

"Everyone says," Mori said, "that you must be a coward. Only cowards survive battles where everyone else dies."

Tears glistened in Riv's eyes and his chin puckered. He was angry and terrified. Cira nodded and motioned for him to sit down.

"Only people who've never been in combat would say that," Cira said. "I won't bother explaining, but that's a lie. Don't believe anything you hear over the public data feeds." She looked at Riv. "I'm alive because I'm a very good pilot and very lucky." She looked up. "Anyone else?"

"If you can't wait to leave," Ezrem asked, "why'd you come?"

"I was ordered to."

Everyone looked startled. Mori frowned. "Didn't you want to?"

"Honestly, no. After the way I was treated when I left I expected never to be welcome here again."

"Not all of us felt the same," Saysheen said.

"That's shit," Marel said. "You hated Cira's leaving."

"But I didn't hate Cira!"

"Neither did I!"

"Then why did you act like you did?" Cira demanded.

"Because you left. That was loud and clear, you didn't want anything to do with us." He shook his head in dismay. "I just don't understand what was so wrong here that made you want to leave."

"Did you think maybe it had nothing to do with you? That it was something I wanted that simply wasn't here?"

"What isn't here? Home, family...what did you lack?"

"I can't explain."

"Neither can I." He stood. "You left. That was enough for me."

"But—it wasn't that I *didn't* want to be here. It was that I *wanted* to be Armada."

"Has that been enough for you? Does the Armada give you what you need?"

"Yes."

Marel waved a hand as if to say, there it is.

"But why did you have to hate me for it?" Cira asked.

"You tend to hate what hates you," Hester said.

"I never hated you."

"Then *why* did you *leave*?"

"Can't any of you hear me? Can't any one of you understand that what I wanted was something else? There wasn't anything *wrong* here. It just wasn't *all* here."

She searched from face to face for a flicker of comprehension. Saysheen sat rigidly, staring into space. Mori looked betrayed and Riv still wrestled with his rage. The others—except Ezrem—all reflected one another's puzzlement.

Ezrem watched her, though, his dark eyes fixed, knowing.

"Ezrem?"

"You haven't figured it out yourself," he said. "How do you expect us to?"

Cira finished her brandy. This was not going as she intended. Perhaps, she thought, it can't go that way. She set the glass down.

"I'm leaving in the morning," she said. "I have no idea where I'll be stationed or what I'll be doing. If any of you are interested..."

If any of you are interested you can trace me through the garrison at Ozma, she almost said. That was pointless, obviously. "When I left five years ago I thought to myself that I simply did not want to grow old and die on Homestead. When I grounded last week at Ozma I told myself that it didn't matter where I died. I didn't want to live on Homestead. After this stay I have to admit that neither statement is accurate. The fact is, I want to live. I can't do that here. The best I might achieve is a comfortable existence. The only reason I'm telling you this is so that if you continue to resent me, at least it will be for the correct reasons."

She went up to her room, then. She lay on her bed, in the dark, and could only think that morning was such a long way off.

Tory listened to the opening arguments with a distant cynicism. It was obvious what the Armada was doing to Palada and nothing the defense did would matter to the outcome. Well, he amended grudgingly, perhaps Palada might be spared detention. But his career was over. This trial was a cruel formality, an official parenthesis.

Still, the defense advocates attacked the problem as if they had a chance of winning, and Tory admired their effort.

For now Palada's court martial was peripheral to Tory's own interests. He had been to three meds so far and already his file contained enough material to begin his own action against the Armada. He went over and over the affidavits, morbidly fascinated by the catalogue of details he only vaguely remembered. His ribs had been broken repeatedly, as had each of his fingers. He limped slightly when he first got out of bed due to poorly-healed splintering in his left shin. There was evidence—he did not understand the dense language of the analysis that supported this conclusion—that his kidneys had been bypassed and toxins allowed to build up in his bloodstream, to painful effect. At one point his optic nerves had been reversed. He exhibited neuronal damage that manifested as an annoying tremor in his left hand. If he concentrated, it stopped, but he found the sustained attention necessary impossible to maintain. He had been given chemicals to control it.

Eighteen days and his captors had virtually taken him apart and rebuilt him. Ironically, in some ways he was better for it. The healing techniques used actually made his bones stronger. Old scar tissue in his rotator cuffs had been removed. Once he had everything sufficiently documented and promises from enough meds to testify in open court he intended to have his shins repaired and the neuronal damage fixed. Two of the meds he had been to were reluctant. The one who had discovered the kidney bypass was outraged enough to promise testimony.

Beyond that—largely because of it—his last ragged bit of naïveté was gone. He was amused to realize that he had, under all the life-battered accreted stoicism, still believed that such things did not happen in the Pan Humana. If anyone had asked him, before this, if the Armada tortured political prisoners, he would have said, glibly, certainly. But, to his surprise, he had not really believed it till now.

He thought of the corral in Crag Nook, where all those refugees were herded from the tram station, and shuddered. He looked at the defense team, reviewing their data so carefully, and thought that it would not surprise him if after the trial they were all arrested.

That made no sense. He chided himself for his paranoia. Why put on a trial at all if they could act so freely, without accountability?

A show, he answered himself.

Self-evident and totally worthless reasoning.

"Deep thoughts or just a hidey hole?" Jesa asked.

"Hm? Oh, sorry."

"Thought you might want to pay attention to the court."

He nodded and tried to listen. The prosecutor general was making his opening statements.

"—will show how Task Commander Anatol Palada knowingly placed his command in jeopardy, resulting in the total loss of his fighter complement. We intend to show negligence in preparation, malice in his exercise of authority, and disregard for the spirit of Armada regulations in his constant and deliberately obstructionist questioning of Task Commander Micheson's every order, during a phase of operations when Task Commander Micheson was attempting, to the best of his abilities, to make right what clearly had been the result of dereliction of responsibility. We will show—"

"How," Tory murmured, loudly enough for Jesa to hear him, "by carrying out his orders under conditions impossible to manage and with forces disastrously underprepared due to a complete lack of response to requests from Task Commander Palada to the Armada Command, Task Commander Palada was set up to take all the blame for the magnificent bloody nose the Armada received at the hands of a bunch of inexperienced, undertrained Secessionists."

Jesa squeezed his forearm. "Shh! Tory!"

He grinned at her. She glowered and took her hand away. Tory looked over the gallery for expressions of disbelief—

"Hey," he said, startled.

"What?"

Tory pointed. "That's Lt. Kalinge, one of Palada's wing commanders at Finders."

"I thought everyone died except—what's his name?—Alexan Cambion?"

"No, no, Lt. Kalinge survived, too. Odd, isn't? Both wing commanders? But I lost track of her after leaving Finders. She and Cambion were shipped out separately."

"Uh, no, you didn't lose track of her. It's in your notes from before Toliman to go to Homestead, where she'd been sent on leave."

Tory frowned. He hated the fact that Jon had helped Jesa access his notes, but he accepted the necessity. He might have remained in custody longer without that information. More irritating was that he still had lapses in memory, sometimes significant ones. Like this. Jesa held a handslate in her lap with the appropriate entry displayed.

She switched it off and looked at him. "I have to admit, Shirabe, you're thorough."

"Hmm." He looked at Lt. Kalinge. "I wonder why she's here? Who brought her in?"

"Not Palada's advocates. Armada registered her as classified and out of bounds. Special mission or something like that."

"But—hell, she can't help the Armada's case."

The prosecution droned on, but Tory did not listen. He concentrated on Cira Kalinge and waited for a recess. Prosecution finally ended his remarks, the three justices conferred with each other briefly, then called recess until next morning.

He drifted out with Jesa and the other members of the defense team. The corridor encircling the courtroom was rimmed with alcoves and conference rooms, all secured against eavesdropping.

Tory let the others move away from him till he felt sufficiently separated, then headed for that part of the corridor where he thought Lt. Kalinge might emerge.

He spotted her coming out in the company of three other Armada officers. Tory stayed back until he knew where they were going—toward the access to the underground shunt system—then quickened his pace. As he passed them he glanced at Lt. Kalinge, maintaining a carefully neutral expression. Her eyes flickered in his direction but she did not react. Tory kept walking, keeping about ten to fifteen paces ahead of them.

When he glanced back he glimpsed them descending the stairs to the tram platform. Tory hesitated, then followed.

"Where did you go?" Jesa hissed in his ear as he emerged onto the platform. She took his sleeve and pulled him along to a private car.

Tory craned his neck to see Lt. Kalinge, but she was lost in the crowd. Reluctantly, he let Jesa usher him into the car and close the door.

"Don't do that," she said. "You could still get picked up."

"Worried about me?"

"Just slightly. If I lose track of you I lose a lot of background material."

"I'm touched."

The door opened.

Jesa glared up. "Excuse us, this is—"

A woman stepped in and closed the door behind her. "A private car, I know," she said and turned.

Tory started. "Co Albinez...?"

Claye Albinez sat down beside Jesa. "Where are you getting off?" she asked.

"The Royce-Avalon."

She nodded curtly and fell silent.

"Excuse me, but—" Jesa began.

"Please, co," Albinez whispered.

She sat stiffly, eyes down and hands folded neatly in her lap. As soon as the tram began to move she relaxed. When daylight shot through the windows she leaned back, eyes closed, and sighed deeply.

Abruptly, she leaned toward Tory and opened her small case. She handed him a disk.

"What's this?" he asked.

"Alexan Cambion."

"Excuse me?"

"I apologize sincerely for what happened to you on Toliman Station, Co Shirabe. I didn't know about it until a few days before I boarded a liner to come here."

"Why *are* you here?"

"At the behest of the prosecutor-general's office. I'm to testify against Commander Palada on Lt. Cambion's behalf." She smiled bitterly. "It's a nicely composed testimony. I'm to explain how all his injuries and the harsh treatment he received at the hands of the Secessionists are somehow his former commander's fault. I'm here with an escort, who at this time is probably frantic over where I am. I saw you in the courtroom."

"Are Lt. Cambion's injuries Commander Palada's fault?" Jesa asked.

"Oh," Tory said. "Co Albinez, this is a, uh, colleague of mine, Jesa Marlin. We're working together for the time being."

Claye Albinez blinked at Jesa, then shook her head. "I have no idea who's responsible for Alexan's condition, but I doubt Palada had anything to do with it."

"So what is this?" Tory asked, holding up the disk.

"After you left I was—" She frowned as if she could not believe herself. "The Armada slapped a security cordon around my lab. All my work was scrutinized, monitored, all my notes confiscated. My life has been...reordered. I live in the lab. I've had almost no contact with my friends, all my communications are recorded and censored. When I attempted to protest to higher authority I was referred continually to a set of emergency orders and the same damn office and the same idiot in a uniform."

She winced and looked out the window. "Never. This has never—*I* determine my priorities, *I* run my life the way *I* want to. I have never had to tolerate this kind of interference. I don't mind if someone makes suggestions, but nobody *orders* me..."

She stopped and looked apologetic. "I continued working with Alexan because I would have anyway. I've been building a persona encoding of him." She nodded toward the disk. "That."

Tory whistled appreciatively. "What do you want me to do with it?"

"I—have no idea. Armada security will probably get one eventually, but—"

Tory nodded, then reached across to Jesa. He plucked her handslate from her pouch and slid the disk into the storage slot on the back and returned it to Jesa.

"So who *is* he, Co Albinez?" Tory asked. "Did you find out?"

"His code had been overlaid heavily, remember?" When Tory nodded she continued. "I managed to assemble enough of his original structure to start a genome trace. Not quite hopeless without the entire code, but close. Still, you can get into main branches, family trunks, that sort of thing. Narrow the search to a few billions. He helped, though, through the imaging sessions I showed you. I worked at him to recall his father."

Her eyes were bright. "And he finally imaged someone! It was a rough approximation, no fine details, and he filled in a lot of blanks from pure imagination, but it was a *face!* With that I made the trace down to one family. Then I just asked what members of that family had emigrated to the frontier."

"And?" Jesa prompted impatiently.

"Houston Thayer."

Tory frowned, trying to remember. He had done background work on Finders during the task force run, but it had necessarily been superficial. Still, the name was familiar.

"All right, I can find out who he is and how he relates."

"He, or at least a close relative, provided the original genetic material—part of it, anyway. I didn't have time to do much more. But everything Alexan is you now have on that encoding."

"What about his mother?" Jesa asked.

"That had been completely obliterated. Most of the overlay found the strongest match points on that part of the code."

"Why would someone do that?" Tory wondered. "Why remake someone so thoroughly?"

"All I've been able to glean from Alexan's memories of Maxwell has to do with the man's ambition and control. Alexan worships Maxwell Cambion, but it's loyalty founded on fear."

"Fear of what?"

"Failure. Maxwell Cambion had contacts within the Armada which he intended to use to get Alexan placed within it. Alexan didn't follow the plan. Maxwell was not pleased."

"Do you think Maxwell Cambion blocked him?"

"I think it's highly probable." She shook her head, looking slightly amazed. "But it is superb work. Not many people in the Pan could have done it. I suspect..."

"What?"

"It's possible we're looking at seti technology. That may be one reason the Armada is so eager to secure everything."

"Well, we may never know. I'm sure by now Finders has been reduced to its original pre-colony condition. What are you going to do now?"

"I'm getting off before you," she said. "And I'm going to do what I can to appease my chaperons. When the trial is over I'll go back to Toliman and take care of my patient."

"We might be able to help," Jesa said. "If you'd like I can see about getting you protection—"

Claye Albinez laughed. "I'm rather naïve about a lot of things, Co Marlin, but I learn very quickly. Right now no one in the Forum or anywhere else in the Pan will say no to the Armada. The horrid nonhuman seti are at the door and the Armada is our brave and mighty savior. We can't give them authority fast enough right now. But thank you. I do appreciate the offer."

She then turned to gaze through the window, and her attitude shut out further conversation. Tory watched her, frustrated and sad, until the tram slowed to a stop. Claye Albinez smiled at them and exited the car. Tory stared after her until she was lost in the scattered crowds. The tram moved again and he slammed his fist against the wall.

"Tory...?"

"I think it's time you contacted whoever you told me could get you to the front. After the trial it would probably be a very good idea for us to leave."

Cira listened to the prosecution's catalogue of charges as if watching a reenactment of events that no longer mattered. She was anxious about what would come next, but it did not touch her directly. Her former commander was being sacrificed for reasons she did not completely understand. She doubted the general public much cared what had happened at Finders, doubted they would believe it all even if they knew. It was a distant, inconvenient conflict the government found necessary in the aftermath of the Riots on Earth, which were much more meaningful. The Riot was over, calm restored. If, in order to guarantee peace on Earth, war must be waged fifty, sixty, a hundred light years away, then the Chairman, the Armada, and the Forum must know best.

Ens Jamer sat beside her, slouching in his casual dress uniform and looking entirely unconvincing as an ordinary Armada officer. Cira would have preferred that he remain in civilian dress or wear the black uniform of the security division than pretend to be her comrade. All the charade did was lend to the general unreality.

He had met her at Ozma City and had been with her since. He was pleasant, occasionally funny, and thoroughly watchful. Cira did not know why she needed watching, but that was the decision. The trial came as a shock.

Prosecution's opening arguments ended, recess was called, and Cira left, sandwiched between two marines, Jamer just behind her. As they made their way to the tram station she looked up and saw a man walk by, looking at her. White hair, vaguely Asian features—the journalist, Shirabe. He moved on by. He had recognized her, obviously, and just as obviously he wanted to talk to her. He seemed thinner than she remembered.

But she descended the steps to the platform and boarded the tram.

"Small universe," Jamer said. "Wasn't Tory Shirabe with Valico at Finders?"

Cira shot him a look. "You wouldn't ask that if you didn't know."

He smiled. "True. Did it seem that he wanted to talk to you?"

"I didn't know him very well. Why would he want to talk to me?"

"Didn't you advise him on board the *Castille?*"

Cira did not answer. She gazed out the window at the passing landscape, dotted with resort hotels, private buildings, sculpted forests, and worked at ignoring Jamer.

The tram slowed, stopped, and they debarked. Jamer said nothing more until back in their suite of rooms.

"You'll be testifying tomorrow," he said then, sprawling on one of the enormous sofas. "We need to go over what you'll say."

Cira hesitated at the door to her bedroom. "I have no idea what I'll say. I don't even know what questions I'll be asked."

"I do. And I have a good idea what Palada's advocates will ask. Rest up, we can go over it together later."

She considered a number of responses, rejected them all, and entered her bedroom. She sat on the edge of the bed and stared, unseeing, out the transparent wall that gave her a view of the resort grounds. In the distance was the glitter of another resort complex.

She felt restrained, doors everywhere and none she could use. She had never felt so completely out of control. Even on Finders she knew that if she reached Armada forces she would be safe. Jamer disabused her of all notions of safety and control.

She looked up. There was one door...

"I changed my mind," Jamer said as he came into the bedroom. "We can go over it now."

She jumped to her feet, heart racing. "What happens after this trial?"

"You'll be reassigned, depending on how well you perform."

"Perform..."

Jamer gestured toward the main room. "Shall we, Lieutenant?"

A portable reader on the large round table in the dining alcove displayed the text of the prosecutor-general's case against Task Commander Anatol Palada. Cira did not sit down to read it. For such a thorough document it was surprisingly short.

"That's not—" she began, then stopped. "I was going to say that that's not what happened, but..."

"You don't think the Armada resorts to lies, do you?"

"This isn't the truth."

Jamer shrugged. "For our purposes it is." He pulled out a chair for her, then sat down himself. "We have some work to do, Lieutenant. We don't want any mistakes. Understand now, your part in this is relatively small. We'll make the prosecution with or without your testimony. You can't help Palada, but you can cause yourself damage."

Cira looked at him sharply. This was the nearest he had come to directly threatening her and for the moment she felt a glimmer of respect. It was a curious sensation, coming as it did after a long period of vague resentment and a helplessness too insubstantial to even frighten. Since Homestead she had found nothing solid to grasp. Everything she reached for turned to gauze and dust. Even Jamer, with a name and a face and a *presence* against which she might gauge her own condition, had not, till now, seemed real. He was an icon, a symbol, a voice and a set of orders.

She understood, then, the nature of her brief respect. He had just warned her. The perfect herding he had done with her all these days for the moment was set aside and Jamer, whoever he was, had shown her the shape of what was controlling her. To resist, you needed a shape, a substance, otherwise all you had was anxiety and suspicion, which worked against you.

As quickly as it came, the respect changed, overwhelmed by a stronger emotion, one she thought she understood, but till now had never really felt. For the first time in her life, she hated.

She sat down. "All right. Let's go over it. I don't want to disappoint the Armada."

Chapter Ten

Nicolan looked down on the small port outside the ruin of the Cambion compound. The Armada had repaired the damaged pits and expanded the base to accommodate a contingent of marines and two airborne assault groups. From his vantage south of the compound, it appeared nothing had been done to the wrecked towers. Four mobile bunkers covered the approaches to the port. Anything coming at them on the ground or in the air could be tracked easily and, unless it was a large force, taken out with little difficulty.

Nicolan touched his jaw. "Kee?"

"Here, boss."

"Are we in position?"

"Waiting on the word."

"Two minutes."

Nicolan let out his breath slowly and tried to relax. He glanced up through the gauzy blanket of the sensor screen. It was difficult to trust that sensor sweeps from space could not pick them up. He flexed his shoulders, working against a neck cramp that had threatened all morning, and forced his attention to the tactical display to his right. The time counted down in the upper left corner.

Have I missed anything? he wondered. Probably, but he did not know.

Below people moved about among the aircraft, the bunkers, the port tower. How many? A standard Armada marine contingent consisted of a hundred troops, ten engineers, three polycom specialists, and support equipment. Two air wings, comprised of twenty aircraft, twenty pilots, ten engineers, ten ground monitors, two polycom specialists per wing. One hundred sixty-seven people. Maybe one hundred seventy, maybe a few more, it was impossible to tell. The bunkers were automated.

Thirty seconds. He could not get comfortable. He leaned forward, intent.

"Boss?"

"Now."

Alarms sounded in the port. The south-facing bunkers swiveled, fast, very fast. Nicolan checked his tactical display and saw the blip coming from the southeast, also very fast. He glanced out to the horizon but saw nothing yet.

The north-facing bunker swiveled slightly east and on his display he saw blips coming from the northeast.

The heavy e.p. cannon throbbed. The brilliant flashes struck sharp shadows across the port grounds, causing the scurrying troops to appear jerky in the strobe effect. The sound rolled off the mountains, thunderclaps of displaced air, searing gas vortices whipping around the projectors. The atmosphere hummed and rumbled around the guns.

The aircraft powered up, pilots sprinted from the tower.

On the tactical display the attacking fighter groups scattered, still making their way toward the port. The tracks of the e.p. shots lanced through them, but the numbers did not diminish. No hits. Nicolan licked his lips anxiously. Another thirty seconds and the targeting systems for the bunkers would figure out what was going on.

The launch pits erupted in the midst of the port. Each one spewed fire in volcanic bursts. Smoke, debris, broken stone and fire spilled across the port proper. The bunkers swiveled again, but stopped firing. They turned back toward the phantom fighters to the north and south. Nicolan smiled. A human within the base had just overridden the automatic systems. Necessary, of course, or the big e.p. guns might start shooting up the base.

The eruptions continued. The field was hidden by the dense smoke. Nicolan looked at his tactical.

Right in front of the bunkers, too close for them to effectively fire on, the ground opened up. Moles climbs out of the holes, followed by the large diggers. The diggers started on the bunkers with electron drills. The glow of the fusion torches turned the smoke hellish orange.

The moles plunged into the roiling ash. The sounds of small arms fire reached Nicolan.

Now brighter explosions colored the blackness—the fighters going up.

"We're in, boss," Kee said in his ear.

"Mop it up, then. I want the data cores."

A minute later, Kee said, "Feeding you Armada commline now."

On the tactical display everything telescoped and expanded. Nicolan studied the data. The entire Armada network was spread out for him.

"Kee, it's time," he said. "Fighters are coming from Crag Nook and Orchard Crest. Let's finish this and leave."

"Got the cores. We're done."

The smoke drifted lazily eastward now in a thick blanket. Nicolan could see nothing on the field. He closed his tactical down, folded up the sensor shield, and packed it all away. He heaved the pack over his left shoulder and hurried away from the small outcrop, into the deeper rocks.

When he reached his own mole, he tossed the pack in and closed the canopy, then drove back down the narrow trail to the ventilation shaft where a makeshift lift had been painstakingly installed over the last several days—as painstakingly as all the other tunneling that had gone into preparing for the ten minute assault.

Successful assault, he added as the lift descended through the mountain.

The lift halted at the mouth of a narrow passage illuminated at long intervals by greenish biostrips. Nicolan gunned the mole forward. The track was rough, hastily cut in less than five days. He doubted that it would last more than a year; without reinforcement and the necessary quake-proofing, the minor tremors that regularly ran through the mountains would collapse it.

An hour later he emerged into a large alcove north of the Thayer smelter works. Diggers and assorted other equipment waited, their crews watching him expectantly. He opened the canopy, stood, and gave them a thumbs-up.

They shouted, grinning, and hugged each other, then started the job of moving a big plug into place to block the tunnel Nicolan had just used. He hurried to one of the diggers and climbed in.

"Activity?" he asked.

The technician at the monitor glanced up. "The fighter groups are still a minute away. Kee's out of there already and the tunnels are being collapsed. Orbital sensor sweeps have intensified, looks like their doing subsurface resonance scans."

Nicolan touched his jaw. "Kee?"

"Here, boss."

"They're looking for you. What's your distance from target?"

"Eight klicks."

"All right, at ten we're detonating."

"Right."

Nicolan watched the monitors. Twenty seconds before the Armada fighters arrived at the freshly-wrecked port, he gestured.

The rumble of the charge reached them even here. On the display the seismic waves showed like a series of tsunamis racing from the base of the mountains just a few kilometers south of the port. Wave after wave, confusing any subsurface sensing the Armada might use, covering Kee's escape.

Nicolan squeezed his hands into anxious fists. Kee's people were being rocked by the same effect. He hoped their distance and speed were sufficient to keep them safe.

"Tunnels are collapsed at the port," the tech said.

"Get ready to detonate the second charge." He touched his jaw. "Kee?"

"We're at thirteen klicks, all accounted for. Some ride, boss, you should be here. Coming to the turn."

"They are now heading west," the tech said. "Two minutes to mountain shelf."

"Let's pick up the pace, Kee, you're forty seconds behind schedule."

"Imagine a gesture, boss; we're doing the best we can."

Nicolan smiled, gnawed his lip.

The fighters buzzed around the burning port, flies unable to alight on the corpse. Nicolan watched the time tick in the corner of the display, silently willing Kee's group to move faster.

"Under cover, boss," Kee reported.

"Now," Nicolan said.

The second device was larger, linked to a third device near the port, and Kee had left a fourth inside the tower. All three exploded simultaneously. The digger trembled beneath his feet.

"All communication between the fighters has ceased," the tech said.

Nicolan bounced his fist off the edge of the console and hissed "*Yes!*" He patted the tech's shoulder. "Let's get out of here. Kee, we're pulling out. See you back at the shrine."

The plug was in place. Nicolan issued orders and equipment was loaded up and the small train of vehicles moved out of the alcove, down a barely-graded spur to the main road, then south to the smelter.

Nicolan kept watch on the monitors for incoming fighters, sharp seismic disturbances, unusual comm traffic, anything that would show pursuit or imminent attack. His back ached by the time the small caravan reached the foundry. He signaled and received the all clear. The dock doors flew open and the moles and diggers scurried inside.

"Let's move," Nicolan announced over the p.a. "This place has to be empty in five minutes."

The command digger rolled down a corridor, into an over-sized lift. His people hustled the caravan into other lifts, down to the new network of tunnels. The mountains around them were bored out, riddled with passages and chambers, most deep below ground level. The constant rehearsals, mostly surprise drills called whenever Nicolan chose, paid off now. By the time his digger raced down the main tunnel to the command base by the Vohec *qonteth*, Thayer smelter works was abandoned, the accesses sealed off, the personnel and vital equipment scattered under the mountain.

The digger halted and Nicolan jumped down to the floor. He sprinted to the observation tower and rode up to the canopy.

Fio glanced at him from her command console, then turned her full attention back to the tactical displays.

"Kee's group is making their run," she said, pointing.

Nicolan looked at the screen, then out across the plain, though as yet the group of moles was too far away to see. The limited satellite access they had managed to tap into gave them adequate telemetry. The moles were ranged out in a wide arc. A group of fighters had left Orchard Crest and was now making directly for them. They were still well over three hundred kilometers away from Kee's force, but closing rapidly.

"Any comm about the damage to the port?" Nicolan asked.

Fio nodded. "Looks like total destruction. Even the two fighter wings went down from the device Kee planted in the tower. The fireball caught them all."

Nicolan looked up. The soft smear of dust Kee's moles kicked up drifted at the horizon. "Come on..." Nicolan breathed.

"Another group," Fio said. "No, two groups."

Fully forty-five aircraft flew convergent paths toward the moles, most of them less than two hundred kilometers away now.

"How much leeway does he have?" Nicolan asked.

"He has under two minutes."

The moles were now black dots within the clouds they raised. Nicolan grasped one hand in the other behind his back. This was the riskiest part of the entire assault. Nicolan did not like it, had opposed it at first, but—

"Five groups," Fio said.

Nicolan started. On her screens the tracks of seventy-five fighters centered on Kee and his eight moles.

Others emerged from below and gathered to watch.

The moles were clearly visible now. Nicolan walked to the edge of the canopy. Far beyond, black smoke marked the site of the assault, a low, angry cloud.

"Come on, Kee," Nicolan said.

Suddenly everyone not manning a post stood shoulder to shoulder with him and began murmuring anxiously.

As if they had somehow jumped across the intervening distance, the fighters appeared, small black cuts in the sky, expanding rapidly. Bolts of energy leapt from their guns to the ground.

"E.p.s!" Nicolan yelled. "Give them support!"

Several people aimed their e.p. rifles at the fighters and began firing. The moles were so close, Nicolan waved his arms and screamed. It did not seem possible that they would not make it.

One of them burst apart from a direct hit. Then another.

The sky filled with Armada aircraft. Like impossible insects, they swarmed over the moles.

One mole shot under the canopy, slewed sideways. Another made it in. A third.

One more exploded. Hot shrapnel pelted them under the canopy. Nicolan spun around, covered his face, and felt a large chunk careen off his back. When he looked around again the other moles were in. Only three lost.

Only three. Nicolan shook his head, angry.

The fighters were making dives at the canopy.

"Back!" he shouted. "Back! Back!"

A few people had been injured from flying debris and were being carried away from the edge. Nicolan danced away. Bolts of energy churned up the ground around the periphery, but none came through the dome above them. At Fio's station, Nicolan watched the patterns of frustrated warflies as they threatened attack, only to pull back at the last instant.

"All right, everyone down below! Move!"

The remaining moles rolled onto lifts and descended. Nicolan joined the wounded and rode down with them.

Once in the command chamber, he ran toward the moles.

Kee leaned against his, hugging himself. He looked up at Nicolan with wide eyes.

"Hey, boss. Next time I let *you* do that."

Nicolan laughed and wrapped his arms around Kee. The man trembled in his embrace.

Kee laughed once, swallowed. "We lost some."

Nicolan nodded.

"But," Kee added, "they know we're here now."

"And so far they're not attacking."

Kee wiped at his eyes and smeared tears across his cheeks. "Well, that's good, eh? Think maybe you were right then?"

"I think maybe so."

Kee nodded. "I'll be okay, boss."

"Kee—"

"I *will* be okay. Just—leave me alone right now, okay?"

Nicolan walked away, unrelieved. He checked on the injured, talked to the other mole drivers, then went to the operation center.

"Three wings have returned north," Fio told him. "The other two are flying expanding radius patterns, probably looking for other vehicles, maybe tunnels."

Nicolan sat down. Around him his people watched, waiting. The initial euphoria of success had given way to cautious confidence. As he studied the monitors and read-outs, though, Nicolan felt increasingly uneasy. Success, certainly. In fact, a greater success than he had expected. If the Armada wanted a base in the south they would now have to build one from scratch. Cleaning up the port area was going to be expensive. This action had cost them and would continue to cost them.

But it had been expensive for Nicolan's people. Weeks of work in digging tunnels, setting the devices, orchestrating the diversions— they had used three of the five devices they had salvaged from the Cambion compound and he doubted the Armada would again be fooled by the false image projections of attacking fighters—and six people were dead. They had probably sacrificed the Thayer works and now they had drawn the beast to their fire.

All on a gamble that, if the Armada threatened the *qonteth*, the Vohec would intervene. That alone had been the reason for Kee's desperate run out in the open. They wanted to draw them in, make them careless, cause an Incident. He did not even know if the Vohec factory platform remained in the system; there had been no word from them since the second Armada assault. For all he knew the Vohec might have withdrawn completely from Diphda.

He doubted it, though. The *qonteth* was important to them. He only hoped it was important enough for them to actively defend.

Venner stirred his bowl of stew absently and listened intently to the speaker on the other side of the table.

"What I heard was they lost a thousand marines in it. Half a dozen wings went up in particles and not a one got off the ground. They never saw it coming and they never saw them leave, just right out of nowhere."

"What base was this?" Rasal asked conversationally.

"The old Cambion port, down south of here," the man said, nodding. "They had a ready-made base there. Now it's gone."

"Only a thousand marines?" Venner asked. "Base that size, I'm surprised they didn't have more."

"It's what I heard. Now, I didn't *see* it, co. I don't think there *were* any eyewitnesses, except those that hit them, and they a'n't saying."

"So where'd you hear this from, co?" Rasal asked.

'I have an acquaintance works on the physical plant team dispatched to do damage assessment. She told me there's nothing left down there but a burnt hard crater." He lowered his voice and looked around the table. "About time, I think. Armada's been having it too easy so far."

The other diners nodded, muttered vague agreements, and attended their meals more closely. Rumor also said the Armada had spies everywhere and paid rewards for reports of unfriendly words and acts. Venner watched the others around the big table do their best to noncommittally agree. Their sentiments were clear—they hated the Armada and probably wished ten thousand marines had perished—but it was unwise to voice such opinions. Venner smiled at the speaker and raised his glass.

When the man returned the gesture, Venner asked, 'So how long have you been working for Armada security?"

Everyone stopped eating and looked up. The speaker glanced around at them, then glared at Venner. He drained his glass and pushed back his chair.

'I a'n't a violent man, co, so I'll leave before I kill you."

He walked away from the table. Venner nodded slightly at Rasal, who gave a nod to two men at another table. She coughed to cover the gesture and frowned at Venner.

'That was harsh, co," she said.

Venner shrugged. 'Maybe. He just seemed to know an awful lot. Mouthing that way, he had to be either a spy or a fool." He spooned stew into his mouth and washed it down, then added thoughtfully, 'Both."

A few of the others laughed. Venner finished eating and left the tavern.

Thick clouds muted the shadows; it was no brighter than twilight. Up and down the street, lamps glowed under the eaves of shops and in the windows. People kept their gazes lowered, as if oppressed by the overcast. Venner looked up—the roof of his old house was visible four streets away—to the rim of the chimney. Automated e.p. cannon looked down on Crag Nook now.

As he walked along the street he resisted hunching his shoulders and lowering his head. The resolute melancholy of Crag Nook pressed in around him. It was a broken town. The burnt sections remained, untouched and cordoned off by no more than bright yellow strips of official-looking ribbon. People did things, moved around, followed the forms of living, but Venner had not heard a single burst of loud, unrestrained laughter since his return three days before. He had heard unofficially that the population was dwindling. Many had left for the Pan, returning to their several points of origin, to families that may or may not welcome them back, a lot of them second- and third-generation Founders whose Pan families probably would not know them. Quite a number, though, were drifting out onto the plain, going who knew where, determined not to leave Finders.

He wondered idly what those who intended to stay in Crag Nook would do when the Armada finally left.

There were gangs of children now, parentless, learning survival on their own. Venner felt a curious disquiet when he saw them from time to time…

One of his men stepped into the street from a doorway and gestured. Venner entered the vacant shop. A light from the adjacent room outlined the curtained doorway behind the empty counter. Venner pushed through.

The man from the tavern sat on the floor, legs folded under him. An armed co stood in each corner of the small room.

Venner smiled. "Well. How are we treating you? Can I have something brought for you?"

The man glared at Venner from beneath sweat-glistened eyebrows.

"What's your name?" Venner asked, leaning back against the wall.

"Soris."

"I'm Hil, Soris."

The curtain opened and Rasal stepped in, followed by the fourth guard, who took his place in the corner nearest the doorway.

"Soris," Venner continued, "we were quite taken by your story. There are a few questions I'd like to ask you about it, though."

"Why didn't you ask them before?"

"Because you would have lied. My questions aren't the sort you want to answer truthfully around people who might want to hurt you later over what you say."

"Then why should I answer you now?"

"Because, Soris, you have no idea what *I* might do. Now, then. First off, the port by the old Cambion Corporation complex isn't big enough to rate a thousand marines and certainly not important enough to warrant six fighter wings when there are only twelve on the whole planet. The complex was attacked and destroyed during the second wave of the Armada invasion, so it might rate a company of marines, *maybe* two wings. How am I doing?"

"So I exaggerated."

"I know you did. And I understand. Sentiment runs high. If it looks like a victory for partisan forces, why not make it a big victory? Who knows how many coes you might trap into saying something treasonous?"

"I do not—"

"See," Venner addressed the others. "Already a lie." He stepped forward and kicked Soris straight in the nose. Not a hard kick, but Soris's nose bled freely and he fell backward.

Venner waited till Soris righted himself and finished cursing. He pulled a handkerchief from one of his pockets and pushed it into his nostrils.

"Try again?" Venner asked.

"Look," Soris said, voice distorted, "I don't do anything different than many others."

"Do you know them?"

"What? Oh, a few, but...I won't tell you who they are!"

"I'm not going to ask. I want to know about the raid on the port. And I want to know what really happened and how you know. I want to know your sources. No exaggerations this time."

"You'll let me go?"

"More than likely. It really depends on how good your account is."

Soris looked at the bloodsoaked handkerchief.

"You're all alone here," Venner said. "All I want is the truth about the raid."

Soris daubed his nose and shrugged. "It was a surprise attack. The garrison was wiped out. The tower, the launch pits, everything. What's got them worried is they think the raiders took a data core."

Venner raised his eyebrows. "Really? Now, *that's* far more interesting than a thousand dead marines."

Soris frowned uncertainly. "The blasts took out a couple of fighter wings, that's true enough. They followed the raiders, though, south, and found them dug in right next to the seti shrine."

"Sounds like a very well organized attack."

"I don't think it'll happen again."

"Probably not, but then it doesn't have to."

"What?"

Venner smiled. "All right, let's go over it again."

"I just told you—"

"Once more. I might not have heard everything the first time." He slid a broad-bladed knife from its sheath beneath his overcoat. "Again, co. I don't want to miss any details. Particularly, I want to know who did it."

"I don't know."

"Maybe between the two of us we can come to some kind of intelligent guess."

Soris surged to his feet and lunged for the doorway. Rasal thrust her arm out, extending a half-meter long black stick. The tip contacted Soris at the sternum and gave a loud snap and a bright blue spark. Soris jerked sideways and fell against the wall.

Venner straddled Soris's legs and sat on his thighs. He held up the knife so when Soris's eyes focused again the blade was the first thing he saw. Soris pressed back against the wall.

"I don't want to miss any details," Venner said. "And when you finish telling me all about the raid, then you can tell me all about who you work for."

"Lt. Commander?"

Cira looked up at the aide. "Yes?"

"Commander Perse will see you now."

Cira stood, tugged the hem of her tunic, and stepped through the door into the commander's office. She stopped before the desk and waited for recognition from the woman on the other side.

"Sit," Commander Perse said without looking up from a handslate in her lap.

Cira glanced over the office. Like the rest of Crag Nook, little had changed since her last visit fifty-one days before. Physically, at any rate; things seemed tidier. A second polycom had been linked to the first. Otherwise only the officer behind the desk differed.

She had short grey-streaked brown hair and deep laughlines. Her tunic was open at the collar, but in no way did she seem lax or informal. Cira knew nothing about her other than she had replaced Captain Laros a few days after Cira shipped back to the Pan.

"Welcome back to Finders, Lt. Commander," Perse said abruptly. She dropped the handslate on the desk and looked directly at Cira.

"Thank you, sir."

"Are you pleased to be back?"

"Surprised, frankly. I expected a different posting."

"Surprised, too, to be on the ground instead of in a fighter. *I* would be in your case. I have orders for you that frankly puzzle me, but I'm in no position to question them." She frowned thoughtfully, then sighed. "We suffered a raid four days ago that cost us three hundred and eighty casualties and our one port facility in the south. We didn't think the Secessionists had the capability to do something like that. Our mistake." She shrugged. "Even if we'd assumed they could, it might not have made any difference. It was a very professional assault. At least we now know where they are. It doesn't do us a lot of good, though. They've built their base right underneath a seti artifact."

Cira waited. Commander Perse was clearly uneasy. Her teeth tugged briefly at her lower lip.

"According to the original charter, humans were allowed to settle the northern hemisphere and exploit it and the system any way they chose. However, Diphda is within the Vohec *Qonoth* and that artifact is theirs. The colonists weren't allowed to touch it or even allow it to come to harm while Finders was in their care. As far as we're concerned that agreement stands."

"So if we just go in and attack we might be risking conflict with the Vohec."

"Exactly. It's that simple and those Secessionists know it. It wouldn't surprise me if they wanted us to attack them."

"Could we just isolate and contain them?"

"If we were staying here indefinitely, sure. We're not. I don't know when we're leaving, but we are."

Cira frowned. "Then what difference does it make?"

Perse folded her hands in her lap. Her mouth twisted as if something malodorous hovered beneath her nose. "They may have acquired a data core from the port."

Cira blinked, surprised. She had not heard about this. Data cores gave access to the Armada networks. Codes could be changed, passwords altered, a variety of blocks put in place, but ultimately a core provided solutions to any and all of these measures. There was no way to tell how much the Armada might be compromised because of this.

"My instructions," Perse continued, "are to send you into the general population to try to infiltrate and find out if that's true and if true, attempt to either destroy it or determine what use it has been put to."

Perse did not look away. Cira was very still while she thought about it and Perse gave her the time. Finally she nodded.

"I understand."

Perse nodded slightly. "The general situation here is worse than when you left. We're managing to transship the loyalists, but most of the population is staying. I don't think they're all Secessionists, but they see Finders as home. We're being eaten at by continual guerilla action, some of it very good. Someone is trying to form a coalition of all the partisan groups, we don't know who. We'd like to know and I have someone else working on that. But there are loose ends everywhere and it's becoming intractable. I understand that you made contacts with locals during the initial wave."

"I brought them in, yes. The Hersteds."

Perse nodded. "We've been using them as informants. They'll be assigned to you if you think necessary."

"I trust them."

Perse raised her eyebrows. "See Sergeant Palker for the rest." She stood and came around the desk. She took Cira's hand. "I wish..."

"Thank you, sir. I'll do what I can."

For a moment Perse's eyes showed gratitude. Then she just looked tired.

"Dismissed."

Cira walked outside and leaned against the rail above the tram station platform. A tram waited to be loaded, troops milling about. Automated emplacements kept watch on the parapets. It was very clean.

Sergeant Palker emerged from the tunnel and glanced up at her. A few seconds later he joined her on the balcony.

"Lt. Commander Kalinge?"

"Yes, Sergeant."

"Welcome back. I just got word to outfit you."

Cira nodded. "Do you know where I can find Rollo Hersted?"

"He's in town right now, but he's due back around dusk. If you'll come with me I'll show you where you're bunking." Halfway down the stairs, he said, "Congratulations on your promotion."

"You know about that?"

"I remember you. You were a lieutenant when you shipped out."

"Thank you. Right now, though, I feel like it's a consolation."

Palker laughed. "Could be worse. They might've posted you at Etacti."

"Oh? What's it like there?" He gave a look and she added, "I've been out of the loop for some time."

"Oh. Sorry. Well, it's turned into a slog. For a while they thought the place was going to collapse, just roll over, I don't know why. But resistance increased and some serious skirmishes changed all that."

"Do you think we'll give it up?"

"I wouldn't want to sound defeatist, but some ground just isn't worth the cost, if you understand me."

"Quite well, Sergeant."

The east wall of the tunnel was a honeycomb of warehouses and barracks. Their bootsteps echoed off the high arching ceiling.

"What has it been like since I left?" Cira asked as they mounted the stairs to the next level above the platform.

"Not what I expected," Palker said. "First ten, fifteen days we had all we could handle with securing the cities. The riot here flared up twice after you shipped out, but by the second one we had most of the emplacements mounted up top." He thumbed in the direction of the chimney rim. "That shut everything down fast enough. Since then there's only been isolated instances of sabotage, ambushes, theft. Police disturbances, nothing more. Here we are."

He led her along a row of cell doors, opened the eighth one and the light brightened to reveal a standard cabin.

"Till we can find you something better," he said, grinning.

Cira stepped in. Her duffel lay on the cot.

"What about now, Sergeant?" she asked. "What's it like now?"

"Eerie." He folded his arms and leaned against the door-jamb. "Coes drift out, never come back. The population has dwindled by a third. The streets are safe now, these past ten days. There are at least twenty partisan groups between here and Emorick. At first we didn't worry about them much, but lately a lot of them have been forming alliances. Most of them are moving north to Emorick." He grimaced. "Can't move in small numbers outside the towns. Partisans ambush anything that looks remotely Armada."

"They're moving north. But the worst raid took place south."

"Truth is we weren't expecting that. We gutted the Cambion operation down there, didn't think anybody had survived."

"Cambion. What do you know about them, Sergeant?"

"Not much. Maxwell, he was the head of the operation. From what the locals say he was a sharp one for business. Other sources tell us he was one of the prime movers in the Secession."

"Was?"

"We think he's dead."

Cira sat down on the cot. "Why would a Secessionist leader send his son to serve in the Armada?"

"Mmm?"

"Alexan Cambion. I served with him on board the *Castille*. He was the other wing leader in the first assault by Task Force *Valico*."

"Alexan—the one we shipped out same time as you?"

She looked up. "What?"

"Sure, I thought—he came off one of the refugee trams, all beat up and mindwiped. Didn't know himself anymore. The only reason we found out his name was a journalist recognized him."

"Shirabe?"

"That's the one."

"Alexan is alive?"

"Well, I wouldn't—look, his mind was thoroughly blanked. Not a bit of memory left in his head. He was going back for rehab, but to tell you the truth—you say he was *Maxwell's* son?"

Cira nodded absently. "He was afraid of disappointing his father."

"Well."

"You say he got off a refugee tram? From where?"

Palker frowned. "As a matter of fact from south of here. The only thing there is—was—the Cambion Corporation mining complex." He blinked, then shook his head. "Like I said, Lt. Commander, this place is eerie."

Cira stood. "Where can I find Rollo Hersted?"

"He's due back—"

"I don't want to wait till then, Sergeant."

He straightened. "Sure, I know where he is."

She wore a long local overcoat and a wide-brimmed hat when she left the tram station. Sergeant Palker's directions took her easily to a tavern near the street where she had hidden with the Hersteds the night of the riot.

Cira studied the streets as she went. It was disconcerting how vast a difference small changes could make. Damaged buildings had been boarded up or leveled, the streets cleared of debris and cleaned, yet instead of the vitality that had before erupted into violence she found morbidity. Few people walked the streets and of those none looked up. They seemed like people in mourning.

The tavern—the *Omnigyre*—was dimly-lit and crowded. No one gave her a glance when she entered. Rollo occupied a booth to himself far in the back. He watched her approach, his big hands cradling a mug on the table before him. She slid in across from him.

"Hey, co," she said.

"Cira."

"Rollo."

"I never thought I'd see you again."

"I didn't think they'd send me back here. How are you?"

He shrugged. "Been better, been worse. At least I've got something to occupy my time."

"How's Becca?"

"I don't know. How would you be?"

Cira thought about it, suddenly anxious to be as honest with Rollo as she could. "Strange, I suppose."

"Hm. She's that, all right. Stays in her room most of the time." He frowned as if suddenly pained. "She'd probably like to leave Finders if she could."

"Rollo, I'm sorry—"

He raised his right hand. "Don't. We never blamed you. Far as I'm concerned you were fair with us."

She licked her lips. "I need to ask your help."

"You can always ask."

She glanced out across the tavern. No one paid any attention. The general noise was not high, but Cira did not think anyone was listening.

"They've given me a mission, Rollo. They want me to go south to find out who did the raid on the Cambion port. They want me to try to get something back, something they're not even sure was taken."

Rollo looked thoughtful. "The Armada's leaving, aren't they?"

"You know about that?"

"It only makes sense. Nothing they do makes sense unless that's the case. No reinforcements, no field campaigns, no attempts at negotiation."

Cira nodded. "Yes, they're leaving. I don't know when."

"Soon enough. What difference does it make to them what the partisans might or might not take? After the Armada leaves they can't use it anyway. Not against the Armada."

"True."

"Then why are they sending you on this mission?"

"Because I'm supposed to die on it."

Rollo was quiet for a long time. When he looked up he wore the hint of a smile. "Then I suppose I'll help you. A co shouldn't die friendless and alone."

Venner studied the map and toyed with his cup. He looked up when Rasal came back. She scowled at him and he returned a bright smile.

"I'm glad you're back," he said. "I've been going over our options."

Rasal shrugged out of her overcoat and dropped it on the counter with the others. "No more like that," she said.

Venner stretched, then tapped the map. "It can only be Maxwell's boy, Nic. Hard to imagine he's alive, but who else could have done this?"

Rasal pulled a chair to the opposite side of the table and sat down across from him. She laid a pistol out and folded her arms. Venner raised an eyebrow.

"No more like this, Venner," she said. "What you did to Soris— that wasn't necessary."

"Oh?"

"No, it wasn't. It was cruel. I won't have another."

Venner gestured at the map. "We have more immediate things to discuss."

"You do another like that and I'll kill you."

Venner blinked at her with mock dismay. "But why?"

"You're a shitfull cold fuck, Venner. You'd be better off as organic material for reworms. Soris long since told you everything he knew and more than we needed and you kept going. You like it. And if you do it again around me I'll kill you."

"There, now," he said, grinning, and reached quickly across the table to pat her gently on the wrists. She did not move. Venner pointed at the map. "Business, Rasal. We've got agreements from all the most important factions in Crag Nook. As of now Liss can count on the support of an army of at least thirty-one thousand." He winked. "Not bad for reworm material, eh?" He chuckled. "Now if we can get this one—Nicolan Cambion—then I think we've done our job."

After a pause Rasal nodded. "Sure."

"The problem is getting there. The main access to the old Cambion works is the tramline and that's solid Armada. Can't go down the Tameurla, not right now. I'm sure they've got a regiment around that site."

Rasal stood. "I know a co that can get us on the tram."

"Why, Rasal! I never guessed you were so well acquainted."

"It might be a good idea to send word to Cambion that we want to meet. If what Sor—if what we heard is true he's not holed up in the mines, but down by the shrine."

"Would you see to it, Rasal? I mean, since you know the people..."

She nodded.

"Good," Venner said, standing. He came around the table. As she turned to go over to the provisions he gripped her arm. "I'll make sure I never do it around you again, Rasal. I didn't realize you were squeamish. But a word in your marvelously attentive ear: next time don't warn me." He patted her shoulder affectionately. "Now why don't you see about sending that word you mentioned. I want to talk to young Cambion in three days."

She hates me, he thought as he watched her walk away. If I'm not careful she will kill me.

Would that be so bad?

What if she knew about the others? One by one he remembered them, each one a co who had worked for Cambion or Armada security or both, each one part of the system that had hurt him. There were a few left—Rike, certainly, Maxwell's chief butcher, and Maxwell himself, though likely he really was dead—and Soris had probably been one, he could not remember clearly, but he might as well have been. Rasal did not know. It was none of her concern, really, but she would think so and…actually kill him…

He drew a deep breath and tried to imagine death. All he could manage was a colorless nothing, sensationless and utterly boring.

But quiet, he thought, and painless…

I'm not right, he thought, not since Lt. Kalinge messed me up…there are drugs that would make me right, in the Pan…but then I wouldn't be able to finish what I have to do…

He grinned and pulled the map around to study it again.

The Cambion mines spread through those mountains like cracks in glass. The main tramline was only the most obvious way to get to them, and the easiest, but there must have been dozens more. His maps did not show any others. He wondered how many people Nicolan might have with him. He scratched his cheek absently. Was Maxwell with him?

He pulled on his coat and headed for the door.

"Where—?" Rasal began.

"I'll be back," he snapped and hurried out.

He ran from the door, across the vacant street and between two buildings. There he waited and watched the door he had just left. The building had housed a tailor, with tenants on the second floor, which had been burnt half away. The windows were covered in sheets now bearing graffiti. Beams, empty doorways, part of a wall jutted up into the night air.

Rasal did not emerge. Venner grunted and continued down the gangway, out into a small courtyard formed by four buildings, through another gangway into the next street. Three blocks west brought him to the ribbon that marked the boundary to the condemned section. There were no guards, but he was careful to keep to the darkest shadows.

The sky was fairly clear and scattered stars winked within the framing chimney rim. Red lights on the gun emplacements formed a constellation of their own.

The streets were almost empty. He remembered nights before the Secession when people crowded Crag Nook's hostelries and omnirecs and taverns and nightclutches and poured through the street in thick rivers. He missed it, though he had never cared for crowds. It had saddened him when he had to work to end what Finders had become, was becoming.

He turned up a narrow alley, stopped, and glanced back. Nothing. He walked on, stopped and turned again. Empty street.

Two children sprinted suddenly from one doorway to a another building. Venner's pulse quickened for a moment, his hand automatically reaching for the pistol in his coat. Then he sighed, slowly and purposefully, and continued down the alley.

He reached the street before his old house and looked up at the roof visible above the outer wall. The windows he could see were dark. He went on past, to the next alleyway, and along the wall. In the blackness he felt his way until he found a depression. Glancing left and right, he pressed his fingers into the edge. Mortar crumbled away; he found the keypad. Quickly he punched in the access code. The door opened for him with a faint grinding.

At the end of a short hallway he came to the inner door. Another keypad glowed faintly. He entered his code and stepped through into his house.

The basement smelled musty. He stumbled twice in the dark before he found the stairs. He drew his pistol and went up.

Faint light outlined the windows, silvered the floor of the long foyer. Venner stood still, listening to the silences around him, feeling strange and oddly unwelcome. He had liked this place, had even made a diagram of it with the idea of recreating it elsewhere, after he retired.

He shrugged impatiently and went to the second floor. All the doors stood open. He passed by the bedroom where he had punished the trespassers and went straight to his room. He stepped in.

The equipment was gone. He grunted sourly. Of course it was gone. He chided himself for thinking that anything might remain. The Armada took everything when they took.

Staring at the bed, he leaned against the jamb. Why, he wondered, had he come back then? The maps stored in his polycom were only a pretense. Standing here, the whole house lit like dust, monochrome, he felt immersed in nostalgia. Nostalgia drew him. *Nosta*, a return...*algia*, pain...a return to pain, a painful returning, and it did hurt to be here, where he had been hurt. He wondered sometimes how he had managed to do the work he had done for fifteen years and escape the kind of intimate pain that finally found him here. Till then, always the betrayer, never the betrayed.

It would be nice to let it go...

The difficulty was that he did not know why.

They were going to kill me...why? My own people...

Physical pain was brief and could not be clearly recalled, but these wounds of the psyche would heal, if at all, only with completion. Several components in that process were finished. He had hurt the Armada, upset their system of agents on Finders, starting with Co Harrias, which had been a surprise even for him. He wondered if Sean had known about her. He had dealt with those parts of Maxwell Cambion's organization that he could reach. He had manipulated partisans, damaged associations, inflicted pain where it seemed appropriate. Completion neared. All that he required was an answer to why.

Is that what I wanted from Soris?

He turned away from the room.

Someone stood at the end of the hall, near the head of the stairs. Venner dropped to one knee, brought the pistol up.

Two pistols flashed almost simultaneously, flooding the space with brief, brilliant light. Venner rolled to the right, into his old bedroom, and listened for the sound of his assailant.

Venner scurried, crablike, to the bathroom door. He pressed against the wall and checked himself over for injuries. Nothing. He smiled, almost laughed.

He listened. A board creaked. A few seconds later he heard the soft brush of fabric on skin. Venner held his breath, strained to hear more. The sound that came was a faint tick, nothing he could identify, except that it was in the next room, just beyond the door—

He whirled around and fired. He saw someone strobed in the flashes, one two three shots, the wall burst open. The man moved, fast, damnably fast, rolling, and collided with Venner's legs. Venner felt himself fall backward. He slapped the floor, all the air gushed from his lungs, and his skull bounced and set sparks dancing behind his eyes. Reflexively he started kicking, working his legs, up down, back and forth, finally rewarded with a solid contact and a heavy grunt. Hands clawed at his coat, trying to get a hold. Venner still held his pistol and swung it down, blindly. One hand jerked away instantly. Venner kicked again. The body fell aside.

He lunged for the door, tried to somersault through, but sprawled gracelessly over the floor. He stood and turned.

The attacker bodyslammed him back through the bedroom door, into the hallway. Venner brought the butt of the pistol down hard, twice, before he hit a wall and fell. He swung the pistol up to fire but this time a boot jammed his arm against the wall and his fingers opened; the gun flew away.

Venner kicked again. He could barely see, only a shape wrestling in the dark to snare him, so his kicks were blind, but he kicked with desperation and connected at least twice solidly. The man staggered away, groaning.

Venner crawled to the stairs. His legs shook, and he half ran, half fell down to the foyer. At the foot of the stair he groped for his other pistol, tucked in his boot, and aimed it up the stairs.

The attacker appeared and Venner fired. He saw him in the flash once, then did not see him again. Plaster fell from the ceiling.

He waited several minutes, frozen in place. Finally he moved. He got to the basement door, descended backward, then ran, still blind in the dank basement, for the exit. He fell over something that felt vaguely like a chair, kicked it away, then made the door.

Outside he waited again, listening. Nothing. But there had been nothing before...

He reached the street and ran.

Sean explored the house stiffly, pistol in one hand and lamp in the other. Venner was gone. Sean sighed and went back upstairs. He opened his medkit and started stripping off his clothes. He checked himself carefully and, amazed, found no broken bones. His torso felt bruised, though, and his left knee burned. He applied a salve to the worst points, then wrapped the knee. That would require a physician or at least the medunit on his ship.

He dressed and sat in the spare bedroom, going over in his mind what he had just done. A simple assassination and he botched it. Intentionally.

I don't really want to kill Venner, he thought sourly. He wondered whether, had the order come from the Secessionist side, he would have succeeded. Venner was dangerous to everyone. But the order had come from the Armada and he did not feel inclined to obey.

"One last chore for the old masters," he said to the walls.

No one seemed very dedicated to the task anymore. When he had returned he sensed the change in mood among the officers, even among the marines, a shift in priority. He guessed—correctly, he discovered—that the Armada was preparing to abandon Finders. That did not explain the ambivalence. Even when he had been given this assignment it had been with a degree of distraction, as if his accomplishing the mission was irrelevant. But he accepted the assignment because it gave him access to data, one last chance to dip from the well of Armada information before he declared his own independence.

They did not even know it *was* Venner. Someone, they said, was organizing the factions, putting together a large partisan army. They wanted it stopped. Sean had dug through files and discovered an incident in the tram station offices involving then-surface commander Captain Laros. That had been Hil Venner. Shortly thereafter, the tram explosion had crippled the connection to Emorick for nearly twenty days. After that, after he realized just who he had been sent to eliminate, he followed the trail of reports of sabotage. Hil had been very busy. Then suddenly it stopped and the first reports of a migration of partisan groups north to Emorick started. Venner was working for Jonner Liss now.

Was. Liss, Sean discovered, wanted Venner dead, too. Now that the coalition Venner was cobbling together for him was nearly complete—complete enough for Liss's purposes—he did not want a—how had he described it?—"a renegade psychotic loose in the mine field."

So. Neither side wanted Hil alive.

And I let him live, he thought. The truth was Sean did not believe Jonner Liss ought to have such an army.

But what if Hil takes it for his own?

No, he decided, that was too unlike Venner. He could assemble coalitions like this, but he could never run one. All this had accomplished was to make sure the Armada could not subdue and control Finders. Even an army of thirty plus thousand partisans could do little to get the Armada off the planet and nothing to get them out of the system. In a way, Hil Venner had chosen a side. Before Sean.

He felt guilty about the whole thing, an exotic sensation he had not experienced for a long time. Compounded guilt. He had followed Venner all the way from his hiding place to this house and might have finished the job at any point along the way. Added to that was the guilt at betraying an old colleague. Multiple betrayals at that. After all, Venner had been set to die originally for Merrick's sins. Sean smiled grimly at that thought. He had been discovered—almost—and the corps had sent janitors to clean up the mess. Only they identified the wrong co. Armada security knew they had a breach, but had not known exactly who. No wonder Venner was working so hard for the other side.

His head whirled with the choices he had made. At a future point he would have to kill Venner. Someone would. For now, though, he thought it better that Venner played the part of a spoiler, keeping everything in a state of flux.

Maybe. Or maybe I'm just sentimental, he thought.

He packed up his gear and left the house.

Cira stepped from the small, clean hospital room. Rollo waited a short way down the corridor, hands tucked in his deep pockets. She did not want to speak to him now so walked the other way, slowly.

"Do you wish to visit anyone else?" the troll asked, coming alongside her.

"No. I want to be alone."

"If you require assistance—"

"I know the code. Thank you."

The troll scooted ahead and disappeared around the next corner.

The corridor widened at the end into a waiting room. Saffron light filtered through blinds. Cira sat down and stared at the window, unseeing. After a time she heard Rollo's long, even tread approach. He sat down across from her, hands still in his pockets.

"I'm sorry," Cira said.

"You didn't do it."

"I promised you that everything would be all right."

"Some promises—it's the promise not the keeping that matters. That was one."

Cira shook her head. "No, I meant to keep it. I'm surprised you'll even talk to me."

"It wasn't your fault."

Cira wanted to argue with him, make him angry and accept his blame. But if Rollo intended to blame her he would, without pretense. As little as she really knew him she felt she knew this about him.

"Does she speak to anyone?" Cira asked.

"No. At least now she feeds herself. Right off she wouldn't take food."

Cira shook her head, dismayed. "The scars aren't visible."

"They're too deep."

They sat in silence for a time. Cira had sat by Becca for nearly half an hour, at first wordless, waiting for Becca to speak, then making conversational gestures that never became anything more, finally lapsing back to stillness.

"They sent me home from here," Cira said suddenly. "I spent seven days with my family. What used to be my family. You can't see the scars there, either, but the cut goes deep. Deep enough to sever."

"You're still welcome to be Hersted."

"Thank you. I'm not sure I deserve it."

Rollo shrugged. "When you think it's right." He stood. "I hate this place. It smells dead."

Cira nodded and rose. "Let's get started."

"South?"

"South."

The hospital was built into the wall of the chimney, one reason perhaps why it had been untouched in the riots. The tram station was a kilometer west and the walk took them through neighbor-hoods of fine houses, the old homes of merchant Founders and community leaders and, perhaps, a few members of Vested fami-lies. Many were empty now—abandoned in the first evacuations, or even before, Pan loyalists coming home at the first sign of familial disapproval—many occupied by squatters, and only a handful still lived in by original residents.

Cira said nothing all the way back to her barracks room. She sorted through her things, chose what she wanted to bring along, and packed them. Then she led the way to the quartermaster.

She drew field rations, weapons, powerpacks, field tents, medkits, a field comm—the quartermaster raised his eyebrows but did not question her. A few minutes later Commander Perse showed up.

"You're leaving today?" she asked, glancing over the equipment.

Rollo looked up once then returned to checking things out and packing.

"Yes, sir," Cira said. "I've got enough information here."

"Do you? Well. Very good, then."

"How long do I have, Commander?"

"If you're not back in five days we'll count you missing."

Cira nodded and continued working. She stripped a heavy s.p. rifle down, checked it carefully, reassembled it. The clicks and snaps filled the silence.

"My family will receive my investment?"

"Also your uniforms, any commendations, and an official testament."

"I would appreciate it, sir, if you would oversee that part. My family has difficulty understanding why I left for the Armada any-way. If it helped them make sense of it…"

"I'll see to it."

"Thank you, Commander."

Perse hesitated, glanced at Rollo. "I'm sorry. This hasn't been a very clear action, Lt. Commander. Many of us are finding it diffi-cult to define what's appropriate."

"I appreciate that, Commander. As I understand it we have to take it one order at a time and hope it adds up to something." She looked directly at Perse. "Whoever gave me this mission knows exactly what its purpose is."

"I'm sure they do." She extended her hand and Cira grasped it, tightly, briefly. Perse stepped back. "I'll have Palker see you safely on your way."

Cira watched Perse leave and pitied her.

"Think we got enough?" Rollo asked.

Cira looked over the assortment and shook her head. "But it'll have to do."

"Five days, she said. The Cambion mines are more than three hundred klicks south."

"I know."

"Not a lot of time to do anything."

Cira flashed him a grin. "Depends on what you expect to do."

"Why would anyone want you dead?"

She thought about that for a long time while she finished the inventory. "Not dead. Gone. Out of the way. Dead is a guarantee. They made me lie about a fellow officer, lie about the action here, and threatened to discharge me and force me to go back to my family if I didn't cooperate." She shook her head, amazed. "They understood that about me. That the idea of going home was worse than…was worse."

"So you cooperated. So?"

"I still know the truth."

"Who'd listen?"

"Honestly? I don't think anyone would."

"Then—"

She shrugged. "Maybe we'll figure it out before we die, Rollo."

"Five days a'n't a lot of time."

"That's the Armada's timetable. Not mine."

Chapter Eleven

Tory pressed back against the bulkhead and shivered. The undiffused blue-white light made harsh shadows beneath each detail in the un-adorned bay and did nothing to alleviate the cold. He tried not to look up, and concentrated on the wide hatch twenty meters across the time-stained floor. The bay vaulted a good forty meters high to a webwork of bare beams and cables and sharp lights that reminded him of incarceration.

An old troll skittered across the deck, a faint red light blinking intermittently on its blocky body. Tory stiffened, but it did not seem to notice him. Its motors whined; it needed repair. Tory blew out a cloudy breath and wondered how much else down here in the belly of this station needed repair. Certainly the environmental controls. He wrapped his arms across his chest.

The hatch opened, releasing a brief cloud of vapor. Jesa stepped out and waved him in. Gratefully, Tory picked up his pack and hurried across the bay. The umbilical was warmer, almost normal temperature.

"Oh, yes," Tory sighed and smiled. "Where did you find this freezer?" he asked, thumbing the hatch.

"You go where you have to. I've got us passage—"

"Us?"

She pushed him along. "Yes, 'us'."

"But—"

She stood with her hands on her hips, eyebrows raised, expect-ant, challenging.

"All right," Tory said. "Why?"

"Because *you* can't journal any of this. *I* haven't been so enjoined and I don't like using secondhand data."

"Very practical. Anything else?"

"Honestly?" Her eyebrows rose.

"Of course."

She raised her hand and ticked each point off on a finger. "I'm not sure you'd come back. I'm not sure you'd send anything back. I'm not sure if I'd get you to the front only to have you vanish in the Seven Reaches, leaving me with nothing to show for all the favors I've called for you."

"You have one digit left."

"I'm reserving that one," she replied, dropping her hand.

Faintly disappointed, Tory nodded. "You're probably right. Shall we meet our Charon?"

She gave him a quizzical look as he walked on up the umbilical.

Tory entered a cargo hold as harshly-lit as the bay he had just left. A couple of old, slow drudges, their mammoth bodies scored and dented, moved crates into webbing. In the center of the hold a small, slim man watched, referring to a handslate as each crate came aboard through the much larger cargo hatch. Jesa edged by Tory and he followed.

The man turned at their approach. He smiled and nodded to Jesa, then looked appraisingly at Tory. He came up to Tory's collarbone. A short mat of reddish hair covered a head that seemed too large.

"Shipmaster Cav Democlitus," Jesa said, "this is Tory Shirabe."

He thrust his hand out. "A pleasure, Co Shirabe. I follow your work, I like it."

"Thank you." Tory glanced at Jesa.

"My policy," Democlitus said, guessing at Tory's silent question, "is to know exactly what I'm carrying. I won't take a commission otherwise."

"But if anyone can get you out," Jesa added, "he can."

Democlitus grinned. "Getting you out won't be a problem. If you ever want back *in*, though…"

"One impossibility at a time," Tory said.

"Any luggage?"

Tory hefted the pack on his shoulder. "Just what I'm carrying."

"Mine's already stowed," Jesa said.

"How many in your crew, Shipmaster?"

"Just me. Once in a while I'll take on some temporaries, but I like quiet runs, all to myself. Where exactly in the Distals are we going, Co Shirabe?"

Tory looked at Jesa. "You didn't tell him?"

"My rules," Democlitus interjected. "Deniability. If I don't know, I can't tell Armada security. I wait till the last minute. That way I can decide on the spot."

"If you decide no?"

"You find another ship. If I decide yes, security is we leave immediately and everyone who should know is already on board."

Tory thought about it and nodded. "Not bad."

"So," Democlitus said. "Destination?"

"Finders."

Democlitus nodded, frowned thoughtfully. "Might have to take a roundabout route. Last time I was there it didn't appear the Armada planned to allow much traffic."

"That's where I need to go."

"Then I'll take you. No guarantees on time, though."

"I'm not sure that's particularly important."

"Good. Co Marlin knows where the cabins are, she can get you bunked. If you'll excuse me for now." He lifted his handslate and resumed his inventory.

Jesa nudged him toward an open-cage lift. It rose to the next deck and they stepped into a long passageway. Narrow service access hatches lined both bulkheads for fifteen meters, then four steps took them up into a wide common. The corridor resumed on the opposite side, this section with stateroom doors.

"Further on," Jesa said, pointing forward, "is the bridge. Meals are taken in the common, all automated. It's a pretty bare bones ship."

"Does it have a name?"

Jesa smiled. "*The Pope In Exile.*"

Tory laughed. "I take it you've used him before?"

"On a few occasions. He's really very good. He's been running contraband back and forth across the Secant since just after the Riot." She palmed open a stateroom. "Here. Your home till we can get you to more dangerous surroundings. I'm right across."

Tory dropped his pack and examined the small cabin. Fold-down cot, fold-down desk, comm, hygienic cubicle, closet. He turned once around and stopped, facing Jesa in the doorway.

"Jesa—"

"Thank me after we cross the Secant. Get settled in, I'll go check our departure schedule."

The door closed. Tory sat on the edge of the cot, suddenly very tired and more than a little anxious. Palada's trial was still going on. Tory had testified on the second day, thirty minutes that did not, in his estimation, do much. That had been three days ago and it seemed clear that he was no longer needed. In that time Jesa had managed to impress him with her resources. He felt like a package, though, being passed from point to point.

Eight hours later *The Pope In Exile* left the station. Tory was relieved when Democlitus made transition with no Armada inquiries. Then he fell into a dreamless sleep.

When he awoke he used the cube, dressed, and went into the common. Democlitus sat at one of the low tables, eating and scanning a handslate. The Shipmaster looked up and nodded politely.

"The 'chef does a fair job if your palate is simple," he said. "Anything fancy it might get creative on you."

"Take my chances, eh?"

"Something like that."

"I'm not hungry right now." He sat down across from Democlitus.

The Shipmaster switched off the text. "You want to talk?"

"I think so. How long do you estimate till we reach the Distals?"

"From here, six days. My first stop is Denebola. What I find out there decides how I go on. When I came back this last time the Armada was concentrating on three systems—Diphda, Eta Ceti, and Skat. They already had Beta Fornax and Gamma Hydras, and they'd broken off from Markab and Kappa Pegasus. It looked like they might retreat from Etacti, too, but that was questionable."

"And Skat?"

Democlitus shrugged. "I think they've lost interest. I think what they want now is to hurt the Distals, make it hard to rebuild, and maybe damage their standing with the seti. They can't possibly retake those systems, most of them were leased from the Seven Reaches. Skat's the temporary capital of the Secession, till Markab recovers, so I think the Armada will pound it till they're bored and leave."

"Finders?"

"I don't know anything about Finders. Communications from there isn't very good, which doesn't sound hopeful. Same situation with Holdkeep, Gamma Hydras. I have a bad feeling."

"Breakfast without me?" Jesa came into the common and went directly to the autochef.

"A bad feeling?" Tory pressed.

Democlitus sat back. "Are you familiar with Millennium?"

Tory's neck tingled. He glanced at Jesa, saw her back stiffen. "Yes and no."

"You know the official version?"

"Sure. Local pathogen mutated into a rapidly-changing recursive infection, killed ninety percent of the population before mutating back to a dormant form. The Armada isolated and contained the system, all traffic in and out stopped except for essential biotech personnel—"

"None of whom," Jesa added, sitting down beside him with a plate of food and a cup of coffee, "have ever been located."

"—and the plague was allowed to run its course. The only thing habitable in the system now is the transit station and a research facility monitoring the remaining population, all of whom are sterile."

"Do you believe it?" Democlitus asked.

"It has the quality of complexity and technical plausibility."

Democlitus grunted. "So you don't believe it."

"I didn't say that. It's one of the most popular conspiracy theory subjects ever, but just about everyone has given up on it. Twenty-six years is a long time not to turn up any new evidence. Now we have the Secession."

"There are a couple of things about it that struck me," Democlitus said. "Do you remember the name of the Task Commander at Millennium?"

"Riordan," Jesa said.

"And his second?" When neither journalist said anything, he grinned. "Micheson."

"Coincidence," Jesa said.

"Maybe. I was working then on a supply ship, running provisions to the system. Nearest we ever got was the outer perimeter, but you get to talk to crew and word gets out. Before the Armada descended on Millennium and sealed it from the rest of the Pan, there had apparently been an incident with the local militia involving an Armada cruiser. There were a dozen different versions of what started the trouble, but the governor tried to take over all Armada garrison functions. He threw the local commander in detention, had militia disarm the garrison—not a very impressive feat, really, the garrison only had a thousand marines—and he declared Millennium an independent polity. The Armada cruiser *Capricorn* was ordered to cut off traffic to and from the surface and isolate the transit station. The *Capricorn* was attacked and badly damaged. Next thing Millennium knew there were three hundred Armada ships in system and they were completely isolated."

"An early secession?" Tory said. "But, there were journalists on Millennium."

"Any of them live?"

"I don't remember…"

"And the name of the shipmaster of the *Capricorn*?"

"I don't—"

"Palada."

"You're suggesting," Jesa said, "that there was a massacre."

Democlitus nodded.

"Why? I mean, a whole system?"

"More to the point, Co Shirabe, is why again? Because the same things are happening in the Distals." He shrugged. "Now, I'll get you into Finders if you really want. But you have to know that you might not get back out." He stood. "Excuse me, coes, I have some chores to tend." He walked aft.

"Well," Jesa said around a mouthful of food. "That was cheering. You know, I've been using him now, on and off, for almost three years and that's the first time he's ever mentioned that he knew anything about Millennium. When this is over I'll have to sit him down and do a full interview."

"He doesn't know this is one your pet projects?"

"Mine? We worked together on Millennium, if I recall. You were just as obsessed as I was."

"You didn't answer me."

"No, I don't mention that to anyone unless it bears directly on my research." She raised an eyebrow at him. "I see that you don't admit anything either."

Tory shrugged. "We did what? Two thousand plus interviews? We went through all the public records and a good number of sealed documents, traced shipping logs, retired Armada personnel, families of Millennium colonists. Four years and what did we find? Nothing. Once the Armada went in, no confirmation of anything other than the official version. I was on the verge of believing it, too."

"What stopped you?"

"You have to ask that after the month I've just had?"

"Good point."

Tory looked toward the hatch through which Democlitus had left. "He might be making it up."

"Did that sound made up? A lot of it matched what we uncovered."

"And a lot didn't. His conclusions—"

"Are the same as mine. I never found any proof, though." She studied him narrowly. "But you followed Palada. That's why you were in Valico, wasn't it?"

Tory shrugged, then, under her continued stare, he nodded. "He'd been shipped to a backwater. Valico isn't much of a posting for an officer of his years and experience. I thought perhaps he might be fed up enough to tell me something."

"Did he remember you?"

"I didn't think so at the time, but in retrospect he made it terribly easy for me to get access to material."

"What theory about Millennium did you come up with that makes more sense than Shipmaster Democlitus's?"

"I didn't. What I saw on Finders would substantiate more than deny his story."

Jesa frowned. "What do you mean?"

Tory leaned forward. "We grew up believing the Armada was there to protect us. Sure, things go wrong, it's a big bureaucracy, lots of people with their own agendas, but for the most part they're the good guys. Right? We believe—*want* to believe—that they're basically the same as anyone else in the Pan Humana."

"So?"

"That's the problem. In many respects, they *are* just like anyone else in the Pan Humana."

"I'm not sure I follow."

"Sure you do. You just don't want to. In the face of imminent danger, how many of your principles are expendable? The horrible, alien, monstrous seti are corrupting humans in the Distals, turning them into things we won't recognize. What are you willing to do to prevent that from spreading? More to the point, what are most of the people you know willing to do?"

Jesa's jaw flexed.

"So," Tory continued after a moment, "the Armada is really the personification of all our fears. And they have guns. I don't believe there's anything they wouldn't do to fulfill their obligation."

"Murdering humans is not their obligation."

"It is if it means protecting the *idea* of human. Any deviation is intolerable. Secession is a clear sign of disease. Surgery is called for."

Jesa shook her head. "So...I gather that means you believe Shipmaster Democlitus."

"Maybe. It depends on his reasons for telling us."

"So why would he make it up?"

"So we might change our minds, not try to go to Finders."

"He could just refuse."

"No...I've known a lot of these independent shipmasters. If they say they'll take you on a run they won't back out unless you tell them to, even if they think it might cost them their ship. It's like they have something to prove to the universe."

"So are you going to change your mind?"

Tory grunted. "No. Maybe change ships when we find out what the situation is, let your friend off."

Jesa nodded, swallowed coffee. "This isn't bad for autochef, you ought to eat."

"Mm."

"What's wrong? Second or third thoughts?"

"No...not exactly. I'm still trying to make sense of what I believe."

"You mean about the Armada?"

"Partly. But it's not just the military. We make assumptions and forget we make them until they're discredited. Until my arrest and...treatment...by Armada security I think I would have believed that what happened at Millennium was an aberration, the actions of officers without official sanction. That kind of thing just doesn't *happen* in the Pan Humana."

"For the most part it doesn't. Or at least it didn't."

"Right. It doesn't have to. The Pan is *comfortable* if nothing else—and it's a *lot* else. Nobody wants to challenge it, nobody feels the need to question the way things are run. Hell, they don't even realize that it *is* run, that decisions are made daily that keep the machinery tuned and engaged. Those who *do* question it are seen as oddities—intellectual purists, radical hermits, maladjusteds—their arguments are entirely matters of philosophy because nothing seems to be broken."

"Nothing *is* broken, though."

Tory looked at her sharply. "Then why would a Millennium happen? Why the Riot? Why the Secession?"

"Surely you're being rhetorical?"

"Before all this I would have answered my own question like this: the Pan Humana is a machine, designed and built and maintained to do a certain task. It does that task better than any previous example of its kind. But a machine built to do one thing cannot, without considerable redesign and refit, do something else. Therefore, it cannot accommodate different systems it was never designed to accommodate. If people try to force it to do so, casualties will result."

"And what's wrong with that description now?"

"Nobody in the Distals tried to force the machine. They tried to leave it."

"So...?"

"Machines don't do things out of fear. You can't threaten a machine. Those are organic reactions. And that's the only reason for the Pan to go out into the Distals and do what it's doing—fear, panic, jealousy—all organic causes."

"Which means—"

"It's not a machine. So there's no logical reason why it cannot accommodate what it's trying to destroy."

"You're saying all this is a choice?"

"Somewhere, at some level, absolutely."

Jesa finished her breakfast silently. Tory leaned back and gazed at the ceiling, trapped for the moment in the recomplicating web of his own reasoning. He did not notice when Democlitus returned, when Jesa accompanied the Shipmaster forward, returned, left again, and finally said something about being in her cabin for a nap.

Tory wandered to the bridge. Democlitus hunched over a navigation console, his face a rigid mask of concentration. The bridge seemed cramped with equipment, though there was ample deck space. The only light came from the innumerable monitors and gauges, light which seemed to pool in the center of the space and radiate back out to smooth all shadows.

Soon enough, Tory mused, they won't be able to accommodate you, either, Shipmaster. You're the uncontrolled element, the treasonous messenger, the string that binds what the Pan wants cut loose, gone.

He thought of all the independents he knew. The life was glamorized in the poplit, but there was nothing easy about it. Ships crewed by one or five or fifteen coes, working ten times harder than any co aboard one of the big megacorp liners just to keep the fees balanced between stations. No one went hungry or without shelter or access to a rich cultural datapool in the Pan, but that did not mean everyone did whatever they wished without cost. Basic commodities existed for everyone and, Tory knew from his few historical researches, what defined basic in the Pan would in past eras have been considered a standard of wealth. But over and above basic, nothing was guaranteed. Shipmaster Democlitus lived a truly luxurious life by virtue of what he could do. It was a precarious life, though, and demanded constant, hard labor, attention to detail; dedication which most Panners found both exotic and perverse. Because what he did allowed him participation in mainstream life as well, he did not share the social stigma attached to radical hermits, freeriders, returnists, nids, and other fringe entities who rejected the lifestyle of the Pan. But he was not far from such status.

They were a threatened group, too. Shipping grew more and more automated, caravans of huge robot freighters moving vastly more tonnage per run than a ship like *The Pope In Exile* could ever hope to. Independents existed more and more in the cracks left by standard shipping. Exotic merchandise—not a little of it illicit seti items smuggled over the new border—and schedules made on the spur of the moment, a shipment overlooked and required, whimsical passengers on what they assumed to be adventurous jaunts, courier services that the megacorps runs could not or would not accommodate. Fewer independents made more profit from such trade and, Tory imagined, once the Secant was concretely established, fortunes might be made in smuggling. The independents were moving into a final brilliant state before nova, and the end of life as they knew it.

Then there was the role they had played in the Riot. Many people, Tory knew, blamed the independents for bringing the setis, for enabling the rioters, for sponsoring and supporting the Secession. No doubt, many independents had participated—but Tory knew better than to paint an entire group with the same brush.

Tory had seen this all along and never before thought it through. It was too easy to simply assume that nothing much would ever change. Things might get more difficult, but so what? The independents would not be allowed to disappear altogether. The novelty alone...

At Denebola Tory remained on board. Jesa accompanied Democlitus out. Tory watched from the observation room above the cargo hold as the drudges began moving crates from their webbing back to the conveyor and out of the ship. Democlitus had six drudges, large clumsy-looking things that nevertheless moved gracefully and efficiently. *The Pope In Exile* also boasted three trolls, one of which supervised the unloading in Democlitus's absence.

Jesa and Democlitus returned on the second day. Democlitus carried a small case under his arm and went straight to the bridge. One of the drudges brought into the hold a single large nacelle. The other drudges stowed themselves in their service niches, the umbilicals retracted, and *The Pope In Exile* left the station.

"We're going to directly to Markab," Democlitus explained. "I've got a delivery to make there. Evidently Etacti is being abandoned. Armada units have been transferring to Diphda for the last seven days."

"The Armada got hurt before at Etacti," Jesa said. "Do you think it happened again?"

"I'm not making any guesses. We can find out more at Markab."

"How long?" Tory asked.

"Three days." Democlitus raised a hand. "I know, I'm behind schedule, but I have to take a roundabout route or chance running into Armada units." He returned to the bridge.

Jesa patted Tory's hand. "We'll get there."

"You could have gotten off at Denebola. It might have been safer."

She shrugged. "And miss all this?"

Tory looked at her. She smiled confidently. "Jesa, have I underestimated you?"

"Probably. Most people do. But I don't take it personally. It's part of the job."

"Job..."

"Listen, Tory, I want you to know...I think you're one of the best. I always scan your material and try to figure out how you figured it out. You're..."

"Don't. I never take compliments very well, even when they're genuine. They muddy my thinking, make me sloppy. But thank you."

She nodded, looking uncertain. "You know, you don't have to stay all to yourself." When he gave her a surprised look, she stood and shrugged. "Just a suggestion. Nothing personal."

"I didn't think you wanted the complications. Last time—"

"Forget the last time. This is different." She touched his hand lightly. "It wasn't *you* I left. You were—you were fine."

"Let me think about it."

"You've got three days."

He watched her go back to her cabin, a mixture of anticipation and resentment fueling his imagination. There had been no formal ending. For a time Tory assumed they might pick up where they had left off. Eventually he stopped thinking about it; the possibility faded to inconsequence. The idea appealed to him now with surprising force and, effortlessly, he remembered details from before.

Why now, though? he wondered, and resented her for taking so long, an irrational resentment, he conceded, since he had taken just as long. Why now?

The question engendered another reaction, not as strong as the first two, but a permeating substance coloring everything as it rose to consciousness. Suspicion.

Which left him with only one sane answer. Tory laughed to himself. With all that had happened, it seemed absurd that denial should be the only sane response remaining to him.

Alexan smiled at the procession of people that walked through his room. Many were acquaintances, coes he had met once or twice, forgotten till now. A few were more than acquaintances, likewise forgotten till now, but for different reasons.

Claye stood to one side, leaning back against the wall, watching. He felt as if he were showing off for her, displaying a talent he had forgotten he possessed. Memory, he decided, is a talent not equally shared.

He came to the end of the parade and raised his hand. The last five stopped and turned toward him, politely expectant.

"These are the core," he said to Claye, although she knew already. "These are the ones who were instrumental."

Claye greeted each by name. She was excited, he could tell. This was the first time they had all been gathered together.

"Lovander Mipelon," she said, nodding, "Ambassador Tan-Kovis, Co Maxwell Cambion, Co Houston Thayer, Lt. Cira Kalinge."

Alexan felt a peculiar pride at the last. Cira had been the last person he recalled, with Claye's help. For several days she had been his constant companion here, talking to him, nursing him, helping him fill in blanks. He glanced at Claye. She had helped him through all this, painfully rebuilding memories, even the memory of his father, Houston Thayer, a man he had never known. But Claye had been able to provide a name, something of a personality, and an explanation.

"Thank you all," Alexan said.

Cira and Houston smiled brightly. Maxwell grunted. Both the setis bowed.

Alexan reached out and touched Claye's hand. "Thank you, most of all."

Claye seemed anxious, uncertain.

Alexan sighed. "Maxwell took me for his own when Houston died. I don't know how that happened, but I'm grateful to Maxwell for that. He used seti technology to remake me into his own son, a privilege for which I'm both flattered and resentful. Mipes and Kovy made sure I could still be my own person and Cira enabled me to do exactly that. Maybe if she'd had a little more time she might have brought me all the way to myself. But Claye completed that, so it's worked out." He cleared his throat.

"I've brought you all here now, though, at Claye's behest. She wants to ask you all questions. I'd appreciate it if you'd answer her, truthfully."

"Why should we?" Maxwell snapped.

"Because I asked you to. You owe me, Max."

He shrugged. "If you expect an apology—"

"Just answer Claye's questions."

"Don't be a shit, Max," Houston said. "Go on, Co Albinez."

"Thank you," Claye said. She stepped forward. She seemed stiff, overly-formal, hands pressed together before her. Even her speech was strained, unnatural. "Maxwell, you have expressed several times what your intentions were in creating Alexan. Do you have anything to add? Did you know the Secession was coming? How long has it been in the planning?"

She droned on. Maxwell answered perfunctorily, almost reluctantly. A part of Alexan understood the technical part of what he saw. The enormous amount of data Claye had gleaned from him in the past weeks had gone into constructing a program from which all that Alexan knew served as a platform from which probabilities could be deduced. Each of the personas Claye now interrogated were based on highly-modeled projections and informed with details that Alexan had always known yet had never pieced together into the kinds of answers Claye now sought. In effect, she was asking for answers that were extremely precise assumptions of what these people knew.

The nature of the questions disturbed him, though. This was a military interrogation. Realizing this, Alexan knew that Claye was not the interrogator. Her model was being used.

When neither seti answered any of her questions, Alexan was perversely delighted. Claye—the Claye projection—became frustrated and irritated. The voice changed, became more strident.

"The emperor's wardrobe is disappearing," Houston Thayer said.

Claye turned on Alexan. "Are you doing this?"

"Doing what?"

"Blocking me."

Alexan looked at Lovander Mipelon and Tan-Kovis. "I don't know. Your models are based on what I know of them. Now that

I think about it, under these circumstances the real ones probably wouldn't answer you, either." He smiled. "So I suppose the answer is yes, in an indirect manner."

Her hands rolled into fists. "Stop it. Let them answer."

"But—"

"He cannot," Tan-Kovis said.

Claye whirled. "Why?"

"Because we are not based, as he has assumed, on models you have built. We are separate models introduced into your system that were stored in Alexan's mind, an invasive program."

"What...?"

"We've been observing all this, all along, and operating through your systems. By now, we've spread into your main dataspheres. You'll never get us out. Not to worry, though, we have no intention of damaging you."

"Then, why?"

"Information. It's the only universal commodity. Communications is a constant within and between civilizations. We long since have isolated the data we wanted and encoded it within normal communications. It has been in your vernacular 'smuggled' to the Distals and beyond, to the Reaches. All the while you have been working on Alexan to restore his memory, this program has been teasing out bits of your larger dataspheres and sending them out. By now we know a great deal about you."

"Then—"

"Alexan was never Maxwell's tool, although Maxwell thought so. He was a courier. Now he's made his delivery."

Alexan stared at Tan-Kovis. The Ranonan looked at him with eyes that, for all their strangeness, seemed to offer sympathy.

"It was an opportunistic arrangement, Alex," the seti said. "If Maxwell hadn't done what he did to you, perhaps this would never have happened. We *did* sabotage enough of his intentions to assure that you would, as we said, set your own goals. But on the off chance that something like this happened—"

"But I've succeeded," Alexan said.

Tan-Kovis nodded. "It seems so. The program has run its course and purged itself from your mind. You're free of us. It seems you're free of Maxwell."

"There's only one more thing to be free of, then." He smiled. "Thank you."

Claye looked from Alexan to the two setis, back and forth, torn between them. A voice absolutely not Claye's shouted, "You have betrayed us!" But Alexan could not tell to whom this was directed.

"It's all right," he said. "I'm fine."

"*You're* fine!"

"Alex," Lovander Mipelon interrupted, which curiously froze the Claye projection.

"Yes, Mipes?"

"An order for your summary execution has been transmitted. You're to be terminated at once, all records from Co Albinez's work sealed."

"Oh. Well, there's nothing I can do about that. I'm stuck."

"This is a private dialogue for the moment," the Vohec said. "We have isolated this time frame. We cannot prevent them from terminating you. You're not a program that we can copy and save, either. You *will* die. But we can preserve a model of you. In fact, Co Albinez has done just that."

"So I could exist like you? A shadow?"

"There would be continuity after a fashion."

"They'll hunt you down and purge you eventually."

"Likely."

Alexan shook his head. "Then thank you. But no."

"Then may we offer you a death not of their choosing?"

"You can do that?"

"The node that contained this program is still in place. An embolism. Deny them the last bits of your consciousness."

Alexan looked at the other three. "I'm glad to have known you all." He glanced at Claye, then nodded to the two setis.

The room faded quickly to black. A moment later he forgot everything completely, even that he had forgotten, and nothing remained.

The Markab Transit Station was little more than a core two kilometers long with extensions growing out from the central cylinder, on its way to becoming a small world, but for now only a skeleton. Several sections were new, a few mangled by explosions. Tory studied it on a flatscreen in the common as *The Pope In Exile* approached.

The planet, Maron, appeared an inhospitable moil of dust and stone, a thin wisp of atmosphere haloing its limb like heat mirage.

"We made it," Jesa announced. She sat down beside him and gazed at the screen.

Ships docked at the ends of the arms. Tory had never seen a station in such early stages of construction. It looked so vulnerable, everything normally hidden in a skin of metal and polymers open to space.

The Pope In Exile maneuvered through a cloud of small defensive craft and berthed.

"This is your chance to see what the Secession is like without the Armada buzzing around," Democlitus said. He handed both of them transponders. "If I need you back here I'll signal."

"Where are you going?" Tory asked.

"I have a delivery to make, co. We might have a couple of days here."

People jammed the station. Many slept in the corridors. The humid air implied an overtaxed environmental system. Medstations proliferated. Tory recognized the varied accents of several worlds. Conversation seemed fixed on refugees and the status of the station and other systems and how many more people they could support. Omnirecs and nightclutches had been turned into hostels and hospices.

Tory watched Jesa stop and speak quietly and professionally with several coes on the way to the shunt. With each conversation her face hardened.

At the shunt they waited ten minutes. Finally a car arrived and they squeezed in with eight others. Jesa found his hand and held it tightly during the ride, then let go when they emerged into a main circuit.

Even here, as spacious as the circuit was, people crowded together. Jesa worked her way among them, Tory in tow, toward an ominrec still operating independently.

They had to wait for a table. When they finally fell into the cramped booth, Jesa leaned her head back, eyes closed, and blew out a long breath.

"Not what you expected?" he asked.

"More," she said. She wiped her forehead free of sweat. "This station can't handle many more."

"We could go back to *The Pope In Exile* and wait for Democlitus to return."

She shook her head absently. "No, not yet."

He frowned. "You're recording all this."

"Of course." She tapped her middle finger against the menu. "Nothing but stew. I suppose I should be surprised they even have that."

"This isn't a cheap war for them."

"Is that disapproval I hear in your voice?"

"I don't know."

"You don't think I should record? What am I suppose to take back to show for my efforts? Your gratitude?"

"Is that sarcasm I hear in *your* voice?"

"Damn right." She glared at him. "The favors I called in to do this were expensive."

"Then why did you do it? You didn't have to."

"I didn't have to get you out of detention, either. Some things you just do because..."

He waited. She turned her attention back to the menu.

"Just because," he finished for her, "they're right?"

Jesa nodded. "It would be nice to be acknowledged for that."

"That's a separate reason."

A man appeared at the edge of their table. "Sorry, coes, no food. I can offer you beer."

"Beer?" Tory asked, dismayed. "Isn't that kind of an exotic commodity to have in these times?"

"No, it's cheap to make. We use excess gasses from the recycling system, yeast from the waste disposal—"

Tory held up a hand. "Never mind, co. I'd rather not know."

The man grunted a near laugh. "You're not from Maron."

Jesa shook her head.

"Well, I'll tell you," he said, "unless you're part of the Council, you'd be just as well off on board a ship."

"Are there more refugees coming in?" Jesa asked.

"Word is we've got a load coming from Holdkeep. A caravan slipped through the cordon."

He looked around suddenly, as if someone had called him, then faded away into the crowd. Tory pushed himself to his feet. Wordlessly, Jesa followed.

Two armed guards stood at the umbilical to *The Pope In Exile*. "No admittance, coes," one of them said.

"This is our ship," Jesa said.

"My orders are 'no admittance'."

"Till when?" Tory asked.

"Till they get changed."

They pushed their way across from the umbilical and pressed against the bulkhead.

"Now what?" Tory complained.

"We wait."

Tory grunted and slid to the deck. The throng moved sluggishly before him. Through a shifting forest of legs he could see the pair of guards.

"I suppose," Jesa said, "we shouldn't have left the ship."

"I don't know. We wouldn't have had such marvelous stew on board." She smiled and he added, "And you wouldn't have gotten more material to market when you get back."

"Are you angry with me about that?"

"I don't know. It just seems rather mercenary."

"And you've *never* been mercenary!" She scowled. "You know, one of the things I always admired about you was your tenacity. You never let anything get between you and a story. I miss that."

"Jesa..." Tory began.

"I think the Armada stripped more than your memory out of you, Tory. We put that back, but this...I don't know if we can."

"I *wouldn't* have put peoples' lives in jeopardy for a story!"

She looked at him oddly. "But you used to do it all the time."

"I—there was no way to avoid certain situations."

"What? Oh, Tory! Of *course* there was. Quit being a journalist. Very simple, very elegant. Step out of it, don't participate in it at any level. No one would be put at risk, then, by your actions. Of course, no one would be helped, either."

She held his hand. Tory concentrated on that. He did not know what Jesa wanted, nor what he wanted. It was easier to accept what was offered, each gesture for itself. Maybe the cumulative result would make sense.

He dozed and came awake to the chirping of their transponders. Jesa jumped to her feet. She offered her hand again and he pulled himself up.

The same guard stepped forward again. "No admittance—"

"We've been summoned," Tory started.

"Let 'em in, goddamnit!" Democlitus bellowed from the umbilical. "They're my crew!"

The guard seemed uncertain for a second, then stepped aside.

Tory expected to be stopped all the way up to the lock of *The Pope In Exile*. When he stepped on board his relief was palpable.

"What happened?" Jesa demanded.

"Got requisitioned," Democlitus said. "The Secessionist Council is drafting all independents. Refusal means getting your ship impounded."

"Requisitioned for what?"

"Whatever needs doing. In this case, escort service for the refugee caravan out of Holdkeep."

"But—" Tory began.

Democlitus waved him silent. "When they found out I was going to Finders anyway, they changed my duty. I'm a courier again. So we're going."

"When are we leaving, Cav?" Jesa asked.

"Soon as I'm reprovisioned," Democlitus said.

Tory felt the last tatters of his fear drift away. What was left seemed inadequate motivation to either go on or go back. He shook his head and went to his cabin.

"Tory—" Jesa called after him.

He closed the door without answering.

The Pope In Exile embarked a few hours later. Tory stayed in his stateroom most of the day. When he came out the common was empty. He ordered a meal and sat down to eat it.

Democlitus came in from the bridge.

"Another fourteen hours and we'll be on final approach to Diphda," he said. "I've been sampling comm traffic. It's busy in that direction. I should warn you that I might not get you through."

"Get me close, I'll find someone who can."

"That's not very complimentary, Co Shirabe."

"I'm not in a complimentary mood, Co Democlitus."

The Shipmaster scowled. "What's your problem? You're getting everything you wanted. It's not reasonable to think you won't get everything you don't want."

"I'm not in very reasonable mood, either."

"If you like. I'll be on the bridge from here on in."

"Co Democlitus."

"Yes?"

"Did you know Jesa was recording everything?"

He shrugged. "I thought as much."

"Including this voyage, you, your ship, everything that's been done so far."

"That's her job, isn't it?"

"Why are you being so understanding? She releases all her material you'll never be able to work in the Pan again."

"If you're going to deal in treason you shouldn't be judgmental about betrayal. I don't really care. I'm not planning on going back, except illegally."

"You're not taking Jesa back?"

"She hasn't contracted me to. I took you both on with the understanding that you would make your own ways back—or, at least, she would, since she didn't think you would want to. If she can find someone willing to take her back..."

Tory laughed, startled, and Democlitus returned a conspiratorial grin.

"I see what you mean," Tory said. "It's all an issue of contracts for you."

"Exactly, co. Now if you'll excuse me."

A thick strip of equipment and troops hid the horizon, four hundred meters out. Nicolan estimated three thousand marines and more than enough assault vehicles, but personnel came and went daily. In the six days since the raid neither side had fired on the other. The Armada base grew, Nicolan's people stayed underground, watching. As expected, Thayer smelter works had been seized, but tunnels Nicolan's people had begun before the raid were quickly completed and nothing really changed.

No word from Lovander Casm, either. Nicolan walked away
from the operations area, nodding to those he passed, stopping to
speak to a few. All show, he thought, all mask.

Kee came toward him, waved. Nicolan smiled. For the first
time since the raid he saw energy in Kee's face. Not quite the casual
optimism he once displayed, but better than sullen fear.

"Just received a message," Kee said. "Maybe a breakthrough.
Something new, anyway."

"From...?"

"North. Jonner Liss."

"Oh." Nicolan tried to cover his disappointment. Where were
the Vohec? He nodded toward his command digger.

Kee seemed not to notice Nicolan's reaction. "A courier approached
the compound outpost," he said as they stepped up into the vehicle.
"Liss has been gathering together all the partisans, forming an alliance."

"All of them?"

"Most. The courier said he's got agreements from all the larger
groups and a lot of the others. Close to forty thousand coes."

Nicolan poured two cups of coffee, handed one to Kee, then
sat down. "Forty thousand. To do what?"

Kee blinked. "Well, I imagine to fight. One cohesive force—an
army—obviously has a better chance than hundreds of little guerilla
bands. You know, strength in numbers, unified goals, stuff like that."

"Sounds reasonable."

"But not to you?"

Nicolan rolled his eyes. "Forty thousand coes with s.p.s and a
few transports won't beat an Armada occupation force. Four hundred thousand won't. Think about it, Kee. Actually, a hundred
separate guerilla bands have more chance. It costs more to track
them all down, it expends enemy resources, bleeds them slowly. I
imagine the task commander would love having all our partisans
gathered together in one place."

Kee looked down into his coffee. "Liss's negotiator wants to
meet with you, talk it over."

"Huh. What's to talk?"

"I don't know. Maybe you should go find out."

Nicolan looked up, startled at the edge in Kee's voice. "All right.
We'll meet, we'll talk."

Kee relaxed visibly, then looked embarrassed. "Sorry, boss. I've been under a little strain lately."

"Me, too. I wish Maxwell were here."

"You've been doing good on your own."

"Hm. Maybe."

"Not maybe."

"I miss him."

"That's different. I miss my parents, too. Well, I miss my mother. Pater was—pater was pater, never seemed to give a shit."

"You miss him, though."

Kee nodded. "I miss him." He gulped coffee. "You never talk about your mother."

"Didn't know her. She died when I was about two hundred and fifty days." Nicolan grinned. "I always believed she must have been incredible. She tolerated Maxwell enough to have a child with him. But aside from a gene template and a holo I don't know anything about her." He cleared his throat. "Where is this meeting supposed to happen?"

"In the compound. I thought that would be safe, neutral ground, not likely to be any Armada nearby."

"You already set it up?"

"Of course, boss. It's my job to know what you want before you do."

"Kee, you son of a—"

"Co Cambion," the comm interrupted.

Nicolan turned. "Yes?"

"New activity topside."

Kee followed him back to the operations center. Fio pointed. On the monitors several large transports were hovering at the northern edge of the Armada base.

"More troops?" Kee wondered.

"Looks like it," Nicolan said. "When is this meeting supposed to happen?"

"Two days."

"We'll be there." As Kee hurried off, Nicolan watched the transports with gnawing helplessness. "I want everyone prepared to evacuate, Fio."

"I'll pass the word," she said.

He looked over at the dedicated commlink where he had hoped to receive word from Casm. Still blank.

The trail cut its way through the mountains about five to seven hundred meters up, a winding, cracked path that occasionally led inside the rock, as if a great worm had bored it out. Cira was drawn again and again by the view across the plains. The strangeness of it—orange-to-greenish sky, yellow and red clouds, black foliage over ocher soil—still shocked her naked eyes. The corrective goggles were no better, the colors as startlingly false as the world was startlingly different. She opted for reality and negated the correction.

At dusk on the fifth day Rollo pointed south to a blackened crater. "The Cambion port," he said.

Cira tapped her goggles and read the range. Even at eleven kilometers it was an impressive sight. Radiation appeared faded almost to normal levels, but she would not want to be close for very long. The medkits could handle large doses, but she wanted to conserve them.

"Another day, two at most," Rollo said.

"Sooner. I feel exposed out here."

Rollo shook his head and chuckled. "You're going to walk me to death."

"You were born and raised here, you're going to tell me an outworlder is going to outwalk you on your own world?"

Rollo shook his head. "I'm not going to tell you anything."

Palker had sent them down a service shunt that paralleled the tramline. They got out at one hundred forty kilometers—the limit of Armada security—and walked an access tunnel to the eastern slopes of the Hobics. Cira was glad and troubled. She wore Founder clothes, she felt comfortable in Rollo's company away from the now-oppressive formality of the Armada. But she was not direct-linked. The field comm provided an uplink, but it was not realtime, not full sensory. They sent her out to spy alone, unsupervised, unaided.

She was relieved that the Armada has sent out few infiltrators. The partisans had little experience with them, then, so her chances were good. So far they had relied on locals, and not many of them. That bothered her, too. It was as if they simply did not care what the partisans did.

Rollo tapped her shoulder and pointed out to the east. Cira studied the landscape for movement, but saw nothing. "What…?"

"The land," Rollo said, pointing again.

She saw it then and amped the magnification. Too far to clearly resolve, sickly yellowish streaks, a different shade than the soil, broke up the black ground cover. It was a small area, maybe a patch five kilometers across, and nearly forty kilometers away. Cira shrugged and continued walking.

At sundown they climbed up off the trail and found a perch a few meters higher. Rollo attached the sleep rolls, then peeled open rations for both of them. The chameleon fabric matched the look of the rock and they huddled within the warm folds, watched the stars appear fitfully between breaks in the cloud cover, and ate.

"Did you ever find out what became of your family in Emorick?" she asked.

"Mater Ghasa died. Those left joined Liss. They didn't say whether they kept the name." He shifted, settled. "You said you're severed from your family. What about the Armada?"

"I was required to bear witness against my old commander, the one I came here with originally."

"What was he guilty of?"

"They said negligence."

"What do you say?"

"He embarrassed the Armada."

"Oh. Then I guess they found him guilty."

"I don't know. After my testimony I was put on a ship and brought back here."

"Then I suppose you really don't have a family."

"Maybe I don't need one."

"Maybe. I've known a some coes who didn't. A'n't for me, though."

"What would you do, Rollo, if you lost Finders?"

"Do you think that's likely?"

"It's possible."

"Then…I suppose I'd go somewhere else. I don't know. It's hard to imagine losing a whole world."

No harder, Cira thought, than losing a whole family.

In the morning, they packed up and continued on. Cira set a
brisk pace. Her muscles had never completely acclimated to Finders, she had ached almost from the moment she had stepped from
the shuttle, but the pain continued to diminish. It would probably
never disappear altogether, but she did not mind. With each step
she knew she was not home.

Rollo took the lead, keeping about four meters ahead of her.
The trail rose and fell, rose again, then turned inward, leading them
through another tunnel. Cira had lost count of how many of these
wormbores they had gone through. This one was short; light shone
clearly at the end, visible from the entrance.

Rollo reached the end, stopped, and backed up. Cira unslung
her rifle.

"Shit…" Rollo whispered, his voice small and hollow in the
tunnel.

Cira moved up behind him. He lowered to a squat and she
could see the trail beyond him.

The rock was black with energy scoring. She followed the streaks
up the slope, almost thirty meters. Here and there bone curved
away from the cliff, uneven masses that had once been humans
stretched out and burned into the stone, the molten remains of weapons and equipment, scattered up from the trail, all inside the margins
of the burn. She counted twenty-five, but she could not be sure.

She worked her way around Rollo, hugging the cover of the
trail edge, till she could peer downslope. At first she saw nothing.
Then she spotted the broken vehicles far below, just off the road.
Armada transports. She switched to IR but saw no traces of life.
The battle had been fought, the site abandoned.

"Come on," she said, standing.

"This must've happened early on," Rollo said, checking his radiation detector.

Cira nodded, scanning the rocks higher up.

"I wonder who they were," Rollo said.

Cira took the lead. Five hundred meters further on they found
a tunnel entrance that led into the mountain. Deep within light panels shone dimly.

"Probably connects to one of the Cambion shafts," Rollo said.

"Then that's probably where we want to go."

Rollo sighed. "We don't have to do this, Cira."

"No. But what would we do instead?"

"I'm only stating a fact."

Cira smiled. "So we both know we did it by choice?"

"Something like that."

"Thank you, Rollo."

She stepped into the tunnel. At twenty paces she heard him follow.

Tory stayed on the bridge. Democlitus weaved in and out of a thickening forest of Armada patrols as they drew closer to Diphda. *The Pope In Exile* possessed a catalogue of fake registries and identities, complete with manifests, transit permits, and false port logs. Democlitus probed the approaches, searching for the gaps in the blockade.

"That's Diphda, there," he said, indicating a big red star on one of the monitors. "That's from the old Arabic, *Al Difdi al Thani*', the 'Second Frog'. The Romans called it *Rana Secundus*, but the way the whole system has been worked I think they should have given it the ancient Chinese name, *Too Sze Kung*."

"Why? What does that mean?"

Democlitus grinned. "'Superintendent of Earthworks.'"

Tory smiled. "Do you know the history of all the systems you visit?"

"Hell no, there's too much. But some of them—like this one—invite inquiry. This system is the source of a lot of attention right now." He chuckled. "For the Pan I think its other name has bearing. To the Greeks it was Beta Cetus, which became the Arabic *Al Dhanab al Kaitos at Janubiyy*, 'the Tail of the Whale'."

"So tell me, Ahab—"

Democlitus held up a hand. He stared intently at another monitor, then made a few adjustments.

"We're being hailed again," he said. He released another data package to answer the hail and leaned back, fingers laced over his stomach. "This one's not accepting it."

"How far out are we?"

"Too far…just under four-tenths of a light year, but it may as well be four light years." He glanced at Tory. "I'm going to have to ask you to leave the bridge, Co Shirabe. I don't care much for an audience under these circumstances."

"But—"

"I'll route a datafeed to the common, you can watch from there."

Tory nodded and went down to the common room. He keyed a flatscreen. There was little to see from the direct sensor feed. The polycom "corrected" the distortion of translight and presented him a tableau of stars. He asked for an abstract and the screen showed him a grid, Diphda at the center, ship positions relative. Two ships moved after them. Democlitus changed course for a direct plunge into the system. Tory wondered how fast *The Pope In Exile* was, then realized that the question was irrelevant—Armada patrols would be thickest near the perimeter.

"What are you doing?"

He looked up as Jesa came toward him. "Watching the final act of our play. We're about to be captured."

Jesa frowned and studied the flatscreen thoughtfully. She shrugged and turned toward him.

"Tory, I'm not going to apologize. I don't think I did anything wrong—"

"Did I say you were doing anything wrong?"

"I wanted honest material."

"Which time and which piece are you referring to?"

"This time, these pieces. I'd like to have worked with you again, but I didn't think you were open to the idea."

"Not open? Or untrustworthy? Maybe I never intended to stay gone, maybe I intended to build a grand comeback on the corpse of the Secession." He grunted. "That sounds about right. Might have worked, too, if I gave a damn about the Pan anymore."

"You're not objective anymore."

"If I ever was."

"Oh, I suppose that means I never was, either."

"Listen to your tone of voice. Of course you're not. Look, you don't need to apologize—"

"Shut up, Tory. I said I won't apologize. But I don't want us to end up on bad terms. We didn't hate each other when it was over the last time. I did not intend to hurt you or offend you. If this had worked out as I'd hoped we very likely would never see each other again. Ever."

"Sentiment, Jesa?"

She winced. "You're not going to let this be easy, are you?"

He laughed dryly. "No. It hasn't been easy on me. You weren't arrested, detained, and *manipulated* like I was. I hope you never are, but it has one thing to recommend it. When you come out you have perspective."

"On what?"

"The nature of the real."

"Philosophy, Tory?"

"Hm. Touché." He leaned forward. "The one thing I always thought set me apart from everyone else—including you—was my talent for differentiating the real from the presented. I produced my journals, shaped them into coherent forms, and put them into the feeds, and coes all over the Pan took the information I fed them for reality. *I* knew better. No matter how well I put the material together, how deep I went into a topic, how much detail I uncovered and layered into a journal, *I* knew it wasn't real. It was a journal and that was the only real part. Everything else about it was a construct, a deduction, an opinion, an interpretation, a conclusion—a presentation of what I thought was representative of reality. But it wasn't *the* reality. That was something else, something *I* knew about that *they* never would. And I'd look at other journalists' work and feel, deep down, that I knew the difference."

"You didn't?"

"No. After Armada security finished with me and I recovered, no small thanks to you, I understood that my mind worked like a journal and everything I saw and heard filtered through that lens. All I saw was what was presented. Everything I believed about the Pan Humana was just a presentation. Like Palada's trial."

"Like Millennium?"

"And Finders and the whole Secessionist war."

"And...us?"

"Especially us, Jesa. In all the time we were lovers did we ever have an unguarded moment, a time when we weren't tailoring our words and actions to protect our careers and sustain an illusion?" He grunted. "Maybe that's why we didn't hate each other when it ended. It never got real enough to matter."

"That's pretty cold."

He shrugged.

"So what do you think is real, Tory? How do you tell?"

"I don't know. Maybe there's no way to know. But I don't think recording it and playing it back is the way."

Jesa watched him for a long time. Tory wondered if he should apologize. He reviewed what he had said. Too harsh? Off the mark? Hard to say.

She stood suddenly. "I think you're full of shit, Shirabe. Recording it and playing it back is the only way to know. It's called remembering." She walked back toward the staterooms. "If you'd still like something real to remember I'll be in my cabin."

Her door closed and Tory stared after her. He glanced briefly at the flatscreen—the Armada ships seemed to be closing slightly. He lay back on the couch and started laughing.

"How dare I try to be sane," he said aloud.

He rolled to his feet and went to her stateroom.

When she opened the door to his second knock, he said, "What would you say if I asked you to stay out here with me?"

"In the common—?"

"No," he barked. "In the Distals."

She blinked. "Why?"

"Well—I don't know. I'm curious. What would you say?"

"Probably no. But I'll give you the benefit of a doubt. What reason could I have to stay out here?"

"There's me, for one."

She grimaced.

"Maybe not," he said. "If the Secession succeeds and the Distals form a government and survive as a community…"

She raised an eyebrow, curious. "Y-yes?"

"They'll need journalists."

"Now that's not bad. I'll give it thought. Are you coming in?"

"Am I welcome?"

She stepped away from the door and waved him in.

He smiled and took a step forward. The deck jerked away from his foot and he pitched into the room. A heavy ringing sounded all around him.

Over the p.a. Democlitus said, "Apologies. We're being fired on. I'll try not to be hit again. But just in case, you'd better prepare to abandon ship."

Chapter Twelve

"The anvil of day."

The voice came out of the darkness ahead, deep and thick, made larger by the echo of the widening tunnel. Cira did not try to find cover. Obviously they could be seen. She chided herself for not switching to IR after they had left the last of the light panels, thirty meters back. Another ten meters in darkness and she would have...

"The anvil of day!"

The phrase sounded familiar. Her pulse raced. It was a recognition sign and Rollo evidently did not know it. She heard him breathing just behind her and to the right. Though it was black she still closed her eyes...

She remembered a wall in Crag Nook, not far from the tram station, Rollo at her back. "Forges the metal of night," she said.

"Come forward."

She reached up, pretending to adjust her goggles, and switched on the IR. Fifteen meters down the tunnel orange, blue, and red shapes coalesced against the dark. She counted five of them, two aiming rifles, one standing in the center of the passage. Cira moved cautiously toward them and stopped.

"Greetings, coes," she said. They all nodded silently, waiting. "We're Hersted. I'm Cira, from Crag Nook, and this is Rollo, from Emorick."

"Emorick?" the leader, the one in the center of the passage, said.

"It's been near sixty days," Rollo said. "I left when Govanchi and Liss started dividing it up."

The man nodded. Cira made another adjustment on her goggles, engaging the compensators. The false colors changed into a flat grey, green, and black image. He also wore IR goggles; their surfaces swirled in moiré pattern. Below, his prominent cheekbones framed a straight nose above a thick beard. The others looked similar. The weapons were all s.p. except one—Cira recognized the grip of a regulation marine e.p. pistol in the leader's holster. Nothing else about the group suggested Armada.

"Did you pass the bodies?" he asked suddenly.

"Outside?" Cira asked. "We passed a battle site, what was left of bodies."

"E.p. cannon," he said flatly. "Those were good coes. They harassed the road for ten days, I think, before the Armada got bored and brought up a cannon. I miss Rike. He was dependable." He cocked his head to one side. "Are you hungry?"

"Always," Rollo said.

The man spun around and walked through his group. The group bracketed Cira and Rollo, two before, two behind, and they continued down the tunnel.

After another fifty meters the pale glow of a light panel outlined the entrance to an adjoining tunnel. A scattered pile of tailings littered the floor. They stepped up into a much narrower tunnel. Light panels illuminated it at ten meter intervals so it seemed larger.

When the passage opened into another tunnel roughly the size and shape of the first, Cira realized that they had recently cut a connecting passage between them.

She looked left. A rock fall sealed the tunnel.

"Things got shaken up a short time back," one of the escorts said. The others laughed softly. "You might've heard."

She switched off the IR here—too many light panels—but she kept the goggles on enhancement.

"If I wasn't hungry before," Rollo said, "I will be after this walk."

The escorts laughed again, still quietly.

Tunnels split off irregularly, most of them dark. Equipment, broken or forgotten, lay against the passage walls. Cira felt the faint touch of ventilator breezes. At one point the tunnel floor came up sharply, almost a meter high. Cira followed the line of the crack. It looked like the tunnel had been bored from opposite directions and here, at the join, it did not match up, an error in geometry. They climbed to the unconnected sister tunnel and continued on.

After nearly a kilometer, the passage widened into a circular chamber containing a pair of boxy cars. The tunnel continued on the opposite side, another passage led off to the left, a strip of railing running down its center.

The leader turned to them. "Your weapons. Give them to Kolit."

A thick-set man, half a head shorter than her, stepped toward Cira. She automatically tightened her grip on her rifle.

"If you don't," the leader said, "we'll kill you here."

Reluctantly, Cira handed the rifle to the one called Kolit. She unslung her belt and gave him that, too. When she reached to her boot for the knife he shook his head and went to Rollo. She swallowed dryly; a short, heavy s.p. was tucked in her pack and two more pistols were hidden in her coat. Rollo, similarly armed, only surrendered rifle and belt.

They boarded the second car, their weapons with Kolit and the leader in the first. The cars rolled down the tunnel. The display in her goggles told her they traveled sixteen kilometers. The cars emerged into a large grotto.

Floodlights illuminated scattered pockets of people across the vast floor. The rainlike patterings of many hands doing many things filled the chill air.

"We opened this pit about fifteen hundred days ago," the leader said as they stepped out of the cars. "Never did much with it. Future intentions, a central point from which to expand the shafts. It's not on any of the active maps, which made it attractive. If they check old surveys they'll find it, but... "

Kolit wandered off with their weapons. The leader pointed in the opposite direction.

"Food," he said.

"Who are you, co?" Cira asked.

"A ghost." He grunted, shook his head. "Call me Max. We'll talk later."

Cira stared after him.

"Max," Rollo said. "Maxwell Cambion?"

"Once," one of the others said. "After Downer's Cove he says it's just Max. Come on, I'll see you get a place to bed down."

"I didn't think anybody'd survived Downer's Cove," Rollo said as they followed him toward a makeshift field kitchen.

Their guide waved at the grotto. "This is all that did. Minus a few who've wandered in and joined us."

"What were you doing up in that tunnel?" Cira asked. "Seems a little out of the way."

"Max goes up there every other day. Those were our people who died on the shelf." He glanced at them over his shoulder. "What were you doing up there?"

"Heading south," Rollo said.

They stopped at the kitchen. Smoke wafted in complex patterns around the lights from the cookers. The air filled with rich odors.

"Looking for the coes who took out the port?"

"The idea appeals," Cira said.

He handed them plates. "My name's Rhonson. Help yourself to food. You can roll out your bedding right over there."

"Thank you, co."

"Welcome."

He walked off. Rollo blew air.

"Maxwell Cambion," he said. He checked a cooker, moved to the next, and dipped the ladle.

Cira nodded. They ate standing up, right by the kitchen. Rollo filled his plate again and finished. Then they went to the area Rhonson had indicated. They unrolled their beds near a cluster of coes who watched them indifferently. Cira noted how well armed they seemed to be—family-engraved s.p. rifles for the most part—then ignored them.

"I'll be back," she said and wandered off.

She imaged details through her goggles. The pit was unnaturally symmetrical, the walls smooth overall, though cracks and irregularities gave it a rough finish look. Besides the one by which they had entered she counted three other tunnels. One appeared large enough for a regular tram line. A collection of moles and diggers—damaged, oft-repaired machines—stood near this opening. About twenty coes bedded down around them. A short distance away broken trolls, consoles, and scrap piled against the wall. Near the center of the grotto a ring of tables surrounded a stack of polycoms and assorted other equipment. Flatscreens lay on the tables. Max and Rhonson hunched over one with three other people, talking intently. Small bands of coes, from different families judging by the designs on the few family rifles she saw, hugged the walls all around. Cira counted roughly two hundred coes, no group larger than twenty-five, most only six or seven. Opposite the kitchen stood a pair of salvaged biomonitors and four standard infirmary beds, three of them empty.

The occupied bed contained a woman. Cira shuddered at the sight. The co's eyes stared up, glazed over by milky cataracts, and a purplish discoloration streaked her cheeks. Clawlike hands, the tendons and veins painfully clear through blotchy skin, absently gripped and released the thin sheet. Cira looked up at the monitors. Blood pressure low, heart rate low, blood sugar levels much too high.

"You a med?"

Cira turned to the man behind her. He looked tired, frustrated. She shook her head. "What's wrong with her?"

"Don't know. We seen a few in the last twenty days, mostly from out in the plains. One of them kept saying the land did it, said something about a new kind of swamp." He winced. "We don't have any swamps on Finders."

"It looks…"

His eyes widened, for a moment encouraged. Cira felt ashamed of herself.

"I don't know. It looks horrible. Any of them survive?"

"No. And I don't have the facilities to do a thorough autopsy. We burned the bodies."

"I'm sorry."

She left the area, troubled.

"Don't be reluctant to express your admiration," Rhonson said, coming up alongside her. He smiled.

"This isn't the group that did the port," she said.

"No. We're just survivors."

"You said Downer's Cove?"

He nodded. "A marine force took the town. When we arrived they were trying to take the Cambion shafts above the town. Max took charge of the defenses and we held them off."

"Marines?" Cira said, incredulous. "With what?"

"Electron drills. It was a new shaft, we had a lot of equipment on-site. Have you ever seen what an electron drill does to stone? Well, imagine what it did to the marines." He shrugged. "We held for five days. Then the power conduits were cut and the Armada flew air strikes. Not many of us got out."

"There can't be much left of the town."

"There's nothing left of the town. When we left—when we withdrew—it was like melted glass."

She pointed. "Is this supposed to be the start of a new army?"

He winced, looked over at the shabby operations center. "Max would like to think so."

"You know better?"

"He—there's nothing left but the forms. He lost his son in this."

"I know. I—" She clamped her mouth shut, feeling suddenly very vulnerable, very foolish. She almost said she had served with him, that they had flown together in Armada service. She thought of Alexan and felt a bitter resentment. She had accepted his death. Now—

Rhonson seemed not to have noticed. "Nicolan was in the main tower at the Cambion compound when the strikes came. We've been back there. Nothing's left but corpses, a lot of them unidentifiable except by genome match, and we can't do that."

She looked at him. Nicolan? "His son…"

"Nicolan. Good co, that one. He was our primary liaison to the setis. He's the one beat the Armada the first time, sent them running." He shook his head. "You said you were from Crag Nook. What's it like? What's happening there? And Emorick?"

"You'll have to ask Rollo about Emorick, though what I've heard it's not much different." She described the riot and the subsequent Armada take-over, the sullen mood of the town now, the damage, the death. It puzzled her a little how dispassionate she sounded, as if beaten herself.

Rhonson asked a few questions, listened intently. They arrived back by their billet.

"We'll talk more," Rhonson said. "If you decide to stay we'll return your weapons in a day or two. Don't ask me why, that's Max's decision. We have no way to tell who's trustworthy or not, so it's just a ritual. Sometimes that's all you have left."

He walked off then and Cira sat down on her bedding. Rollo had gotten another plate of food.

"This is sad," Cira said. "This can't be all, can it?"

Rollo shrugged. "Do we stay or go on?"

"We'll stay a few days. I'd hate to try to find my way out of here. They've obviously cut new tunnels."

"By the look of them I wouldn't trust half these coes on a street in daylight."

"I believe Rhonson when he says they aren't the ones who made the raid on the port. They don't look like they could do anything very effectively."

"Maxwell Cambion, though, is another thing."

"He said Maxwell's son's name was Nicolan."

Rollo nodded. "That's right."

"Did he have a brother?"

"Not that I heard of." He stretched out on his bedding. "At least we a'n't moving for awhile." Soon his breathing deepened.

Cira watched. Max drifted from polycom to table, spoke to one or another of his aides, stood very still for long minutes, then drifted within the perimeter of tables. His face never changed expressions. Once he looked toward her, but turned away. Coes occasionally left one group to join another, talk for a time, then return. The grotto was deeply still, troublingly quiet with so many people; the sounds of motion but few voices. A mournful place.

She dozed off, jerked awake, then dozed again.

She came awake to the sounds of excited voices. Her chronometer informed her she had slept five hours. Rollo was sitting up.

Half a dozen coes stood at one of the tables. Maxwell, Rhonson, and Kolit faced them.

"What?" she asked.

"They came in a few minutes ago," Rollo said and indicated the largest tunnel. "Max got excited."

Cira sat up, rubbing her eyes, and stretched briefly. Max nodded emphatically and the new arrivals grinned. Max spoke to Rhonson and Kolit, who then left the circle, Kolit heading toward the vehicles, Rhonson to one of the small groups.

"I'm hungry," Cira said, standing. She went over to the kitchen. Two men were preparing a cooker, adding rice and lentils. They looked up and nodded greetings. Cira took a plate and filled it with a thick pile of noodles and white paste.

"What's happening?" she asked.

"One of the patrols come back," the younger of the pair said. He seemed boyish, much younger than Cira, despite a scar on his neck. "Hitchy's, a'n't it?"

"Hitchy's," the other one affirmed. "Found something, obviously. We'll know soon enough."

Cira rejoined Rollo. As she finished her food, Rhonson came toward them. He stopped at the foot of her bedding and squatted. "We're going to a meeting," he said. "Under the compound. Do you want to come?"

"Meeting with what?" Rollo asked.

Rhonson grinned knowingly. "Maybe with the coes who did the port."

"Maybe?" Cira questioned.

"Won't know till we meet them."

She set the plate aside. "Wouldn't miss it."

"Good. See Kolit, he'll give you back your weapons. Be at the main tunnel in one hour."

"Why would he trust us?" Rollo asked.

"He doesn't. Whatever's happening, he thinks we might be part of it. We'll be watched."

"Ah. So everything's normal."

Cira chuckled.

When they gathered at the designated area Cira counted twenty-five others, plus Max and his two close aides, Rhonson and Kolit. Looking at their faces she wondered how many of them would leave at the first excuse, if any of them would fight for Max or if they stayed here only because they had nowhere else to go. Most shuffled restlessly, avoiding eye contact, and clinging tightly to their rifles. A few carried themselves like veterans.

Max consulted with Rhonson quietly, then suddenly walked to the mouth of the tunnel, turned, and waved them onward.

Venner checked the map on his handslate again. Sections of the labyrinthine passageways beneath the Cambion compound were blocked by fallen stone. The shockwaves from the explosions had rearranged much of the old order and threading his way through the remaining maze required close attention.

Few light panels remained. Lamplight swam over the walls from the group behind him. Ten coes, including Rasal. He wondered if he had brought enough or too many. He had no idea how many would be at the meeting.

"Doesn't matter," he whispered.

"What?" Rasal asked.

He glanced at her, annoyed. "Nothing."

"How far?"

He studied the handslate, then the passage walls. "We're one level above the tramline…two hundred meters south…"

"I don't care much for this."

"Hmm? You're a Founder, I thought you were all born underground."

"I lived in Emorick all my life. My mother taught at the academy."

"Where is she now?"

"Dead."

"Oh." He looked away. He hated peoples' declaration of loss. No matter how plainly and unsolicitously they told him, he always felt that they blamed him or wanted his sanction. He did not want to know. Asking seemed polite conversation, but it was a trap under certain circumstances. He resented them for eliciting the small spark of guilt he always felt in the presence of loss.

He thought occasionally that his mind was recovering, that sanity might be returning. Once in a while, unexpected pangs of guilt stabbed, coupled with a memory of some injury he had inflicted. But it passed quickly and when he examined his feelings, he found nothing to support the notion that normalcy might return.

"How far?" Rasal persisted.

"Uh…another level up…less than a kilometer."

"Up…none of the lifts are working."

"Optimism, Rasal. We'll climb another shaft."

She scowled at the walls and nodded.

A series of sounds like pebbles on water mixed with pouring sand echoed around them. No one moved. In moments quiet returned, except for the slightly more audible breathing of the group.

"Ghosts," Venner said. No one laughed.

How simple, Max thought, how so sickly simple, if everything had done what everything had been supposed to do. The tunnel was dark for the most part, like the rest of what was his, dark, a shape, empty. He still saw the momentum it contained. The sullen footfalls around him, echoing off his walls, hurt to hear. Trams, shunts, lifts, diggers, moles, life breathed into stone, all at his insistence. He had envisioned all this and started building, working a world, clay in palm, to make it move to his mind. First Houston, then Liss, and Alexan...damned Alexan, without him the only thing Max had was a half-finished shell and nothing solid but luck to keep it going. So simple, Max shook his head, so sadly simple, the boy always did what he was told, strived to please, hurt himself to meet Max's demands, and at the last, when it really counted, he came back perversity itself, nothing the way Max had wanted it, chance deviation, an ill-considered streak of independence, years of planning and manipulation and now there were dead bodies all over Finders. None of it should have happened this way. He strode on down his tunnel toward his mines, amused that those he went to meet did not even know he still lived. Amused, unsmiling, never smiling, cannot smile, damn virus, damn neurons, damn face. Nicolan understood, Nicolan saw beneath the ungiving skin, the dead muscles, but Alexan always wanted a smile, worked harder to make Max smile than on anything else, and Max simply could not, so simple, so serenely simple, the brain sent the signal, the face did not respond, stop trying. He did not smile. He did not frown. He never wept. Bodies burned in front of him, flesh ran like mercury, blood vaporized in brief bright reddish clouds that burst from exploding corpses. The town sagged beneath the battle. Five days, six days, he forgot, the atmosphere around them thick black, choking dense. Left, right, one foot after the other, I cannot smile but I can walk. Alexan disappointed him, Michen ran off who knew where, the seti abandoned Finders, Nicolan died, but somebody hit the Armada hard, *some*body boiled them where they stood, *somebody* hurt them badly one time, just like Nicolan had done with the first task force, ridiculed them with defeat, how I miss Nic. A shunt waited around here, one that still functioned, one he and Rhonson had found and repaired; Rhonson, good engineer, good friend, terrible judge of character, look at those two he dragged along on this mission, that one, the female, reeks Armada, a spy, a bomb in our belly. Max shrugged. No trouble to kill her if she moved wrong. The big co with her, though, a Founder, curious that he's a friend to an Armada *agent provocateur*, an assassin, an infiltrator. Not fair to judge too harshly, no telling what Crag Nook may be like now, might be the only way to make it. He can be as easily punctured and deflated. So simple. So systematically simple. Walk, walk, where is the shunt, walk, walk.

Sean waited patiently as the big Vohec ship approached. A signal inquired about his ID and condition and he requested permission to come aboard. The behemoth moved closer and enveloped *Solo*.

An escort brought him to Lovander Casm's chamber. Lovander Mipelon and the Ranonan, Tan-Kovis, were there. Sean greeted them politely.

"We approach Finders," Casm said. A holo appeared before him. Sean studied it briefly and nodded; it confirmed his own observations. "The data flowing from our infiltration of Armada and Pan Humana governmental systems continues. Either they do not know about it yet or they cannot shut it down."

"They know about it," Sean said. "They don't want to damage their systems by an arbitrary shutdown. They're integrated to a high level."

Casm inclined his head. "Then that explains these ship movements."

Armada vehicles formed clusters within the Diphda system, all maneuvering around the task force command ship. It certainly looked to Sean like preparations for a pull-out.

"How long," Mipelon asked, "do you think it will be till they close our access?"

"Not long. You might have another few hours of dataflow. What do you intend to do with the people left on Finders?"

"Nothing," Casm said. "If they survive and there have been no violations of our charter, there is no reason to remove them." He looked at Sean. "Your intervention at Etacti was clever and irritating. Our understanding of the Armada suggested that if Etacti fell then they might abandon Finders, certainly before now. With Etacti still resisting, they would be forced to cling to Finders."

"And neither has happened."

"Not entirely by your efforts. The access Ambassador Tan-Kovis and Lovander Mipelon opened to Pan Humana data has caused them to react by, evidently, ordering a withdrawal. You could not have known then about this."

"Pardon, Lovander," Tan-Kovis said, "but he did know. We conferred before he arrived at Etacti."

"I just didn't know when your access would open. But given that, this *is* a perfectly predictable outcome."

Casm stared intently at Tan-Kovis. Finally, he said, "We will speak later."

Within the holo the fleets moved.

The interior looked like a giant had picked the compound up whole and shaken it. Rock falls lay over equipment, cracks ran through the floors, loose gear mingled with debris. Nicolan wondered how stable this place was, how safe. Except for the small sounds his people made as they arranged themselves, all was silent. Safe enough probably. Safe enough for a meeting.

In position, boss, Kee informed him.

"Good. Now we just wait."

Nicolan leaned back against the stone. From here, on the partially collapsed catwalk above the old operations area, he could watch the only entrances still open.

Old operations area...it felt so long ago that the description seemed appropriate, but it had been less than seventy days since the first Armada incursion. Seventy days and the world was different, completely, even physically, and would be different again in seventy more.

Got an approach, boss.

"Where?"

Northwest, worker's billet area.

Nicolan fixed his gaze on the balcony one level above the floor, almost directly across from him. Three entrances opened along its length, two of them blocked by cave-ins. The third was a black gash in the rock face. Light flickered uncertainly from deep inside, then grew brighter, steadier.

Someone stepped onto the balcony, rifle balanced in the crook of the left arm. Nicolan stood and waved. The figure returned the wave, spoke back into the tunnel, and more coes emerged.

When they reached the main floor, Nicolan climbed down, joining the three coes already there. They accompanied him to the center of the chamber.

The man standing there, smiling, looked vaguely familiar. His eyes seemed a little too wide, his smile a touch too secretive. Nicolan stopped a meter away.

"Co," he said. "You requested a meeting on behalf of Jonner Liss?"

The man laughed softly. "My, my," he said. "Nic, it's so good to see you. I thought you were dead." Nicolan frowned and the man laughed louder. "You don't know me, do you? Pater never told you about me, I guess. Just as well. My name is Hil Venner and I used to work for Max. I do suspect, however, that he didn't entirely trust me."

"Why wouldn't he have trusted you?" Nicolan asked, a caustic edge in his voice. Hil Venner, whoever he was, irritated him. He thought that this would turn out to be a short meeting, a wasted effort.

"We should carry this conversation on in private."

Nicolan looked around. "Where would you suggest?"

"Mmm. You have a point. Still..."

Nicolan motioned for his escorts to move off and Venner did likewise. Alone now with Venner, Nicolan felt more anxious. Not threatened so much as simply vulnerable.

"Why wouldn't my father trust you?"

"Well," Venner said, "it might be because I also worked for the Armada at the time. I didn't think he knew about that, but as it turned out Co Harias was also an Armada agent. She didn't like me at all." He leaned forward and appeared to examine Nicolan's face. "You know, you're very much like your brother. Except he ended up without a mind."

Nicolan started. "Brother..."

"Oh, that's right! You didn't know about *him*, either! Max kept an awful lot of secrets!" Venner laughed once more. "It's all right, I can catch you up on family history. I had a long talk with Michen and he explained a great deal to me. So *you* hit the Armada here. I'm impressed, I really am."

"I was told you have a proposition from Jonner Liss."

"But don't you want to hear—?"

"Business first."

"Very like your pater. All right. Liss's proposal is fairly simple. We've already acquired the agreement of most of the independent partisan groups—"

Another track, boss, Kee said. Nicolan did not move, allowed Venner to continue. *Coming up out of the Downer's Cove tunnel, slow.*

"—once we have everyone standing behind one spokesman, Liss can negotiate with the Armada from strength. Then—"

"Are all your people here?"

Venner stammered and frowned. "What?" He glanced around. "Yes."

Nicolan touched his jaw. "Cover, Kee." He gestured for Venner to move, then backed toward the jumbled remains of the On Site Coordinating Area.

The west tunnel, the one that once led to Downer's Cove, did not gradually fill with the light of handlamps. It remained black.

"So where are they, Kee?" Nicolan asked.

Right inside the mouth, boss. Got solid IR on them. Big group.

"Stay sharp." He stepped from the shadows of the OSCA. "You in the tunnel! My people are sighted in on you! Come out!"

Three people stepped out. The one in the lead walked stiffly forward. As he reached the center of the staging area Venner began laughing. Nicolan scowled at him, then looked at the approaching figure.

"What a reunion!" Venner shouted.

Nicolan stared, dismayed, at the bearded man coming toward him. The eyes seemed familiar. Then he looked beyond to the other two and recognized Rhonson and Kolit. Even then it took a few moments before he made the connection.

"Maxwell...?"

Venner howled and slapped his thighs. "The family's almost all here! Pity they shipped Alexan back to the Pan!"

Nicolan walked quickly to meet his father.

"Nic?" Maxwell Cambion said wonderingly. He reached out carefully and let his fingertips brush Nicolan's cheek.

"I thought—"

Maxwell's fingers pressed against Nicolan's lips. He shook his head almost imperceptibly. "Hil, I thought you'd gone back home."

The laughter stopped at once. Venner strode up to them. He leaned toward Maxwell, his face pulled by a visible hatred that startled Nicolan.

"Home is death to you," he hissed. "Is that what you mean? You thought I was dead? Is that why you turned me over to the Armada as a traitor?"

"I don't know what you're talking about, Hil."

Tears glistened in Venner's eyes. "I *saw* Harias with Laros! Hurt me, Max, but don't *lie* about it!"

"Harias? With the Armada?" Maxwell shook his head. "I knew we had a security breech, but Harias? It's hard to credit, Hil. Why would I want you dead?"

"*That's what I want to know!*" His face was wet now.

"Co Venner," Nicolan said, "why don't we go sit down and talk."

Venner sucked in a deep breath and stepped back. "With him? I don't think so."

"Hil," Maxwell said. "This isn't very rational. I'm not rational myself. I thought you were gone and Nicolan…"

Nicolan had long been used to his father's inability to change facial expression. He even thought he understood Maxwell's refusal to take neural therapy to correct the problem. Nicolan had compensated by learning Maxwell's other cues. But he had never seen quite this collection of signals. Maxwell's eyes were wide, his mouth open slightly, head set forward from his shoulders. His left hand was raised almost to his waist and the thumb rubbed slowly back and forth across the other four fingertips. Nicolan experienced the effect as amazement and gratitude, a mix of emotions he had never felt from Maxwell.

Suddenly Maxwell turned. "Rhonson! Kolit! It's Nicolan! He's alive!"

More coes came out of the Downer's Cove tunnel. Like watching ghosts come back from Acheron, loosed from Hades' grip, Nicolan stared, afraid to blink.

"You're *happy*," Venner accused. "All the misery you've caused and you're *happy!*"

Maxwell looked at him. "My son is alive."

"This one is! Your other one is not!"

"I don't have another son."

"Alexan, remember? Michen told me all about it, just before I killed him!" He barked a harsh laugh. He stabbed a finger at Maxwell. "What a story! How he ruined his partner, took the man's son away from him—"

"You killed Michen?"

"Yes, I killed Michen. I killed Harias, too, and five others who worked for you then. I killed a lot of Armada. The only one left is Rike—"

"Rike's dead."

"Oh. Too bad." Venner shrugged. "But now I have you and Nic!" He laughed again. "But you never told Nic about Alexan, and Houston—"

"Houston died in a cave-in," Maxwell said.

"—and you did a complete genetic overlay on the boy! Raised him as Alexan Cambion and sent him off to become pater's little diplomat within the Pan Humana. I knew about Alex, of course, but I didn't know all the rest, where he came from and all. Brilliant plan, Max, I applaud the scope! If it had worked you would have had a son on the Armada command staff speaking on your behalf. Finders would have been gifted to him in the event of an Armada victory. If not, he represented a solid pipeline for trade with the Pan Humana. Max Cambion would have been a pivotal figure either way."

"Alexan didn't…" Maxwell looked away.

"Alexan didn't do what he was supposed to do," Venner continued. "He came back here as a fighter pilot! Wrong part of the Armada, he wanted to impress pater by being a warrior! But he got shot down, along with everyone else in the Valico Task Force!"

"Hil, don't," Maxwell said, quietly.

"So," Venner patted Nicolan's shoulder, "you had a brother. A twin, in fact, it's remarkable how much you resemble poor dead Alexan. Nobody knew, of course, it wasn't safe. Alexan had tutors in Emorick, he spent a lot of time off-planet in the transit station, he rarely saw pater—I suppose because pater was busy being pater to you, and that has paid off, you're a credit to your pater—and as soon as he passed the qualifying exams he was shipped off to Armada OTS and, what Maxwell hoped, a brilliant career as a military bureaucrat. Michen told me all about it, Max. Michen did the work, you see, Nic, so Michen had to know everything. Of course, I suppose it's not quite the same as having a real brother. Max never thought of him that way, he was just so much genetic material shaped for a purpose. A throwaway attempt at empire, wouldn't you say, Max? Don't you think that's a good characterization?"

Maxwell brought his hand to his holster and turned, but Venner already had his pistol out and aimed.

"I don't think so, Max," he said, grinning.

Venner lurched forward; a loud crack filled the chamber, then another immediately, and the left side of Venner's head erupted. Blood and bone spattered Nicolan. Blood dampened Venner's shirt. The pistol fell from his hand as he dropped to his knees, then sprawled face down.

Nicolan looked up. One of Venner's people stood several meters away, rifle still aimed where Venner's back had been. By the mouth of the west tunnel a large co was lowering his rifle.

Cira's ears rang from the shot. For a moment she did not understand what had happened. Then Rollo moved—lowered his rifle—and at the same instant she saw one of Venner's people lower her rifle.

Venner lay on the floor between Maxwell and Nicolan Cambion.

Nicolan Cambion...when she had stepped from the tunnel and saw him she could not stop staring. He and Alexan were different, but they were the differences of experience, of living.

Then Venner had begun ranting. She grew feverish with anger.

During the entire trip from Crag Nook, she had been struggling with options. She had few, knew what the Armada wanted for her, but could see little choice beyond following the program and seeing what might happen.

Seeing Venner just now concretized her feelings.

"Rollo," she had said quietly, "that co doing all the talking?"

"Mmm?"

"He's the one. He killed Olin and hurt Becca."

"You're sure?"

"Absolutely. Hil Venner."

Of course, that had been purely a guess on her part, but it was a reasonable one. Venner had been gone when they had returned to his house. He had survived and killed three Armada agents. There had been something disturbing in the tableau he had left and then, when she brought Sergeant Palker back to collect Olin and Becca...she had believed then and now felt certain that only Hil Venner could have done that.

Now he was dead, not only from Rollo's shot. One of the people Venner had arrived with had fired, too, a moment before Rollo. It did not surprise her that others would want him dead. It did not surprise her that he had managed to avoid it till now. She was glad he had, though—for Rollo.

Nicolan held out his hand to Max. Hesitantly Max took it and suddenly Nicolan pulled him into an embrace. For no reason she could identify, it made Cira glad.

The three parties came together then. The woman who had shot Venner in the back seemed to be in charge of her group now—perhaps she had been all along—and joined Nicolan and Maxwell away from the rest. Coes rigged lights, discarded packs. Smaller groups formed. At some point Venner's body was removed. Cira avoided everyone, keeping watch on the three leaders. They spoke for a long time. Finally the woman left to speak with members of her own party.

Cira drew a lungful of cold air and crossed the staging area. Both Cambions looked up at her. "Yes?" Nicolan said.

"Co Cambion...I'd like to speak with you."

"We're a little involved at the moment, co..."

"My name is Cira Kalinge. Lt. Commander Cira Kalinge, of the Armada. I served with Alexan. I thought you might appreciate knowing what kind of an officer he was."

Both men stared at her for several seconds. Then Nicolan, frowning, turned to Maxwell.

"I think this would be a good idea," he said. "Father."

Maxwell stared at his son for a long time. Finally, he nodded.

"Please," he said to Cira. "We'd like very much to hear."

Cira set down her pack and rifle, sat cross-legged before them, and started talking. It felt very good.

The evacuation moved swiftly. The mutagens the Armada had released into the soil spread out of control. Cira explained to Nicolan that the agro potential that three generations of reworms and accompanying modifications to Finders' mineral-rich soil were not being undone so much as that one of the by-products of the chemical rape endangered the cohabitants. Slowly, Finders would turn poisonous. She had recognized the infection in Maxwell's camp, in the purpling face of the blind woman.

From the Vohec ship Nicolan checked the role of ships coming up from Emorick, saddened by this final indignity. The Armada had pulled out, suddenly and inexplicably. For three days Founders celebrated, believing they had won. Then the field reports from Orchard Crest and the agro stations came in. The Armada's parting gesture to an intractable world—slow death. The pettiness was almost laughable.

He signed off on the role and left the command platform. The lighter gravity gave him a spring in his step. At least he welcomed that. Back in space, and not altogether unhappy about it.

As he descended the ramp to the connecting concourse he looked right at the huge display of the evacuation fleet. Rahalen carriers took in the transports from the surface. The giant ships enveloped the smaller craft, closed up, and moved off one by one. The refugees were spreading all across the Distals. The process had benefits and drawbacks. The collective skills of all the Founders would be welcome by the new state, but it was never easy to absorb refugees. This time the numbers were relatively small—less than half a million—but they would still tax the depleted resources of the besieged systems.

Nicolan made his way to the Vohec platform. He entered the veil and approached Lovander Casm.

"Co Cambion," Casm said.

"Lovander. It is good to see you again."

The Vohec gestured to a seat. "Food, drink."

"Your generosity is recognized." Nicolan poured wine, sipped.

"The evacuation is ahead of schedule," Casm said.

"My thanks. Without your help this would be impossible."

"I regret the need." His inclined his head. "I am curious, Co Cambion. I have studied the action on Finders. I have questions."

"Ask. Perhaps I can answer them."

"Much that the Armada did makes no sense. Wasteful tactics, ill-considered overall strategy. Nevertheless, not without effect. This has been instructive as to what kind of opponents they would be. Your own tactics demonstrated less organization, but more thought. Perhaps because of a limitation of resource."

"True. When you have less to fight with you have to make better use of it."

"You expended most of your heavy weaponry in the assault on the Cambion spaceport. This did not seem reasonable when the main Armada headquarters was in Crag Nook. It was not impossible for you to have moved your materiél there. Was this strike, perhaps, out of a passion for revenge?"

Nicolan shook his head. "No. It was a gamble. The importance you placed on the *qonteth* led me to suspect that you might intervene if it were threatened. I was hoping the Armada would slip and attack us, thereby threatening Vohec territory."

"You were trying to draw us in."

"Yes. It didn't work."

Casm was silent for a long time.

"The *qonteth*," Nicolan said. "It's a problem."

"Yes…"

"A problem seeking a solution."

"You entered it?"

"I did. No one else did. After seeing the same battle restaged for the sixth time I understood what it meant."

"The Vohec have lost only one action."

"Finders?"

"Yes. We were an independent empire. The Rahalen were aggressively forming a coalition, what we call the Coingulate, out of the disparate civilizations of the *Sev N'Raicha*. The Vohec did not wish to join. It came to conflict."

"How did you lose?"

"We did not. We compromised. You will agree, I think, that a civilization is known both by what it will do and what it will not do."

"Y-yes…"

"Histories vary, terms are not precisely comparable. We have studied your history, especially since we accessed the Pan dataflow. Bear with me, then, if I draw crude similes.

"The Vohec have been militarists since before we could leave our own system. You might call us mercenaries, but the comparison is most valid with your Old Earth Swiss Guards. We provided the military for many clients. Contractual obligations are a source of *qonroith*—honor, more than honor. When we met at Finders to decide Vohec membership, the Rahalen mingled their fleets with the fleets of Vohec allies, who themselves had been seduced into the action by the Rahalen. It was necessary to avoid engaging these allies and destroy the Rahalen components."

"I watched the engagement six times. You could have done it."

"No. There was no way to attack the ally of an ally without violating *qonroith*. We could not remain who we are and win that battle."

"So why the *qonteth*?"

"A lesson. A study. We learn. Perhaps one day a solution may be derived that none of us has imagined." He cocked his head to one side in a provocatively human gesture. "Perhaps you will find it useful to run your own lesson, to learn the limitations of what you will do in order to preserve what you are."

"Perhaps." Nicolan frowned. "Are you suggesting that the Pan Humana has exhibited *qonroith* in this?"

"That is difficult to say, since we do not understand what it is they believe they are. Can you add meaning?"

Nicolan shook his head. "I'm afraid not. I'm sorry."

"They are your own kind, though."

"Biology doesn't automatically bestow understanding."

Casm nodded after a time. "Perhaps the Rahalen are correct about you."

"What?"

Casm gestured at the table. "Food, drink. Tell me what you will do now. What do you hope for the future?"

Nicolan lifted a glass, frustrated. He understood the ritual well enough to know he would get no answers from Casm now. That part of the conversation was over. He raised the glass in salute and turned his mind to other things.

Epilogue

"Lt. Kalinge?"

Cira looked up from the flatscreen. For a moment she did not recognize the man standing before her. He smiled brightly, though, and clearly expected her to. His hair was white, but his face was youthful—

"Oh. Co Shirabe."

His smile widened. "I hoped you'd remember me."

"Of course. Sit down."

She straightened in the chair. Her glass was nearly empty. She held it up and a tray floated beneath it and carried it off. "A drink?"

"No, thank you."

The omnirec was nearly empty. Above, people surged to and from on the open bridges between floating platforms. The Vohec ship seemed to be little more than a vast sack of atmosphere with platforms suspended throughout connected by bridges. At first she had found it unnerving, but now she was merely impressed.

"I didn't expect to find you here, Lieutenant."

"Not 'lieutenant' anymore, Co Shirabe. I made Lt. Commander before I joined the Secession."

"Oh? Dissatisfied with the Armada?"

"With all of it. I saw you at Commander Palada's trial."

"Yes. If you can call it a trial. I didn't stay for the outcome."

"They found him guilty of treasonous negligence. I was shipped back to Finders before the sentence, so I don't know what happened to him. How did you get out here?"

He laughed. "I nearly didn't. I was trying to get back into Diphda, to Finders. The Armada had it bottled up so tightly we couldn't get through. Our shipmaster tried three times, was run off three times. Finally he gave up. We ran into the Vohec fleet the last time and they took us on."

"We?"

"Oh. Jesa Marlin. She's a journalist, too." He grinned. "We're going to try to set up a newsnet out here."

"You must be optimistic about our chances."

Tory Shirabe shrugged. "Even defeat is news. But we're persona non gratae in the Pan Humana now. Jesa's last journals about the Palada trial and the Armada's ill-treatment of a colleague—me—won't endear her to the powers that be." He frowned. "She's giving up a lot more than I am. I was given little choice. She still had a viable career." He shook his head. "So what are you doing for the Secession?"

"For now I'm in charge of the Finders militia. I don't know how long that will last, since Finders is no longer a viable habitat."

"Maybe you can help me, then. Do you know Nicolan Cambion?"

"Yes. How do you know him?"

"I don't. But—I found Alexan. I found out about Nicolan when I got out here. I thought..."

"Where?"

"Hmm? Oh. He ended up in the care of a psychometrist. I tracked him down. That's how I ended up a guest of Armada security."

"Did he...?"

"He was never getting out, Co Kalinge. I don't think anyone will hurt him, but let him go? No."

Cira let the information settle within her. For the last ten days details had filled the time, distracted her. Other than the decision—which really had been made for her—to break with the Pan Humana and help the Secession, she had dealt with nothing personal. Logistics demanded her attention, distracted her from her own needs. She let Tory's news open the way a little for the personal, enough that she knew immediately that she was not ready.

"I'll take you to Nicolan."

Tory followed her up the ramp to the bridge. She did not speak all the way to the operations platform. Nicolan stood with Rhonson and Rasal by a tactical display.

"That's him," Cira said.

"Shit," Tory breathed.

"That's what I thought when I first saw him. Make no mistake, though, he's a very different co from Alex."

"Thank you, Co Kalinge."

"Cira, please. We'll get together later, all right? I'd like to talk to you."

"A pleasure."

Cira watched him approach Nicolan. She could not hear what was said, but Nicolan straightened, took Tory's hand, and listened. Rhonson and Rasal moved away politely.

As she was about to turn to leave, Tory reached into his jacket and pulled out a sheaf of disks. He handed them to Nicolan, who held them carefully, like a precious gift.

Cira turned away. She could find out later what that was all about. For now she had to find the space to begin making a new home.

About the author
Mark W. Tiedemann

The year Mark Tiedemann was born, the Dow Jones finally broke its previous high from 1929 by closing at 404, "The Day The Earth Stood Still" premiered, and Isaac Asimov published his *Caves of Steel*, all of which bode weird for a strange life. After that, events took several turns for the unexpected.

Mark has been publishing science fiction and fantasy stories since 1990, a couple of years after attending Clarion with instructors like Tim Powers and Samuel R. Delany. His short story "Psych," was included in the *12th Annual: Year's Best Fantasy & Horror,* and in the last couple of years his has published a few novels—*Mirage* and *Chimera* in the Asimov's Robot Mystery series, *Compass Reach,* volume one of the *Secantis Sequence,* and stand-alone *Realtime.* He has several more novels coming out, especially *Peace and Memory,* volume three of the Secantis Sequence, from Meisha Merlin, 2003.

All these novels have made him a happy writer, which is a Very Good Thing.

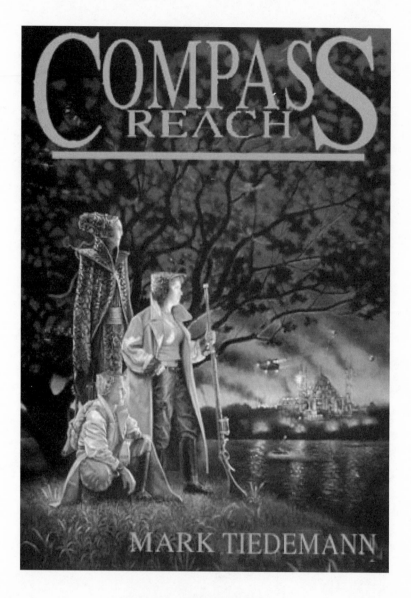

COMPASS REACH

MARK TIEDEMANN

ISBN 1892065-39-8
$16.00

Fargo owes nothing to the Pan Humana. He turned his back on them long ago, when he was stripped of his identity, his class, his position, and all the other ties to human civilization enjoyed by its billions upon billions of citizens. Fargo joined the ranks of the Freeriders. To themselves, Freeriders are interstellar gypsies, the disinvested and therefore the truly free. To most of the rest of society, to the Invested, they are parasites, freeloaders, bums.

But now Fargo finds himself caught up in events that are dragging him back into the folds of human culture and forcing him to choose sides in a struggle to determine the future of humanity in the galaxy. The aliens have come to make treaties, to interact with a paranoid humanity, to bridge the gaps that separate them. They do not understand the resistance they encounter and enlist aid where they can. Among those they pick, Fargo is their most unlikely choice. He is also their most dangerous choice.

To the humans opposed to embracing the new future offered, Fargo is representative of everything they reject, a threat to everything they hold important and fear to lose. He is an outsider, unwanted, unwelcome, in many ways a barbarian, yet indispensable to both sides.

For himself, Fargo has his own reasons for going all the way to Sol, to Earth, into the heart of power.

Fargo has touched an alien mind.

Come check out our web site for details on these Meisha Merlin authors!

Kevin J. Anderson

Robert Asprin

Robin Wayne Bailey

Edo van Belkom

Janet Berliner

Storm Constantine

John F. Conn

Diane Duane

Sylvia Engdahl

Rain Graves

Jim Grimsley

George Guthridge

Keith Hartman

Beth Hilgartner

P. C. Hodgell

Tanya Huff

Janet Kagan

Caitlin R. Kiernan

Lee Killough

George R. R. Martin

Lee Martindale

Jack McDevitt

Mark McLaughlin

Sharon Lee & Steve Miller

James A. Moore

John Morressy

Adam Niswander

Andre Norton

Jody Lynn Nye

Selina Rosen

Kristine Kathryn Rusch

Pamela Sargent

Michael Scott

William Mark Simmons

S. P. Somtow

Allen Steele

Mark Tiedeman

Freda Warrington

David Niall Wilson

www.MeishaMerlin.com